SEARCHING FOR

WHO WAS JANE AUSTEN'S CAPTAIN WENTWORTH?

JANE ODIWE

TIME TRAVELS WITH JANE AUSTEN

ACKNOWLEDGEMENTS

I'd like to thank:

Jane Austen, for her wonderful books and inspiration.

My family, you know who you are, I love you all.

Anne Rice, for many wonderful and inspirational days spent together discussing all things Jane. I've always loved the *Rice portrait of Jane Austen,* so when I was invited to see the painting and hear all about its history, it was a truly memorable experience. I am also grateful to Anne for very kindly granting me permission to reproduce her fabulous portrait for the cover of this book. Thank you so much!

Gaynor, Jenny, Caroline, Penny, Elaine, May, Adalgisa and Jen, for their constant love and support of my writing.

Fellow authors, Sue Wilkes, Juliet Archer, Monica Fairview, Diana Birchall, Kathryn Nelson, Amanda Grange, Laura Boyle, and Victoria Connelly, for their support, friendship and many laughs.

Helen Porter, for her lovely company and for giving me the opportunity to talk to fellow Janeites on her *P&P tours.* http://www.pandptours.co.uk

Laurel Ann Nattress, Vic Sanborn, Julie Wakefield, Meredith Esparza, Maria Grazia, Lori Hedgpeth, Alexa Adams, Nancy Kelley, Laura Hartness, Deb Barnum, Laura Gerold, Margaret Sullivan, *Austen Authors, Historical Romance UK Authors*, and the *Romantic Novelist's Association*, for your friendship, kindness and entertaining blogs.

Jackie Herring and the Jane Austen Centre, for their kind invitation to speak at the *Jane Austen Festival.*

The Pulteney Arms, Bath, for always providing wonderful food, white wine, and a warm welcome.

The City of Bath with all its attractions – my idea of Fairyland!

Last, but by no means least, a huge thank you to:

Every single reader of my books, for it is you who keep me going, provide inspiration, and lift me up with your wonderful letters and emails.

For Olivia, with all my love

FOREWORD

In the summer of 2009, a lifelong dream came true when I moved into a flat in Bath with its views over Jane Austen's garden in Sydney Place, the Holburne museum and Sydney Gardens. The experiences that followed and the consequent dreams that haunted me have been my inspiration for this book.

Anyone who visits Bath today will be as entranced as I was when I first visited the city and there's much pleasure to be had in walking in Jane Austen's footsteps. The Assembly Rooms, the Pump Rooms, Sydney Gardens, Milsom Street, Great Pulteney Street and the Gravel Walk are all visited in her novels, especially in *Northanger Abbey* and *Persuasion*, and can still be seen much as they were in Jane's day. Her novels are responsible for a good portion of the tourists who come to see where Austen was inspired to create many wonderful characters. Janeites flock to the Jane Austen Centre and its annual festival every September, to experience what it must have been like to live in Regency Bath.

Considering that she mentions Bath in all of her novels, and that two of them were largely set in the town, I've always felt it was surprising that so little correspondence relating to Bath remains. But, between 1801 and 1804, none of Jane's letters have survived. Could it be that Bath held the key; that something happened here which changed her life forever?

Persuasion is the most powerful and emotional of her novels, and my own particular favourite. It's always a pleasure to take a newcomer around the town and show them the places that Jane wrote about. It's often said that Jane disliked Bath but I've always felt that if this were really the case, she would not have set two of her most romantic novels here. Letters written in her youth give quite a different picture, and I wonder if the reason she became disillusioned with Bath was because her father died in the city. Thereafter, her life became increasingly difficult as the family's circumstances became much reduced and they were forced to move from house to house.

It's true that Jane's books are not only about the heroes and heroines that fall in love. Bath provided a wonderful backdrop for the characters Jane must have known in real life, as well as those that she invented. Social climbing and husband hunting went hand in hand in Regency Bath, and it's easy to imagine that characters like Sir Walter Elliot and Lady Dalrymple were based on some of the people she observed.

Finally, we may never know for sure who inspired Captain Frederick Wentworth, Jane's hero in *Persuasion*, but that she loved and lost, I do not think there can be a doubt.

Jane Odiwe
June 2012

"*...The quarrels of popes and kings, with wars or pestilences, in every page; the men all so good for nothing, and hardly any women at all — it is very tiresome: and yet I often think it odd that it should be so dull, for a great deal of it must be invention. The speeches that are put into the heroes' mouths, their thoughts and designs — the chief of all this must be invention, and invention is what delights me in other books.*"
"*Historians, you think,*" *said Miss Tilney,* "*are not happy in their flights of fancy. They display imagination without raising interest. I am fond of history — and am very well contented to take the false with the true...*"

Jane Austen.

Chapter
I

On the day that the parcel arrived, I didn't really take much notice at first.

'Now, that's what I call an interesting object,' my father said, putting the brown paper package before me on the kitchen table with a flourish. 'It offers all sorts of possibilities from the exotic to the mundane.'

'Knowing my luck it's more likely to be the latter,' I muttered under my breath. Spearing the top of a boiled egg with my spoon I watched the golden yolk trickle in a glutinous trail down over the striped eggcup, until it congealed in a pool on the blue plate. Aware that he was observing me closely I sensed his silent agitation, as he waited for me to show some sign of interest.

'Full of mysterious promise is that parcel, I wonder what's in it,' Dad persisted, watching me stab a toast soldier into the yolk, until there was nothing left but porcelain egg white like the gleam of a fragile teacup. In an effort to appear uninterested, he went to stand at the sink pretending to be busy. I heard him fill a bowl with steaming water, knowing that I was being watched from the corner of his eye.

'Well, aren't you going to open it?' he said at last, clearly bursting with curiosity.

I wasn't in the mood. I couldn't care less what was in the parcel and I sighed before I could stop myself.

'Is anything wrong, love?' He put down the teacloth and the saucepan he was drying, before sitting down on the chair next to mine. 'You're out of sorts, Sophie. Tell your old Dad. What's the matter?'

The teacloth proved to be an object of fascination in that moment as I avoided the answer and his eyes, taking time to fold the fabric into a satisfying rectangle. Part of me was ashamed to be behaving like a petulant teenager. I was far too old for that but, I didn't want to tell him everything because despite being truly sad for me, I knew that he would also be completely delighted and I couldn't stand the thought of seeing that in his face. The truth was that I'd had my heart irrevocably broken, smashed up like the brittle egg shell lying shattered in pieces on my plate. Everything I'd ever believed about Lucas, our relationship and about our future together, had finally been proved to be false. If I'm truthful, I'd always known that I would find myself sobbing into my breakfast one day, feeling bruised and abandoned. But, that it would come at such a spectacularly low point in my life, I hadn't fully considered. Actually, there were no more tears; I'd gone beyond the crying stage. I just felt completely numb. Telling my Dad, who I knew would be pleased to be proved right about my philandering boyfriend, was out of the question, so I blamed my mood on the horribly unsuccessful job interview of the day before. All I had to do now was listen to murmurs of sympathy.

'I knew there was something, I could just tell,' he said, as he folded me into the warmth of his strong arms. 'Don't worry, Sophie, it'll all turn out for the best. Besides, there's a reason you didn't get the job; it wasn't meant to be and, I've always said, the right thing will come along just when it should. Be patient, time will tell.'

Dear Dad, that's his answer to everything. Fate will play its hand. According to him, we cannot escape our destiny, nor should we try. Still, it was nice to hear some sympathy even if I didn't subscribe to his ideas about providence and divine intervention.

It wasn't just the fact that Lucas and I had come to the end of what was inevitably going to happen anyway, I knew I had to face up to some uncomfortable facts. To be a writer had been my ambition since leaving university, but the manuscripts I'd sent out had always come back, the fat brown envelopes dropping back through the letterbox with the most depressing sound in the world. I'd had a few articles published, seen my name in print and earned the princely sum in six years of what amounted to most people's idea of a six month salary. Yesterday had been my first attempt into the world of work and a "proper job". I hadn't got it. So, what was I going to do now? I had no idea.

'Aren't you going to open it?' Dad persevered, nodding at the package and producing a pair of scissors that he'd obviously had at the ready.

In a way, the thought of the parcel did cheer me up. I've always loved getting presents through the post, but I couldn't see how this could possibly be anything that might improve the sense of hopelessness that was filling every thought in my mind, every pore of my being. I cut through the string and the brown paper layers wound round with so much sellotape, that I'd almost lost the will to finish opening it, before I managed to extract the most exquisite object I've ever received. It was a rosewood box inlaid with mother of pearl, fashioned into simple scrolls and arabesques into the lid and along its sides. There was a small key in the lock, which on turning clicked satisfactorily to release the mechanism that secured it. When I look back now, I must admit I was immediately intrigued. The box was like no other I have ever seen or held since. On opening, the shades of the past seemed to whisper in my ear as a heady fragrance, of orange blossom and frangipani, rose from within its depths. Inside, I found a set of keys bound together with a blue striped ribbon and a letter.

Carhampton Dando
Somerset
Dear Sophie,

How are you, my dear? I hope you are well. Your father's last letter gave me all your news and I'm very pleased to hear that you are still writing!

I hope the box that you have opened will prove useful to you. There is nothing like a fresh place for inspiration and it crossed my mind that you might enjoy a break from your London life, so I am enclosing a set of keys to the house that my father's family have owned in Bath since it was built, which is for far more years than I can remember. Your Grandmother and I spent our summer holidays there from school before travelling to the seaside in Dorset and Wales. Later on, we used to take your mother as a girl, and I think she enjoyed these visits very much until she was quite grown up, just before she met your father and the pleasures of Bath did not have such a hold.

Unfortunately, the entire house is no longer at your disposal as it was divided up when my father wanted to lease out the lower floors. You will have the run of the upper floors, however, and I believe there is only one tenant now on the ground floor. It is some time since anyone in the family stayed in the house and I'm afraid to tell you that there are not too many modern conveniences, but I hope that this will not trouble you too much.

The location is particularly pleasing being next door to Jane Austen's house in Sydney Place, a situation very well positioned for the gardens across the road and a five minute level walk to the shops. Do you know Jane Austen's books? I think you would enjoy them.

I sincerely hope it will prove to be an inspiration for your writing and that you will enjoy as much fun as your namesake in Sydney Place. There was another Sophia Elliot who lived in the house once upon a time and, as a youngster, I remember reading her journal. Anyway, my dear, I know it would have pleased my

*dear sister and, indeed, her beloved daughter, to think that you
might be able to enjoy a little holiday in the famous spa town. Have
fun!*

    Yours ever,
    Great Aunt Elizabeth.

I put the letter down and gave my father a look that told him
I wanted the truth.

'What have you been up to?' I asked quietly, 'Exactly what
have you been telling Great Aunt Elizabeth?'

His ears instantly tinged with pink as he admitted what I
already suspected. 'I'm worried about you, Sophie; you've been
moping about this house for too long. I admit, I did write and tell
her what you'd been doing but it was her suggestion that you go to
Bath. To be honest, I'd forgotten there was a house although your
mother used to talk about it sometimes. Listen, I've a little money
set aside. I want you to use it and I know your mum would have
liked you to make the most of a trip to Bath. You could write that
novel you're always saying you haven't got time to do. What do
you say?'

I couldn't be cross with him. Anyway, it was a brilliant idea
and so generous of him. Besides, what else was I going to do? I
didn't want to hang around the house, feeling completely
depressed, or go out and experience the misery of bumping into
Lucas and Lily in Camden High Street confirming the fact that they
were seeing one another. I didn't want that above everything else.
At that moment, I wanted to believe in all Dad's nonsense about
fate and destiny. To be as far away from London as I could get
seemed a great idea and Bath was a place I'd wanted to visit for a
long time. In fact, ever since I'd read about it in *Persuasion*.

My favourite book has always been Jane Austen's *Persuasion*
and it's been the comfort blanket of my life which I know sounds a
bit dramatic but, if ever I'm feeling fed up, it's my novel of choice.
What I've always done when I can't face the world is to retreat into
its pages and spend some time with Captain Wentworth. Oh, I know

how that sounds and every one of my friends thinks I'm completely mad, but the truth is that Frederick Wentworth is my idea of the perfect hero and, let's be honest, the idea of a man in uniform goes a long way to help numb those real twenty-first century feelings.

Just as perfect and to complement this handsome sailor there's no one quite so faultless as Anne Elliot, the love of the Captain's life. The fact that she shares my family name, has been disappointed in love and also lost her mum at a time when she was most needed, makes her seem very real. But that's where the comparisons end. I don't have a lot else in common with Miss Anne Elliot of Kellynch Hall in Somerset. I am not sweet and good, nor do I live in a stately home in 1815. Anne is the kind of person I would love to be: gentle, modest, and intelligent. I'd like to think I've got a brain but, as for the rest, I know I have a habit of being outspoken. I'm always saying the wrong thing and putting my foot in it, a fault the lovely Anne would never commit. Above everything else, I'd like to find a guy who adores me as Fred does Anne and experience that kind of enduring devotion for myself; a burning passion with a forever love.

I took the train. There was nowhere to park in Bath that wasn't going to cost a lot of money and Dad said that he thought most places could be reached on foot. I liked the idea of walking. I badly needed some exercise especially as those New Year promises to keep up my gym subscription had disappeared when I saw just how much it had gone up. It wasn't until the Abbey and Pulteney Bridge came into view that the age or the beauty of the place really struck me. However, by the time I was striding over the narrow bridge's footpath, the novelty of architectural views and the effort of walking had worn off due to the number of people crossing who seemed to think I was invisible and kept walking into me or my luggage. Dragging my suitcase on wheels and weighed down with another bag stuffed full meant I had no time to stop and look at all the shops along the bridge, though it crossed my mind that even if I found nothing else to do I could happily spend a month in retail therapy.

But when I reached the island at Laura Place, I had to stop. In *Persuasion*, the Elliot's snobby cousin, Lady Dalrymple, lives there with her daughter, Miss Carteret, so I paused for a minute trying to imagine which house it was that they occupied. Great Pulteney Street lay ahead, magnificently grand like some dowager duchess putting out her best jewels on display. Its length seemed interminable, but I kept my eye fixed on the Holburne Museum at the end knowing that I was to turn off before I reached it.

Sydney Place is no longer the quiet spot that Jane Austen must have known and the traffic, which roars past day and night, is as loud as any in London. That was the first illusion shattered, although I felt really thrilled at the idea of living next door to the house of the writer who had penned *Persuasion*. The thought that perhaps some of Jane's genius might permeate through the walls to inspire me was exciting. As I walked up the pathway of the imposing Georgian house I looked across to next door looking for any sign of life, but the shutters were drawn like sleeping eyes preventing any glances at the soul within.

I'm not quite sure what I'd expected really, but I felt faintly disappointed once through my own front door. It was hardly Jane Austen heaven. In the dim light, I could see scuffed magnolia walls and a blue nylon carpet stretching down the passageway to sweep up the elegant staircase. A torn paper shade over an electric bulb hung just behind the fanlight above the door and smells of rotting vegetation from recycling bags in the corner did nothing to improve my first impressions. It was then that I wondered if I'd made a huge mistake.

Chapter
2

On the left was the entrance door to the ground floor flat, which gave no clues to its owner apart from the fact that it was painted a very tasteful grey. I'd just picked up my stuff to go upstairs when I heard the handle of the door start to turn. I didn't know what to do and, holding my breath, I stood for a moment with a fixed grin on my face waiting for the person on the other side to open the door. The handle rattled again but, to my relief, no one came out. Knowing that I looked a complete mess after my journey, I must admit, the thought of meeting anyone just yet filled me with horror, so I stealthily crept up the staircase as quietly as I could and let myself into the flat.

If I'd been disappointed before, now I was devastated. It was the pungent smell that hit me first, a mixture of stale air and damp, of rooms having been shut up for an age. I couldn't see it was so dark, but I managed to stumble my way into what must have once been the drawing room. It was a sizeable space with double doors dividing the room beyond. Heavy, damask curtains closed against the three floor-length windows on the opposite side emitted fat sighs of dust to powder the air when I touched them and rattled on brass rings like a wheezing, bronchial chest as they were pulled aside. I unlatched the wooden shutters, top and bottom, and threw them back to send sparkles of light from the sun streaming through the murky windows to gild the ancient objects and faded furniture inside. Struggling with the locks, which were screwed tight, the windows protested against being opened, but at last they gave in and fresher air filled the room.

I felt suddenly overwhelmed. The fact that I was on my own struck me with a force. I'd never been completely by myself before. Even at university I'd always been surrounded by people and friends. Why on earth had I thought that coming to Bath was such a good idea? Right then, all I wanted to do was pick up my phone and call Lucas. But, I couldn't ring him. I couldn't give him the satisfaction that I needed him and still wanted so much to talk to him.

And then my phone rang. It made me jump – the stupid ringtone Lucas had chosen for me all those months ago reverberated through the air with a suitably fake rendition of "our song".

'Hi Babe, how are you?'

His voice still had the power to make my heart leap even if I'd always hated that particular "endearment", which I was convinced he used simply because he couldn't remember which girlfriend he was talking to, and I knew when I spoke that my voice would tremble.

'I'm okay, Lucas.' Did I sound as brave as I hoped? I knew I should have ignored the call understanding, all too well, that later on I would be cringing at my responses, as the words I should have said would come to me instantly with amazing clarity. 'Lucas, I don't know how to thank you enough. Since you left my life I feel wonderful, everything's just been incredibly brilliant and I've never felt better!' But, of course, for now I couldn't think straight, I was a gibbering wreck.

'It's so good to hear your voice, Sophie. I've really missed you, baby. How about we go out tonight? I was thinking we'd go into Camden for a pint, watch a band and top it all off with a night of love. What do you say?'

It was the "night of love" that gave me the courage. Even though my voice was trembling I'd found a new strength, plus he'd sounded like such a sleaze. 'I can't do that, Lucas, and I don't think there'd be any point. We've been over it all so many times and nothing can change what happened. I don't want to see you again.'

Silence. I knew he was thinking he could just talk me round. He'd always been completely arrogant.

'Sophie, you know you don't mean that. Come on, you're overreacting. Honestly, there's no one else. Lily means nothing to me. How many times have I got to say it? You know you've only ever been my girl, my one true love.'

An image of Lucas and Lily loomed, the memory of the last time I'd seen them together. Starkly lit by spring sunshine, like a framed painting in a gallery, her blossom-white arms were draped over him, in sharp contrast to her rippling, auburn hair that tumbled over his face. Silk sheets, limbs entwined – the image was a picture indelibly etched in my mind.

Summoning up all my courage I took a deep breath. 'No, I've made up my mind for good this time. I don't want to see you again; I don't want to hear any more excuses. I'm not in Camden, so please don't come looking for me. I'm sorry, Lucas, but I need to be on my own for a while.'

And then I pressed the little red button, cutting him off forever before I could change my mind. Burying my phone at the bottom of my bag, I was determined not to cry or to waste any more time thinking about him. Snatching up a plump, velvet cushion from a winged chair by the fireside, I threw it across the room. Sending yet more dust clouds glittering into a shaft of sunlight, I felt a moment of triumph before falling and flopping into the seat like a discarded rag doll.

I took a good look at my surroundings with a sinking heart. It must, at one time, have been a very elegant room, I considered. Jane Austen certainly would have felt very much at home in it judging from the Regency furniture, the clock on the mantelpiece and the gilt candlesticks scattered everywhere. The place just needed cleaning, that was all, and as there was no one else to tackle that but me, I had to stop feeling sorry for myself, dismiss the idea of running back to Camden on the first train going to London and actually do something about it. Some activity would also help to keep me warm. At least the weather was reasonably mild for April; the fireplace had coals laid in the basket and more in a copper bucket. Perhaps if I could get it going later when it was bound to get a lot cooler, all would not be lost and, I could heat up the place.

The whole flat seemed trapped in some kind of time warp. Through the folding doors was a rather austere dining room with a large, polished table in the centre and Sheraton style chairs. Beyond this room was the kitchen and small scullery where I could find nothing useful, except beautiful china that looked too good to use along with some silver cutlery. Unpromising items, (such as a rusty mousetrap, a washboard with a scrubbing brush in a zinc bucket and the only object recognizable as a vacuum cleaner) all looked like museum pieces, the latter blowing up with an alarming blue spark and a puff of smoke the second I plugged it in. So, Great Aunt Elizabeth had meant every word. I wasn't going to find any modern conveniences.

Up two flights of stairs I found the attic rooms were locked but on the floor below were a further three bedrooms, the largest of which had the same view onto the front of Sydney Gardens as the drawing room. It also had a wonderful tester bed with four posts and curtains to keep out the draughts. I instantly fell in love with it. There were clean sheets and blankets in a linen press by the window, still smelling faintly of the lavender sprigs tied in bundles that lay between each one. Silk lampshades on the bedside lights looked left over from the last war and a Regency toilet mirror on the dressing table was draped in muslin and ribbon. It all looked very pretty, but for a layer of dusty felt on the silver brushes arranged with precision along the top of the table.

I was beginning to feel hungry and not knowing where to start with sorting out the place, I decided to go out and find some lunch. I'd left my bag in the living room so I rushed back downstairs with renewed enthusiasm. It would be great to get out for an hour or two and I knew I'd have more energy once I'd eaten. The vast looking glass above the fireplace twinkled in the light, its old, silvered surface distressed in places giving the impression of almost seeing through mist. I quite liked the effect, I thought, as I ran a comb through my hair: it gave a softer look to my face.

I've never been quite sure what happened next, although what followed later gave some sense to the extraordinary experience, but I suddenly felt goose pimples all over and the strange sensation of warm breath on my neck, almost like a whisper in my ear. I felt a piece of my long hair pulled sharply at the nape, as if it had been snagged in the clasp of a necklace, which was impossible because I wasn't wearing one. It was a natural reaction to spin round and to put up my hand to touch my hair but, of course, there was nobody there. It was only when I turned back again to the mirror that I imagined I caught a fleeting impression of a moving reflection in the murky glass, white and fluttering. Passing silently out of the open door behind me, scenting the air in wafts of orange blossom and frangipani, I glimpsed a cloud of muslin, a flurry of ribbon and a white satin shoe.

Chapter 3

By the time I'd got beyond the front door and out into the sunshine, I'd decided that not eating was responsible for my overactive imagination and dismissed all thoughts of misty spectres in mirrors as hallucinatory visions brought on by a lack of sustenance. To have lunch at the Pulteney Inn round the corner struck me as a genius idea and turned out to be a spectacularly brilliant decision. Smells of home-cooked food wafted under my nose, reassuringly, as I entered the pub, making me feel more ravenous than ever. Whilst toasting myself in front of the wood-burning stove, the landlady, Lara, chatted away entertaining me with tales about the history of the place, whilst I sampled a bowl of her delicious homemade soup and crusty bread. The few locals gathered round the bar seemed friendly and all eager to learn what I was doing in Bath and where I was staying.

'I'm writing a book,' I said, knowing that this was not the entire truth, but saying it made it seem much more real and I'd quite decided that I was going to be inspired enough by my surroundings to write one.

'You're an author!' Lara exclaimed. 'How exciting. I couldn't possibly even begin to think how to write a book; you must be so clever. What's it about?'

'Well, I'm staying in Sydney Place, next door to Jane Austen's house and it's a novel inspired by her writing. I've hardly started; it's just a germ of an idea. I'm not exactly an author yet. I've had one or two little things published and, to be honest, I'm still learning.'

'Well, everyone has to start somewhere. I love Jane Austen's books and you're certainly in the right vicinity. I know the house you mean, that place has been empty for years,' said Lara, tucking a blonde curl behind her ear, 'except for the ground floor, of course. Have you met your neighbour? Actually, you might have spotted him. He was just leaving when you came in.

I shook my head. 'No, I don't think I saw him and I haven't met him yet.'

'You would have remembered if you'd seen him,' said Lara. She lowered her voice, her blue eyes twinkling as she spoke. 'He's very striking, if you know what I mean. It's difficult to describe exactly, but there's a sort of presence about him. My sister is always talking about auras and he's definitely got one of those. He's tall.' She laughed. 'Tall, dark and handsome ... and single, I think. I wouldn't mind him living downstairs from me if I hadn't got Martin.'

I laughed too. 'I shall go and knock on the door and introduce myself then, see if I can borrow a cup of sugar.'

'Well, I'm sure you must need some help with something if you're just moving in. Don't you need any shelves putting up?' She laughed again. 'You know, he might be "handy".'

'Shelves are something I definitely don't need. The place is stuffed full. I feel as if I've dropped into a Jane Austen novel and that the last time the place was occupied was about the same time. Don't get me wrong, it's got promise and it's full of beautiful things, but it's filthy and the only vacuum cleaner has just blown up.'

'We've got a spare one if you want to borrow it,' Lara offered generously. 'Have one on permanent loan, if you like, we never use it. I'll get someone to bring it round, then perhaps the handsome Josh can carry it upstairs for you.'

Lara did make me smile. 'Thank you so much. That would be wonderful though I am sure I can manage.

'I'll send it as soon as you like.'

Half an hour later I was back at the flat, armed with dusters, the promised vacuum cleaner and an array of chemicals guaranteed to blitz the place of ninety nine per cent of all known household germs. I worked so hard that my Dad, or anyone else who knew me, would not have recognized the cleaning machine I became. It took three hours but, at the end of it, the living room, kitchen and bedroom positively gleamed. My bed was made, its curtains having come up beautifully for a good beating, and I'd managed to light a fire in there, so it would be quite cosy by the time I was ready to collapse for the night. I arranged all the blue and white china on the plate rack in the kitchen; the sink, surfaces and floor were all scrubbed and smelling pleasantly of disinfectant. I even managed to light the ancient gas stove and felt the kind of satisfaction that I'm sure every proper housewife must feel, when all is in its place and neat as a pin.

I left the living room until last. By pulling the sofa nearer to the fire and positioning the little tables so that I could just set down a cup or a book without having to get up, I transformed the whole room. The flames licked up the chimney with a pleasing crackle and I felt for the first time that I might enjoy myself in Bath, after all. I was just reuniting a porcelain shepherdess with her shepherd on the window ledge when I heard a noise below, the sound of movement and the bang of the front door shutting. The clock on the mantelpiece was striking the hour, I remember hearing five chimes as I looked out at the gloomy scene. Huge, dark clouds that threatened rain had replaced the earlier sunshine and the day, which had started so spring-like and uplifting, had completely returned to wintry dreariness. And then I saw him. Well, I saw the back of him, which was the next best thing. He was tall and broad shouldered with dark, curly hair waving over the upturned collar on his jacket, his blue jeans showing a lean physique. My neighbour was standing on the broad pavement outside waiting for the traffic to clear and fiddling with the catch on an umbrella, as large raindrops started to fall out of the sky. He seemed to be looking for something, checking his pockets, before putting up the huge, black umbrella that obscured any chance of a glimpse at his face. I could see what Lara meant; he definitely had something about him even from the back. It was then that I noticed that he'd dropped something, white and crumpled, but I couldn't decide whether it was really something or nothing. I didn't quite know what to do. I didn't want to bang on the window because he'd instantly know I'd been watching him and as it was I felt a little like I'd been spying on him. I watched him cross the road. He was heading off in the direction of Sydney Gardens opposite. I don't know what possessed me at that moment, but before I knew what I was doing, I snatched up my coat and keys, ran downstairs and out through the door.

I picked up the wet object and it unfurled in my hand like a fortune-telling, cellophane fish from a Christmas cracker. It was a man's glove with long fingers made of fine, white kid. Finely stitched, clearly hand-made and soft to the touch, I was immediately reminded of a glove I'd seen before. Captain Wentworth's glove. There's a scene at the end of my favourite *Persuasion* film where Captain Wentworth takes Anne Elliot's hand. It's the most romantic gesture that unites them finally, at the end. The kiss that takes place afterwards has nothing on the way he covers her small fingers in his large ones, and it was this image that immediately jumped into my mind. I looked up but could see nothing of the mysterious Josh. Clutching the glove in my hand, I dashed between the cars and headed for the gardens. It seemed strange that anyone should wish to go walking under dripping trees on a dismal afternoon, but I couldn't think where else he might have gone. I walked up the tarmac paths, under tall pines and horse chestnut trees, but I couldn't see him. Just past a stone bridge I thought I'd found him, but it turned out to be a man fast asleep on a bench in a Roman temple, cradling a tin of lager, oblivious to the world. His dog, tied by a string to the belt on his coat, slept across his feet as they both sheltered from the rain.

Then I saw Josh in the distance disappearing between white railings. I called out, but he didn't hear me, which was just as well because it came out as a really pathetic whelp. And, I know it will sound vain, but there was a part of me that didn't want him to turn round and see me. My hair, always a problem in damp weather, I knew was now hanging limply round my face in frizzy curls. The sleek, straight look I preferred having vanished with that first spot of rain and that first hint of damp in the air. I nearly turned back, especially as the rain was bouncing off the path and gurgling in the gutters. Yet, I'd come this far and I wanted to see where he was going in such a hurry. I followed the path to the white railings, which turned out to be a bridge over the railway line. Onward and upward I hurried keeping him just in sight before he finally disappeared. The only way he could possibly have gone seemed to be screened by hedges but, as I approached, I saw a white cast-iron gate hidden in the greenery. I must admit to feeling a little uneasy at this point. The gardens were deathly quiet and felt more than a little eerie. I was totally and utterly alone. All my Mum's advice about never going into parks by myself came back with a flash. I could easily be murdered and no one would know anything about it. I looked behind me, but there was not a soul around so I pushed the gate open and stepped down onto to the canal path. I didn't want to go any further, I couldn't see my neighbour anywhere and there was something very melancholy about the place. Under a beautiful cast-iron bridge, studded with moss jewels upon its stone façade, a ribbon of jade water snaked slowly along to the echoes of dripping water as two seagulls swooped in a race to the end of a long, dark tunnel.

I was getting soaked through; it was time to go home. I turned, walked up the steps and put my hand on the gate. It opened with a rasping scrape and as I placed my foot to step through the entrance back into the gardens, I thought at first I'd been hit so hard that I reeled and clutched at the gate to steady myself. The world went black and then so dazzlingly bright that I was blinded. I instinctively closed my eyes and how I managed to stay upright I couldn't later figure out, but the greatest shock came when I opened my eyes again. From my place, half hidden behind green bushes, I saw a scene that made no sense.

Chapter 4

I half wondered if I'd stumbled across the filming of a Regency drama, but there were no cameras or anything else to suggest a film shoot and, what was stranger still was the fact that the day was bright and sunny. As real as any moving image on a cinema screen men, women and children paraded, along gravel paths I no longer recognized, parasols and walking sticks in hand. Vibrant cloaks and pelisses gave a glimpse of the white muslin dresses fluttering back in the breeze beneath them and a hundred straw bonnets, feathered and flowered, were tied under the pretty chins of flirting girls in a myriad of silken, ribbon hues. The objects of their smiles looked equally wonderful, bowing before them, in breeches, frock coats and boots. I was rooted to the spot, my heart hammering in my chest, and a thousand questions running through my mind. As the image became sharper, so I became more aware of myself. I still held the glove, though the hand that held it wore a glove of its own. It wasn't my hand, yet it moved with me, and was fixed to the pale arm which disappeared into a long sleeve, pointed at the wrist. I touched my cheek, and brushed the brim of a straw bonnet where a silk ribbon was tied in a bow under my chin. As my senses kicked in the rigidity of bone-stiffened silk, tightly laced about my body, made it difficult to breathe properly. A crisp, cotton petticoat was layered next to my skin and over that, I discovered an outer gown of fine, diaphanous muslin. A square shawl with a floral border, draped over my shoulders, complemented my beautifully tailored coat of soft, apricot wool. To complete my outfit, a reticule of silk satin, embroidered with a basket of roses, was suspended from my wrist on knotted strings. Looking down at my feet, I was glad that at least they were comfy in leather half-boots, even if every other part of me felt squashed and pummelled into shape.

There seemed no explanation except the one that immediately popped into my head. I must have gone back in time, I said to myself, but just having that idea was so ridiculous I dismissed it at first. Slipping the glove into the reticule, I took a step on shaking legs. The trees around me were moving. My feet were taking steps, one in front of the other, but I had no sensation of movement in my legs. I seemed to pass over the grass, over gravel pathways, hovering six inches above the ground without feeling the surface below my feet. The sun felt warm, everything appeared so intensely brilliant that bright tears smarted in my eyes because the light was so fierce. When at last my feet touched the ground my hesitant first steps soon quickened into quite a pace, which felt no more peculiar than wandering around Sydney Gardens dressed in nineteenth century costume would be at any other time. Feeling really uncomfortable and totally self-conscious, as the bonnet on my head wobbled about unnervingly, I wondered how on earth anyone would ever get used to this feeling of being trussed up like a Christmas turkey. I hadn't a clue which direction to take; the gardens looked so unfamiliar until I came out from one of the narrower walks onto a wider path. I recognized the museum at the end, but even this looked different with its rotunda style front for a bandstand and wings of boxes on either side, hardly recognizable to the building I'd seen with its modern additions of glass and ceramic. The exit lay ahead and I was just wondering what might happen if I made it back to my aunt's house in Sydney Place, when two young women came rushing through the gate talking nineteen to the dozen. One of them waved energetically before running towards me, holding onto her hat with one hand as she hitched up her long skirts with the other.

'Miss Elliot! How pleased I am to see you,' she cried, taking both of my hands in hers. 'You are well, I hope, though I must add, you are looking a trifle pale.' She hesitated and I felt her clear hazel eyes, almost amber in their luminosity, sweep over every inch of my face. 'Miss Elliot, I must admit you do not look quite yourself.'

No, that was for sure, I thought, being completely uncertain how I looked. It was very confusing. I felt like me but I really couldn't be completely me, I decided, because here was a stranger who knew me.

The girl whose broad smile reached her twinkling eyes had round rosy cheeks like a painted doll and unruly chestnut curls dancing under the brim of her bonnet in the breeze. Dressed in a plum, velvet pelisse which looked rather worn in places, but suited her dark colouring so well, it was cheered up by a smart, cream, Kashmir shawl with details in crimson and cobalt. Like that of her companion who caught us up, her clothes were neat but clearly not as new as mine. Just as I was struggling to find the words to speak, her expression swiftly altered, the fine arched brows above her lively eyes knitting anxiously together, as her face loomed in and out of focus.

'Cassy,' she called to her companion, 'Miss Elliot is unwell. Help me!'

At that precise moment, I felt the world sway. A wave of nausea rippled through me as the ground seemed to be trying its hardest to meet the sky.

'Quickly, Jane! Let us support her between us.' Cassy acted swiftly, taking an arm and bearing the weight, as my legs buckled. Jane took the other side and the girls managed to lead me to the nearest bench.

As if time was moving, one moment I could see the gardens I'd left behind, and the next all was changed. Shifting in layers, the past and the present overlapped for a moment and I was left, feeling queasy, unable to focus on anything. Gulping back deep breaths of air, the feeling that I might be slipping back to my own time gradually disappeared. Jane and Cassy were talking to me, but their muffled voices were sounding far off like echoes coming from a long tunnel.

'Oh, Miss Elliot, you've come back to us.' Cassy said, as she waved smelling salts under my nose. 'You've quite given the Miss Austens the fright of their lives.'

'We thought we'd lost you,' Jane added, 'I'm so glad you're still here.'

I was feeling so wretched that at first, the enormity of what I was experiencing didn't sink in. An incredulous idea about the identity of the girl formed in my mind, as I recognized that she was one of the world's greatest writers, a novelist of such genius that her books are still being read and loved two hundred years after her death. Even then, when the thought slowly surfaced and registered that Miss Jane Austen herself was talking to me, I couldn't really equate that iconic figure with the slim, finely featured girl that took my hand between both of her own. I'd only ever seen one small portrait of Jane, which showed her as unsmiling, a rather stern looking spinster in a mobcap. Yet, the girl at my side seemed just like me. I saw a young woman whose love of life sparkled in her eyes and danced at the corners of her mouth.

Her sister spoke. 'Are you recovered enough to walk, Miss Elliot? We will escort you.'

I could order a chair to collect you from the ticketman at the gate,' Jane added, 'We need to get you home where you may recover by the warmth of a fire.'

I knew that I couldn't stay sitting mute any longer, but I didn't want to betray myself as soon as I started to speak. I opened my mouth only to close it again. Then, just when I thought I'd never talk again, I heard my voice ring out loud and clear.

'Oh, please, Miss Austen, Miss Jane, pray do not be troubled. I am quite well.'

It felt surprisingly natural and I knew I'd got away with it judging by the expression on their faces.

'I did not eat very much this morning and I fear my unsteadiness is as a result of my fastidiousness.'

It was out before I could stop it. I repeated the sentence in my head. Had I really just spoken those words? I could only be grateful that it felt as if I had.

'That is a relief of some kind,' said Jane. 'I had begun to think you were really ill. But, at last, the colour is returning to your countenance ... "your pure and eloquent blood speaks in your cheeks!"'

I hadn't a clue what she was talking about.

'Just like your namesake,' added Cassandra. And when I looked at her blankly, she said, 'Are you acquainted with Mr. Fielding's novel, Tom Jones? It's one of Jane's favourite books and she is always quoting out of it.'

Cassandra looked at her sister with a mischievous glance and in a stage whisper pronounced loudly, 'Between us, I think Miss Jane fancies her own scarlet cheeks could be compared to those of Tom's heroine, Miss Sophia Western.'

'Not only of my cheeks,' Jane continued, pursing her lips, but of my sweet mouth also.

"Her lips were red, and one was thin,
Compared to that was next her chin;
(Some bee had stung it newly)" ...

'Of course, strictly speaking, that's Suckling not Fielding, but nevertheless, I am sure they both had me in mind when they wrote that description.'

We all laughed.

'Well, Miss Elliot, I am glad to see you better and if we cannot assist you, we can at least keep you company,' said Cassandra.

'And very pleased you will be to have our society when you learn our most exciting news,' added Jane. 'Our dearest little Charles is coming home. Except, of course, he is not little at all being at least six feet tall and thinks himself a very grown man, indeed.'

'He is very nearly three and twenty,' interrupted Cassandra, 'but, Miss Elliot, it is impossible to think of him as anything but our baby brother.'

'As soon as he is able to get off his ship, he is to come here,' Jane continued. 'Such excitement! Not that I ever really think returning to Bath is quite like coming home. If we were in Steventon where we used to live, there would have been a great party with all our friends and neighbours to celebrate the Peace. But our old home is no longer ours and those days of youth and comfort are quite gone.'

'I understand how you might miss your home so much,' I said. 'I must admit, I did not want to come to Bath and I do not know when we might return.'

I had spoken without consciousness; yet, I was sure what I was saying must be true. And the thought emerged that somehow I'd slipped back in time to experience the life of my ancestor. I surely couldn't be addressed as Miss Elliot for nothing, but the idea that she had known Jane Austen was such an exciting one that I could hardly take it in. What on earth had happened to me?

'Oh, Miss Elliot, then you understand completely,' said Jane, 'but, at least we can visit Steventon though it might as well be inhabited by strangers for all that I feel at home in it.'

I saw Cassandra frown at Jane and a look pass between them that Jane clearly understood.

'My brother James has the rectory now,' she continued, ignoring her sister's expression, which entreated her to be more reserved on the subject.

'Jane, I am sure Miss Elliot does not want to hear our family concerns,' Cassandra rejoined. 'Come, if you are feeling better, perhaps we could all continue with our walk.'

I nodded and we rose together to link arms, once more assuring my companions who were looking at me anxiously that I felt absolutely fine.

'Tell me more about your brother, Mr Charles,' I said.

'He is in the Navy, serving as a second Lieutenant on the frigate, Endymion,' Jane replied, bright-eyed once more. 'Charles has already had a taste of adventure on the high seas and won a little prize money for his efforts, though he will never be rich if he always spends it on his sisters. The topaz crosses that Cassy and I always wear in the evening were bought with his very first rewards. He is such a sweet, generous-hearted brother to think of his sisters above everyone else. How he will manage coming home to a house populated by three women and my long suffering father, I cannot think, but we are all so excited to be seeing him again. Later on, my father has planned a trip to Devon and beyond. Charles will be coming with us. The days cannot pass too quickly for me, Miss Elliot, I confess.'

'I have always wished I had a brother,' I replied.

'We have several we could share with you.' Jane paused, as if picturing them all in her mind. 'I am sure we could let you borrow one if you ever need one, though they do have a habit of running off to some far flung place just when you need them most. I've planned many a time on being a stowaway in a sailor brother's boat, but they would never agree to it. Heavens, it's as much as I can do to escape to these gardens.'

Although her manner was light-hearted, she'd expressed more than a hint of frustration. Their brothers were free to go off whenever they wished. I couldn't imagine such restrictions, unable to go where I liked. Even taking a stroll in the park was clearly seen as daring.

We were walking round one of the bowling greens and past one of the entrances to the Labyrinth, a maze, which Jane said she had had the pleasure of getting lost in on two occasions.

'I cannot imagine how you came to lose yourself when you must have walked into it almost every day,' said Cassandra with a smile, 'or how such a predicament could have been at all pleasurable.'

Jane looked wistful. 'I wasn't lost to the sensations of nature, exquisite in sight and smell. I assure you, I was never happier when confined within those yew hedges, brilliant after a storm.'

Cassandra caught my eye and grinned. 'My sister is inclined to be whimsical, Miss Elliot. I promise you, the Labyrinth must be the design of a child and, for all its secret corners, is not a place to easily lose oneself. I wonder at Jane's capricious mind, there is no limit to her inventiveness.'

It was then that I felt the first spots of rain. The sun had disappeared behind a blanket of cloud.

Cassandra sighed. 'Oh, dear, all this talk of storms; I knew I should have brought the umbrella.'

'It is just a little rain. April is almost here and showers like these are to be expected, nothing to regard,' said Jane. 'But, Miss Elliot, you must not get wet or you may become ill again. I really urge you to think about us helping you home.'

I'd been feeling more and more comfortable and I'd stopped worrying about what I was going to say because it just happened without me having to think about a single sentence, but now I knew the real test had come. Waves of anxiety washed over me. What would I find when I reached my aunt's house? Would Sophia Elliot's family be there? If anyone were to see through me, it would surely be my own ancestors. Perhaps they would guess something was not quite right. But, as frightened as I felt by the whole ordeal, I was excited to see them and experience a glimpse of Sophia's life.

We were at the gate and then dashing through a gap between the smart, black carriages rolling round Sydney Place to reach the other side of the road. The buildings looked so new, the characteristic Bath stone almost white and the railings painted not their customary black, but bright blue. Everything had the appearance of spruce elegance; the houses gleaming like newly painted doll's houses. And the streets were full of people, the unfamiliar sounds and sights ringing through the air. The heavy rumble of carts and drays, the bawling of newsmen, muffin-men, and milkmen, and the ceaseless clink of pattens on the neat pavements, confirmed the truth that I was in a place that I could just recognize, yet was completely unknown.

The Miss Austens shook hands, begged that we should meet again soon and disappeared next door. The lion's head knocker on the door in front of me looked ready to open its golden mouth to roar and I had to muster all my courage to take it up and strike the door.

I panicked. I didn't feel ready; I wasn't at all certain what to do or how to react. I willed myself to turn and dashing back over the road, I decided that if I could get back to the gate where it had all started that would be my best escape. People walking past me through the shaded, dappled paths started to fade, as the present and past appeared to fuse for a moment, dream-like in translucent transparency. I could see the gate ahead, one moment in sharp focus, every detail magnified. But, in the next second it disappeared, just as quickly, evaporating like wisps of smoke, elusive and ethereal. As I reached out for it in desperation, grasping at nothing I could physically hold onto, it appeared in sharp focus once more. I held on tight, willing myself to feel the cold touch of iron, pulling with all my strength and at last I felt it open.

I found myself standing in the pouring rain at the bottom of the steps by the canal side, just as I had been moments before I'd passed through the gate. I must have dropped the glove at some point and couldn't find it at first, until I realized I was actually standing on it. I couldn't begin to think about my strange experience with anything approaching common sense, but I knew I didn't want to go back through the gate. Deciding that my best course would be to follow the canal path, it didn't take long before I reached a set of steps that led up to the main road with its hum of traffic and the sight of people going about their business looking reassuringly normal.

I let myself into the house. My first thought was that I must be brave and return the glove to its owner. It would be rude if I didn't introduce myself, so I knocked, but there were no sounds from behind the immaculate, grey painted door. I'd just have to try again later.

Sitting by the fire to dry out, I kicked off my shoes and watched my damp socks steam on a footstool before the flames as I tried to understand what had just happened. The time by the clock on the mantelpiece said half past five, which surely couldn't be right. I'd been away for at least a couple of hours. But when I thought about any time travel books I'd read, time didn't ever behave, as it should. Had I really visited the past and met Jane Austen and her sister? Somehow, voicing those words in my head made it seem so unreal. I couldn't explain anything. It was very unsettling and I wasn't sure how much I did want to think about it. That sense of unease, and the feeling that somehow I was not alone made me long for some other company. There were noises in the silent flat, which I know sounds like a contradiction. The creak of floorboards and scratching in the wainscot I put down to the possibility of nesting mice but, the tread of footsteps on the stairs, the rustling of silk swishing along the floor and the click of a door shutting softly, were all sounds that I could not easily explain. I closed the shutters as dusk fell and lit the candles in the sconces on either side of the huge looking glass before settling back into the winged chair. I felt my eyes grow heavy and sleep steal over me as I gave in to the comforting sounds of the fire crackling and the ticking of the clock. But not for long: other noises soon had my eyes open and staring into the darkened room. The sound of footsteps stealing up behind my chair froze my limbs to rigidity and pinned me to the seat. Wide-awake with a thumping heart I listened intently, trying unsuccessfully to convince myself that all I'd heard was a noise from the flat below or from next door. To my absolute horror, when I finally plucked up the courage to look behind the wing of my chair, I saw the door move as if someone had just pushed it open and heard the kind of ghastly creaking you might only hear in the scariest films at the cinema. Acting on impulse, I grabbed a heavy, gilt candlestick from the mantelpiece and crossed the room at speed to peer into the corridor beyond.

'Is anybody there?' I called weakly. Eerily silent, all seemed quiet in the dark hallway. The resounding, pounding beat of my heart made me jumpy and I couldn't get past the feeling that somehow I was not alone. Scolding myself for getting carried away, I put my sensible head on and considered the fact that in an old house like this there were bound to be all sorts of noises caused by old timber shrinking and expanding, and gales howling through the gaps in the antique joinery. Returning to my chair, I gave myself a stern talking to before I sat down and switched on the lamp. Candlelight was a little too atmospheric, I decided, and the light that pooled across the tabletop and over Great Aunt Elizabeth's rosewood box was comforting. But the reassurance lasted no longer than the time it took my eyes to alight on a small, leather-bound volume, lying next to the rosewood box as if it had always been there. I was sure I'd never before set my eyes on this small pocketbook that proved on opening to be an ancient journal, but to consider what that meant was an idea I didn't want to contemplate. It surely was the case that I'd merely overlooked it.

Opening the diary with trembling fingers, I saw three names inscribed in three very different hands on the inside cover and then I didn't feel quite so frightened any more.

Firstly, in a flowing style in brown ink, neat and perfectly formed, were the words: *This book belongs to Sophia Elliot of Monkford Hall, Somerset, January 1st 1802*. She was the namesake my Great Aunt had mentioned, and I felt for sure it had been her body I'd inhabited earlier though just thinking about it had me doubting that my strange experience had really happened. I remembered my mother talking about this ancestor, telling me that I'd been named for her. I'd often wondered what she was like, but I knew nothing more. Mum always said there had been portraits of Sophia in the family, but sadly they'd all been lost or sold many years ago before she was of an age to save them.

Secondly, in pencil, with many flourishes on the capital letters, my grandmother had written: *This book belongs to Dorothy Elliot, Mandeville House, Stoke Road, Crewkerne, April 7th, 1950.* Keeping the name of Elliot in the female line, my grandmother had declared, was a family tradition that had been in place for hundreds of years passing from daughter to daughter. Thankfully, each generation had married happily to understanding men who never baulked once when their own names were rejected in favour of their own. Elliot women could trace their ancestry back to Tudor times according to Dorothy Elliot, but whether those first ladies had felt as passionately about their heritage, we would never know.

Thirdly, written by my mother in an expressive, artistic style in blue fountain pen ink: *This book belongs to Caroline Elliot, Flat 3, 36, Lennox Place, London, December 11th, 1976,* but was clearly written when she was young, the letters larger and expressed with a creative flourish. Perhaps written when she was at art school, I wondered. Seeing mum's handwriting brought back memories of her shopping lists, the recipes she'd copied out on scraps of paper that still fall out of cookery books to this day and, of course, all those precious birthday cards I'd collected. I stroked the ink, held the page to my face, knowing that her hand had been there and had touched the page. I wanted to add my own name, to feel a kind of kinship with the known and unknown Elliot women who had cherished this diary before me. I dug out my pen from the large bag at my feet and wrote my name with pride.

I skimmed through the entries, turning the pages and admiring Sophia's perfectly formed handwriting. January and February seemed to have been fairly dull months for her, I noted. The weather that year had been cold and it had not been possible to go out very much in the Somerset countryside. The family coach had once become stuck in the snow after a ball which meant they had all walked home in their evening clothes, resulting in Sophia being put to bed for a week with a head cold. There were a couple of entries about her father and sister Emma leaving for London with a Mrs Randall, and one at the end of February that intrigued me.

February 22nd: My sister has a new beau; we are told, in a letter received this morning. Mrs Randall thinks it will be a good match and predicts a wedding by Easter. I am so pleased that I managed to persuade my father that I could be left behind. The thought of being paraded about at all the drawing rooms of London like a prize cow fills me with horror. I hope for Emma's sake it is a love match, but I fear in such a short courtship, this cannot be the case.

So, Emma Elliot had been taken to London to find a husband. I could quite understand Sophia's horror at the thought. To be introduced to a stranger and married in a month or two before you knew anything about your partner seemed a barbaric practice. But their whole way of life was something I couldn't relate to and it was hard to imagine the lives of my ancestors. My family had enjoyed a life of leisure, privilege and wealth, but in my Great-Grandmother's time the First World War changed everything. The family fortunes dwindled along with the estates, which had had to be sold. Now, all that remained was a black and white print of Monkford Hall, the manor house that the first Elizabethan queen had given in recognition of services to the crown, which my mother had framed and put in pride of place above what she had jokingly called her other "seat", in the loo. I'd always wondered about the house. My mother said she'd visited it once as a girl, a very long time ago, but there was no one living there now that we knew.

I turned the page and started to read the next entry, completely absorbed in this fascinating little book. To think that Sophia had written the diary was incredible and the fact that she shared my name made me feel an instant connection.

'Sophie,' whispered a voice with warm breath in my ear.

I literally jumped out of my chair. Spinning round I could see no one. I knew there could be no physical being attached to the soft, female voice I'd heard coming from the alcove where the corner cupboard, with its shell-shaped recess, stood. Was it my imagination or was the display of teabowls and silver teapots gleaming with a ghostly glimmer?

'There is no one here,' I said out loud to myself. 'I'm just not used to being alone in a big, old ... quite scary place, now it's dark.'

I plumped up the cushion on my chair, thought about sitting down again, but instead picked up my bag.

'I think I'll just pop out for a walk,' I announced to the room as calmly as I could, not wanting to admit to myself that I just couldn't stay there a moment longer.

Chapter
6

When I stepped outside the darkness felt intimidating, and I didn't
feel quite so brave about the thought of walking around by myself.
I needed company like I never had before and so I took the short
walk round the corner to revisit the pub. It was Friday night, which
meant the place was heaving with locals. They all seemed to know
one another; the air was thick with conversation and laughter as
they all celebrated the end of another week at work. One or two
people nodded and smiled in recognition. They'd been there at
lunchtime and had evidently settled in for the evening. Making my
way to the safety of the bar, I perched myself on a tall stool and
managed to catch Lara's eye.

'How's it going?' she asked, opening a bottle of white wine
and pouring me a glass.

'Surprisingly well,' I said, almost convincing myself and
resolving to keep my weird experiences to myself. 'You wouldn't
recognize it; the place is spotless. Thanks so much, I couldn't have
done it without you.'

'It's my pleasure. I'm glad to help, but I expect you're worn
out now.'

'Yes, I am really tired, and in the great scheme of things, I completely forgot about shopping or eating and suddenly that seems a great idea.'

'Of course, here's the menu. I'll be with you in a minute. Have a look and see what you fancy.'

As Lara moved on to the next customer, I scanned the room thinking how much I loved this quirky place with its eclectic décor. There were ancient gas lamps hanging above the bar, their shell-pink lustre shades glowing with light. A painted oar from a rowing boat was pinned into the wall above the be-ribboned, Georgian mantelpiece, flanked on either side by trophies from a bygone age, and surveyed from on high by a print of *The Laughing Cavalier* who sported a furry moustache that someone had clearly stuck on over his own, for a joke. Nobody noticed me and I was quite enjoying the sense of anonymity when Lara stopped again to take my order.

'Oh, by the way, Josh is in tonight,' she said, putting a knife and fork in front of me before diving under the counter for salt and pepper pots. 'I'll introduce you to him in a minute. Then you won't have to sit on your own.'

I looked to where she was pointing but before I could ask her exactly where he was, she was away upstairs to see to food orders. Presumably, she meant he was sitting on the other side of the bar, which was sectioned off in another room and I couldn't see anyone at first. It was gloomy on that side, except for the glow of a fire in the grate. Then a figure moved forward, I could just see a blue-jeaned leg jutting out from a table. He bent down to pick up a leather bag and I got a glimpse of a profile, but Josh might as well have been a silhouette in a miniature portrait for all I could really see. Well, Lara had promised an introduction, so I'd just have to be patient. I wished I'd brought his glove with me and then, at least, we'd have something to talk about.

My Thai fishcakes arrived, fragrant with lemongrass, accompanied by wedges of crisp potato and soured cream that had my mouth watering. I was hungrier than I knew, savouring each bite as Lara looked on with a grin. She glanced behind her into the other bar and I guessed that she was checking up on Josh.

'I won't call him over until you've finished,' she said. 'I don't think you'll thank me for an introduction whilst you're eating.'

I smiled. 'Thanks. No, I don't really want to meet my new neighbour with bits of coriander stuck between my teeth!'

'Quite right. First impressions are always very important. And, it would be lovely if you could get to know one another. He always looks a bit lonely, and I never really see him with anyone. I don't think he's got a girlfriend.'

I could feel myself blushing under her scrutiny and was beginning to wonder whether meeting Josh like this would be such a good idea. It would be nice to make friends, but I didn't feel like starting the sort of relationship that Lara was making hints about. I needed to change the conversation, although I admitted to myself that I was curious about him.

'What does he do?'

'He's working on something at the museum over the road.'

So that's where he'd been going earlier, even though it had been an odd time of day when everyone else working were locked in their offices. I couldn't imagine what sort of job he could possibly do, and judging by his clothes and his mop of shaggy curls, if Lara had said he was an actor or a musician I would more readily have believed that.

'Josh organizes exhibitions,' Lara continued. 'He's here on a contract, so it's not forever. He's putting together something to do with Georgian paintings and artefacts; he'll tell you about it himself, I expect.'

'I saw him today, I think. He dropped a glove, out on the pavement. I picked it up and tried to catch up with him but he was too fast for me.'

'Yes, it would be those long legs of his that kept you away. You'd have to run to keep up with him.'

'Are the gardens over the road connected to the museum in any way?'

'Yes, I'm sure they have a connection. I know they're at least a couple of hundred years old, if not more, but I think I'm right in saying that at one time the museum was a hotel. Sydney Gardens were a place of entertainment, what they called pleasure gardens, not quite like they are now.'

'Then Jane Austen herself must have walked in the gardens,' I said, really thinking out loud, casting my mind back to my inexplicable experience.

Lara looked at me, a bemused expression on her face. 'I daresay she did, but Josh will be able to tell you more about it than I can. Have you finished? Come on, you can ask him yourself.'

I saw her turn round, poke her head into the bar behind and say something to a person out of view. When she turned back, the look of disappointment on her face was plain to see.

'I think we've just gone and missed him again, but Martin says Josh was going straight home because he'd got a bit of paperwork to finish. If you're quick, you'll catch him, he's only just left. At least you've got a good excuse to knock on his door.'

I didn't really want to hang around much longer. It was beginning to feel a bit like being at a party where I was the only person who didn't know anyone and I couldn't expect Lara to chat to me all night. On the other hand, the prospect of going home to knock on Josh's door didn't seem very tempting either. By the time I walked round the corner, I chided myself for being silly. What harm was there in just knocking on the door and saying hello? I could just hand over the glove and say I found it in the street, though how I'd get around the problem of telling him that I knew it belonged to him, I couldn't decide. He'd think I was some kind of weirdo for spying on him if I told him. There was only one answer to my problem. I would just walk past his door and on up the stairs to my flat and try to forget all about it for the time being. In any case, I'd have to think hard about what I'd say and right now I was so tired, I couldn't think straight.

However, nothing could stop me feeling guilty about it still being in my possession. I turned to the box that Great Aunt

Elizabeth had sent me. Out of sight would be out of mind. I popped in the glove closing the lid quickly before I could think about what I'd done. Somewhere in the deep recesses of my mind, I knew there was little possibility of the glove ever making an appearance again. And, although the idea that this was very wrong crossed my mind fleetingly, I chose to ignore it.

I couldn't resist picking up the journal once again, though the spooky experience I'd had earlier made me hesitate, for a second, until I told myself not to be so silly. I opened it at the place I'd marked with a silk ribbon and waited. Much to my relief no whispers or haunting visions appeared. I read the next entry.

March 1st: Emma and my father are leaving London this morning. There has been no further mention of Mr Fellowes and their abrupt departure seems somewhat strange. I fear something is amiss.

I wondered if Mr Fellowes had got cold feet or if Emma had refused to marry him. The next few pages were blank and then on March 6th the journal became very interesting.

We are to remove to Bath. Mrs Randall has suggested this expedition to my father in order that Emma might be introduced to Bath society and perhaps find a husband. My father is adamant that she will be married before the year is out.

I do not want to go to Bath and leave my home for months on end. The only saving grace is that Mrs Randall will accompany us, for which I am truly grateful. We are to take a house near Sydney Gardens. Mrs Randall assures me that I will enjoy myself and for her sake, I will endeavour not to disappoint her.

I couldn't help feeling sorry for Sophia. Though I knew her words had been written over two hundred years ago, the sentiments and feelings were so fresh mirroring my own misgivings at leaving everything familiar. The next entry made me smile.

March 10th: We are arrived in Sydney Place. It is not at all like being in the country but the gardens just over the way are very pretty, and I hope I shall be allowed to walk there sometimes. Mrs Randall has lodgings nearby in Daniel Street. She would not be talked into joining us here in the house, saying that she had no wish for people to assume that she was trying to take my mother's place. Dear Mrs Randall, only you would be so considerate. You have been such a comfort since Mama passed away.

It was a strange thought that this was the very house where the family had arrived all that time ago. I could almost feel them around me, hear their conversations, or at least, imagine what they might have been. As the journal continued, Sophia's reticence had given way to youthful excitement.

March 12th: Mrs Randall took us shopping for new muslins, that we might look respectable for a ball at the Upper Rooms. I chose a pretty, tamboured muslin that is to be made up into a round gown and I have black gauze for a new cloak. I also have a new white chip bonnet, trimmed with white ribbon and I find it looking very much like other people's and quite as smart.

March 13th: We went to the Pump Rooms this morning and signed the arrivals book. Mr King introduced us to a family who are also residing in Sydney Place, and I have discovered they are living just next door. I wish my father were not so abrupt in his manner. He hardly acknowledged them. They seem pleasant, respectable people, but I know he assumes they are not worth knowing. They do not appear to be wealthy, though seem genteel enough. The father is a clergyman with a shock of white hair and the mother has quite as many airs as my father, which amused me greatly. I am not sure who felt they were being more condescending in addressing the other. There are two daughters, both very pleasant girls, whom I wouldn't mind knowing better... their name is Austen.

I caught my breath, hardly able to believe what I was reading.

March 19th: I met the two Miss Austens on our morning walk in the gardens today. Miss Jane, the youngest sister, has a most penetrating way of looking at you, which I find particularly unnerving, but despite this her manner is quite friendly. Indeed, her clear hazel eyes continually sparkle with amusement, as if she has just heard of something that is about to send her off into peals of laughter.

So, it was true! I really had met Jane and Cassandra, as Sophia Elliot had all those years ago. I couldn't wait to read more.

March 20th: A ball at the Upper Rooms tonight. Miss Jane Austen and her sister Cassandra were in attendance with their parents. Miss Jane engaged me in conversation when she was not dancing. I like her very much for her intelligence and her wonderful sense of humour. Her sister is also very pleasant, but has not Miss Jane's liveliness, nor her wicked tongue.

March 22nd: A ball at the Lower Rooms – I nearly died laughing at Miss Jane's antics. She teases and abuses all her dancing partners with her quick wit, but the best of it is that they do not realize she is laughing at their expense. We danced every dance and sat down not once.

March 24th: Accompanied the Miss Austens to the circulating library in Milsom Street. I heard all about their handsome brothers today. Edward is a rich landowner, James a clergyman, Frank and Charles are in the Navy, and Henry is a banker!

There was one last entry.

March 29th: I met the Miss Austens in the gardens as has become our custom on our daily walk. They were very excited, because now hostilities are at an end with the French, the Peace means all our brave soldiers and sailors will be at war no longer. I expect Jane's sailor brothers will be home soon. At any rate, we can expect to see whole crews and battalions of young men descending on the town. There is to be a ball held in celebration and I am to have a new headband to wear.

My hand flew to my mouth. I knew exactly what had happened that day and the conversations they'd shared! Frustratingly, there was no more, and I couldn't help but wonder why, though I guessed Sophia had just been too busy to write. How I wished that she'd written more about her time with the Austen family. I flicked through the remaining pages and then one more entry stood out in blue ink as bright as if it had just been penned. On the page marked the last day of May were some lines written in my mum's very familiar handwriting.

May 31st: Is it wrong to pursue what I know my heart must give up? I dare not go back again. But, when I am there, it does not feel like a deception, and I know it is right.

Time is but a shadow,
Too slow, too swift,
But for those who love,
Time does not exist.
I am a shadow, so art thou.

This was most puzzling and the only snippet of mum's writing I could find. It did sound a bit dramatic for a woman who'd always been so even-tempered and calm whilst she lived her all too brief life. What, or rather whom had she contemplated giving up, I wondered? I actually didn't know anything about my mother's life as a girl, though I remembered her talking once or twice about old boyfriends who clearly weren't significant. No, the only person she'd ever truly loved was my dad. There are photos of her when young, but they almost seem to be someone else, certainly no one I recognize. There's one in a frame at home. She's standing by a lake, her long, dark hair flowing back in the wind, her dress billowing out behind her showing lithe and fragile contours. I like that picture because she's laughing, it's a face full of love and hope for the future.

I didn't quite feel comfortable about all the feelings and emotions that seemed to emanate from the yellowing pages of the journal like a forgotten elixir, elusive and intangible, and was about to add it to the contents of the rosewood box when I noticed the edge of a piece of paper tucked in to the binding at the back. Carefully extracting the brittle paper, I unfolded it to find the dust of a dried rosebud wrapped in a piece of lace, a silver medal-shaped coin and what looked to be some sort of subscription card. The medal had an engraving of the Sydney Hotel on it and I wondered if it might be like a kind of ticket, perhaps, to what was now the museum or even the gardens. But the most intriguing object was the subscription card to the Assembly Rooms for the entrance to Cotillion Balls for the price of a pound. The date was April 5th, 1802, and the name Sophia Elliot was written along the top. But, what really caused every hair on my head to stand on end was the realization that it was written very clearly in my own hand.

Chapter 7

I held the card up to the light turning it one way and then the other. Surely I must be mistaken. The brown ink was a mystery, but there was no confusion about the handwriting. Even by comparing it closely with Sophia Elliot's writing on the journal flap, it was evident that different people had written both samples of script. And I did know my own writing as well as I knew myself and I couldn't know anything more than that. Could I?

As I puzzled over the small card that set my heart racing to the point where I felt so light-headed I thought I might pass out, a nagging voice at the back of my mind said that I knew perfectly well what it meant. Yet, this amazing idea was so weird and momentous that if I were to speak it out loud or if I were to tell anyone they would instantly have me locked up. But, I knew I must have been there. I must have owned the subscription card to the Assembly Rooms in 1802 and, in my heart, I knew that the episode in the gardens was not a figment of my imagination, however much I tried to tell myself that it had been. It was time to reassess what had happened. It wasn't very easy because the whole thing just seemed so ridiculous. All I kept thinking was that to prove it to myself, I would have to go back to the gardens and find out. I would pass through the white gate once more, even though the very thought filled me with a sense of foreboding so strong I could almost taste it on my tongue. Nothing could be done until the morning, and inevitably, a fitful night followed with harrowing dreams. Once, in the night, I swear I heard the turning of the door handle to the bedroom, but I couldn't wake up enough or even turn on my pillow to look. When the light speared through the shutters to coax me into opening my eyes, I started when I saw the door was really open. I was sure I'd shut it before jumping into bed, but on the other hand, I didn't feel very sure about anything any more.

I was up and dressed in no time, carefully tucking the subscription card into the back pocket of my jeans. I wanted to do my own research before I hurled myself back through time, if that was in fact what I was going to do, and I knew the Holburne Museum in the gardens might help with my detective work. Just thinking about the possibility of time travel was surreal, but I'd got enough to think about before I made any further attempts!

I found what I was looking for straight away on a glass cabinet shelf, upstairs in one of the small galleries. Full of trinkets, I saw beautiful examples of the enamelled patch and snuff boxes made for the eighteenth century tourists who'd flocked to Bath. Amongst the "Trifles of Bath" were silver subscription medals just like the one I had found and, most spookily of all, several subscription cards for "Dress Balls" and "Cotillion Balls" exactly like the one in my pocket. I took it out for comparison. There was no mistake; it was the real thing, which made me feel very strange.

Ignoring my hammering heart, I explored the upper floors and as I made for the staircase to go down to the café, I passed a large poster at the entrance of the exhibition room showing the paintings, ceramics and decorative items that were to be in the new display, set against an enormous portrait of a Captain Holburne who'd been in the Navy in the 1750s. I will never know what possessed me to do it, but the door was irresistibly ajar. I popped my head round for a sneaky look.

The door made a horrible noise as I leaned on it and immediately a figure appeared from a side door, lit like a silhouette from bright lights at the back of the room. Even as I ran away like some silly teenager, I knew it was Josh even if I hadn't seen enough to make out his features. I would have recognized his physique from a mile away. I'd never moved so fast and almost running downstairs made me laugh out loud, partly because I felt like a naughty schoolgirl, partly to relieve the tension.

Relishing a muffin and hot chocolate in the café with its wonderful views of the gardens all around me, I contemplated and cogitated on the pros and cons of what I was about to do. There seemed so many sensible reasons not to go back and venture through that gate, but I knew that if I didn't, I would always regret it.

Once outside, and through the gates into the larger part of the gardens, I tried to convince myself that I just needed to walk, and have a think about things. At least the weather was better. The whole place had a far friendlier feel about it in the sunshine. When I got to the laurel hedge, my heart began to pound again so I took a deep breath to steady my nerves. I decided to do exactly as I had before. I stepped through the gate and down the steps to the canal side. Everywhere was quiet, thankfully, not even a seagull in sight. I turned, marched up the steps and put my hand on the gate, which scraped reassuringly as before. But, this time, nothing happened. No matter how many times I crossed the entrance, or held onto the gate, placing my foot on the stone threshold as I had that last time, I was disappointed. And that's exactly how I felt, strangely. I felt really let down and as I walked home I began to doubt that what I thought had happened last time, about actually travelling through time, was for real.

I didn't want to go home. I was feeling really fed up. It was being on my own, I decided, that had given me all these daft ideas about talking to Jane Austen in 1802. It was time to forget all that nonsense and do something else. I'd been in Bath for two days, but

I'd seen nothing of it yet. I veered off back down Pulteney Street, thinking that I would walk into town, do a bit of sightseeing and pick up some shopping on the way back. But where should I go first? I wandered towards the imposing Abbey, immediately recognizing the scene from my favourite *Persuasion* film.

Just walking through the revolving door under the Pump Rooms sign was as good as stepping back in time and it did look as wonderful as I'd hoped. A sea of tables dressed in crisp white linen stretched the length of the room, each decorated with arrangements of white lilies scenting the air, along with the evocative aromas of Earl Grey tea, pungent morning coffee, the fragrant smells of cake and toasted Bath buns. From the lofty ceiling, a dazzling chandelier glittered above the throngs of tourists. Spangled with strings of crystals like sprinkles on winter cobwebs, every pendalogue dripped prisms of rainbow light to illuminate the glossy hair of a young girl, or to wink in a clinking, silver teaspoon. Fringed, terracotta hangings in the Regency style framed the long windows and, on the opposite side, the brass dogs in the fireplace gleamed against the dark marble of the chimney-piece making the perfect foil for the rich green of a potted fern. There was something so very English and genteel about the whole place, not quite Jane Austen perhaps, but lovely, nevertheless. The room was buzzing with chattering people whilst a trio on the stage entertained everyone with music from a piano, viola and violin. Presiding over it all was the statue of Beau Nash who along with the portraits of stern gentlemen looked as if he might climb down from his stony pedestal at any moment to remonstrate with the table underneath him, a noisy family who were gathered to catch up with their gossipy news. At the water fountain in the bow-windowed alcove, a man in fancy livery was dispensing water into glasses. A little queue was forming and there was a lot of laughter and pulling of faces as people decided whether they liked or disliked the taste of Bath's spa water. I made my way to the counter, pulling off my gloves and hat and leaving them to one side. The steaming water frothed from an urn into the mouths of copper fish, green with verdigris, as the Pumper filled the glasses placing each one before reticent customers. He put one before me with an enquiring look. I couldn't really come to Bath and not try the waters. After all, I was sure Anne and Captain Wentworth had managed, as had Jane herself, so I handed over my money. I must admit, I wasn't thrilled by the smell and I did end up holding my breath so that I couldn't taste the warm, sulphurous liquid. But, I managed to get to the bottom of the glass, which I felt was an achievement, though I wasn't sure I was going to do it again. I was just about to leave when I was suddenly aware of someone standing too closely behind me, right by my elbow, wedging themselves in between the person next in line and myself. I think I probably looked a bit cross when I turned round, but I was sure that they were rudely barging in.

'Does this belong to you?'

I started and stared, both at the glove in his hand and the face looking down at me. Although I'd never seen this face before, I immediately recognized the mop of chocolate curls. Registering the lightly tanned skin and deep velvet eyes; brown as the bed of the brook I paddled in as a child, I watched sensuous lips curve into a smile revealing white teeth. I'm sure my mouth fell open in surprise.

'I'm sorry if I made you jump,' he said, 'but I just saw your glove fall to the floor a moment ago and someone tread on it. The next thing it had been kicked to one side, and I thought you might not notice, or find it yourself.'

I managed to say thank you, but I couldn't utter another word.

'Are you sure you're okay? You know, you look really pale. Would you like to sit down?'

I couldn't believe my eyes. It was Josh whatshisname. Though I hadn't seen his face before, I knew the rest of him so well. Standing right next to me, he was so close, I could have put a finger up through one of those long, loose curls that tumbled in dark, unruly waves. I could just imagine what Lara would have said about his leather jacket, the silver chain he wore round his neck and his snug fitting jeans. I admit I was slightly over-awed; he had such presence. He was one of those people that command attention, who everyone stares at when they enter a room. His large, expressive eyes were looking at me in concern, but he smiled again, a sort of funny, half smile that just hinted at a sense of humour. I was shocked, utterly dumbfounded. I just kept thinking, he must wonder if I'm totally stupid as I stood with my mouth open doing a very good impression of the copper fish on the water pump behind the counter. It was so unexpected.

'Have you come for your usual, Mr Strafford?'

'Yes, line them up, Toby,' Josh said, thumping the counter, 'I'm ready and willing!'

Toby, the pumper, poured three glasses of spa water and placed them before Josh. I watched him drink the first, draining the glass without flinching once. I noticed his hands, like artist's hands I thought, with long, slender fingers. He looked at me again with those eyes that seemed to acknowledge the effect he was having on me and he winked playfully.

I felt myself blushing but, at last, I found my tongue. 'You're not going to drink them all, are you?' I asked, before I realized that I'd actually spoken my thoughts out loud.

He paused to turn and grin at me. 'Every morning without fail, I'm here to take the waters. Isn't that right, Toby?'

'That's correct, Mr Strafford,' replied the pumper, with a tone that suggested a certain pride in what he obviously thought was a very admirable habit in his customer.

'But, do you actually like it?' I persisted. Drinking one glass had been quite enough as far as I was concerned.

Josh licked his lips and grinned, his eyes sparkling mischievously. 'Don't you?'

I wanted to say yes. I know that sounds ridiculous, but I really wanted to agree with him. I hesitated.

Picking up the next glass, he threw back his head in a theatrical manner and I watched his throat move as the liquid disappeared. 'One to go,' he cried, dashing the glass down noisily upon the wooden counter top.

Then he suddenly leaned towards me, which surprised me so much that my immediate reaction was to back off, but there was nowhere to go as I was up against the edge of a tall column. He buried his face in my hair and I remembered thinking how sorry I was that I hadn't had a bath or shampooed my hair that morning, but hot water was something in short supply and I'd just had a quick wash. Thank goodness I'd drenched myself in perfume, I thought.

'The water is disgusting,' he murmured, 'but don't tell Toby, it would break his heart.'

I couldn't help but laugh. Toby, I noticed, was on the other side dispensing more water to hopeful clientele. Josh now turned away looking straight ahead as if there had been no communication between us, all innocent and quite like a small boy who has just been very naughty.

'Can I get you another?' he asked, with a twinkle in his eye, just as Toby passed by.

'Oh, no thank you, but it was delicious,' I said, loud enough for Toby to hear and be rewarded with a smile.

'I'm Josh,' he said, putting out his hand very formally, the smile friendly, but less conspiratorial.

I should have said, 'Yes, I know, you live in the flat below me.' But I didn't. Why didn't I do that one thing that would have made everything simple? Perhaps if I'd explained, it would all have been fine. But, I didn't. And, I knew why. Because the irony of the situation was that he'd gone out of his way to return my glove and as I had gone out of mine to steal his, I was feeling very guilty. So, I put out my hand and pretended I knew nothing about him instead.

'Hi, I'm Sophie.'

'Are you here on holiday, Sophie?'

I hesitated. 'Yes, I suppose so.'

'Are you not very sure?'

'Well, it's a sort of working holiday, meant to be, anyway.'

'I'm intrigued. Doesn't sound much like a holiday if you're meant to be working.'

'No. Well, I haven't really started doing anything very much. I plan to, of course.'

I looked down at the floor, knowing that I wasn't making very much sense, or being very forthcoming and thought how boring I must sound. By the time I looked up again, he was checking his watch and looked as if he had had enough. 'Well, Sophie, I have to be getting back to work now. It was nice to meet you.'

'And you. Thank you for retrieving my glove.'

For a moment, I wished he'd ask for my number, or question me about where I was staying, though I was relieved when he didn't. I wasn't sure I could feign surprise when he realized we lived in the same building. Watching him depart, I saw him weave his way through the tables of middle-aged ladies nudging their friends and casting admiring glances at him as he passed by. Well, at least it was over, for the time being. However, the thought struck me that if we ever did meet in the pub, it might be pretty embarrassing if Lara were to start talking and he'd be sure to realize that I already knew about him. I would just have to avoid them both was all I could think.

I left as soon as I could. I didn't want him to think I was following him, though I had to walk that way myself, and I saw him turn right by Upper Borough Walls. I couldn't see anything of him by the time I'd got that far up and turned the corner and, in any case, I needed to head off for the supermarket. I selected a couple of ready-meals that I could heat up in the ancient cooker, thus avoiding the necessity of going to the pub and bumping into him. Adding grapes and clementines, milk, butter, a camembert cheese and a loaf of bread, I selected a bottle of wine from the chiller cabinet, feeling rather decadent.

I took my lunch, a plate of crusty bread and cheese, into the sitting room and filled one of the beautiful lead crystal glasses I'd found in a kitchen cupboard with the cool, gold wine. I thought about the meeting I'd had with Josh. He seemed nice; and then scolded myself for the use of that insipid word, which Jane Austen surely would not approve of after she made Henry Tilney tease

Catherine Morland about it in *Northanger Abbey*. I admitted to myself that I liked Josh. He'd really cheered me up and made me realize quite how much I'd begun to miss human contact.

I felt guilty about the glove and stared at the box on the table, imagining I could see through it to the contents within. Perhaps I should just be brave, come clean and tell him the whole truth. Now I'd met him, I could just say how I'd tried to return it, but he'd never been in, or something like that. Taking it out of the box, I turned it over in my hand. I've always loved the smell of leather and the touch of the fine kid made me lift it to my face to stroke it against my cheek. I wondered who it had belonged to, and if it had been some illustrious captain in the Navy in Jane Austen's day, perhaps Captain Holburne himself. Slipping my fingers inside, I hoped to get a sense of its owner.

I was feeling very light-headed from the wine, but the sensation that the room and all my surroundings were beginning to blur grew stronger. I could see the looking glass above the mantelpiece quite clearly and hear the distinctive tick of the clock, but now I could see that there were flames in the unlit grate, which was strange, as I'd not even raked out the coals from the night before. The light from the windows shone very luminously, forcing me to blink back the tears that welled at the overwhelming brightness. When I brushed them aside, I could see that although the room had reverted to the dim afternoon light of before, now there were other people in the room with me.

I stared at them, not knowing quite what to feel. Even though I had
no idea who they were; I didn't feel frightened immediately, it was
as if they belonged in the room. I can't explain it any other way, but
I felt a part of the whole picture. There was a man standing by the
windows talking to a lady who looked so familiar, I immediately
felt at ease even if I couldn't think why. Dressed in a long gown of
dark, printed cotton, her grey hair curled under a lace cap. The man
in breeches with a dark blue coat over a frilled shirt wore his short
hair brushed forward and was very animated as he talked, waving
his arms about. I couldn't hear what they were saying, but it clearly
had something to do with the very pretty girl who sat on a chaise
longue on the other side of the fireplace. Dressed in sheer,
embroidered muslin, she wore a silk shawl around her shoulders
with her hair swept up onto the top of her head in elaborate curls
that fell around her face. A pink slipper nudging under her hem was
beribboned with a silk rose, which trembled as her foot tapped up
and down with more than a little impatience. As if trapped in a
dream that felt far more real than any dream I'd ever had, I watched
them become more than the shadows they had appeared at first.

Then, to my great shock, the gentleman turned to me and spoke. For the first time, I could hear him.

'And, where have you been all morning, Sophia?'

Tall and with an imposing air, his whole appearance suggested fastidious observance of fashion. From his carefully dressed "Grecian" hairstyle and elaborately tied neckcloth stiffly arranged above an exquisitely embroidered waistcoat, down to his coat and tight, moulded breeches cut with precision, I wondered how he would manage to undress. No wonder he had such a pained epression – his breeches were clearly causing him grief.

'I've been out walking in the gardens with the Miss Austens, Papa,' I heard myself say.

'Yes, I saw you in company with them from the window. They are a respectable enough family, I suppose, if one wishes to be in society with a country curate and his spinster daughters, but a clergyman is nothing in society. He has no influence or importance, and no one wishes to know him better. His daughters will frighten away your suitors if you allow them any kind of intimacy. Such independent creatures, and what airs they give themselves considering their questionable position amongst the noble families of Bath. As for the mother, who lets everyone know of her far distant connection to the Leighs of Stoneleigh, her society is intolerable. I heard her braying at someone in the Pump Rooms the other day, pronouncing in a loud voice that she is very proud of her aristocratic nose. Gentlefolk do not have to degrade themselves by resorting to such devices in order to get introductions. If you see them again, I would prefer that you cut them.'

I stared, not knowing how to answer the disagreeable man that I had just addressed as my father, but whilst I hesitated, the words were already being spoken.

'I have an engagement, Father, with the Miss Austens on the morrow. I am looking forward to it very much and I have every intention of fulfilling their most kind invitation.'

The room was suddenly quiet except for the ticking of the Sèvres clock on the mantelpiece and the fire crackling in the grate, which at that moment seemed to be the dearest sounds in the world for their domestic familiarity. The gilt clock, with its painted pastoral panels, was the very same clock left behind in that other time. At that precise second, it prettily chimed the hour with four silver strikes of the bell, as if we'd all paused to hear it.

'Father is quite right,' said the young woman seated in the winged chair by the fire. This must be Emma, I thought. 'If you are seen going out and about with the Miss Austens, your ability for attracting suitable attachments will be negligible. I am sure they cannot help being so very poor, but they already appear to be very much left on the shelf. Spinster sisters for company will do you more harm than good if you wish to find a husband. You should not be in such a hurry to ruin your chances of matrimony.'

She was obviously worried about what effect Sophia's friendship with the Austen sisters might have on her own relationships, and it was clear that this was really behind Emma's defence of her father's outburst.

'I am certain that being friends with two such pleasant young women cannot have any detrimental effect on your ability to attract the very best of suitors,' I began. 'No young man truly interested in marrying you is going to be concerned with anything or anybody connected with me. Besides, you know yourself, whenever we are in company, heads turn to stare at you. You must have more partners at a ball than any other girl in the room.'

I did wonder if this was entirely true, but I guessed Sophia was probably doing her best to soothe her sister.

The lady sitting opposite on the chaise longue had remained silent during these exchanges, and although her eyes were sometimes averted from the conversation, she didn't look in the least embarrassed. She was obviously used to the confrontation and knew them all well.

Mr Elliot stood in front of a pier glass set between two windows and tweaked a curl into place on his forehead before admiring his reflection in profile, first one way and then the next. 'Mrs Randall, may we have your opinion on the subject?'

She looked up and gave me a smile, making her vivid blue eyes sparkle. I knew straight away that she loved Sophia as a mother loves her child. I had the sense that I knew her well, but could not explain it.

'I think that the Austen girls are fine companions for Sophia, Mr Elliot. I understand your concerns, but intimacy with a respectable gentry family who have aristocratic relations, as you stated yourself, cannot be harmful. Perhaps they will be visited by some of their distinguished connections, who may have sons on the lookout for a pretty wife. Let us not be persuaded against the acquaintance just yet by reservations that cannot be justified.'

Mr Elliot turned from the glass to address Mrs Randall. 'I suppose there can be no real objection to you seeing these people occasionally, but you must understand, Sophia, that I only have your best interests at heart. You and your sister are not getting any younger and suitable husbands must be found.'

Something about the way he made this last pronouncement, as if his real concern was ridding himself of the daughters he clearly thought were a burden, produced a shiver all over to make every hair on my body stand on end. That was his priority, to see the girls married and as soon as possible. Their happiness seemed secondary, even an unnecessary consideration.

'We have shopping to do this afternoon, do you remember, Sophia?' Mrs Randall rose, fixing me with a look that suggested if I should like to make my escape, here was a chance.

'Of course,' I answered, feeling for the first time that I had actually spoken for myself. 'I will be ready in a moment.'

I remembered just in time to curtsey before I left. All the bobbing up and down, the formality of behaviour and the strain of being so attentive to everything, not to mention feeling that I was about to burst out of my clothes was making me feel as if I wanted to say something outrageous, swear out loud and tear off my corset. I made my way up the next flight of stairs, my heart thumping in my chest. I wasn't sure where to go but I could still hear the murmur of voices downstairs, so I opened the door that was mine in the time I'd left behind. Of course, I might have known it was Mr Elliot's as it was the biggest room with the view over the gardens. There were an enormous number of looking glasses of varying sizes adorning the walls and a dozen carefully arranged wigs on the dressing table, which made me immediately wonder if he had any hair at all. I quickly shut the door and investigated the next room. It could be mine I thought, taking in the gowns hanging from a tall press and noting the floral, enamel boxes upon the washstand, but there were no definite clues. With fear and panic rising inside, I was suddenly aware of clipping footsteps upon the staircase. My first instinct was to hide behind the door, but I realized how stupid I would look if I were discovered. And then, before I could do anything else, Emma flung back the door and marched in.

'What are you doing in here?' she demanded, her face flushed red with anger.

'I took a wrong turn,' I muttered, without thinking. I could have kicked myself for being so silly.

'If I find you have taken anything belonging to me, you will be in more trouble than you can imagine,' she hissed. 'You know you're not allowed in here. Now, go away!'

Hurrying out of the room, I was only too pleased to be gone. I had an idea that Sophia and Emma did not share the close relationship that their neighbours did. It was a pity, for I felt sure that they were missing so much from having each other to confide in.

The last room at the end of the corridor turned out to be Sophia's bedchamber. It was half the size of any of the others, but had an interesting view looking out onto the short row of Daniel Street with the stables in between. There were only three houses built along the road, (Lara's pub being one of them) which seemed very strange to see. The backs of the houses down Pulteney Street looked much the same even if they did look out onto open spaces and distant crescents curving loftily above Bath.

The small, half-tester bed was not one I recognized, but the dressing table and oval toilet mirror were the very same that still occupied a corner of my bedroom in that other time. I sat down with relief, glad to have a moment to myself. Peeling off my gloves, I opened my reticule to safely store them before venturing out again. There to my surprise was the white glove safe inside, but there was something else which made me curious. At the bottom of the bag was a small, netted purse, rounded off at both ends with tassels. I reached inside to fetch it out and, in doing so, pulled out the white glove before I could prevent it from happening.

Chapter
9

Time paused, and the glove floated in slow motion to the floor. I
bent down to pick it up but even as I did so, I knew the spell had
broken. As I raised my head, the room started to revolve at speed.
I shut my eyes to stop the world from spinning and felt the warmth
from a strong, flickering light upon my face, but it was so bright I
knew I had to wait until it was over before attempting to look again.
When at last it stopped, I found I was sitting on the very same seat
in the very same room. The past had vanished, evaporated as
quickly as mist warmed by the rising sun on a summer meadow. It
was as if time had not altered and as the images so fresh in my head
faded into nothing, I looked about me.

I knew this must be one of the spare rooms that I had not
investigated, largely because it was filled mostly with oddments of
furniture, books and pictures that had obviously been stored to save
being sorted out. I was sitting in the middle of a mountainous
muddle piled high on every side. I looked at my wristwatch and
knew that the hands had hardly moved. It was only eleven o'clock.
I'd been away for ages and yet, time here had stopped. The white
glove lay upon the floor at my feet and it was then that I began to

question its significance. I recalled that I'd been holding the glove in my hand on the very first occasion I'd stepped back into time in the gardens. Was this the key? If I put it on again, could I return? Would time roll back to deposit me in this house with the family who'd lived here so long ago? I didn't know if I wanted to do it again. I was feeling very strange, a little faint. I realized that there was something truly inexplicable happening and, I also knew that above everything else, I wanted it to happen again. I braced myself as I slipped my fingers inside the glove. Even as I did so, and as much as I willed it to take me back, I was not surprised when nothing happened. Perhaps there were only so many chances or perhaps the glove was not powerful enough on its own.

Whether I was right about it being some sort of passport to the past, I couldn't be sure, but I wasn't going to relinquish it just yet, even if I knew that was wrong. As I sat wondering what to do next, I spotted the edge of a familiar object down on the floor trapped beneath a stack of picture frames. The remains of a disintegrating reticule frayed at the edges, the cream satin aged to a dull grey, could only be the one I'd held moments before pristine in its newness. I picked up the frames two and three at a time to release the forlorn object from the dusty floor. When I got to the last, the final picture frame that pinned the reticule in place, I knew before I brushed away the layer of thick dust on the glass that I'd found something of more importance than the remains of a fabric bag. In its gesso and gilt frame, the portrait of a young girl smiled at me in her best bonnet and blue gown. Signed in the corner, the pencil had faded too much to make out the name of the artist, but a name I recognized had remained clear enough to read.

'Oh, Sophia,' I cried out into the silent room, 'what do you want with me?'

The portrait was a delicate watercolour and quite a substantial size. I took it downstairs into the kitchen and gently wiped away the years of grime from the glass and frame. Sophia Elliot was sitting on a rock at the seaside with her hands clasped together in her lap and her half boots crossed at the ankles resting in the sand.

Happiness beamed from her as brightly as the sun shining down upon her features, on the bathing machines, the stone cottages and the line of cliffs in the background. I longed to know more. It was a picture that begged to be admired and hung up for all to see. There was a little piece chipped off the glass in one corner where the frame was broken and I wondered if it were possible to mend it. Carrying it with great care, I propped it up on the mantelpiece in the sitting room and remembering the white glove, I took it out of my pocket to pop it inside the rosewood box on the occasional table, telling myself that I would return it to Josh soon, but not just yet.

Suddenly, feeling completely exhausted, all I wanted was my bed. I'd just lie down for a moment I thought, as my eyes closed instantly the second my body sank into the plump, silk eiderdown. When I awoke, it was morning. Bright sunshine streamed through the lace at the windows. I'd slept right through the rest of the day, on into the evening and all night long, without once waking up. I felt amazing, really rested and rejuvenated like I couldn't remember feeling for a long time. I ran a bath in the cold, green-tiled bathroom that must have been the pride and joy of the Edwardian Elliots with its nod to *Art Nouveau* in the floral majolica tiles above the washbasin. I used every last drop of hot water, but there was enough for a decent soak. After crumbling in some bath salts from a glass jar on the shelf, which still smelled faintly of eau de cologne, I slipped into the steaming water to wash my hair and have a think. In the vivid light of day, I automatically began to question what had happened the day before, but this time I didn't dismiss it completely. This second experience had been far more measured than the first jolt back in time, but possibly that had something to do with my increased receptiveness to the whole episode. What would it be like to really interact with those people, to live with them, I wondered? And if I tried to get back again, would I be able to get used to that feeling of not quite knowing myself and becoming used to the separation of my mind and body, the body that didn't quite seem to be my own?

I dried myself as quickly as I could, hopping about on the chilly, lino floor before wrapping myself up in the dressing gown I was now so pleased to have brought with me. Thank heaven for the twenty-first century hairdryer, I thought, as I sat down at the dressing table. Drying my hair and trying to coax it into a style that didn't look completely hideous seemed to take forever and by the time I'd finished, I couldn't decide whether it had been worth all the effort. There was a moment as I scrutinized my reflection when the green eyes that stared back at me didn't look quite like my own. There was an impression of fuller, darker brows, and of lustrous curls framing the face that looked back at me. A flash in time; it was over in a second. For a moment, I saw my mother in the curve of my cheek and recognized my grandmother's hair rippling back from her brow, echoed in the waves of my own locks that refused to be tamed. Generations of Elliot women seemed to smile at me as they gazed back through the mirror from their own particular time. I glimpsed a powdered wig profuse with roses and feathers, above the glitter of diamonds encircling a white throat and a spangled, damask sleeve. I saw yellow taffeta and a cap to match, a dab of rouge on an ivory cheek, concealed in another moment with the flick of a fan from a dainty wrist. Creamy flesh pillowed over the stiff bodice of a silk corset studded with satin bows, its owner dressing her ringlets with a practised hand, adjusting a flower to fall over her forehead. Within a fleeting heartbeat, the ephemeral kaleidoscope of images flickered into life and was gone. But, the feeling of kinship with every one of them felt as if I'd been given an extraordinary invitation to join a unique, secret society. It was time to get dressed, to go out and seek the adventure my ancestors were calling me to embrace.

Sophia's picture greeted me as I entered the sitting room, her eyes following my every move around the room. It looked a little sad to see the glass and frame in such bad repair, so I thought I would start by heading into town with a picture framing shop in mind. Finding some brown paper and string in one of the dresser drawers in the kitchen, I wrapped it up before grabbing my jacket and heading downstairs feeling grateful that it wasn't too unwieldy an object to tuck under my arm. I'd just put it down to unlock the front door when it opened by itself, making me jump backwards in surprise. There was only one person who could possibly be opening the door, I realized, but even when I'd registered this thought, it was still a shock when we came face to face.

I was struck dumb and I knew my face was as scarlet as the fringed scarf Josh had draped round his neck. Even so, I thought how much it suited his dark colouring as one or two strands of those glossy curls nestled in the swathes of fabric round his neck. He looked almost as astonished as I did.

'Can I help you?' he asked, looking at me so searchingly with his dark eyes that I found it difficult to maintain eye contact.

'Oh, I know you,' he said, just seconds later before I could answer, as his expression changed to one of smiling recognition. 'You're the girl from the Pump Room. Are you living here? I've been hearing the occasional footsteps upstairs, and Lara at the pub said someone had moved in.'

I managed to nod my head, but I was blushing more furiously than ever and feeling the heat on my cheeks like a furnace blast from an open oven door.

'I'm Josh Strafford,' he said, 'your neighbour from the downstairs flat. This is such a coincidence, don't you think?'

'Sophie Elliot,' I said, holding out my hand, and then regretting it instantly because it seemed so silly and formal to be shaking hands. But he didn't shake my hand. He took it and kissed it like some Regency suitor in a romantic novel.

'I'm very pleased to meet you, Miss Elliot,' he said, with a mock bow and in a very serious voice, obviously thinking I was a complete noodle to be behaving so ceremoniously.

I giggled because he looked so solemn, but it did break the ice.

'That name has a most familiar ring. Are you related to the family that own the house?' he asked in such a direct way that I was taken aback.

I nodded again, a little hesitantly this time, wondering why he wanted to know.

'It's just that I've found some of the Elliot family whilst doing some research. I'm over at the museum across the road, temporarily, putting together an exhibition celebrating Georgian Bathwick and its inhabitants. I've got lists of people who were in the area at the time and I was interested to find out who was living in the house during the early eighteen hundreds.'

I nodded. 'I'm the great-niece of the lady who still owns the house which has been in the family since it was first built.'

'Wow, that's amazing!' said Josh, who looked genuinely impressed. 'The family had a manor house, I believe ... Monkford Hall in Somerset.'

'The family seat,' I said, smiling at his round-eyed expression. 'We don't have it anymore. To my knowledge it passed out of the family after the First World War. They'd lost all their money by then and after the war there was nothing to be done, but sell it.'

Josh looked genuinely disappointed. 'Oh, that's a real shame.'

'Yes, I know, but I imagine great houses must be such a financial drain and always cold. I couldn't imagine living in one, could you?'

Josh didn't speak, so to cover the awkward pause I just carried on talking. 'My mother always kept an old print that gives an idea of what it must have looked like in its heyday. I understand it's still a private house. I always think it was a shame that she never got to see it again, or have another look inside. Mum died some years ago so she'll never see it now.'

'Oh, that's so sad,' he said.

As I looked up at him wondering why I was telling this virtual stranger about every aspect of my family history, the thought then struck me that there was a very remote chance that I might be able to visit the house, though I seemed to recall that the Elliots I'd met in the past were to be in Bath for some time and not about to travel. How wonderful it would be, I thought, if I could go back to visit Monkford Hall and walk in the footsteps of my ancestors.

I suddenly realized that Josh was staring at me. 'I haven't

upset you by talking about your family, I hope.'

He must think I'm not all there in the head, I thought, as I became conscious that I'd been standing mute with a faraway expression on my face for longer than I should.

'No, not at all.' I felt so embarrassed I picked up the painting in an effort to disguise my flame-red cheeks. 'I was just going out. It's really nice to meet you, properly. Of course, I know we met before and everything, but ...'

There didn't seem to be anything else to add and what I'd managed to say hadn't come out at all the way I'd wanted it to. I moved forward and then the agony was prolonged a bit further by the fact that we both went the same way and did that sort of dancing thing where you can't quite get past each other. The hallway wasn't very wide as it was and it was getting very ridiculous as we hopped about, until Josh put his hands on my shoulders steering me towards the door. I mumbled my thanks and opened it without looking back. Call me paranoid but I was sure he was watching me as I marched away, cheeks on fire. I didn't hear the door shut straight away and I could just picture him with a puzzled expression, making a mental note to avoid me at all costs in the future.

I could still feel his hands. I'd noticed his hands the very first time we met and the touch of those long fingers on my shoulders stayed with me as far as Pulteney Bridge. It was quite a good feeling really, even if I was dying of embarrassment inside. Since I'd been in Bath, I'd had no real physical contact with anyone. I tried not to think about Lucas who instantly popped into my head, and my thoughts turned to home and my Dad, instead. We'd agreed to text rather than phone so I could save on money and the only phone call I'd made to him from the railway station seemed so long ago, even if in reality it had only been a couple of days. Walking into Bath, I found a nice card for him in a shop by the Post Office and wrote a little note to go with it, something suitably sentimental that I knew he would enjoy. Then, by the time I'd stopped someone to ask about where I might find somewhere to get the picture looked at and been directed to Walcot Street where the little picture framing shop was to be found, I'd begun to regret the idea of getting it mended, it was so heavy to carry. But they were so lovely in the shop, and said it could be left in their capable hands to pick up at a later date. Reluctantly, I left it behind feeling as if I'd somehow abandoned the real Sophia to a set of strangers she didn't know. I wandered up Walcot Street to the church where I spent a few minutes looking round. Two American ladies stopped and asked me if I knew the location of Jane's father's grave. It's funny how people talk about Jane Austen as if they know her and her family, but I suppose there's something about the way she draws you into her books which makes you feel you know her quite like a friend. I'd no idea that Jane's father was buried there or that her parents had married at St. Swithin's. We found his tombstone and an inscription that explained that he'd died in 1805 and was buried in the crypt. It made me feel very sad to think of Jane and her sister grieving for their father, a family of women left to fend for themselves in a city where they were surrounded by wealthy visitors on holiday. I remembered hearing somewhere that Jane had disliked Bath and I wondered if this had been the real reason. My knowledge of Jane's life didn't extend much further than the books she'd written. It would be a good idea to buy a biography and find out a little more.

I needed some shopping so turned tail to walk back down the hill into town to the supermarket and wandered down the aisles selecting some chicken pieces to roast, a jar of Dijon mustard, a garlic bulb and a bunch of tarragon, new potatoes, French beans, and of course, the obligatory bottle of white wine. I'd missed my lunch and was feeling ravenously hungry, a state that seemed to be an ever-increasing problem since I'd moved to Bath. It must be all that time travelling, I said to myself, though even saying the words in my head seemed crazy as I stood at the very ordinary checkout loading my 'bag for life' with purchases. Doubt that any of it had actually happened and that insanity of a kind had actually taken hold, hit me once more. I couldn't explain any of it. When I was there it was as if I belonged in that time, and the present seemed remote. Being here in this supermarket with people around me going about their everyday shopping felt just as real and the past seemed a figment of my imagination. But I was beginning to feel that all this analyzing about what was going on was doing my head in. I didn't want to think about it any longer.

I let myself into the flat. There was a piece of paper just poked under the door, which I knew immediately could only be from Josh. I opened it not quite knowing what to expect.

Chapter 10

Dear Sophie,

I've been going through the catalogue of exhibits this afternoon. I've just popped over on my break because there's a painting here I'd like you to see that I think might interest you. I finish work about five, so if you'd like to come over to the museum then, I can show you.

I hope you didn't think I was too intrusive today – I apologize, I'm just a very nosy person.

Anyway, if you'd like to, I'd love to see you. Just ask for me at the desk and someone will show you the way.

Josh.

Oh dear, he'd obviously mistaken my earlier vacant musings for wounded sensibility. He'd been direct, but I hadn't thought he was being overly inquisitive, just very interested and I'd really enjoyed the fact that he'd wanted to talk. I wondered what the painting could be that he wanted to show me. I felt very curious despite the pangs of gnawing hunger, so I grabbed a biscuit before deciding to postpone eating until I returned.

The lady at the reception desk was clearly expecting me. Whether it was my imagination or not, I cannot say for sure, but she seemed to take a great interest in my appearance. Looking me up and down, staring at my embroidered bag and my slouch boots, she appeared to be memorizing every last detail to tell her colleagues about the girl who had come to see Mr Strafford. I knew exactly which way to go, but of course I pretended that I didn't know where I'd find him. She took me upstairs leading me to the exhibition space that was starting to look much more promising with one or two pictures on the walls or propped up along the sides and empty glass cabinets placed in a line waiting to be filled with exciting objects. We stopped at the door of a room at the back, just off on one side. Josh was seated behind a desk; his head buried in what looked like a good deal of paperwork. The room was dim, only the glow from his laptop was giving out an eerie, but totally inadequate light.

'Mr Strafford, you'll ruin your eyesight,' the receptionist scolded in a playful way, and switched on the lamp in front of him.

'Oh, I've been meaning to put it on for ages, the time has just run away with me this afternoon,' he said, pushing back a handful of curls from his forehead. He looked up and our eyes met. For the first time I looked straight back at him hoping that I didn't look as out of my depth in this place as I felt. Don't get me wrong, I'm not stupid, and I love anything historical, but I wasn't an expert, not like him. It unnerved me just a little, especially when I admitted to myself that I wanted him to think I was intelligent and worthy of his interest in my family.

'Sophie, you came!' he announced brightly and he sounded so pleased that I felt myself grin with pleasure.

'Thanks Alison,' he said to the receptionist, 'what would I do without you?' Alison almost fainted with delight, even when he handed over a pile of post. 'Would you mind taking care of these for me?'

The effect he had on Alison was the same I'd witnessed in the Pump Room on the other women. She gazed at him with sheer adoration as if he'd just given her the crown jewels for her own personal safekeeping.

'Can I get you any tea for you and your guest?' she asked.

'No thanks, Alison, we'll only just be a moment.'

Satisfied that she was no longer needed Alison beamed at him again before departing, albeit rather reluctantly I felt, with the vast pile of letters.

There was an awkward moment when neither of us knew what to say.

'You said in your note that you had a painting you wanted to show me,' I said, breaking the silence. It was so very quiet in the room, which was making me feel more nervous than ever.

'Yes, I think you'll be really interested to see it. I've done a little research; it was sold in an auction at Monkford Hall sometime in the early 1900s.'

He said no more and gestured towards the exhibition space. I walked out of the room and on the opposite wall in front of me I could see a large oil painting that I must have walked past on the way in. Its subject was of two women in Georgian dress and the plaque at the bottom of the painting was inscribed with a title and the date, 1782.

'The painting is of your ancestor, Mrs Elliot of Monkford Hall, and her cousin Mrs Randall,' Josh said. 'Do you know anything about them?'

'No, not really, I don't know anything very much about the family. I should think this was one of the paintings that had to be sold in an effort to raise some money before it all had to go.'

I was mesmerized. Mrs Elliot stared out of the painting looking every inch like an older Sophia with her hair bundled under a satin cap. She had a kind face.

'Poor Mrs Elliot died in childbirth in 1788,' Josh continued. 'I looked her up in the archives. She had three daughters, Emma, Sophia and Marianne. Her last child was a stillborn son.'

'All I know is that I was named after her middle daughter. It's so sad to see her looking so young and full of hope without any idea of her future fate.' I was moved emotionally by her story, but not entirely by the portrait of Mrs Elliot alone. The painting fascinated me in a way that made me feel most peculiar. It was the likeness of Mrs Randall that intrigued me most of all, for I knew her face almost as well as I knew my own. I had that feeling again of goose pimples all over, accompanied by the sensation that Josh and I were not the only people in the room. I stared and stared unable to say a word.

'Is anything the matter?' asked Josh. 'You look as if you've seen a ghost.'

'I have,' I muttered inaudibly.

'The painting of Mrs Elliot reminds you of someone, I can tell.'

I shook my head. 'No, it's not Mrs Elliot's portrait, but Mrs Randall's that is remarkable. She is the very image of my mother. It's quite uncanny. I wish my Mum were alive to see it, she'd think it so funny to see such a resemblance of herself all dressed up in satin.'

I couldn't tear myself away and I couldn't imagine why I had not realized the likeness before, but then the Mrs Randall I knew was twenty years older than the lady who gazed at me with the same wistful expression my mother always wore. I'd not seen my mother grow older, and it seemed to me that perhaps twenty years in those days left a far greater impression on a lady's looks than it would now. Mrs Randall was seated on a mahogany chair and dressed in a gown of steel-grey satin with a vermillion shawl around her shoulders. An organza cap covered her hair, ruched and ribboned in front to match the frills about her throat and the fabric at her décolletage. Mrs Elliot looked just as elegant on a matching chair with a tasselled cushion in russet silk. There was a table between them where tea was being made. A silver teapot, sugar box and milk jug took pride of place beside a steaming kettle with blue and white teacups scattered over the tabletop. But there was one more surprise, which really set my heart beating so fast I was sure Josh would be able to hear it. Behind them on a desk was a box that

I recognized. Made of rosewood and inlaid with mother of pearl, the lid was open and a pair of white gloves was draped over its edge.

'Oh dear,' said Josh, 'the last thing I wanted was to upset you.'

'No, I'm not upset in the least, not the way you mean, anyway. In fact, I'm thrilled.' I turned to look at him again, and was met once more by his frank expression, his dark eyes showing concern. 'Thank you so much, Josh, for inviting me to see the painting. I'll have to text my dad and tell him. He'll think it's wonderful.'

'And you're not too disturbed by it?'

'I am, but in a good way.'

'Well, thank you for coming, Sophie.' He was still looking at me as if he thought he'd done something dreadful. I suppose the surprise must have shown in my face, because he reached across and took my hand holding it between his two large ones. 'You still look in shock and I'm thinking it's all my fault.'

I didn't move my hand. I couldn't for one thing and for another, he'd started patting it softly as if he were trying to get my circulation going or something. It felt lovely and I felt cherished, which sounds silly, but I really did feel that he cared.

'I'm absolutely fine, but I suppose I'm a bit hungry,' I said at last. 'I haven't really eaten very much since breakfast.'

He let go of my hand. 'Sophie, you should have said. Look, I feel totally responsible. Will you let me take you for supper? My treat. Lara does the best food this side of the bridge and it's not far to go. We can be eating in ten minutes.'

I wanted to say yes, but I didn't really want to go to the pub. Besides, Lara and the rest of the locals might put two and two together making up something about our relationship that just wasn't true, and I was worried that the glove might be mentioned. I was feeling very guilty about it and didn't know quite how I was going to resolve the situation. As time was moving on, it was getting increasingly difficult to return it to him. I couldn't think how I was going to explain that I had the glove and to be perfectly honest, I wanted to keep it just for a little bit longer.

'Would you mind very much if we didn't go?' I said, thinking quickly. 'I've got some chicken at home that needs cooking and I'd love it if you'd share it with me.' I wondered if that all sounded a bit intimate as soon as I'd said it, but Josh answered without any hesitation saying he'd love to have supper with me.

We left straight away and headed home. I was enjoying his company and he did seem a nice guy, but even as he took my arm to guide me over the road, I had a memory, as clear as if it had happened yesterday, of Lucas being similarly attentive when we first met. Well, I was sure someone as good-looking as Josh would have a string of casual girlfriends anyway and I was not about to let my guard down. Not that he appeared to be attracted to me in any way. He seemed genuinely friendly, but I felt a sense of detachment about him that I couldn't quite explain.

I left him in the sitting room with a glass of white wine, whilst I got the chicken pieces ready smothering them in Dijon and arranging the bunches of tarragon in the tin. I hesitated over the garlic, but then broke it up and added that too. It wasn't as if I was going to be kissing him or anything and I told myself off for even having the thought. The French beans and potatoes were set in saucepans with a covering of water ready to be put on later, so I made a quick detour to my bedroom. I ran a comb through my hair, sprayed on my favourite perfume and persuaded myself that I didn't look too haggard.

When I came back into the sitting room Josh was standing by the fireplace. I could see at once that he was admiring the clock on the mantelpiece, not staring at his reflection like Lucas would have been.

'This place is wonderful,' he enthused, 'it's got such an amazing atmosphere.'

'You're very polite,' I said, 'but what you really mean is that it's like being in a museum. I doubt it's changed very much since the very first Elliots' occupation.' I didn't add that actually I knew for a fact it was little altered. Apart from the modern sofa and the odd chair, most of the furniture was a couple of hundred years old.

I perched like a timid bird on the sofa and gulped at my wine. All of a sudden I realized I was alone with a man I hardly knew and one who seemed so sophisticated that I felt utterly out of my depth. He relaxed into the winged chair looking completely at ease.

'So, do your family still live in Somerset?' he asked, putting his glass down on the little table next to him.

'No, London ... Camden. How about you? Where's your family?'

'Dorset.'

'Oh, lovely. I always associate Dorset with holidays. Which part?'

'Lyme Regis. Well, just outside on a cliff-top overlooking the town.'

'Oh, I love Lyme. I always think of Jane Austen's *Persuasion* and Louisa Musgrove falling off the Cobb.' As soon as I'd spoken, I wished I hadn't. I was sure he was going to look at me blankly like most guys do when you mention Jane Austen. And even if they've heard of her or about any of the books it's most likely to be *Pride and Prejudice*. Plus, it's a sad fact that most men think all you're interested in is Colin Firth or Matthew MacFadyen in wet shirts and tight breeches, which is only partly true.

But he didn't look at me. He simply closed his eyes as if he were trying to remember something. 'There was no wound, no blood, no visible bruise; but her eyes were closed, she breathed not, her face was like death.'

I was utterly astonished at Josh's quotation. 'You know *Persuasion* very well!'

'It's a favourite book of mine. I studied it when I was younger and had a part one year in the school play.' He cleared his throat and stood up, fixing me with those dark eyes that twinkled with amusement. His voice was soft and he spoke to me as if he meant every word. 'You pierce my soul. I am half agony, half hope. Tell me not that I am too late, that such precious feelings are gone forever. I offer myself to you again with a heart even more your own than when you almost broke it, eight years and a half ago.

Dare not say that man forgets sooner than woman, that his love has an earlier death. I have loved none but you.'

I felt my cheeks grow warm and in an attempt to cover up my blushing face, I burst into spontaneous applause to which he bowed deeply.

'I played the part of Captain Wentworth, you might have guessed. That's some letter he wrote. It really is one of the most beautiful love letters I ever read.'

I laughed. 'Possibly because it was written by a woman.'

Josh grinned and nodded. 'I can't deny that, but do you mean to say that you don't think men capable of writing romance or pouring out such heartfelt feelings in a letter?'

He was looking at me so seriously that I knew I couldn't be flippant. 'I suppose I don't really know. No one has ever written me a love letter. Maybe there are guys out there who could write the equivalent of a letter like that but, if there are, I've never met one. Anyway, I'm not sure it would be quite the same in a text or email. I think romance died with the laptop and the mobile phone.'

I felt I'd said too much, that there was more than a hint of bitterness in my voice, so I excused myself to go and turn on the hob and rattle the saucepans as if I was busy. The chicken was beginning to smell delicious though my appetite seemed to have left me. The trouble was I didn't really feel at ease with Josh, and I just felt that everything I'd said so far must sound pathetic. Trying to think of a topic of conversation that would make me feel less like an idiot, I collected a couple of plates, selected some cutlery from the dresser and turned to see Josh standing in the doorway watching me.

'I'll take those,' he said. 'Where would you like them?'

'There's a Pembroke table in the living room. I thought we could pull that out and eat there as the dining room is a bit chilly.'

I followed him with placemats, napkins and water glasses to the table behind the sofa. Josh put the plates down, tucked his hair that was flopping into his eyes behind his ear and pulled out the table, securing one of the leaves in place. Relieving me of the placemats he started laying the table. He seemed happy enough as he arranged everything carefully, so I turned back to the kitchen, stabbing a fork in the potatoes and putting the beans on. I fetched out the chicken pieces, leaving them to rest on a beautiful willow meat plate, then made some gravy and drained the vegetables which I assembled round the crisply roasted meat. Satisfied with my presentation, I carried it in thinking that at least I might impress with my culinary skills even if I might not with my conversation. I nearly dropped the plate when I saw what Josh was doing.

He was sitting in the chair next to the little table where I kept the rosewood box. But it was not on the table; it was in his hands. I held my breath.

'This is such a beautiful box,' he said, studying the decoration along its side.

The key was on the table, and I remember thinking how I'd replaced the glove but hadn't locked the box again, being too distracted by the painting of Sophia and my thoughts of getting it mended.

'I've got this really strange feeling of déjà vu,' he said, a frown wrinkling between his brows. He stroked the surface of the box with those long fingers as if he were caressing something or someone precious to him.

'You have seen it before,' I answered, putting the food on the table, 'in the painting you showed me this afternoon.' I hardly dared watch in case he opened it.

He stood up and to my relief he put the box down, turning to me with an excited expression. 'Oh, gosh, that's incredible. Then, it's at least two hundred years old. It's still here looking exactly as it did then. That's the strange thing about old objects, isn't it? They have an eternal existence, at least if they are looked after. Doesn't it make you feel weird to think about that? You and I will come and go, as others have done before us, but this box will remain long after we are gone.'

'Yes, it's a peculiar feeling to think about that. It's like when you go into an old building, or an ancient church that has stood in the same place for hundreds of years. I always think about the people who must have lived there or who sat on the same pews. There's a sense of time not being so long, somehow, if you think about the lives of the objects in a place and the people who used them.'

Josh joined me at the table. 'Yes, I know exactly what you mean. And it's not just objects or buildings that have that effect on me. Landscapes, especially those that are unspoiled can make me feel the same. I have often stood on the end of the Cobb at Lyme and wondered about all the people who have gazed out over the water, watching the same view as they admired the lines of cliffs. Things change, of course, but the basic lie of the land and the rhythm of the sea is hardly different from when Captain Wentworth and Anne Elliot took a stroll along the top of the harbour wall.'

'You talk about them as if they are real people,' I said, with a little laugh. 'But I feel like that too. It's what made her such a fantastic writer, I suppose. You love the characters and they are so true to life, you feel as if you know them.'

'Of course they're real, I don't know how you could suggest anything else.' He raised his glass. 'Thank you, Sophie, for this truly, incredible meal. To you,' he said, clinking his glass against mine, 'and to Anne and Fred!'

I started to feel much more at ease and was glad that the meal was proving to be as delicious as it looked, even if I still could not face eating too much. There was silence as we ate for a minute or two, but it didn't feel like an uncomfortable pause brought about by a lack of conversation. Josh was clearly enjoying his chicken.

'I've forgotten what it is to eat home-baked food, a fantastic roast like this,' he said. 'I can never be bothered myself. It's a real treat and you are an amazing cook.'

It was lovely to be praised even if I knew the chicken had practically cooked itself and that I really felt I'd cheated by buying ready prepared vegetables. But then, it was nice to feel that I was good at something.

'How's the writing going?'

Somehow, I'd known that feeling wouldn't last. 'How do you know about my writing?'

'Lara told me you're a writer and that you're in Bath to be inspired.'

'The truth is that I haven't even really started.'

Josh nodded sympathetically. 'Well, you haven't been here very long. It's a novel you're researching, isn't it? What's it about?'

I didn't know exactly, but I really didn't want him to think I was clueless. 'Yes, it's a novel inspired by Jane Austen, but also a kind of personal exploration.'

'Semi-autobiographical?'

'Not really, it's an historical novel, though there will inevitably be some of myself that will reveal itself, I'm sure. Don't you think anyone who writes a book leaves a little of themselves in the pages? I'm sure Jane Austen did.'

'Do you think she was Anne Elliot, then? And if so, who was Captain Wentworth?'

'Mmm, I don't know about that. I've always wondered if it was the theme of the book, of love being lost and found again, that was more important. Besides revealing the snobbery of Anne's father and some of the people in Bath that she so obviously wanted to expose in all their awfulness, I imagine that she wanted to write a happy ending for herself – perhaps with the man she'd truly loved, whoever that might have been. Someone told me that she wrote *Persuasion* when she was dying. She knew she was never going to marry at all, let alone marry the man who Captain Wentworth was based upon.'

'Somebody is bound to have a theory about it. I do know that the time she spent in Bath is shrouded somewhat in mystery. She wrote endlessly to her sister, but for some reason there is a complete gap in the correspondence between 1801 and 1804. Nothing, not a single letter, not even really much writing! "They" say that her sister burned them all.'

'I've always wondered why she placed her most emotional novel in Bath. I remember reading that she disliked Bath but, if that was true, why would she set her most romantic book here? And why the mystery? Do you think she had a love affair or something?'

'That's it! Josh thumped his fist down on the table in a triumphant gesture. 'That's what you should write about, a novel about Jane Austen's unrequited love. I bet you could find masses of information for research, here in Bath.'

I couldn't help laughing at his enthusiasm and I was surprised how closely his ideas mirrored my thoughts. It set me thinking. Maybe there might be a way I could find out what I was curious to know, as well as find out more of Sophia's story. But there was only one way to discover what I wished to know about my ancestor and that particular method would, of course, involve the use of a certain white glove. Yet, I knew that I was feeling very uneasy about still having it. And I also knew that in the unlikely event of Jane Austen ever choosing to confide in me, I would never betray her secrets.

'I expect someone's already done that, anyway. But, I really would like to find out more about her life. I'd like the answers to a few questions I have. Everyone has their own idea about Jane Austen and I'd like to explore that in some way.'

The meal was over. I hadn't any pudding to offer, but Josh said he couldn't eat another thing, thanking me again for a lovely meal and for my company.

'It was so lovely of you to ask me to supper. I'm always on the move with my job and I don't usually get to meet anyone much, let alone be invited home for a meal.'

'I really find that hard to believe. I would have thought there'd be females falling over themselves to take you home.'

I could have bitten off my tongue the moment I'd said it.

He gave me a long look, almost quizzical. 'Would you?'

I felt my cheeks burn. 'Well, I just meant that women always seem to hone in on blokes on their own. It's like a primeval instinct somewhere between wanting to mother and ensnare them.'

Josh regarded me from under dark brows, his eyes questioning. 'Is it?'

My friends at university used to despair because I never did know when to shut up, especially when it came to conversations with the male sex. I had a habit of saying totally inappropriate things at the wrong time and I knew I'd just made a classic one. Josh was really staring at me now. I couldn't believe what I'd just said. All I kept thinking was that he would assume I'd lured him to my flat in a sorry attempt to seduce him. Suddenly, it seemed terribly important to inspect my fingernails in minute detail. When I finally glanced at him, he looked away as soon as our eyes met. I stood up to start clearing the table. It wasn't my imagination. There really was an awkward silence now.

'I'll wash up,' said Josh at last, rising to pick up the plates I'd collected together.

'Oh no, please don't, I'll do them later,' I said. I was starting to wish he'd go. All my feelings of self-doubt and of being an absolute failure at everything were returning. I just kept thinking how he'd probably tell the lovely Alison at the museum all about his narrow escape from the lecherous clutches of his neighbour who had delusions of becoming a writer. In my head, I could see them laughing. 'No, I'm sure you've got other things to do, places to go.'

Everything I said just seemed to make it worse. Nervously, I rubbed my forehead and ran my fingers through my hair desperately trying to think of something to make it better. My face must have given away how I was feeling, because in the next moment I heard his voice, soft and gentle.

'Oh, I'm sorry, you've had a long day, and I've talked you to death just now.'

I'd only gone and made it worse. I didn't know what to say to put it right so I kept quiet. The silence in the room was deafening.

At last, Josh spoke. 'Well, I must be going now, I've still got a bit of work to do, and I promised to catch up with an old friend later,' he said, avoiding my eye and taking out the plates. He reappeared moments later, standing at the door with his jacket over his arm. 'I'll leave you now to get some rest. Thank you very much for having me.'

He sounded so formal, almost solemn. As I approached, he seemed to lurch down the passageway for the front door and opened it before I managed to get anywhere near him.

'I'll see you around, then.'

I managed a smile. 'Yes, see you around.'

I felt a bit deflated when he'd gone. The sound of his door shutting made me feel worse and all I could think about was how he must be congratulating himself on his early escape. Then I told myself not to be so silly, that he'd probably got stuff to do, as I had, even though I knew I'd practically told him to leave.

I'd got a book to write and I hadn't even started. It wasn't going to be easy having no laptop, internet connection or even a pen and paper, but I thought I'd start with a bit of thinking about my characters. The heroine, obviously, was going to be a lot like me, but I was having a bit of trouble with the invention of my hero. Despite every effort, I couldn't see beyond a naval uniform. And I'm slightly ashamed to admit, the breeches figured quite prominently too. My eyes strayed to the little table. Opening the rosewood box, I took out the white glove looking for inspiration. It was then that I heard Josh's door shutting downstairs, and the front door being opened. What happened in that short window of time, I'm not sure how to explain, but a sudden pang of overwhelming guilt made me shove the glove in my pocket, grab my coat and run downstairs.

Chapter
11

Only once did it cross my mind that Josh would think I was some kind of obsessed stalker as I ran up the road after him. But, I convinced myself that all would be forgiven when I handed over the glove. Thinking about the ideas for my novel had made me resolve on doing the right thing. I wasn't going back to interfere in the lives of people I didn't really know any more. The past was better left alone and if I was intent on writing a book of fiction, I must use my imagination, not rely on any event that might have happened in real life. To do so would be cheating, somehow, and I knew if I did go back in time once again that the experience would completely colour my writing. That wasn't to say that having a glimpse into the past hadn't been useful. My mind was full of the images, sounds and smells that I could bring forth just by touching the glove. I was careful not to handle it too much again. It was safe in my pocket. Quite how I was going to explain to Josh what I was doing with it was another matter, but I was determined to hand it back to its rightful owner.

The light from the street lamps lent their dim beams to shimmer in rosy blushes as if dashed by an artist's hand in ripples on the dark pavements, wet with rain. I saw Josh turn left at Pulteney Bridge, but by the time I reached the same spot, I'd lost him. Drawing my coat closer about me, I forged ahead buffeted by strong cold blasts roaring up from the river as it foamed over the weir to churn and froth. There were a few people crossing making their way towards town. I thought I caught a glimpse of him at the end of Grand Parade, but even though I started to break into a jog again I could hardly keep him in my sight. On reaching the Abbey, I saw the silhouette of his dark head framed in the light from a streetlamp. Towering above everyone else, his mane of curls distinguished him as he moved quickly along Cheap Street. Then he disappeared, but as I reached the archway opposite Union Passage, I realized he must have taken a turn. There were lights glowing from the Pump Rooms, so I turned left and crossed the pump-yard. Josh's unmistakable figure could be seen in the glass of the revolving door.

There must be some sort of function on, I thought, and hesitated before I stepped onto the quadrant putting my hand out to stop the door from moving like a carousel. I looked through the glass, but I couldn't see Josh. The dark, heavy doors needed all my weight to move them, but once I'd got them started they swiftly seemed beyond my control to stop. Very quickly, the doors picked up a frightening speed and started to spin so rapidly it was impossible to make any attempt to get out. Faster and faster they turned, moving with a force all of their own. No matter how much I shifted my weight to lean against the one behind, nothing would slow the increasing acceleration of the revolving doors. I clung onto a brass rail with fear, shutting my eyes tight because I felt so giddy and nauseous. It was only when the sensation completely stopped that I dared to open them. Even then it was a few moments before I could take everything in.

I might have known that I'd passed back through another portal, a doorway through the present into the past. This time, though not exactly comfortable and feeling completely disorientated, I knew as I examined my dress, my hands and my feet, that I had returned to be Sophia Elliot once again. It was daytime and morning, I guessed. The sun was streaming in bright yellow shafts through the long, glazed windows, illuminating the ladies' ethereal muslin gowns to angelic brightness, casting shadows over the wooden floors and glittering dust motes to sparkle through the air. Mr Elliot, Miss Elliot and Mrs Randall were less than two feet away. It almost broke my heart to realize the resemblance of that lady to my dear mum, but though the likeness was extraordinary, there were enough differences to see that she was someone else entirely with a whole different set of mannerisms. She even moved in a different way and I supposed that was partly why I'd not noticed the similarity before. Thankfully, they were far too busy talking to be much bothered with me, so I could wander at leisure and have a really good look at everything.

Although I felt I was in familiar surroundings, the Pump Room was far less fussy than the tearoom that I knew. The chandelier still shimmered, but the room was pared back in appearance. The long windows were naked of fabric, unlike the swarm of bodies who paraded about the room in fashionable dress unhindered by tables and rout chairs, which were ranged along the walls for those who wished to observe. The clamour of voices all talking and gossiping on the subject of one another seemed much the same, punctuated with an occasional silvery laugh rising into the high ceilings. It was quite a sight.

I'd hardly registered where I was when the figure of a tall man stepped up, smiling as if he recognized me. I smiled back. There was something familiar about him though I had no idea who he could be. What struck me most about him, despite the fact that he was very good-looking, was his tanned face. It seemed so incongruous amongst a sea of pale faces. He bowed.

'Miss Elliot, I see you have found my glove. I cannot thank you enough, wherever did you find it?'

I remembered to bob a curtsey, which also gave me a moment

to realize that the white glove, that had been in the pocket of my jeans not five minutes ago, was now in my hand. He immediately held out his hand to take it. What could I do? I had no choice but to hand it over. The thought struck me then that I might very quickly be sucked back through time, as the glove was no longer in my possession, but to my astonishment nothing happened.

Our eyes met. I relaxed. He had such an easy manner and a friendliness that made me feel almost as if I knew him.

'Ah, my sisters approach,' he said. 'They have been attending to my mother and father.'

Of course, this had to be Charles Austen. He wasn't in uniform and I realized then that he probably didn't wear it when he was off duty. He'd come to Bath for a holiday, to be with the family he had not seen for a while.

The Austen family stopped to shake hands. Mr and Mrs Austen smiled very cheerfully. His white hair was almost silver and his kind, hazel eyes, reminded me so much of his daughter Jane's. Mrs Austen's piercing eyes scrutinized my face as she looked shrewdly from her son to me and back again.

'Will you be attending the ball at the Rooms on Monday evening, Miss Elliot?' she asked, as if she could guess what we'd been talking about. 'I daresay you will. Young people love to dance, do they not? Of course, I cut quite a figure in my youth, you know, but nowadays my legs prefer to sit it out. I'm not as strong as I was once, you see. My poor heart flutters in the most alarming way at any exertion that it doesn't like. "Be still my beating heart", is apt to come to mind, though indeed, it's rapid throb stems not from any longing of the heart, but mere incapacity.'

Not only did I privately think she looked as strong as an ox, but I was also aware that during this speech, Jane, who was standing slightly behind her mother, was raising her eyes heavenward in a gesture that was so naturally comic it was all I could do to keep a straight face. Thankfully, Jane's mother seemed totally unaware and had other distractions.

'Come, Mr Austen,' she said, 'I see Doctor Bowen and I

simply must know what he thinks of this rattle of a cough that's plaguing me.'

She took his arm and moved off at speed, leaving Jane, Cassandra and Charles all looking at me with their sharp eyes seeming to penetrate my every thought.

'I do hope you will be attending the ball, Miss Elliot,' said Charles.

I felt very conscious that I had no idea of the answer to this question. No voice came, no involuntary thought. The feeling that I was merely inhabiting another body had entirely gone. The only way I can describe it is that I just felt like me. And when it became clear that Sophia was not going to be talking on my behalf, I realized that I couldn't stand there any longer without saying something.

'I hope so too, Lieutenant Austen, but I do not know of any firm plan to attend the ball.'

'But you must come,' Jane said. 'Come with us if your family are not attending. I'm sure Charles would like it above everything else.'

Charles blushed slightly at her remarks, immediately bowing before excusing himself, saying he had just caught sight of a fellow sailor he'd promised to see.

Cassandra was quick to scold her sister. 'Jane, you are a terrible tease. Poor Charles has not been home for five minutes and he is the butt of your merciless jokes.'

'I was not teasing,' contradicted Jane, 'I should think my brother would enjoy Miss Elliot's company at the ball very much. And, you see, I am always right about these things. His feigning embarrassment is just a trick so he does not have to talk to us. Besides, he would not have asked as much or taken himself off so quickly, looking half so discomfited, if there were not a grain of truth in what I said.'

It was my turn to feel somewhat uncomfortable. I felt I was witnessing the sharper side of Miss Jane Austen's tongue.

'Forgive me, Miss Elliot,' said Cassandra, putting her hand on my arm in a confidential manner and talking quietly in my ear, 'but my sister has a habit of matchmaking, or at least, she is always attempting to make matches, as I know to my cost. It will be her undoing, and she will create more mischief than happiness by such interference. Please do excuse her boldness.'

Jane's retort came at once. 'I do not attempt to make matches where it is clear there are none to be found. But I have an eye for those where there are true feelings of the heart. I pride myself on my ability to spot such matters. Besides, Cassy, you must admit yourself that Charles lights up like a torch whenever Miss Elliot is near.'

Cassandra smiled. 'You must forgive our rude way of running on so, Miss Elliot. We are not used to very refined company having been closeted away most of the time in the country with no one but ourselves for society. You must not be frightened by Jane's outrageous behaviour. She does not mean it, truly.'

'I will speak for myself, if I may, Cassandra,' said Jane, taking my arm and her sister's in an affectionate way. 'If I were a betting person, I would stake my reputation on the fact that despite having met her but two days ago, my dearest brother Charles will not only dance with Miss Elliot at the ball on at least two occasions, but that he will seek her out again and again. What do you think of that, Miss Elliot?'

I hardly knew what to say and for once my tongue, which has a habit of running away with me, was still. I was surprised. Jane was so outspoken. She wasn't the timid, quiet spinster I'd expected, not at all how I thought she'd be, but then, if I thought about how little I really knew about her, perhaps that was not surprising. What did jump into my head was another book of hers that I'd enjoyed reading. Emma, whom Jane herself had written was a heroine whom "no one but myself will much like", was a young woman who made it her business to interfere in the love lives of the characters of Highbury village. But surely, sweet Jane, the clergyman's spinster daughter, could not share any of the characteristics of Miss (matchmaking) Emma Woodhouse.

I spoke truthfully. 'I do not know how to reply, Miss Jane.'

'But, do you like my brother?'

What could I say? 'I do.'

'Then there is nothing further to be said on the subject. Come, let us take a turn and be admired. And when we have had enough of this insupportable crowd, where we will not find one genteel face among them, we shall take ourselves off to the Crescent to breathe the air of better company.'

We laughed. It was impossible to be cross with her, she was so funny. Before we'd walked very far, however, Mr Elliot and Mrs Randall appeared. Mr Elliot didn't acknowledge the Miss Austens and I felt mortified for them. Jane let go of my arm. I think she knew I felt embarrassed, but I only saw her move away with her sister, as if this was a situation she had encountered many times before. Happily, it was only a moment later that I saw her turn with a wave goodbye and a mischievous grin, an expression that told me in no uncertain terms that she was not upset in the least.

Mr Elliot made no reference to the Miss Austens whatsoever. It was as if they were invisible. I could only hope they didn't feel too offended and looked forward to seeing them at the ball, if I didn't get a chance to see them sooner.

Chapter 12

My first night in Regency Bath was very strange. Wandering about the house felt both extraordinary and familiar, but I couldn't help hoping that when I went to bed I might wake in the morning to find it had all been a weird nightmare. Jane's brother had Josh's glove and I couldn't think how I was going to get it back or how I might return to my own time without it. I didn't sleep very well and as I tossed and turned in the early hours of the morning, it seemed to me that I was not really alone. Lying in the dark under stiff cotton sheets, I felt sure I heard snatches of conversation in that very room. As in a dream, I thought I could hear the sound of stifled giggling along with whispered, confidential chatter.

'Dolly, have you got any money left? I've seen a lovely hat in Jolly's and I only need another three shillings.'

'Only another three shillings! Lizzy Elliot, you'll be the finish of me. We won't be able to go to the dance if you spend what we've got left on a hat you don't need. And then you shan't be able to dance with that young officer who's home on leave.'

'Oh, he's a vision, isn't he, Dolly? And, quite as handsome as your Royal Navy sweetheart!'

I opened my eyes. It was only there for a second, but the impression of two young girls pinning their hair into rollers, as they lounged upon twin beds adorned with pink satin eiderdowns, was like a snapshot from a 1940s scrapbook. There were silk stockings hanging over a chair, cotton camisoles and pretty, belted dresses on hangers, dangling from a picture rail. There were felt berets on a wig stand, perfume bottles and a crystal bowl complete with a swansdown puff, which left a powdering of pink dust upon the surface of the dressing table. As I glimpsed the scene in a trance, the sound of a siren loudly wailing made me jump up to look round. The strange images and sounds vanished in the blink of an eye. It was almost a relief to see Sophia's room sharpen in focus again. The Chinese embroidery glimpsed through the looking glass on the opposite wall and the painting of birds and flowers trailing on sinuous branches across the room, had the effect of making me feel as if I was lying in a garden and, along with the muslin flapping in the breeze at the windows confirmed my existence in 1802. I couldn't explain what I'd just seen, though I wondered if my fervent wishing to be in my own time had somehow projected me enough for just a few seconds to deposit me in my Grandmother's time. I remembered my Great-Aunt Elizabeth referring to her sister Dorothy as Dolly, the name she always used with such affection. I couldn't help wondering what they would have thought if they'd happened to see me. Would I have looked like a ghost to their eyes, or a shadow hovering above the bed? There were so many questions I had about this whole business of passing through time. Did time move forward? Or were we all just fixed in our own layer of overlapping moments, existing side by side, all in the same time. But the more I thought about it, the more confused I felt. All I knew was that when the light of the morning sun filtered over the shutters into my room, I had not returned to my own time and I couldn't help feeling both trapped and disappointed.

At breakfast next morning, I decided to make a bid for freedom. I knew if I could get out to the gardens I might have a chance of seeing Jane and Cassy, but Mr Elliot had other ideas saying we had an engagement that couldn't be missed. William Glanville, a distant cousin by marriage, had arrived in Bath on the previous afternoon and had invited us to visit.

'You are to make yourself very amiable in the company of this gentleman, Sophia, for the sake of your sister,' he said. 'He is a widower who has made it known amongst the acquaintance of our circle that it is time he thought about marrying again. He is rich, the owner of several properties in the land. His largest estate is in the north, a gothic castle, that I am sure would satisfy all the romantic notions of any young woman.'

I breathed with relief. It was impossible not to think of poor Sophia being paraded before this Mr Glanville like a prize cow being led to the slaughter, but at least, it seemed she might be spared the ultimate sacrifice. That unenviable lot would be left to her sister Emma to fulfil.

I was surprised to find that Mr Glanville was not the grieving widower, but young and good looking, appearing to be both charming and very hospitable in an old-fashioned way. He was confident and dressed expensively in clothes that were cut to show off his tall, slim figure. I thought of all the men in my own time that I knew, and decided I was definitely a girl with a preference for nineteenth century manners.

'My dearest cousins, I am so delighted to make your acquaintance once more. It has been too long, but I hope we will make up for lost time now we are together in Bath. Tell me, have you visited the theatre yet?'

Emma lost no opportunity in speaking up, blushing pink as she spoke. 'No, Mr Elliot, we have not yet had that pleasure. Is there a play that you would recommend?'

'Why, *"The Rivals"* – Sheridan's masterfully funny play is a wonder not to be missed. I am certain it would be to your taste. I know young ladies like a romance, and those two heroines, Lydia and Julia will not disappoint. I shall arrange a box if you would like it.'

'Oh, Papa, may we?' Emma was smiling and happier than I'd ever seen her. Mr Elliot agreed to the idea, but Mr Glanville rapidly moved on to other subjects. He shared his love of poetry, not forgetting to ask our opinions on our own favourites, which had me almost scratching my head in remembrance of schooldays and appropriate poems. When he talked about his anticipation in dancing at the balls, I began to think that perhaps Emma could do a lot worse than marry this man who would at least be able to give her a comfortable life and who seemed to share an interest in like-minded passions.

When we found ourselves back at Sydney Place, Mrs Randall sought me out, saying that she was delighted by the visit, confiding that the summer before he'd married had been a time when Emma's first hopes with that gentleman had been disappointed.

'You were away at school, so I daresay you knew little or if you remember at all, but we expected a match for your sister then.'

'No, I do not remember.'

'It was the talk of Bath. Mr Glanville sought your sister out at all the dances during the first month of the season. Everyone admired Miss Elliot, she was in her bloom and as pretty as a picture. But when Miss Ancaster came along with her family estates and fortune, we knew that Emma's hopes would be dashed. Your sister's dowry and lineage could not possibly compete, though I shall always say that on beauty alone Emma won the day. I do believe your sister suffered when he withdrew. Did she never write to you about her disappointment?'

'Possibly she did, but I cannot recall the letter,' I said truthfully. 'So, Mr Glanville made his choice based on wealth and gain and not on the suitability of a partner by any other means.'

'Only a foolish young man would have acted to the contrary,' admitted Mrs Randall. 'But, now his wife has been in her grave these last twelve months along with her poor dead babe, perhaps he is ready to start looking about for someone to take her place. This invitation is very encouraging, though, in any case, as a family connection I am sure he would have sought our acquaintance.'

'I hope for Emma's sake, everything will turn out as she hopes.' I wanted to add that I would find it very difficult, if not impossible, starting all over again with someone who had not even wanted to marry me in the first place, preferring to choose someone who had more money, but tried to remember that my own thoughts were modern ones. Their way of going about courtship and marriage was accepted by everyone. I'd read Jane Austen's novels over and over again to know that much. And I didn't know quite what to think about the charming Mr Glanville any more.

When Mrs Randall left me, the impossibility of my escape from the nineteenth century began to hit me with a force like a blow to the head. I hadn't really wanted to come back again, I'd wanted to sort things out with Josh, and now, I didn't know if there was any chance of doing either.

The sound of a gong calling everyone to dinner broke my thoughts and as I passed the cheval glass in the corner of my chamber, I caught a glimpse of my reflection in the mirror. There was something about the eyes I recognized, but the face that stared back was not mine even though it moved in just the same way. I stuck out my tongue, trying to catch out the vision in the glass. Why I was so astonished when my mirror image did the same, I don't know. I remember thinking how much more of myself I seemed to be able to see in Sophia's face, in her figure and in the way that she walked, and for a single moment, I could not remember anything about myself or the life I'd left behind.

The afternoon light was fading into early evening twilight and the glow of candlelight could be seen through windows across the meadows in the curve of the Paragon and beyond to all the terraces and crescents of Lansdown lit up like tiers in a vast amphitheatre. The talk at dinner touched upon one subject only, that of Mr Glanville and of the honours Mr Elliot felt by being received so cordially.

'Family connections remind one of our place in society and it will be to our great advantage to be seen in the company of our noble cousin. Blood and good breeding will always find one another. Emma, you behaved very prettily this afternoon. And, I am sure it did not escape the attention of our host that you are in very good looks.'

'I flatter myself that I take after you, Father,' Emma answered, with a smirk. 'Indeed, I have often traced my features in your handsome portrait at the Hall, and I am blessed to have the luck to witness that face whenever I stand before the glass.'

'And Sophia has equal good fortune to look like her dear mama,' said Mrs Randall.

I chanced to look up from the plate of food that I wasn't entirely certain about. Everything had arrived on the table at once. Arranged symmetrically on white gilded Wedgewood with a laurel motif, the mahogany table gleamed under candlelight, bearing plates of salmon with bulging, glassy eyes, jellied tongue glistening with gelatine, Florentine rabbits complete with heads and furry ears, oily mackerel in a sea-green sauce, a quivering white blancmange, and the only dish I was tempted by, a syllabub, like a dish of snow topped with crystallized flowers. I hesitantly tasted the cold mackerel that stared at me balefully from my plate. Was it my imagination or was the green gooseberry preserve that covered it doing more to disguise the fact that the fish had not seen the sea for quite some time?

Mr Elliot looked me up and down through his quizzing glass in such a way that I very quickly returned my gaze to my plate. 'She does, indeed, and whilst she may never equal her sister in handsome looks, she has got over that most trying age and there is an improvement in her complexion, which was rather sallow. At least, Sophia has the advantage over her sister Marianne. The last time she came home from school, she had a nervous tick that rendered both eyes a most unattractive shade of puce. I do hope she will be improved in the summer.'

Whilst smarting on Sophia's behalf it occurred to me that I didn't really know about this other sister Marianne, youngest of the Elliot girls and fortunately for her far away at school.

Mrs Randall looked at me as she spoke up with a kindness that made me warm to her even more. I felt sorry for Sophia, but at least Mrs Randall seemed to have her best interests at heart.

'The Elliot girls will be admired wherever they go, not only for their beauty which they all share, but for the qualities inherited from their parents whether they take the form of physical and intellectual attributes or whether they are hidden in other talents that make up a person's character. Those qualities of sense and amiability in Mrs Elliot, that made her the dearest cousin and friend to me, are the treasures that lie within them all. I witness those traits every day and am constantly reminded of her quiet strength.'

I struggled to eat as much of the cold fish on my plate as I could. The second course arrived with plates of roast beef and duck, as well as apple pies and custards, but my appetite had gone.

Mr Elliot turned the conversation to Monday's ball. 'Mr Glanville will be in attendance and has made his request that we should be there to join his party.'

That wasn't quite how I'd remembered it, but I felt sure that Mr Elliot would find some way of putting himself forward. The thought of the ball filled me with dread, and as Emma spoke excitedly about what she was to wear and which dances might be performed, all I could hope was that the tedium of an evening spent with the Elliots might be relieved with some conversation from Jane and her brother Charles.

Chapter 13

Time seemed to pass slowly before the ball. Over the next few days it was impossible to get out. I was thwarted at every attempt to escape; I saw nothing of the Miss Austens and could only hope that Mr Elliot hadn't upset them too much. On Saturday morning Emma spent the entire time trying on dresses asking my opinion about which gown she should wear for the ball and how to dress her hair. It was impossible to concentrate on anything. As far as I was concerned, there was only one thing to think about. I had an idea that if I could get to the gate in Sydney Gardens, I might be able to get back to my own time. It was the only hope I had. After nuncheon, I chose my moment carefully, when Mr Elliot's snores resounded loudly from his favourite chair and when I knew that Emma and Mrs Randall were closeted away upstairs discussing gloves and fans. I slipped away out of the house and across the road.

It didn't take long to find the white gate, although I knew as soon as I saw it that it was hopeless. The gate was locked, and in my heart I knew it had been a futile exercise. Without the glove, it was impossible. There was nothing for it, but to return to the house.

I wandered along the gravel paths trying to convince myself that I'd been given an opportunity that most people only dream about. But the world was changed beyond anything I had ever imagined, and I tried not to think about the fact that I could be imprisoned there forever. I felt so completely alone.

It was then that I heard a voice calling me. 'Miss Elliot, you are not lost, I hope.'

Charles Austen was hurrying towards me. I had to smile. 'Lieutenant Austen, I have not yet ventured into the Labyrinth, and can safely find my way home, thank you.'

I wondered if I'd sounded rude, but I didn't want him to think that I was a helpless female who couldn't walk round a park without needing male assistance. He touched his hat and I thought he might walk away, but then he seemed to change his mind.

'My sisters are clambering up Beechen cliff this afternoon,' he said. 'I must admit I had not the energy for such a jaunt today. I wanted peace, solitude, and a level walk.'

There was more than a hint of laughter in his voice. I wondered if he was finding it difficult being in the company of such strong-minded women after being on a ship completely dominated by men. When I thought about Mrs Austen's apparent hypochondria and her interfering ways, I could understand why a profession that took you away from home for months and even years at a time might be such an inviting one.

'I enjoy being on my own, and the gardens are so convenient,' I began.

'Do you always prefer your own company to that of being in society?' His face looked serious for the moment, though his dark eyes twinkled as if there were some hidden secret only he delighted in.

'Oh no, but I do love to have time to think,' I said, knowing that this was perfectly true, 'and I can never think so well in a room full of people as I can on my own.'

'Your thoughts mirror my own, exactly. And even if you do manage to slip away with your thoughts in a crowded room, there is always someone who wants to know just what you are about. In my house, Miss Elliot, it is impossible to have private thoughts.'

I imagined that it would be far more difficult. At least in the twenty-first century you could be in a room full of people watching television and no one would know whether you were far away with your own thoughts or whether you were taking in everything on the screen. It was much more difficult in a time where conversation ruled the day and where you needed to be taking notice of what was being said at all times so that you could respond. I was learning how different it was to have your attention constantly demanded. Opinions were always required, and yet, I was beginning to feel that the only opinions considered worth having were those that matched everyone else's.

'Being out of the house and walking are what I enjoy when I need to think,' I said. 'And, if you can walk and see nature in all its glory; that is all to the better. When I am at home and can only see the grey buildings of the town, I long for the countryside. To see vast landscapes with fields stretching away before you lifts my spirits like nothing else.'

'Forgive me, Miss Elliot, but I believe I have been mistaken in thinking your family home is in a country village in Somerset.'

I suddenly realized what a silly mistake I'd made. 'It is in Somerset,' I said, thinking quickly, 'but we are often in London for the Season, and then the countryside seems so far away.'

Oh dear. I knew he was looking at me with a puzzled expression, and as I didn't know what else to say, I thought now might be the time to move on.

'Would you take a turn with me, Miss Elliot?' Charles Austen held out his hand, and I couldn't help noticing the tan leather of his gloves, suspecting that he kept his white ones for more formal occasions. 'Take my arm, like my sisters do.'

Without another thought I held out my hand, which he took up linking his arm with mine. We walked in silence and I wondered what he could be thinking about, if he was enjoying the chance to have a few private thoughts without being asked about them.

'It's good to be walking on dry land again,' he said at last. 'I do not have the opportunity for much exercise when I am away at sea. Of course, on the occasions when we put into port, it's a different matter. I love to go exploring if I get the chance.'

I looked up at him and smiled. 'Your sister told me that you are a lieutenant on the Endymion. Is the life of a sailor as adventurous as it sounds?'

'Miss Elliot, my life on board ship has been an exciting one thus far, and I have travelled to many parts of the world that I never thought to see. I have been extremely lucky.'

'But it must be a perilous one also in times of war.'

'The life can be dangerous, but not all my duties involve fighting at sea, whether it be attacking gunboats or capturing privateers. A while back I had the good fortune to accompany Prince Augustus to Lisbon for the sake of his health. The climate is milder and the young prince was to spend winter there. I spent three pleasant days in Portugal's capital and found my royal passenger to be jolly and affable!'

'But the conditions on board ship, they cannot be as comfortable as one might enjoy at home, can they?'

'Not perhaps as home comforts might be, but the accommodations are very adequate. It is true, life in the Navy would not suit everyone, but like my brother Francis, it suits me very well. If I could convey to you, Miss Elliot, the sense of pride I feel when we put out to sea and the great satisfaction felt by us all when the tasks our Admirals set for us to do have been accomplished, you would comprehend my devotion to the job in hand. And, once engaged in our mission and our duties, any sense of danger or peril just disappears.'

'How wonderful it must be to have a career where you feel your every action makes an important difference.'

'Well, I do not know that I have yet proved myself to be indispensable, but I hope I will establish in time that my superiors were right to believe in me enough to set me on the road I have chosen. With luck and hard work I hope to make my mark. The opportunities to make a career in one of the noblest professions are there for the taking. I am not rich yet, Miss Elliot, but one day, I trust there will be a chance to earn my prize money.'

'Your sisters told me that you have earned some prizes already, but that you spent it all on them.'

'It was nothing to spend a little to see the delight on their faces, I can assure you. My sisters do not have much in the way of treats or luxuries and when I saw the topaz crosses all I could think about was how much delight they would give.'

'Your sisters are very lucky, I think, to have such a thoughtful brother, Lieutenant Austen.'

'You do not have any brothers, Miss Elliot?'

'No,' I answered. 'I always wished to have one.'

He said no more. We walked on with our own thoughts as we came back around the gardens to the entrance once more. I'd enjoyed being with him. He made me feel safe and I knew instinctively that he was someone I could rely on. I'd never had a brother and hadn't Jane said I could have my share in one of hers? As we said goodbye, and Charles repeated his wish to see me at the ball on Monday, I reflected on the fact that despite wishing I could really go home, I had enjoyed a lovely afternoon.

The day of the ball held the promise of the first truly warm spring day. Blue skies and sunshine lifted my spirits and I tried not to think about how I might never be able to return to my own time again. I'd stopped trying to work out how I was still able to be there without the glove I'd managed to give away, and although apprehensive about what might happen next I couldn't help feeling curious and even a little excited at the idea of going to the ball. Jane's books were always full of balls, and I longed to know if the reality would be as satisfying as my imagination. A Mr Mancini arrived in the afternoon to dress our hair. As I sat and listened to the plans for frizzing and curling Emma's hair, it struck me that one thing has not changed very much in two hundred years. The anxiety that goes hand in hand with cutting and arranging hair and the horrors of placing your trust in someone, who could as easily be responsible for making you look completely hideous or stunningly beautiful, have not changed. When the tongs came out, the smell of Emma's hair being singed into rolls of artificial curls was enough to send me running. Thankfully, my own curls needed only piling up on top of my head. Mr Mancini seemed to understand that I would prefer a more natural, simpler style, pinning my long hair into place and threading through an arrangement of white gauze flowers on a silk ribbon. My gown was laid out on my bed along with a beautiful fan in silk and spangles. The dress, in a shade of apple green silk, was ruched around the décolletage and on the short puffed sleeves. There were long kid gloves and a fringed stole, and I couldn't help but be pleased with the way I looked.

I met Emma coming out of her doorway as I came out of mine. She looked wonderful, and I told her so.

Her eyes travelled lengthways from the top of my hair to the bottom of my gown. 'Thank you, Sophia. I believe I was correct in choosing the blue satin after all. Green is such a difficult colour to wear, is it not? And Mr Glanville always favours me in blue saying it brings out the matchless sapphire of my eyes. He always notices things like that, you know.'

'I am sure that Mr Glanville will not be able to resist you, Emma. I hope you will enjoy a dance or two with him.'

'I'm sure I shall, but pay heed. Should he ask you to dance, you must refuse him. Is that clear?'

I had no intention of dancing with Mr Glanville or anyone else for that matter. I hadn't a clue how to dance, and as I thought about the number of times I'd watched any kind of Regency dancing on television, I wondered if I might be able to fool anyone if I was forced to get up and join in. The thought didn't fill me with confidence and my hesitation to speak seemed to agitate Emma even more. As she waited for an answer, her eyes narrowing in suspicion, I finally nodded.

We were all to gather in the drawing room before the carriage was called. Emma ignored me as she perused the paper. Unless her father was in the room she didn't seem to have much interest in anyone else, and I was beginning to learn that he was always last to make an appearance. Candles were just being lit when Mrs Randall bustled in through the door.

'Girls, what a picture you look! Do get up and let me see you twirl. Your dear mama would have been so proud. Well, we're almost ready; there is just one small matter to attend. I have your new monthly subscription cards here for you to sign and then I can hand them into your possession.'

Despite the warmth of the fire and the glow from the candles in their sconces, I felt a sudden chill.

'Sit here, dears, there is ink and a freshly mended pen, and the light is quite good enough.'

I waited for my turn, and then sat down at the little table before the window where beyond the half closed shutters I could see the darkening trees in Sydney Gardens opposite. Dipping the pen in the ink, I carefully wrote my name and when I'd finished felt my heart pitter pat at the recollection of seeing it just like this in another time and place that now seemed so far away.

It was something of a magnificent spectacle to see all of Bath decked out in their finery at the Upper Rooms. The place was full, every passage and staircase bursting with giggling debutantes, dour matrons, and gambling card-players, waving to other revellers in recognition as they tripped along in the tide, washing them through the doors of the ballroom, the tea and card-rooms. Our party headed for the Octagon Room. Whilst Mr Elliot and Emma jostled for the best view by the fire, simultaneously grabbing the finest place from which to be admired, I glanced round to take it all in, committing to memory the beauty of the women dressed in bright silks and white muslin, the splendour of the men in dark evening dress. The looking glasses over each mantelpiece captured a cluster of fractured images displaying a handsome head, the eager glances of a young girl, or the silk-shod foot of a nimble dancer in each pane of scalloped, rococo glass. Plumes nodded, satin rustled and diamonds glistened under chandeliers sparkling with candlelight. In the glowing room incessant chatter was the order of the evening, the rising hum of expectant voices reaching a crescendo as the rooms filled. A low guffaw, a crystal laugh, and the distant tuning of instruments were the sounds I caught above the rest. Candles guttered as the noise of a hundred voices, all talking at once, rose in the heat, along with the scents of orange blossom, jasmine and lavender, masking those other smells of warming humanity, which had my nose wrinkling at the sour odours seeping from cloth, stale with sweat.

I had a very good view of the door and saw the second that the Austens arrived. Wearing white muslin with a glossy spot, setting off her slender figure, Jane dashed through first, child-like in her movements, her bright eyes alert. With her hair swept up into a pretty arrangement of twisted silk, several tendrils escaped from her cap, kissing the base of her neck as she moved. As she quietly observed all before her, I couldn't help wishing I could read her thoughts. I wondered if she, like me, would be storing away the evening's conversations to be brought out and examined for inspiration later on. Also in white, her pretty sister came in next wearing an elegant muslin embroidered at the hem. Mr and Mrs Austen followed in their wake, dressed in their comfortable country clothes, both smiling and bowing to all their friends.

I almost didn't see him at first. Charles came dawdling along at the back stopping to talk to his friends, to listen attentively, or laugh out loud at a shared joke. I imagined they must be other sailors from the way he greeted them. Dressed for the evening I couldn't help staring as he nonchalantly strolled across the room. Every detail of his appearance sharpened into focus. Dark curls fell on the high collar of his black coat, cut to display a flash of white silk waistcoat with buttons faced in pearl, that led the eye to the swell of satin where his breeches began. Defining his muscular legs, they finished at the knee where silk stockings delineated the curve of shapely calves leading down to a pair of gleaming dancing shoes. He looked beautiful if I can use that word to describe a man, and I knew I was not the only woman in the room who glanced his way or sat up in their chair. I wasn't standing near the fire, but I felt the rush of heat on my cheeks as I stared. Something about the cut of his dark coat emphasized his broad shoulders, and the crisp cotton kerchief at his neck exaggerated his tanned features making him stand out from the crowd. His air of self-assurance might have come across as arrogance in anyone else, but to me, he simply looked perfect lighting up the room with a personality so magnetic, he seemed to draw everyone around him. The family took up station by the fireplace opposite. Jane glanced across with a smile, and I saw her point me out to her brother. Our eyes met across a sea of people and Charles smiled broadly. I cannot say what made my heart flutter at that moment, but I felt he'd curled a finger round my heart. I couldn't sustain his gaze and looked away.

'Who is that fellow over there with the Astons?' said Mr Elliot, making me feel instantly cross that he couldn't even remember his neighbours' name.

'I'm sure I have no idea,' said Mrs Randall, looking at me as if she were sure I could supply the answer. 'He is a very fine looking gentleman. Perhaps he is a relation of the Austen family; a noble peer, I daresay, by his attitude and deportment.'

I spoke out. 'He is the Miss Austens' brother, Mr Charles Austen, lately returned from his duties at sea as a lieutenant on the frigate Endymion.'

'Oh, a sailor,' uttered Mr Elliot, turning back with utter disdain. 'Well, I suppose a clergyman's son has to make his way in the world as any other. But he should be careful about giving himself such airs or he will be sorry when he is found out to be a nobody; a person of obscure birth. I might have guessed he was no gentleman for his face is the colour of my mahogany secretaire.'

'The Navy has done so much for us that I am convinced of sailors having more worth and warmth than any other set of men in England,' I said, but even as I uttered the words I felt sure I was repeating something I'd heard spoken before. They came out so naturally that I couldn't stop them.

'I suppose the profession has its uses but I have my own objections to the Navy's place in society. Men who would never have been raised to honours in the past are now moving in the same circles as their betters, though I can assure you not one would find a friend in me. Besides, I could never be seen consorting with such weather-beaten creatures. A sailor is old before his time; a man's youth is cut off in its prime. They are exposed to every sort of foul weather and as a consequence are as wrinkled as a walnut and not fit to be seen.'

I was just thinking that this speech had more than a familiar ring to it when I chanced to see that its effects on two people standing less than two feet away had been both painful and mortifying. Unknown to me Jane and Charles had walked over from their place on the other side of the room. They'd obviously heard every word judging from their expressions, though they both assumed smiles as soon as they saw that I, too, was quite horrified by the conversation that had just taken place.

Mr Elliot did not acknowledge them for the second time and I saw Emma turn, linking her arm in his to lead him away. Mrs Randall smiled at my friends, but followed the other two, so I was left alone to think how I could possibly apologize for their abominably rude behaviour.

I didn't know what to say or how to start. I couldn't bring my eyes to look at Charles even though I knew he was looking at me intently and was very thankful that Jane was the first to speak.

'Well, is there anyone here worthy of our notice, do you think?' Her face was alive with humour, her words peppered with irony.

'Only the first-rates, eh, Miss Elliot?' Charles declared with a smirk and a wink.

I knew they were teasing, but I couldn't decide if their comments were in reaction to my family's rudeness, or an allusion to their pompous and snobbish behaviour, and I didn't know how to reply.

'And speaking of which, Miss Elliot,' he continued, 'do you see the lady over there in white whispering in the ear of the gentleman that she insists is her nephew? That's the Dowager, Lady Nethercott.'

'Oh, goodness,' I said, hoping to sound suitably impressed,

though from what I could see she was dressed in sheer, clinging muslin, a style for young women half her age with the bloom of youth painted on her face with a heavy hand. Her companion was gazing at her in a way I thought unlikely for a nephew to look at his aunt.

'Do you mean the old lady both nakedly and expensively dressed, exposing far more bosom than she ought at her age?' quipped Jane.

'Hush, my dear sister, please lower your voice! No one is old in Bath or can expose too much flesh!'

'Charles, you have quite misled Miss Elliot,' Jane scolded. 'My dear friend, it is clear that my brother has picked her out for amusement.'

Charles grinned. 'Well, perhaps I did, but you seemed to share your part in the joke.'

'Now look, our neighbour cannot think what to make of us,' said Jane taking my arm. 'Shall we start again? Let us pretend that we have not yet been introduced. Miss Elliot, it is a delight to see you again. You remember my brother Charles, I think.'

I nodded, unable to suppress a smile, and plucking up the courage to look up found him gazing steadily at me, a flicker of amusement crossing his face. 'You have not forgotten me since Saturday, I hope, Miss Elliot.'

It was my turn to smile. 'No, I remember you very well.'

'You saw Miss Elliot on Saturday?' asked Jane, looking from one to the other of us.

'Yes, we happened to bump into one another in Sydney Gardens. Unfortunately for Miss Elliot, she was craving solace and quiet. That she did not find it is quite certain, as I am afraid I rather forced her to enjoy my company and urged her to take a turn with me.'

'I remember you saying that you had no wish to go out walking that day,' Jane continued, searching her brother's face. Her eyes sparkled in a most teasing way. 'But, perhaps the sight from an upstairs window of a pretty girl entering the gardens quite changed your mind.'

'I think perhaps it was not so much his choice of companion that led him into the gardens as much as the desire to find a level walk,' I said, before she could insinuate anything more. 'I believe you were climbing up Beechen Cliff, Miss Austen, a jaunt that requires both stamina and endurance. You would have to be a very good walker to contemplate such exercise and perhaps the idea of such a testing ramble proved too much for some.'

Jane laughed. 'How refreshing it is to find someone who can tease my little brother as well as I can. What do you think, Miss Elliot? Will he dare to give us his opinion? I cannot wait to hear his answer.'

'I will have you know that I am an excellent walker and any time that either of you would like the challenge of a walk up that noble cliff, I will be only too pleased for you to witness my vigour and fortitude in the accomplishment.'

'Miss Elliot, how can we refuse him?'

'I do not think we can.'

'No, indeed. Charles, let us meet very soon. Miss Elliot, I hope if you have no other engagements that you will be able to accompany us. I expect my sister will join us also, and if the fine weather continues, we should consider a picnic.'

'Miss Elliot, do you think you would be able to come?' Lieutenant Austen, I discovered, had dark brown eyes flecked with amber and gold, at once attentive and almost hypnotic as he held my gaze.

'I hope so, though I am not certain of our present engagements.'

I could sense Jane watching us. 'I must speak to Cassy at once, as I am sure she will be most interested to learn of our scheme. We must fix a date.'

She was gone in a moment and for the first time I felt slightly uncomfortable. I didn't know how to explain it, but I knew I was attracted to Charles. I also knew it wasn't right to feel like that. It felt like a secret I'd never be able to share. I didn't belong in this time and Charles, I was sure, would have no interest in me. But, I didn't hesitate when he asked me for the first dance, which I was certain had been prompted by Jane. It was just a dance, after all.

'I would be delighted.' The words were out before I could stop them. I tried not to think about what a disaster it might be, though I kept remembering that the dances I'd seen always seemed to have such complicated shapes, lots of turning and crossing in circles or figures of eight. We'd had country dancing lessons at school for a while. I would just have to do the best I could.

'Come at once,' chided Emma, suddenly appearing at my side and hissing in my ear, 'Mr Glanville has arrived and if I'm not there to greet him because of your flirting with a social upstart, I shall never forgive you.'

Lieutenant Austen bowed, and as I allowed myself to be wrenched away, I hoped he hadn't heard her. I couldn't help feeling sorry for myself, or more importantly for Sophia. When I thought about how I'd always longed for a sister or a brother I hadn't imagined it could be a relationship based on cruelty. The only comforting thought was the fact that I knew the reverse could be true. The Austen sisters clearly adored one another and I knew Charles felt the same way about his siblings. I loved the way they were constantly teasing one another and sharing jokes, not with any sense of humiliating the other, but each one knowing that they did so out of affection and love.

We could see Mr Elliot in the distance, standing with his cousin at the entrance to the ballroom. Both seemed oblivious to the fact that they had forced everyone else to a halt as the huge number of people spilled out across the reception hall. As Emma and I approached, the sea of whispering faces seemed to part as people stepped aside to let us through the throng.

'Oh yes, those are the Elliot girls. The family is with Mr William Glanville, you know. Rumour has it that he's looking amongst his own for a new wife!'

Emma heard them and smiled broadly. She stood very erect displaying her long white neck to perfection and sallied forth as if she fully expected to become Mrs Glanville within the week.

William Glanville seemed very pleased to see us both. With the pleasantries out of the way, he asked Emma for the first dance. As he took her arm to lead her into the ballroom he suddenly turned to me.

'Miss Sophia, do take my other arm. I insist on your dancing with me after your sister, and I will brook no refusal.'

I didn't know what to say. Emma would be furious if I said yes and Mr Glanville was urging me to accept. My silence only seemed to make him think that I'd agreed to it.

'I shall look forward to our dance very much. If I may be allowed an observation, Miss Sophia, I would say that the hue of the gown you are wearing this evening is most becoming. I am no poet but your jade eyes are beautifully enhanced by apple tones.'

Needless to say, after this most embarrassing outburst, mine were not the only eyes to appear an altered hue. Emma's were quite pea-green with envy.

Chapter
15

Charles came to claim his dance. I needn't have worried about not knowing what to do, though I began to think that hours spent watching Colin Firth dancing Mr Beveridge's Maggot were not going to do me a lot of good. This dance was really energetic, more like the country dances I'd learned at school. Fortunately, only one couple started at a time, which gave me a chance to watch what they were doing. William Glanville and Emma led the dancing and as I tried to memorize the steps and figures, Charles demanded my attention.

'Do you enjoy dancing, Miss Elliot? I must admit, it is my particular delight and the activity I miss most when I am away at sea. Indeed, whenever and wherever we disembark I will always head to the nearest assembly as soon as I can. No matter how tired after a voyage, a night of dancing always increases my spirits. My sister Jane always laughs at me about it, but to tell you the truth, she is just the same.'

'I enjoy dancing very much,' I replied truthfully, but had to suppress a smile when I thought how shocked he would be by the dark nightclubs I knew where not only the music was very loud, but where a partner might take you closely in his arms. Yet, somehow, looking at his expression, I had a feeling that if Charles Austen were suddenly catapulted into the twenty-first century, he would quickly get used to the idea. But thinking about my own time was no good, I had to prove myself in his, and I knew that I desperately didn't want to let him or myself down.

All I could hope was that I wouldn't disgrace him. I needn't have worried; Charles took command. That air he had, a natural confidence in his own ability, coupled with charm that positively glowed from within, shone through even more so on the dance floor. All eyes watched us, which was unnerving, but once I felt confident about the steps and figures, I was able to really enjoy myself. Once or twice our eyes met. I had that feeling of indescribable excitement again. It felt fantastic and I hadn't experienced that in such a long time, though I scolded myself for my ridiculous behaviour. What on earth was I doing? I was practically flirting with Jane Austen's brother! But when Charles whispered that my dancing was wonderful, I felt I might burst with pride. I hadn't thought it would be so energetic or exhausting and I was glad when it was the turn of the other couples to lead the way so I could get my breath back.

It was on one of these occasions that I spotted Jane on the other side of the room. She really had a talent for dancing. Nimble on her feet and so graceful, she skipped and smiled wreathing her way down the set. But, as I watched her laughing, her eyes bright and sparkling, all of a sudden her expression changed and her body language conveyed more than any words could say. She froze and her darting eyes clouded in recognition at the tall, fair-haired man standing next in line to dance with her. He was clearly making her nervous. I couldn't see him well enough to make out individual features, but I could see he was very good-looking. I saw Jane studying the floor intently before she looked up to flick her head the other way, thus avoiding his lingering glances. There was a moment of hesitation; a clear delay, and a faltering behind the beat of the music for just a split second before she allowed him to take her hand and when she did, that was when I saw the sparks fly. They held each other's gaze, Jane's head tilting at an angle displaying her long white neck. It was as if they were joined by an invisible cord and for a long time they did not take their eyes from one another. Not a word passed between them, but every glance spoke volumes. In the next second, I saw her raise her chin defiantly and as she gaily danced along the line as if nothing had happened, I noticed neither one of them looked back or sought the other out again. You would have thought they were strangers, yet I knew I was not mistaken. If they were not lovers now, I was sure there had once been a very strong attraction. Though neither had spoken to the other, I had no doubt they knew each other intimately.

My attention elsewhere, I nearly missed my step. Thankfully, Charles saved the day, grasping my hand and sending a frisson of pleasure coursing through me. By the end of the dance, my cheeks flamed, my breath taking a few moments to steady. Charles, of course, looked very cool. His slightly heightened colour made him look more handsome than ever and, unlike me, he seemed to be no more out of breath than when we started.

After the dance finished, I sensed neither of us wanted to part straight away.

'Thank you, Miss Elliot,' he said at last, touching my arm briefly, but enough to send a little shock of desire running through my veins, 'it is rare to find a partner who dances with such grace and ease.'

I was so pleased. 'The delight was all mine, Lieutenant Austen.'

'I hope you will not think me presumptuous to ask for another.'

'I would love to dance with you again,' I said, even knowing that although I'd got away with it this time, I might not do so a second time. It was a risk worth taking, and however much I told myself I should not dance with him again, I knew there was nothing I'd rather do.

The musicians were tuning up again. Lieutenant Austen

bowed and I curtsied as prettily as I could. He was about to take my hand again when we were rudely interrupted.

'Miss Elliot, what a delight it has been dancing with your sister. And now, I hope you will enjoy our promised dance to which I have so looked forward.'

Mr Glanville took my hand. It was done so swiftly that I couldn't protest. Charles's expression altered, he no longer smiled, and after a curt acknowledgement he immediately walked away. I could only trust that he would come to my rescue later on, but all hope vanished when he didn't turn to look in my direction or reassure me in any way. As I walked to the floor with Mr Glanville I saw Emma glaring angrily, her lips pressed together in an anxious attempt not to reveal her true feelings. I silently mouthed an apology, but she didn't want to see that I wished to be anywhere else but dancing with him or holding his hand that gripped mine far too tightly. Doing all I could to put him off, I avoided his eyes and his questions, but he seemed as keen as ever.

'You have been hiding yourself, Miss Sophia,' he said, 'and it is a great pity for it is rare to find such a dancer to complement one's own abilities. I should never boast of my own talent for dancing, of course, but my friends tell me of their envy. Sir Archibald Anson, a very dear acquaintance, declared he should never wish to be caught in a quadrille alongside me for fear of being put at a disadvantage. And he, my dear, has had lessons from the great Mr Wilson himself!'

'I have little experience in dancing, Mr Glanville, and am as likely to tread on your toes as the next young lady,' I answered, determined at once to show how very bad I could be. I hesitated on the next call, managing simultaneously to jump onto his gleaming slipper and smile as if I was totally unaware that I'd committed such a dreadful crime. Watching him wince had me biting my lip, and at least Emma looked placated for a second or two. But neither ignoring him nor abusing him seemed to stop him being as attentive as ever. As the last note struck I ran away, conscious that he was about to repeat his request to dance again. I thought he might follow me, but fortunately, Emma was waiting. She looked furious and wishing to steer clear of her, I dashed away losing myself in the throng.

The ballroom was very crowded and it took some time to squeeze past the multitude of people who stood at the sides observing the dancers. I didn't quite know where I was going; the card room was full of people and I just wanted to be on my own. I was making my way along the corridor in the crush of people when I caught sight of Jane. Trying to reach her I was swept along, my feet hardly touching the ground as the crowds surged in two directions. Spotting a gap, I slipped and dodged my way through until I almost caught up and was about to call her name when I noticed she was with the same man she'd been dancing with earlier. He was urgently whispering something in her ear though she didn't look at him or communicate in any way. I couldn't see their expressions, only the backs of their heads. There was a flash of movement, their fingers brushed with lightning speed, and I glimpsed a piece of paper pass between them before they abruptly separated, she to the ballroom, and he to the card-room.

I didn't know what to think. I couldn't help feeling curious about the reasons why they couldn't talk to one another openly, but it was none of my business, and I decided I must put any speculation out of my head. There could be all sorts of reasons why Jane and a handsome young man were corresponding in such a clandestine way, and then told myself off for imagining that a love affair must be the reason.

Opening up the pair of double doors to my right I decided to take a chance and found myself in the tearoom, which was empty. Preparations had been made for the influx of thirsty dancers who would be arriving within half an hour to take tea. I sat down amongst the tables scattered with teacups and closed my eyes savouring the peace and quiet. The sense of relief at having escaped was sublime until I heard the door scrape open.

Chapter 16

To my enormous surprise, it was Charles who poked his head round the door. 'I thought I saw you come in this direction. Please tell me to go away if you'd rather not have any company. I cannot help thinking that you wish to be on your own again.'

'Oh no, I would welcome your company, Lieutenant Austen. Please come in. I admit; I came in here to escape, but not from you.'

He took the seat next to mine and stretched out his long, muscular legs. I remember thinking how he seemed to make the entire room come alive with warmth and brightness like the candles that burned in the sconces, sending haloes of candlelight to fall softly on his features and on the dark curls waving around his face. I noted the firm contours of his face and his grave, serious expression that almost hid the humour that bubbled away behind the deep tawny eyes. Struck once more by his sheer physical presence Charles made me feel dainty and tiny by comparison, a distinction that reminded me that we were so very different. Poles apart in every way and yet I felt there was a connection between us. I sensed it and I began to think that perhaps he might too. He was studying my face again, watching my mouth, which made it twitch with nerves. I wanted to bite my lips.

'Is it Mr Glanville you wish to avoid?'

I nodded. 'I do not want to dance with him again for fear my sister Emma will never speak to me again.'

'Ah, I see. If not for your sister, you would choose to dance with him.'

'Oh, goodness me, no! He is a pleasant enough person, but he is … a little eager,' I said at last, trying to find the words without betraying any modern sensibility.

I looked up to see him smiling. 'I cannot blame Mr Glanville for wishing to dance with you.'

'Well, my sister would prefer that I did not dance with him at all. I think between them, she and my father have designs on him. He is a widower, you know.'

Charles smirked. 'Yes, I have heard he is looking for a wife.'

'My sister is looking for a husband and I think it a very likely match.'

'And you, Miss Elliot, are you also looking for a husband?'

I caught that expression of his again, the serious one with the evident hint of mirth around his mouth just waiting to break out into a laugh. Was he teasing me again?

'No, I am not. Marriage where love has no place is not for me, I confess. There is far too much of that sort of thing going on here in Bath and it is not to my taste, I can assure you. Husband hunting could never be a sport for me. Until I fall in love with someone I believe truly returns my affection, I shall not contemplate it.'

'You are in a very happy position to have that choice, Miss Elliot.'

'Well, whether I truly have that power remains to be seen, but I do not think my opinion is one generally shared amongst the people with whom I am acquainted.'

'I am certain your ideas are well-considered, Miss Elliot, and I think it wise to trust to your own judgment in these matters.'

'And, what is your opinion, Lieutenant Austen? Are you intent on marriage? Do you seek love or the pursuit of a suitable wealthy alliance?'

'I would like to marry one day. But, I have my way and my fortune yet to make. Even if I wished to marry, I could not expect to attract a wife. Not perhaps until I am made Captain of a frigate of my own will I consider matrimony as a serious prospect.'

'So, I understand you will not allow yourself to fall in love until you have been promoted.'

Charles threw back his head and laughed again. 'Well, Miss Elliot, you may prove me wrong. I think, however, that what I meant to say is that, I feel it would be best to wait before I form any attachment that I could not immediately honour. However, I do not think that my sister would necessarily agree with the idea of waiting to marry. Jane has expressed her thoughts on this matter having witnessed at first hand the misery of what can happen when two people are forced to wait for want of fortune.'

I wondered if he was going to tell me something about Jane's mysterious friend. 'Was Miss Jane in love?'

'It was my sister Cassandra who fell in love and became engaged before her fiancé went to sea as a chaplain. They hoped his position might find him preferrment with Lord Craven, but poor Mr Thomas Fowle died of yellow fever in San Domingo and was buried at sea. His death afflicted us all; he was as another brother to me.'

'That is a very sad tale. I cannot think how your sister must have been affected.'

'For Cassy, I believe, she has never fully recovered, although she bears her loss with dignity and fortitude. But, her nature has always been more reserved and I am not sure if she would ever have been encouraged to any folly by marrying early or before our parents thought it right, whatever the outcome.'

'Something in what you have said makes me think that Miss Jane is a different character.'

'Cassandra is prudent, well-judging – she has the calmer disposition of the two. My sister Jane is very open with a happy temper, vivacious and passionate in all her pursuits. If she were to fall in love, we would all know about it, I think.'

'And if you were to fall in love, Lieutenant Austen?'

'You are a very bold inquisitor, Miss Elliot. But, since you ask, the fact that it is impossible for me to contemplate the marriage state just yet, means that I will do everything in my power to insure love doesn't happen.'

'Do you mean to say that you might deny your feelings? If, for example, you were to fall in love against your will, if it happened without you knowing so that you had no time to consider it, what do you think would happen then?'

Charles paused. I met his eyes, which were contemplating mine. 'I enjoy the company of pretty young women, I love to dance and even to flirt a little, but I do not have the luxury of time to make really lasting friendships. I tend to rely on my sisters for companionship when I am at home.'

'I think you have very successfully evaded my question. What of your feelings, Lieutenant Austen?'

'I like to think I am an open-hearted person, Miss Elliot, with all the correct feelings of affection, but perhaps it is just a matter of not ever having met the right person who inspires the sort of feelings you describe. I admit; I have little idea of how it might feel to be in love. I have not had the luck to fall in love … yet.'

'I think that a fair answer. And I daresay, it will be your fate one day. I am certain there must be someone for everyone. When you least expect it, love will strike!'

'In the meantime, could I persuade you to another dance, Miss Elliot?'

'No persuasion is necessary, Lieutenant Austen. I should love to dance.'

If possible, the second dance was even more fun than the first. We both relaxed and the need for polite chatter all but vanished. We moved together so well, he was a wonderful partner and such a good dancer, that I felt completely at ease. I couldn't think of a time when I'd enjoyed myself so much.

Mrs Randall was waiting for me as we came off the floor. She acknowledged Charles before excusing us, saying that my father wished to speak with me.

'Thank you, Miss Elliot,' Charles said. 'I hope we shall see you very soon. I know my sister is full of schemes for her expedition up to Beechen Cliff.'

I knew that we should not be able to dance again. In all of Jane's books it was considered most inappropriate to dance a third time in one evening. It made me like him even more. Such "a good-looking, gentleman-like, pleasant, young man," was the phrase that sprang to mind.

'Miss Elliot, I must speak to you,' Mrs Randall said quietly. 'I wish only to advise you as I believe your mother would have done, but I think you should be on your guard. Your friends, the Austens, are very amiable, genteel sort of people and I believe your dear mama would have had no objections to the friendship with the sisters who are well-informed, intelligent girls. However, I cannot help the observation that Lieutenant Austen has singled you out for two dances this evening and has been most particular in his attention to you. Your father would not approve of such a marked interest, or of such a connection.'

'I have only danced with him, Mrs Randall. We are not about to be engaged!'

'Be that as it may, you should be cautious. It is a daughter's duty to marry well for her family's sake as well as her own. You and your sister will make exceptional matches, marriages that would have made your mother proud and happy, allowing you to partake in a life of privilege and wealth. This is what she wanted for you, Sophia, to take your place in society. Do not damage your chances of happiness for a few moments of foolish frivolity. Do you understand, my dear?'

'You think Lieutenant Austen is trying to court me? Really, Mrs Randall, nothing could be further from the truth. He has no wish to marry. He told me as much. No, he is too busy proving himself in the Navy; he has no intention of doing anything so foolish as to fall in love. My father's fears and your own are completely groundless.'

'He might not do anything so foolish as to fall in love, but your defence of him just now leaves me feeling no more assured of your ambivalence toward Lieutenant Austen than before we started this conversation.'

Mrs Randall was looking at me with a most anxious expression. Despite the fact that the real world I knew was dimming into nothingness like the wisp of a dream on waking, I saw and recognized in her the traces of my own mother. I couldn't help thinking about her and of how her life had been cut tragically short, robbing her of the chance to see her only child grow up, both denying us the friendship and love that forms such special bonds between mother and daughter. Sophia and her mother had been denied that relationship also. And, whatever I thought of Mrs Randall's interference, even I could see that she had Sophia's best interests at heart. There was only one way to reply. I took her arm in mine as we crossed the room.

'Mrs Randall, I know you speak to me out of kindness and concern for me. My mother, I am certain, would have spoken to me in just the same way. I thank you from the bottom of my heart for standing in her place and I promise, I will never give you any cause for alarm or worry in regard to matrimony or anything else!'

Mrs Randall made no more comment, leaving me at Mr Elliot's side before hurrying away to see to Emma. I knew I was changing, being taken over, body and soul. I was not myself and yet, I felt more like the person I should be than ever before. I was Sophia Elliot of Monkford Hall and the snobbish, vain and irascible Mr Elliot, I hardly knew, was as much my father as if I had known him forever. My own time and the people who belonged there were fading like the moving pictures on an old celluloid film.

I'd so enjoyed the ball after all, though the real pleasure had been in spending time with the Austens, particularly Charles. When Jane called the next day with an invitation to go for a picnic to Beechen Cliff on Thursday, I didn't hesitate. Getting permission to go would be another matter, but I decided it might be best if I didn't mention that Charles would be coming with us. I stressed the fact that I would be going for a walk with the Miss Austens and was extremely vague about all the rest.

Thursday morning arrived with delphinium skies and sunshine. I'd been awake since the early hours thinking about the pleasures of the day to come and was soon dressed, hurrying down to the kitchen to beg whatever provisions I could for the picnic. Mrs Potting, the cheerful cook, let me have the seed cake she'd baked the day before, plus half the tray of muffins that had just come out of the oven, even giving me napkins and a basket to carry them in.

Thankfully, Mr Elliot and Emma felt happy about leaving me behind to go for their usual walk to the Pump Rooms. Emma's desire to see Mr Glanville was very obvious and all I could hope was that he would be similarly attentive for all our sakes. They made a brief enquiry about my plans, but I knew neither of them was interested. Mrs Randall had not yet arrived from her lodgings to question me about where I was headed, so I looked forward to the day with mounting excitement. Sitting in the window of the drawing room, which looked out over the gardens, I knew I should be able to have sight of the sisters coming out of their door. But, as the time passed and no one came, I began to worry.

I ran downstairs looking for the housemaid, Rebecca, who soon told me that no one had called. Grabbing my pelisse and bonnet and hoping they'd forgive my impatience, I let myself out and presented myself at the door of number four.

'You've missed them, Miss Elliot,' said the harried looking maidservant. 'They left this last half hour, at least.'

I could hardly hide my disappointment. 'Did they say where they were going?'

'Up to Beechen Cliff, as far as I remember, Miss, though goodness knows why they want to go tramping up there in the mud and mire. Wait a moment, Miss Elliot. I'll ask Cook, she'll know for sure.'

The flustered maid tripped away down the corridor and I saw her vanish through the door at the bottom. I was left standing in the hallway, unable to believe that I was really in Jane Austen's house. I caught my reflection in the looking glass on the wall. It still gave me a shock to see it wasn't my own, yet try as I might; I couldn't quite remember how I ought to look.

The console table had a gentleman's black hat upon it. It looked just like the one I'd seen Charles wearing on that day in Sydney Gardens and I wondered if it belonged to him. Casting a furtive glance down the hallway I decided to risk picking it up to take a closer look. I saw them straight away. Where the hat had lain was a pair of gentlemen's white gloves.

Then the door opened. The maidservant returned, rushing along the corridor with a beetroot face and barely audible from her huffing and puffing. 'Yes, Cook says they're not expected back until this afternoon. I'm sorry; Miss Elliot, I'll tell the Misses Austen that you called. Good day.'

I was dismissed, and disappointed. I couldn't think why they hadn't called. Had I misunderstood? But, I was sure I hadn't misheard and it was definitely the right day. It all seemed so strange. I stepped outside feeling really dejected. Perhaps Charles was embarrassed that he'd danced with me twice, or felt he'd singled me out too much. All that talk about love must have frightened him and he was letting me know in no uncertain terms that I should keep my distance. I was sure it must be something like that, though I felt hurt that even Jane had not called to try and explain about the reasons for now wishing to go on their own.

I knew then that I didn't want to stay. I took the glove out of my pocket and turned towards Sydney Gardens where I knew I would find the white gate, hoping it would be unlocked. Yes, I know it was so very wrong of me to have stolen it, but the opportunity presented itself and I found I couldn't do anything else.

Chapter 17

Finding myself back in the twenty-first century was an enormous relief. The transition was as smooth as passing through a time portal could be, almost like walking through a garden gate at any other time. What was more, I felt energetic not drained like on previous occasions. I'd made a lucky escape even if I felt sad about leaving my friends, and in particular, I was sorry that I might never see Charles again. My heart tugged with an ache I didn't want to recognize when I pictured him in my mind. But, perhaps it was for the best and if I was honest with myself, I knew I shouldn't really be there interfering in their lives. I'd felt a dangerous attraction to Charles and the more I thought about it, the more I reconciled myself to the fact that I'd done the right thing. I'd got carried away for a moment. After my relationship with Lucas the last thing I needed was to be falling for someone else, especially a guy who lived in another time zone. Just thinking about that made me realize how ridiculous the whole episode had been and brought me instantly back down to earth.

It felt like coming home when I reached the flat and once I'd picked up some shopping I resolved on starting to work on my book. I'd need to do some research, which I fully intended to do, but right now I wanted comfort, some soothing consolation. Picking up my old battered copy of *Persuasion*, I decided this would be the best place to start if I wanted to get things right in my head, and hopefully, it would also provide some inspiration or insight into Jane's world. Spending the next few days reading and making notes was good therapy for the pangs of regret that surfaced every time Captain Wentworth's name was mentioned or when Charles popped into my head. But I knew that locking myself away was not going to accomplish anything. I decided that joining the library would get me out into the real world, and help enormously with my research. Besides, I'd started feeling lonely, and I needed to see people again.

The very next morning I set off into town. I strolled along Pulteney Street in the sunshine thinking how lovely and familiar it all looked. Peeking into the windows of the charity shops, I was unable to pass by without looking at all the books on display. Suddenly, the sight of an old volume, opened up at the frontispiece, grabbed my attention and when I saw it, I felt goosepimples all over. I just had to go in. It was fetched out of the window at my request, and the red, cloth-bound book put into my hands. What struck me with a bolt of recognition was the engraving; a portrait of Jane Austen that I'd never seen before. Dressed in sprigged muslin, and carrying a parasol, there was the Jane that I knew. It looked like a photograph, but I suppose that's because it was in black and white. Younger, a girl of about fourteen perhaps, but with the same intelligence sparkling in her eyes and a hint of a smile lighting up her face as if amused by her thoughts. My eyes were immediately drawn to the text of the book and in the preface, one paragraph stood out above all others.

Hence the emotional and romantic side of her nature—a very real one—has not been dwelt upon. No doubt the Austens were, as a family, unwilling to show their deeper feelings, and the sad end of Jane's one romance would naturally tend to intensify this dislike of expression; but the feeling was there, and it finally found utterance in her latest work, when, through Anne Elliot, she claimed for women the right of 'loving longest when existence or when hope is gone'.

So, the book was not going to give up any secrets about Jane, and it seemed I was not the only one to think that *Persuasion* must tell the tale of her one great love. I couldn't wait to read more and looking through the pages saw that it also contained copies of her letters, which I'd never read in their entirety. Flicking through, I couldn't find anything about Charles apart from his date of birth on a quick look, but guessed there must be more hidden within its pages. I must admit, there was a part of me that didn't want to know what had happened to him, but I knew I could no longer avoid knowing the truth. I handed over my money, popped the book into my bag, and headed into town.

I'd just reached the bridge when I ran into Josh. When I say I ran into him – I did see him coming towards me for a few yards, but I could do nothing about it. There was nowhere to hide on the pavement. He'd seen me too and once he'd waved at me, I could hardly turn round and run in the opposite direction. I wanted to, of course, but the thought that the last time I'd seen him I'd made an awful impression made me stubborn enough to want to change that. I was determined that he would see a person who was totally indifferent to him and not at all like the man chaser he'd assumed.

'Hi, Sophie, I haven't seen you for a while. How are you doing?'

'I'm very well, thanks. And you?'

'I'm well, busy with the exhibition, of course.'

There was an awkward silence, a feature that seemed to be increasingly prominent in our conversations. Josh smiled. He looked as if he might say something else, but then scratched absently at his cheek.

'Right ... well, I'm just going to the library,' I said, tugging my bag up to my shoulder.

'Oh, I see. I'm just out on a lunch break.'

I made a move to go and he spoke again putting out his hand, touching my sleeve.

'I'd love it if you'd join me. Would you come? I really need to ask you something, a favour. It would mean a lot.'

It was impossible to refuse him, and I felt I ought to at least try and prove my innocence. He was being so nice and I must admit, I'd been feeling a bit lonely. I was also more than a little intrigued so I found myself accepting. I could always do my research later.

'C'mon, we'll go to the pub. It's such a nice day, we can sit outside.'

My heart sank at the idea of going to the pub, but when we walked inside together Lara was very well behaved. Her face betrayed no symptoms of suggestion and there wasn't even so much as a raised eyebrow as she took our order. That is, until Josh left me for a moment to talk to a neighbour. I tried to avoid speaking to her and looked the other way pretending I was interested in something on the opposite side of the bar. Lara was pulling a pint, her eyes on the glass, but I knew as soon as I saw the biting of her curling lips, that she was struggling to keep herself from smiling.

'So, I hear you've met Josh at last,' she said, glancing up at me with a mischievous grin.

I could only give her a look that I felt expressed total nonchalance on my part. 'Yes, I have.'

'I wondered why I'd not seen you for a while,' she said. 'I understand from him you've been enjoying cosy suppers together, that you've cooked for him. Is that right?'

I don't know what made me smile then, but she was being so daft and conspiratorial about everything. 'It's not like that,' I protested, shaking my head. 'Josh and I are just friends. No. We're merely acquaintances. We hardly know one another, we've only really just met.'

'Does time alone determine how well you know someone or whether you fall in love with them? Seven years wouldn't be enough for some people to know each other and seven days are more than enough for others. Martin and I were in love after a week, I certainly didn't know him.'

'Isn't that seven days or years stuff from *Sense and Sensibility*?' I asked.

Lara grinned. 'It might be.'

'Well, be that as it may, I am not in love with Josh. We are not in the process of knowing one another in any way. He's probably just returning the favour of the one, single supper that I cooked for him.'

Lara raised her eyebrows at that and lowered her voice. 'Well, he hasn't taken his eyes off you since you walked in. He might be talking to someone else, but he certainly isn't paying them much attention.'

I don't know why I turned round, but I did and she was right. Josh was staring at me, really looking me up and down, but he was talking all the time. Not about me, that was clear and I don't think he even realized he was staring or that I was looking at him. It was unnerving and all I could think was that I must have a huge grease spot or worse down my front. He suddenly caught my eye as I smoothed down my top. His eyes followed my hands and back again to my face. I was mortified. He would only think I was trying to give him the eye or something equally, hideously suggestive. If only I could go home.

Josh came back over to the bar then, picked up our drinks and smiled. 'Shall we sit outside?'

We settled ourselves opposite one another on a bench-table in the little patch outside, where the profusely stuffed hanging baskets considerably cheered up the view of the disparate backs of the houses down Pulteney Street. One of the fascinating things about Bath's architecture is how the rear of buildings differ so much, rambling all over the place, quite unlike their neat, classical fronts. Well, they held a particular fascination for me now. I didn't know where else to look. It was becoming apparent that Josh's eyes were now studying my face, but I couldn't spend all afternoon looking at Pulteney Street. Our eyes met.

'I hope you don't mind me saying so, Sophie, but you do look very lovely today.'

How could I mind? Wouldn't anyone love to be told that they looked very lovely? Even if something about the way he said the words reminded me so much of Charles. The thought and everything connected with Charles seemed like a recollection to a dream I'd once had sitting here in my modern world. The frustrating thing about this double life I was leading was that one blotted out the other with alarming rapidity. Those feelings that I'd never really travelled backwards or forwards through time and that it was all part of some trick being played by my mind were rising again.

I muttered my thanks and took a large gulp from the glass of iced white wine I was drinking.

'How's the exhibition coming along?'

'It's going really well. Actually, I was going to ask you something, but I'm not sure you'd really be interested.'

The April sunshine suddenly felt unseasonably hot. I felt a trickle, like a teardrop of liquid slide down my spine.

'Oh? Ask away.'

'There's to be a launch party.'

He's going to ask me if I'll waitress or something, hang coats, I thought, wondering how on earth I'd be able to get out of it.

'It's a party for the exhibition. I wondered if you'd like to come.'

My first instinct was to summon up some excuse, but then I thought that wouldn't be very fair of me. I wanted to see the exhibition and perhaps I'd meet some new people. I didn't feel like meeting anyone, to be honest, but I'd spent too many years reading magazines telling lonely women how to improve their social life. Even knowing that people only talk to the people they know at a party, wouldn't shift the idea that I might meet someone just as lonely who could cheer me up.

I couldn't help the picture of Lucas and Lily surfacing in my mind. The moment when I'd realized that the two people I trusted most in the world had betrayed me flashed before my eyes. I'd blamed myself at the time, thought the fault lay with me and I'd felt compassion for their plight even as I'd witnessed her slender arms clinging to his tanned body, both of them locked together in the writhing throes of passion. I was feeling really awful now. London beckoned.

'Yes, I'd love to,' I lied, and then thought about how I seemed to spend most of my time not being very truthful, either to myself or to anyone else.

'I thought you'd like to see the portrait in situ amongst all the other exhibits and see it being admired, as surely it will be. And besides, there is to be another surprise, something I've not told you about.'

'Oh, what is it?' I was immediately intrigued.

'I told you, it's a surprise. My lips are sealed, even if you do agree to come. Will you? I'd love you to be there.'

I nodded with as much enthusiasm as I could muster. 'That's really kind, Josh.'

The sun suddenly felt very hot, triggering a whole box of reminiscences I'd thought were safely buried. I remembered last April on a day like this one, when I'd thought Lucas and I were so in love. Memories of lying amongst a carpet of bluebells wrapped in one another's arms were so sharp; I could smell the heady perfume of the violet bells. But visions of Lucas and Lily blotted out the sea of blue, replaced by an ocean of billowing white sheets. He was kissing her tenderly, just as he used to kiss me.

'Sophie, I know it's none of my business, but you seem really sad.'

'I'm fine, really,' I said, until I noted the look of concern on his face and the kindness in his dark-fringed eyes. I felt tears pricking behind my eyelids. What on earth was the matter with me? A tear rolled down my cheek to collect in the corner of my mouth.

I licked the salt away and brushed at my cheek.

'You look as if someone just broke your heart.'

He was being so lovely it was impossible to stop the floodgates from opening. The tears really flowed then. I couldn't do anything to stop them. Josh jumped up from his side of the bench and came rushing over to mine, fetching out a tissue to dab softly at my damp face.

'Do you want to talk about it?'

I shook my head and willed myself to stop. I certainly didn't want to talk about it and I didn't want to think about it any more. Besides, however I was feeling, it was a little ungracious of me to accept Josh's invitation to lunch and then cry all over him. If it wasn't too late, I knew I'd have to do something about that. He proffered the tissue, which I took, blowing my nose as discreetly as I could before donning my sunglasses so that no one could see how red my eyes were. I felt his arm steal round my shoulders pulling me gently towards him and it was such a natural, empathetic gesture, that I found myself leaning into him, nestling my head just against the base of his neck where it met his collar bone in a pillow of firm, smooth flesh. I shut my eyes and felt the tender touch of his arm about me, his chin resting lightly on the top of my head with those corkscrew curls flickering in the breeze like stolen kisses about my cheek. I felt the pulse in his neck like a tiny heartbeat. His striped tee shirt smelt freshly laundered, a hint of something tropical, creamy coconut meeting a touch of citrus on his skin like chocolate melting with lime.

I might have known that Lara would choose that moment to bring out our lunch. I sat up promptly, like a teenager who's just been discovered by her mother in the act of kissing her boyfriend.

'Two Caesar salads with chips to share,' she said. I knew she was looking at me, but I couldn't raise my eyes from the table. 'Can I get you anything else?'

I couldn't speak, Josh answered for us both in the negative and as soon as she'd gone we picked up our knives and forks. Sensing an air of awkwardness between us, I wished I hadn't broken down or let myself lie all over Josh. He'd really think I was throwing myself at him now. And, I also knew I would have to start a conversation if I was going to get this whole outing back on any sort of comfortable footing. I contemplated a chip on my fork and put it down again.

'So, what happens now with your work?'

'Well, I've got a few weeks to finalize the exhibition, but then after the launch I'll be a free agent. I suppose I shall have to start looking around for another job.'

'Will you be wanting more exhibitions to do?'

'I'll take whatever interests me, to be honest. Something usually turns up. Though lately, I must admit, I'm getting a bit fed up with this nomadic lifestyle. I sometimes think how nice it would be to have a permanent job, nine to five. To wake up in the same bed, in the same flat for more than six months together would be something of a luxury.'

'But, it must be exciting being able to travel around and see new places all the time.'

'I have enjoyed it very much but lately, I've felt it's not really taking me where I want to go. I don't know ... it's just at the moment, I feel as if I'm not living in the real world.'

You and me both, I thought. Josh paused again.

'How about you, Sophie? Is the writing going well?'

I could have lied, but for once decided to tell the truth. 'No. I can't say it is going that well at the moment. There are too many distractions for one thing and I still haven't got past feeling that I'm on holiday. I do find Bath very inspiring; I just need to be a bit more disciplined about my work, I suppose.'

'Yes, nigh on impossible, if you're in holiday mode.' Josh put down his fork to squeeze my hand. 'Don't worry, you'll find your muse. I know you will, Sophie, just keep the faith. I think you're probably still soaking up lots of stuff that you're going to bring to your novel. Being here in Bath is surely all part of your research. You've got to give it a chance. I'm sure it will write itself when the time is right.'

It was lovely to feel I had a friend, someone who believed in me. 'That's exactly how I feel. Thank you, Josh, it is nice to have someone who thinks I might be able to have a go. I do want to be a writer so much though I'm not sure I'm going to achieve all my goals. The chances of being able to live off my writing are very slim, I know. Sometimes I think I should just go and find a proper job so that my Dad doesn't have to help support me any more. I long to be free, to be independent.'

'You can understand how frustrating it must have been for a woman like Jane Austen, can't you?'

I thought about Jane and her sister both tied to their parents because they didn't even have the option of getting a job. 'At least, Jane was beginning to learn that she could make money from her writing. The true tragedy is that she never knew how much her books would be loved, or how independent she might have been had she been able to live in another time. Oh, it's too sad to think about.'

'And even more reason why you shouldn't give up! What would Jane think if she thought you were going to fall at the first hurdle? If you can't do it for yourself, you've got to do it for her because all her opportunities to write as many books as she wanted were taken away. You've got to keep going for Jane and Captain Wentworth, for all the chances that she missed and the love she was denied.'

That last statement had my eyes smarting once again. 'Oh Josh, you're right.' And I would add one more person to that list, I thought to myself. My own, dear mum who sacrificed so much of her own career to bring up her daughter and who never got the chance to fulfill her dreams of becoming an artist. It was time to think about how I was going to start.

'Come on. Let's go for a walk. I think we're in need of inspiration.'

'Where shall we go?'

'Do you really need to ask, Sophie? Where might the power of conversation make the present hour a blessing indeed?'

Of course, a stroll along the Gravel Walk only reminded me more than ever of that other gallant man in my life, Charles. Not that we had ever strolled along there together heedless of every group around us, seeing neither sauntering politicians, bustling house-keepers, flirting girls, nor nurserymaids and children, like Anne and her Captain at the end of *Persuasion*. I wondered if Jane had snatched a turn along the Gravel Walk with the man she'd loved. But just thinking of Jane and her novel kept a certain gentleman of the Navy in my mind. Though Josh was funny and he kept making me laugh despite my low spirits, I couldn't help be reminded of the walk to Beechen Cliff that had never taken place and wondered for the millionth time what it was that had caused the Austens to change their mind about calling.

Josh and I walked side by side. Sunshine fell through the leaves of tall trees in dappled spots of gold, like coins of light, on the cool path as we passed the higgledy piggledy backs of the houses in Gay Street. Josh talked about his dreams and then listened to mine. By the time we'd walked to the Royal Crescent and then back down again to the flat, I realized a whole afternoon had passed by.

I was feeling much happier as I let myself into the flat. Josh had really cheered me up and I was able to think about things much more clearly. One fact was indisputable. Everything I'd experienced as Sophia had already taken place a long time ago. It was probably the case that I was feeling her emotions, seeing her memories. My senses had tricked me into believing that I was attracted to nothing more than a whisper, a veil of an apparition, a shade. The feeling of ghosts in the house was such a strong one that the idea couldn't be dismissed, even though I would normally have said that I'm a fairly level-headed person. I felt them all around me, which you'd think would be enough to send you running, but the connection with them was so intense, that I knew they meant me no harm. The house was full of my family, those who had known and loved me, as well as those who had lived before me. Yet, Charles was as real to me as Josh had been today. For a moment, they fused in my mind. Both living and breathing, both physically resplendent in youth and manliness, I could summon them both in my mind's eye, vital, thriving, alive, despite the two hundred years that separated them.

Chapter 18

I was feeling so much happier and had really enjoyed Josh's company, but I was glad to get home. I knew that the time was right, that I must face whatever would be found in the pages of the book I'd bought and with a second sense knew that it was not likely to be easy reading. The afternoon sun had disappeared. It felt decidedly cold in the flat, reminding me that although summer was on its way, it definitely hadn't arrived just yet. I lit a fire, pulled up my chair in front to toast my toes in the hearth and fetched out the book. I started to read a page at a time determined to read every one. But, it was a weighty book and I knew it would take more than one evening to read. Not only that, I knew I was avoiding the truth. The fire roared in the grate, the heat of the flames warming the star-like petals of the lilac bough Josh had picked for me, scenting the air with their fragrance.

Skimming the pages impatiently trying to find any mention of Charles's name, as soon as I turned over the correct leaf, it immediately jumped out at me in black print burning itself into my brain. And I knew, despite the cheerful fire, why I instantly felt chilled to the bone.

During these years, Charles Austen was long engaged in the unpleasant and unprofitable duty of enforcing the right of search on the Atlantic seaboard of America. Hardly anything is said in the extant letters of his marriage to Fanny Palmer, daughter of the Attorney-General of Bermuda, which took place in 1807.

Written there was all I needed to know. I'd guessed all along that something must have happened to prevent Sophia and Charles becoming more than just friends. My sensible head told me that if their friendship had been anything else, I would have known something about it and that there would have been some history in the family. The truth was that Charles had found the love of his life and married. That didn't stop the immediate questions about what had happened and I couldn't help wondering why Charles's wife or his marriage were not mentioned in the letters, giving rise to other feelings. Had Jane been disappointed by his choice, I wondered? In any case, I now knew that Sophia must have been disappointed because in my heart, I recognized that she must have fallen in love with him.

A week passed by during which I started to write again. I wasn't quite sure where to start, but having equipped myself with a new notebook and a vast file of paper, the ideas started to flow. I knew straight away that the experiences I'd had were going to be recorded. I wanted to write about meeting Jane and Charles even if no one else would ever read about what was to me such personal knowledge. The only problem was that although I'd decided that I couldn't see them again, the very act of writing it down made me long to do so.

I didn't see anything more of Josh. He was out early in the morning working long days and sometimes didn't seem to be around at all. I knew he was working hard on the exhibition and in any case, I was so busy now I was caught up with my own writing and research that I didn't really have much time to give him a thought.

Monday dawned with a formidable purple sky and rain sheeting down as it only seems to in Bath, the perfect day for staying inside and writing. I'd just settled down with a steaming mug of Earl Grey tea, books and papers to hand on every surface including the sitting room floor, when there was a knock at the door.

I knew it could only be Josh, and was slightly disconcerted by the thumping of my heart as I opened the door and the fact that I was altogether a little too bothered about what he might think of my scruffiest trackie bottoms and a baggy jumper with more holes than the colander on the draining board in the kitchen.

'I'm having a break and giving myself a day off,' he said. 'Are you busy?'

'Erm … not really, come in and have a cup of tea,' I said, knowing that he'd instantly see my work strewn all over the floor.

'So, you've started the book, then?' he asked immediately, in his typically direct way. 'Sorry, Sophie, I've completely interrupted you, haven't I?'

'Well, I'm very happy to be interrupted,' I said, grabbing armfuls of paper, picking up books three at a time off the sofa and chairs to put out of the way so he could sit down. To be honest, I didn't want him to be looking at it and even though I'd not known Josh for long, I knew he was going to be really curious.

'When can I read it?' he said immediately and when I turned from thrusting it all up high in the cupboard in the alcove, managing to simultaneously drop half of it at the same time, I could see him grinning at me.

'Maybe, never.' Suddenly, I couldn't bear the thought of anyone reading it, least of all Josh.

'I knew you'd feel like that,' he said, helping to pick up the papers. 'I haven't done much writing myself, but I'm reliably informed that it's a bit like baring your soul or standing naked in the high street before asking everyone if they like what they see.'

I laughed out loud partly because of the ridiculous and hideous picture of myself, trotting around without clothes in the middle of Bath, that I conjured up in my all too lively imagination and partly because he was so right. Watching him shuffle the papers together like a news presenter, I hoped he hadn't been able to glimpse a word.

'I just came to ask if you've seen the Jane Austen display at the Fashion Museum yet and to see if you'd like to come with me,' he continued. 'They've got the film costumes from every adaptation ever made, and I thought if you hadn't already seen where Jane danced, you'd like to see that too. The Fashion Museum is in the Assembly Rooms. I know you'll love it because they filmed so much of *Persuasion* there.'

'No, I haven't been to see the display,' I said, quite able to look truthfully into his eyes. 'I'd love to go. Can you give me a minute to change?'

We agreed to meet downstairs when I was ready. I felt suddenly excited about going though I knew seeing the Assembly Rooms would be strange without carriages rolling before the doors depositing muslin-clad dancers and frock-coated gentlemen bent on the card room. Pulling on jeans, a jumper and a belted trench coat as defence against the weather, I was ready for anything, but I felt some of my timidity returning as I knocked on Josh's door.

He thrust an umbrella towards me with a grin as he opened the door. 'I've equipped myself for Bath, you see. I wish you'd make use of it.'

'I certainly will, Captain Wentworth,' I answered, recognizing the quote immediately and grinning back. 'Anne Elliot might be my heroine, but I'm not about to decline the offer of a good umbrella like she did.'

I did wonder if that sounded like I'd paired us up as a couple, but thankfully, Josh didn't seem to take much notice. He insisted on holding the umbrella for both of us and grabbing my arm in his, pulled me closely to his side as the rain thundered down above our heads. He was in great spirits and by the time we were walking up Bond Street, he'd pointed out everything of interest from the shop they'd used in my favourite film version of *Persuasion*, representing Molland's coffee shop, to the faded paintwork that still exists on the building of what used to be the old circulating library in Milsom Street, which Jane herself must have visited. Taking a turn into Quiet Street and rounding the corner onto Gay Street, we climbed ever higher, unable to pass the Jane Austen Centre without visiting the giftshop where Josh treated me to a book. I chose *Cooking with Jane Austen and Friends*, a sumptuous volume, which had my mouth watering at the fantastic recipes. Josh suggested we break our fast by sampling some hot buttered *Crawford's Crumpets*, washed down with a cup of Peking tea in the Regency tearoom upstairs, and in such surroundings we felt we'd escaped from the hustle and bustle of town life below. At last, much refreshed and rejuvenated, we set off up the steep incline and on reaching the Circus at the top, we marvelled at the beautiful curves of the buildings, the hand-chiselled frieze running around the Doric columns with decorative emblems, every one depicting something different. A short walk along Bennett Street and we reached the Assembly Rooms. Although recognizable, the additions of modern life made the past seem remote and so far away that it was almost like I'd never been there before.

The display of costumes was fantastic. Original gowns of satin, silk and muslin were displayed side by side with the film costumes, the light dimmed to preserve the fragile fabrics, and every case offered a treat. I recognized many as worn by my favourite actors and actresses. The first case showed costumes from *Sense and Sensibility*.

'So, who do you identify with most? Are you Elinor or Marianne?' asked Josh. He was looking at me quite intently and I felt myself blush, as I admitted what I'd not vocalized to anyone before. I was glad the place was empty so no one could hear.

'Marianne,' I said without hesitation. 'I'd love to be more like Elinor, but I admit, I am far too much of a romantic to be as sensible.'

'Your heart rules your head, then?'

I stared at Marianne's bonnet, a wonderful straw confection

with peach ribbon and a feather to match, and knew that I longed to wear such a frivolous item. 'I suppose it does. I know that I don't always think before I act, a fault that Marianne had too. And, I'm sure most people who know me would say I'm a bit of a drama queen.'

'You're being a little unfair to yourself – that's just your own opinion. I haven't known you for long, but from what I've seen, I'd say that you combine the best qualities of both Elinor and Marianne. I'm convinced Jane Austen was writing about dual aspects of her own personality and don't we all share that to some extent? We have a 'sensible' head that regulates our behaviour and one that makes us act impulsively, rashly. In any case, I always prefer people who are open myself. Jane made a point of saying that often enough in her books. Even Mr Darcy said that disguise of every sort was his abhorrence. A personality who is not afraid to say how they feel is ultimately a warmer person and far more real. There's an honesty about someone who says what they think.'

'I suppose so, though we should always be careful that our impulses don't hurt others, I think, or make them feel uncomfortable.'

I hoped Josh couldn't see my red cheeks. I moved on hoping I'd cool down. Hiding so much from him made me uneasy.

Look Josh, here's one of Mr Darcy's shirts,' I called out, hoping to distract him and change the conversation. 'I always wonder what Jane would have thought about the wet shirt scene she didn't write where Colin Firth plunged into the lake.'

Josh laughed. 'I suspect she'd have had a little chuckle if she knew. I don't see her as a stuffy spinster sitting in a corner, do you?'

'No, not at all, I think she was quite the opposite. I imagine if she were alive now, she'd have a lot of fun helping to cast her heroes too.'

'Oh, now, I love that greatcoat.' Josh's eyes lit up. Mr Willoughby's coat, complete with layers of cape, was displayed next and I couldn't resist asking Josh what he thought about Jane's wild boy.

'Jane clearly knew a handsome scoundrel or two, I think, but I reckon she probably forgave them as she hardly metes out any real punishment for them in her novels, though I suppose in Willoughby's case, he had to suffer knowing that the love of his life was happily married to someone else.'

'That's true. Even William Elliot in *Persuasion* gets off lightly, and would still end up inheriting Kellynch Hall.'

'Yes, but he has to see Anne go off with Captain Wentworth. He obviously hoped to get both the inheritance and the girl too.'

'But, doesn't he go off with Mrs Clay in the end? He couldn't have been that upset about Anne.'

Josh nodded in agreement. 'I think what's so brilliant is that Jane Austen always recognizes human frailty. Not one of her characters is wholly bad or good. It's what makes them seem so real.'

We'd come full circle. In the last case were the costumes used in *Persuasion* and a slideshow flickered on the wall. Amanda Root and Ciaran Hinds smiled out at us, my perfect idea of Anne and Frederick Wentworth.

'There you are, Miss Elliot. Here's your namesake,' said Josh. 'And her costume, which I'm sure would suit you very well.'

I didn't know what to say and stared ahead, admiring the green silk of Anne Elliot's gown looking rather like the one I'd worn to a ball. That had just been some fanciful dream; I was beginning to think.

'Sophie, I hope you don't mind me saying so, but you've got far more in common with your favourite heroine than you know. Just like Anne, you are an extremely pretty girl, both gentle and modest, with taste and feeling.'

I decided he must be teasing me so dropped a curtsey with a prim smile. 'Why, thank you, kind sir, and may I say in return that you appear to be a remarkably fine young man, with a great deal of intelligence, spirit and brilliancy!'

Josh laughed, but then he turned towards me, all humour gone from his face. 'I'm perfectly serious. And I'd like to add that there was clearly more of Marianne about Anne than most people would credit. A young woman with feelings and emotions, just like you. Listen, Sophie, it's none of my business, but I know someone's hurt you. I just want to say that I'm here if you ever want to talk about it, or if you ever need a true friend.'

I was so touched, I nearly wept. 'You're such a gentleman, Josh, in the true, old-fashioned sense of the word, but honestly, you don't know the half of it.'

'Oh, I think I probably know enough about broken hearts to have a little idea. But, I do understand that you are essentially a private person when it comes to matters of love and I promise, I won't pry.'

'There was someone who broke my heart,' I said, wondering if I really wanted to tell him more. 'He went off with a friend of mine. I loved her as much as I loved him.'

'Sophie, I'm so sorry.'

'I'm fine about it now. I'm over it, really. It just felt such a blow losing the two people who meant the whole world to me. My Dad's been so kind and I don't know what I'd have done without him. It's just that lately I've felt really lonely ... lonely and alone. Quite a lot alone, if you want to know the truth.'

I'd never admitted any of that to myself before and I felt a bit embarrassed saying it now, telling Josh all the deep secrets of my heart. I thought I'd better change the subject. 'Thanks, Josh; it's been a lovely exhibition. I've loved seeing these costumes and I feel totally inspired.'

Josh put his hand out to stroke my arm. 'Sophie, I wish I could take all that hurt away and make you feel better.'

He was so sweet; I just wanted to kiss him. And I did. Without thinking, I stood up on my toes and kissed him on his cheek. It was such a spontaneous moment but the next minute, I was totally blown away. Josh's eyes locked with mine. The feeling was so powerful I could hardly look at him. His expression was so intense; it was as if he'd reached inside my soul to touch my heart. It happened so quickly. I felt those long fingers in my hair, his warm lips on mine and before I knew it, we were kissing one another. A long, slow and tender kiss, that took me completely out of this world.

When it was over; it seemed for a minute that neither of us knew what to say. I was completely dazed for one thing and when I dared to look Josh in the eye again, I saw him bite his bottom lip. 'Sophie, I shouldn't have done that; I apologize with all my heart.'

I was in shock. All I remember is hearing the sound of footsteps entering the room only to disappear as quickly and thinking that if I'd been the person to stumble across us locked in each other's arms, I, too, would have beaten a hasty retreat.

I felt Josh's arms loosen and he suddenly looked embarrassed. I really wasn't helping matters and knew I must find my tongue. 'No, don't apologize, it was my fault.'

'It was very wrong of me. I know you're feeling very vulnerable.'

'But, I am quite capable of making up my own mind and I needn't have kissed you back. I admit, it took me by surprise but then I found I wanted to kiss you.'

'And I wanted to kiss you,' said Josh, taking my hand in his, and bringing my fingers to his lips. He turned over my hand planting a soft kiss on my palm. 'Forgive me?'

'Only if you forgive me.'

There didn't seem to be much more to be said and as Josh let go of my hand and started talking about Captain Wentworth's uniform, pointing out the bicorne hat on display, the awkwardness passed. It was as if nothing had happened and though in that moment of madness I'd responded without hesitation, I didn't feel entirely comfortable about what had happened. I felt safer now things seemed back as they were before. I didn't need any more complications in my life right now and clearly Josh felt the same. The episode wasn't mentioned again. He was friendly, but distant, as we walked home under the umbrella being so careful not to make any bodily contact, which was difficult, to say the least. The rain drumming above us on the taut cloth was the only sound. Josh didn't utter another word after we turned onto Green Street. I searched desperately for something to say, but was tongue-tied, only managing a quiet goodbye when we parted.

Chapter 19

The day of Josh's launch party was drawing ever closer and I had a sudden panic about what I was going to wear. The official invitation that Josh put under the door certainly gave the idea of a formal occasion. I'd bought absolutely nothing with me that was going to be of any use at all. I had no choice; I'd have to get some money out of the allowance my lovely Dad had given me for just such an emergency. Well, he might not have seen it as such, but as far as I was concerned, it was important that I made the right impression. That thought led me to another that I didn't quite know how to think about. Josh had asked me to go, had indicated that he'd pick me up on the way over, but it didn't feel like a date and he certainly hadn't asked me as you might if it was a romantic date. Surely, he'd just asked me to go because he was polite and thought I'd enjoy it. He'd probably asked lots of people, I decided, but even so, I didn't want him to think badly of me, and that meant choosing the right outfit. Wondering whether I should go and peruse copies of Vogue and Harpers Bazaar, I also knew that I hadn't got the type of budget that was going to run to a designer outfit. I'd just have to hit the shops and see what was there. We hadn't seen each other since the day of the museum and although I'd promised myself I wouldn't think about what had happened, I couldn't help remembering the sweetness of that kiss even if it all seemed so unreal; like a dream, somehow. I kept going over what he'd said in my mind, but came back to the same idea that it was right not to complicate our relationship. We were good friends and it would be best if it stayed that way.

Sometimes, just very occasionally, it does seem as if the fates conspire to make everything right. For the very first time in my life, I walked into the very first shop I came to and bought the very first dress I tried on. A flowing floor-length dress in dove-grey jersey, with silver beads embellishing the halter neck strap, seemed to present the perfect solution between the formal and the casual. I couldn't believe my luck. Teamed with some flat, Grecian style sandals and long earrings, I actually started to feel quite excited about the party and hurried home with my spoils.

I saw Alison as I turned the corner onto Sydney Place. The receptionist from Josh's museum was knocking on the front door and looked as if she was on an urgent mission.

'Oh hi,' she cried, as she saw me approach. 'Do you know where Josh can be? Only I've been knocking for an age and I've got an important message I know he won't want to miss.'

'I'm sorry I haven't seen him, but if you'd like me to pass it on, I'm very happy to do that.'

Alison looked me up and down, hesitating as if she were weighing up whether she thought she could trust me. 'Can you tell him that Louisa called again? She said he's not answering his phone and she's desperate to talk to him. They just keep missing one another and he was so upset last time.'

She laughed and added, 'He must have it bad. Lucky Louisa. What I wouldn't give to be in her shoes when they get together. Oh well, if you could tell him, I'd be really grateful. I can't think where he's got to today. He's seemed right down in the dumps this week. I'm a bit worried about him, to tell you the truth.'

When she'd gone, I felt really deflated. I couldn't help

wondering who Louisa was or about the message I had to deliver, but it was obvious from Alison's hints that this girl was evidently very important to Josh. I let myself in, dumping my bags in the bedroom before scribbling a note and poking it under his door.

Back upstairs; I stood at the windows watching the sun going down over the park and the shadows lengthening. I suddenly felt very alone in the gloom of my darkening sitting room and couldn't help thinking about Josh. Louisa must be someone special. Was she the reason for the broken heart he'd mentioned, I thought? No wonder he always seemed aloof. Although I was sure he was sincere in wishing to be my friend, I knew that what had happened between us had been a huge mistake, one that he'd never meant to happen. Touching my mouth where his lips had kissed mine so tenderly that day reminded me of the powerful emotion I'd experienced. Why was life so bewildering? I didn't want to fall in love with anyone, so why did it feel as if my heart was trying to confuse me?

My eyes wandered to the rosewood box and opening the lid I fetched out the glove. I'd tried very hard not to think about Sophia and her friendship with the Austens, but it still bothered me that I hadn't had a satisfactory explanation for what had happened on that day when they'd decided not to call. If I had done or said something to upset my friends, I just had to find out. I felt as if I was always running away from life, but I recognized that I was never going to be happy until I knew. What harm would there be in going back? I would find them and set everything straight. And, as soon as I had, also satisfying my curiosity, I would leave again. There was no reason why I shouldn't just be Charles's friend and I ought to make sure that he knew that friendship was all I wanted from him.

I was determined on a course I knew in my heart to be both foolish and irresponsible, but I couldn't help myself. How quickly come the reasons for approving our actions and doing what we like! Five minutes later I was in Sydney Gardens, which looked ghostly with descending mist in the fading light. At the gate, I didn't hesitate. Besides, I was absolutely sure I didn't want to be there when the setting sun disappeared beyond the horizon.

It was daylight on the other side, warm and sunny, which instantly made me feel better. I was surprised at how familiar the gardens looked and though I was feeling a certain amount of trepidation at the thought of seeing Jane and her brother, I was pleased to be back. I'd escaped temporarily from the real world and right now, that was all I wanted to do.

Turning onto one of the quieter paths I passed dense shrubbery on either side of the Serpentine Walk, which at every turn met with shady bowers where climbing plants concealed a lover's seat or a stone statue. The sound of a splashing waterfall led me to a hidden grove where water tumbled over rocks glittering in sunlight and the curving fronds of green ferns dipped their feathery leaves into a gurgling, icy pool. It all looked so magical, like a fairy grotto, and I sat down on the stone seat hidden amongst the greenery to watch a blackbird bathing in the shallows at the water's edge. I wasn't in a hurry and in such a beautiful place; it was impossible to worry about anything. Shivering in the cool shade, I pulled my shawl tighter about my shoulders, before taking a pin from my hair and dropping it into the water to make a wish. I closed my eyes, willing with all my heart that what I hoped most of all would come true. More than anything I wanted to see my friends and feel everything was right between us again. From my seat I could see the entrance to the Labyrinth. Like an enchanted wood, it seemed to be calling me in and I thought I'd take my chance, even though I remembered Jane saying she'd lost herself in the maze on at least two occasions. Green hedges rose high above me as I stepped inside and were so dense it was impossible to see through them. Hurrying along the twisting pathways I wondered if it was a good idea to walk alone, but the place was deserted. Even the gardens had been extraordinarily empty of people. Several times I took a wrong turn at a hermit's cottage or where a wooden pavilion signalled the end of a path and had to double back, but I soon found myself in the middle. There was Merlin's swing, a huge wheel rising high in the air for those brave enough to try it, but there was no one suspended above the Labyrinth today to laugh at those who'd lost their way. A moss-covered grotto with a wooden sign declared an alternate way out through an underground passage. I wasn't sure if I wanted to go that way. It looked dark and gloomy so I turned back on myself, and following a butterfly that flew into my field of vision I entered another part of the Labyrinth.

The butterfly almost seemed to be waiting for me to catch it up. As I ran to keep it in view, I watched the beautiful creature dancing in the sunlight, its fragile wings hovering above the ground before soaring to the top of the hedge to alight on a leaf. Brown velvet wings fluttered to make a display of its white lace, and it was then I realized that we were not alone. I heard a whispered exchange, hushed voices that held such nostalgic sounds of recognition, I instantly felt I was intruding. Before I'd taken many more steps I knew that I'd stumbled upon a lover's meeting and though I really didn't want to spy, I found myself unable to stop staring.

Concealed within a bower of arched trees, with blossoms tumbling in white curtains like confetti to the ground, a handsome fair-haired gentleman sat holding the hand of his girl who was hidden from my view.

'I have never been inconstant,' he said. 'Your heart must understand the truth of all I say. Tell me not that such precious feelings will diminish, that you will cease to love me. I love none but you. Accuse me of self-interest, I cannot deny it. I am guilty of being selfish, I know, but the happiest hours of my life have been those spent with you. Do not blame me for wishing to snatch a few more.'

'I do not blame you, but with everything settled as we know it to be, as things can only be resolved, we will do more harm than good if we do not accept what is beyond our control.'

'If I were a knave, I would plead with you to change your mind.'

'And we both know there lies a path to unhappiness and folly.

This encounter is insanity itself, I cannot think how you persuaded me to meet you today.'

'Yet, you came.'

Silence descended. Oblivious to everything around them, I saw two heads bend towards the other and the young man plant a tender kiss upon his lover's hand. I was rooted to the spot, even though I knew I should leave. If I moved they would hear or see me and know that I'd found them out. That they had no wish to be discovered was painfully obvious. Although the young man seemed to be less furtive, I sensed their anxiety as I caught a glimpse of the girl leaning forward to whisper in his ear. Dressed in a blue gown, which fluttered back in the breeze, I saw her bonnet strings were untied.

The young man spoke again. 'Can we not pretend just for today, that we are as free to love one another as we were all those years ago when we first met?'

'The past seems so long ago, a time in another world. You and I are both changed in every way,' she said.

'But not in essentials, I believe. True, our circumstances have changed and we've had to follow another course to the one we should have desired, but our souls will be forever entwined.'

I heard the girl laugh. 'You are the most amusing gentleman of my acquaintance. Tell me, just how many of the romantic poets are you imbibing these days? Too much poetry can never be safe!'

'I only speak from my heart and if you examine yours, you will know that I speak the truth. I need no poet's sonnet to inspire or declare my feelings. You of all people could never accuse me of disguising my intentions.'

'No, you always were a most forthright fellow!'

Do you remember that first night when we both realized that we loved one another?'

'How could I forget a warm summer's eve, a night sky filled with stars and the beauty of the Kentish countryside all around us?'

'Riding on Queen Mab in the moonlight, we flew like midsummer fairies over the fields and hedgerows.'

'You stole me away from the house like a wicked bandit.'

He laughed. 'I do not recall your protest. Indeed, I seem to remember it was you who urged me to share the horse. No doubt, so I should have to hold you against me.'

'Which you did with no hesitation, sir.'

'And then we found a spot to your liking.'

'I have no recollection of being consulted about the stone temple, dark and enclosed.'

'I took you in my arms and you did not resist.'

'I did not.'

'You did not recoil from the kiss I planted.'

'No.'

'Is it etched in your mind, as it is in mine? Are you able to recall all that we were to one another? I can bring forth every feeling, every sound and smell of that sweet night. The scent of your skin, the soft caress of your lips, and the sounds of a burbling stream making its way to the river are all married as one.'

There was another silence and it seemed to me that the girl whose few words had been so filled with emotion could not speak many more.

'Jane, you pledged your heart to me that night.'

'And it will forever be yours. I shall not break my promise.'

Recognizing him and immediately deducing the identity of his friend, I turned to go; but an unforgiving twig snapped under my foot like a pantomime prop, the sound reverberating in the enclosed space like a gunshot. A glance across confirmed what I'd already guessed. Jane stared straight back at me, fear flashing in her eyes. I'd known it could be no one else before she turned her head, sensing also that this man who held her hand so tenderly could only be one person. I gave her my most reassuring expression, placing a finger on my lips to assure her of my silence before I ran from the lover's scene as fast as I could. There was no doubt; he was the man from the ball and I knew instinctively that he was someone special. Remembering Jane's words about getting lost in the Labyrinth took on a completely new meaning. I didn't wish to think about why they were meeting in such secrecy, sensing that such a question could only have an unhappy answer. I wanted to assure her that I would never say a word, but as much as I wished to promise that her secret was safe, I was undecided about whether I should acknowledge it at all.

I didn't have to wait long. Moments after I found my way out, I heard footsteps running up behind me. I didn't know what to say to Jane, I could hardly pretend that I hadn't seen her and her handsome partner. Words wouldn't come as I also remembered the last time we should have met, and all I could think was how Jane would think me completely dim-witted.

'Miss Elliot, I must speak with you. I wish to offer some explanation,' she began.

She looked very upset and I knew I must put her mind at rest. 'Miss Austen, you do not need to say anything more. There is nothing to justify. Please, do not talk of it.'

She looked as if she might speak again, but I could see the anguish in her eyes.

'Believe me, I mean every word sincerely. I do not want you to enlighten me in any way. I saw nothing out of the ordinary in the Labyrinth today, I promise you.'

'You are too generous, Miss Elliot.'

I took her hand. 'I am so pleased to see you again, dear friend.'

'And I you, Miss Elliot,' she said, clasping my hand with a returning squeeze, 'but though I have been wanting to call, I admit I could not decide what to do.'

'I am sure you had a good reason for not calling on me, Miss Austen.'

'Oh dear, I suspected not all was as it seemed. My dear friend, we would have called if not for the fact that we were prevented. Last Thursday, on the day of the picnic, we met your father as we were coming out of number four. In the way of conversation I declared how much I was looking forward to your company, but he insisted that you'd left for the Pump Room with Mrs Randall. We assumed that you'd changed your mind about our outing especially when we received no note or any explanation. Indeed, we have not known how to proceed.'

'I am sorry, Miss Austen; I must apologize for my father who was entirely mistaken. That was not the case at all. I waited all morning and when you did not call, I came to find you, only to be told that you had already left.'

'Alas, Miss Elliot, we have been at odds, but it seems that neither of us are to blame and at last we are together again. I know one person will be most pleased to hear there was a misunderstanding. Indeed, he's not stopped talking about anything else.'

I knew she was talking about Charles.

'Let's arrange to meet later this afternoon. Would you like that?'

I couldn't have been more pleased and although I felt nervous at the thought of seeing Charles again, at least I would now have an opportunity to show that I considered him simply as a friend.

I hurried home. I wanted to make sure there would be no attempts to keep me from my friends' company and when I heard from Mrs Randall that another cousin of Mr Elliot had arrived in Bath I felt sure they would be calling on Lady Cholmondley as soon as they could. Hoping for a chance to escape whilst they were all otherwise occupied with their illustrious relatives, I might have known my hopes would be in vain.

'Upon my word, Miss Sophia Elliot, will you never learn to discriminate?' said Mr Elliot. 'Or are you only content to fraternize with the lower orders? Surely you can put off this engagement. Indeed, I insist upon you accompanying us.'

There was nothing else to be done. Knowing it was fruitless to argue, I hastily scribbled a note to Jane for the maidservant to take round as soon as I could, and resigned myself to the fact that I should have to go calling with my family.

The visit took place along with the inevitable fawning by Mr Elliot and Emma. Suddenly, Lady Cholmondley and her daughter were their most intimate friends and the talk of the dinner table. Even Mrs Randall seemed excited by the new connection. A week of engagements with our cousins stretched ahead and I wondered if I'd ever get the chance to be free again. If we were not to be calling on them in Laura Place, then we were to be accompanying them to the theatre or to the Pump Rooms. When a returning note from Jane arrived asking me to go with them as soon as I could be free, I couldn't imagine when that time would come.

Chapter
20

A fortnight passed where I saw nothing of my friends. All our invitations were to private evening parties where I knew Jane and her family wouldn't be invited. It was impossible to get out on my own and the weather seemed to conspire against me. On the following Monday heavy rain set in, making me despair of ever walking out by myself. At least everyone left me to my own devices. Emma and Mrs Randall were busy with the kind of plans I was not party to, and Mr Elliot locked himself away in his study with Mr Glanville. An early dinner was arranged for four o'clock and when I walked into the dining room, I immediately sensed an atmosphere, a feeling of excitement and expectation in the air. I wondered if an engagement was about to be announced especially when Emma leapt out of her seat, her feet pattering across the oak boards as she rushed towards me. I'd never seen her look so pleased before.

'Sophia, it is all decided. Mr Glanville is to take a tour along the West Country coast and we have been invited to join him. Is that not the most diverting piece of news you ever heard? I am so excited, I have always longed to see Lyme!'

Mr Elliot looked as thrilled as Emma did at the prospect, but I couldn't feel happy at the thought of leaving my friends.

'When are we going?' I asked, looking at Mrs Randall who of the three still seemed composed.

'As soon as arrangements can be made,' she said. 'We are to travel to Monkford Hall directly, in order that your father may see his steward and leave fresh instructions about what is to be done in your absence. I imagine we will be gone in a day or two at most.'

I thought about Charles and how I'd like to talk to him, although I knew there was little possibility that I might see him before we left. He'd have made me feel better with the sight of one small smirk from the corner of his mouth and with his eyes twinkling at some unspoken joke. If Emma had her way, our bags would be packed that afternoon and we would be gone home to Monkford Hall by nightfall. The idea of never seeing Charles again was one that upset me more than I wished to admit.

'Mr Glanville is to travel on Friday,' said Mr Elliot. 'He did not want to miss the gala on Thursday evening in Sydney gardens, which we shall also be attending. And I think it will be to your advantage, Emma, if he is seen accompanying us. I do believe it is all going on very well. Indeed, one should not expect less from a near relation. Blood and connection finds its level – that is why our cousin has singled us out with such alacrity. There is no one else in Bath with whom he wishes to be so closely associated and he will win his prize yet.'

'Oh, whatever do you mean, Papa?' cried Emma, returning to his side, her face uplifted with an eagerness that suggested she knew exactly what he meant.

'Let us just say that the jewel he is after is in our midst, dearest daughter. I think if you carry on just the way you are, it will not be very long before my allusion will be made apparent.'

I watched him put a hand up to stroke her cheek. 'With your beauty and charm you have captivated all of Bath. There is not a face to be compared with your sweet looks. William Glanville told me himself that he thinks you very handsome and I am sure that everyone has witnessed his attentions towards you.'

I was aware that Mrs Randall had turned to look at me. I caught her gaze and smiled. I knew she was trying to think of something to say which would include my share of the attention, but I think my expression told her it was unnecessary. Besides, I was very grateful to Mr Glanville for occupying so much of Mr Elliot's time, and if he was pursuing Emma, as far as I was concerned that was even better.

'William Glanville is a very well-looking man, is he not? If not for his red hair, I would consider him the most handsome of my acquaintance.' Mr Elliot stood up to stand approximately midway between two looking glasses. From this vantage point, he could admire both his front and back at the same time. 'It is very pleasant to have such a companion when walking. He has that effect upon the ladies, which only a really good-looking man may induce. All eyes are upon him, I declare.'

It did cross my mind at this point that they might not only be staring at him because he was easy on the eye. A fortune and the possession of several large properties make the most unattractive male more appealing. If he's good-looking too, he soon becomes an object of desire.

'Oh, Papa, I am certain that Mr Glanville finds just as much pleasure in accompanying someone who is equally handsome. There is no better effect on ladies than two good-looking gentlemen walking together. I expect they are looking at you just as much, and he is put at an advantage by having such a partner. And, your hair is still as dark as it was when mother was alive. No wonder the ladies are put in a swoon as you go by.'

Mr Elliot moved his head to check his profile, stretching out his neck until any suggestion of jowls or a double chin completely disappeared. With one finger he smoothed his brows into place, and adjusted a curl over his ear.

'I have been extremely lucky. I am fortunate that time has not left its ravages upon my countenance in quite the same way as it has for some of my peers. Generally, it is a fact that a gentleman improves with age as he gets older, a truth, which sadly, cannot be said for the majority of ladies,' Mr Elliot went on. 'When one considers that there is help at hand in the form of cosmetics for the ugliest female face abroad, it is surprising that we do not see more tolerable countenances especially amongst ladies of a certain age. It is little wonder that one seldom sees them walk down the street in broad daylight, and really, I consider it a blessing that we have only to be punished by the sight of such plain women by candlelight.'

'If only we could all be as handsome, Mr Elliot,' said Mrs Randall, looking away wistfully as she spoke yet maintaining a completely serious expression. 'Women are soon old and become invisible when their charms are gone. For myself, I believe in the efficacy of drawn blinds against the harsh light of day when there is no candlelight to grace ageing features.'

Mrs Randall and I exchanged looks and I immediately had to stifle a giggle, for it was very clear that she was having a little fun with him.

'Quite so, dear lady. At least one never sees an aged or repulsive face in the Pump Room,' he replied, without faltering. 'I fear at so early an hour that would be too much to bear. One supposes that the general indisposition of old women prevents them from appearing first thing in the morning.'

'That must offer some comfort to you, Mr Elliot,' Mrs Randall replied, her face giving away nothing of her amusement.

I think Emma sensed something of what was going on for she chose this moment to pointedly change the subject.

'Goodness, is that the hour? I think it must be time to dress for Lady Cholmondley's card party. Mr Glanville has promised to attend.'

'Make haste, my dear. We will postpone dinner for you so that you may prepare yourself.'

'Yes, at once, Papa, and Sophia, you are not to have Rebecca's help first. I have precedence!'

I didn't doubt it, nor did I wish to be prodded and poked about by the housemaid however willing and kind she was to help me dress. I liked to be able to sort things out for myself, as far as I could, and with that thought in mind hurried to my room to get ready before anyone could interfere with me.

The card party was said to have been a great success by Mr Elliot who congratulated himself upon our family having been the centre of attention. Every older widow in Bath was there, and fawned over him every time he opened his mouth and uttered anything at all. William Glanville was also much admired, but having seen that his interests only lay in the young ladies who were there, any older ones contented themselves by giving him their prettiest smiles and pushing their daughters forward.

I was too upset at the thought of having to leave Bath to want to join in the card games and couldn't settle to anything. I wandered about listlessly, which had Mr Glanville hovering at my side more than I wanted. Emma grimaced every time he spoke to me, but the more I tried to ignore him the more persistent he became.

'Miss Sophia, I hate to see you without your endearing smile. You look so unhappy this evening. Let me cheer you. Will you not join my table in a game of cards?'

'I would much rather read a book, Mr Glanville,' I said, trying to think up any excuse I could. 'I admit; I do not enjoy cards.'

'Perhaps you could assist me if you do not want to play. Come sit here by my chair, Miss Sophia. Besides, I am certain you have the knowledge of foresight.'

Puzzled, I joined him reluctantly being urged on by Mrs Randall to do as he bid and so was unable to escape. Emma, Lady Cholmondley and Mrs Randall all sat at his table expectantly, my sister giving me glowering looks at the attention I was receiving from him. He collated the playing cards and spread them out like a fan before me. 'I believe you have the power to choose your destiny. Here, Miss Sophia, pick a card.'

I blushed when I saw that of all the cards in the pack I had managed to draw the Queen of Hearts. Everyone laughed with the exception of Emma, who reddened in fury. Mr Glanville's face remained passive and when he asked me to offer the cards to him, I hardly dared look as he selected his choice. Of course, it was the King of Hearts, as I knew it would be. There was a burst of laughter and an exchange of knowing glances between all the old ladies who sat round the edges of the room. Whatever trickery he'd devised showed immediately in his face as he smirked at the horror on mine, and as soon as I could I moved to the other side of the room. It was either that or further put up with his constant flirting, with Emma kicking me under the table for the rest of the evening.

Chapter
21

Early next morning, I hurried to the Pump Room, following in the wake of Emma and Mr Elliot who were keen to see their cousins. I was desperate to see a familiar face and as soon as we passed through the doors, I looked everywhere to see if Charles or his sisters had arrived. I was anxious to tell them about our travel plans. Knowing there was probably very little chance of meeting up with them at a later date, I remembered that Jane had mentioned a trip to Devon. I wondered where they might be going and clung to the idea that Lyme might also be a place they'd visit. The idea of weeks spent solely in the company of the Elliots filled me with apprehension, although I knew that at least I should have Mrs Randall to spend time with when everyone else would be occupied with the business of courtship. The lure of Monkford Hall was an opportunity I didn't want to miss, however difficult it might be to find a way back to my own time. But, I'd managed before, I told myself and I was sure I would again.

I couldn't get away from the conversation or mentions of the forthcoming tour. Everyone we met had heard the news and insinuated everything they possibly could about a forthcoming marriage between Emma and Mr Glanville. Every time the hints were made, Emma glowed just a little more. Slowly, it was beginning to sink in that we were actually going and that after Friday I might never see Charles again. There was nothing to gain by telling any or all of the Austens how I felt about going, nothing could be changed, but I just knew that if I could tell Jane or her brother that I would feel better. Perhaps Jane would write to me and let me know where they were travelling, but then the possibility of being able to keep up a correspondence seemed very remote if we were to be both moving about. It was highly unlikely that they would be travelling to the same places or at the same time. I had mixed feelings about leaving Bath altogether and to think of going far from the house felt frightening, however much I didn't want to miss the opportunity of seeing Monkford Hall and staying there.

Despairing of seeing anything of my friends as the morning was almost over, I had given up hope when to my enormous pleasure I saw Charles walk through the doors. He was chatting to a lady and a gentleman that made me instantly think that he must be another brother with his dark auburn hair. Jane came along next with a young girl hanging onto her hand and behind them followed Cassandra with Mr and Mrs Austen. Waving as she spotted me, I saw Jane point me out to the child turning her in my direction.

'Miss Elliot, here is my niece, Anna.'

The little girl who looked to be about seven or eight years of age bobbed a curtsey, putting one small foot behind the other before looking to her aunt for approval, which was soon granted in an indulgent smile.

'My brother James is here in Bath with his wife and their two children for a visit. Anna is put to my charge, but we have left her small brother behind today with his nursery maid.'

'I'm very pleased to meet you,' I answered with a returning bob. 'And how are you enjoying Bath, Miss Anna?'

'I'm having a lovely visit, thank you, Miss Elliot. It is heavenly to see Aunt Jane again, I miss her so much,' she said, stepping nearer towards Jane until she felt the arm of her aunt encircle her shoulders. 'I used to see her almost every day and I wish she could come home to Steventon to live with me again.'

'I'm sure you miss her very much, as I will do, too, when I have to go away,' I said.

A frown wrinkled between Jane's brows. 'Whatever do you mean? Are you leaving us?'

'I'm afraid we are, at Mr Glanville's invitation. Believe me, Miss Austen, if it was in my power, I should not go anywhere, but it is all decided. We are leaving for Lyme and will be touring the West Country, perhaps even going as far as Wales.'

'Oh, my goodness, I am disappointed to hear you are leaving so soon and I know someone is going to be particularly upset to hear your news.'

Out of the corner of my eye I saw Charles approach. 'What news is this, Miss Elliot?' he asked.

I couldn't say the words. Jane spoke for me instead. 'Miss Elliot is leaving us for Lyme.'

Charles looked at me with an expression that demanded more detail. 'I did not know you were going away.'

'I did not know myself until yesterday. We are leaving on Friday morning. I do not know how long we shall be gone, or even if we shall return to Bath, but I think our trip will be of some duration.'

'We are going away ourselves in June,' said Jane. 'My mother and father have talked of visiting Dawlish and Teignmouth, which are only a little further along the coast from Lyme. Perhaps we will see each other on our travels. Indeed, you must write to me and let me know where you are for as long as you are able and I shall let you know of our direction.'

'Yes, Miss Elliot, you must write to my sister,' pressed Charles. 'Promise that you will.'

I nodded, smiling into his eyes that looked so searchingly into mine. There didn't seem to be anything else to say. Now that I had told them I felt sadder than ever about leaving.

'Are you to attend the gala?' Charles was studying my face.

'Yes.' Trying hard to appear my usual, cheerful self was impossible. I felt if I stayed there much longer I might cry.

'Let us meet on the morrow and enjoy a walk up to Beechen Cliff as we promised before,' said Jane. 'It would be such a pity to part without witnessing Charles's ascent – a sight to cheer the most dismal soul, if I'm not mistaken. And, it would not be fair for Miss Elliot to miss such a spectacle, Charles. I shouldn't wonder if she hasn't had a small wager on your chances of gaining the top!'

I gave Charles a mischievous grin, as if every word Jane spoke was true. He smiled wryly and took so long to answer, preferring to stare into my eyes that I felt my cheeks grow warm.

'Never fear, ladies, I am more than willing to meet your challenge. You will see me gain the summit and what is more, I shall provide a picnic treat for those who can join me.'

'There, Miss Elliot, now you cannot refuse an invitation of such an exciting and persuasive nature, I do not think,' said Jane, who was clearly trying not to laugh. 'What could be more diverting than the sight of a competent hill walker fairly running up Beechen Cliff with a picnic basket on his head?'

'I shall look forward to it very much.'

James and his wife joined us then and all talk of our plans ceased for the moment. It was fascinating to recognize the Austen features in this brother and though a pleasant looking man, he had none of Charles's air or stature. He had a sensitive face, I thought, and seemed rather ill-matched with his wife, who proved to be irritable and short-tempered. She interrupted the conversation with a demand to be escorted to fetch her water. It didn't escape my notice that Anna looked rather fearfully at her stepmother who scolded her repeatedly for coughing; slouching, and it seemed, for simply being in her presence.

'Anna, do not hang onto Aunt Jane like that and stand up straight. Please stop coughing, my nerves can't abide it, but if you must, hold your handkerchief to your mouth. We will all be ill if you cough so.'

Jane's brother wasn't allowed his share in the conversation.

He'd started listening to Charles, but his wife was not interested in anyone else. 'Depend upon it, James, I would rather not take the waters, but Dr. Bowen has recommended I take three glasses daily and I do not think I should be the person to contradict his prescription. No one suffers more than I do, as you know, and if I could just see this illness off, I daresay, I would be right as rain. Come and procure a glass for me, my dear. The pumper is an ill-natured fellow at best and if he is not watched will shorthand us with only half our due.'

Mr James Austen smiled indulgently at his wife who took his arm and without acknowledging anyone else started to lead him away until recollecting something, she turned and spoke to her stepdaughter. 'Anna, come here and stop bothering your aunt.'

'Mary, she is no trouble, believe me,' Jane said, 'I'll see to Anna, you go and take your water. We may go for a little walk then, so please do not worry. We will have much to occupy us, shall we not?'

Anna beamed up at her aunt, her excitement at being rescued all too plain to see.

'Dear me! What an excellent idea, very good indeed,' said Mary Austen. 'You have such a way with little Anna; she's so attentive to you and I must admit, my nerves are very bad today. I adore my children as much as the next person, but such constant attention is so very wearing.'

'Worry no further, leave Anna to my care,' Jane insisted. 'Have some time on your own with James and we will all meet together later.'

It may well have been my imagination but the atmosphere felt much lightened after they'd gone. The little girl relaxed in the company of her uncle and aunt. Miraculously, her nervous cough seemed to disappear. Charles teased her and made her laugh by instantly producing a coin from behind her ear. She gazed up at him with round eyes and as she begged for more, he managed to produce another. 'What shall we spend it on, Anna? A book for Grandpapa, or a piece of lace for Grandmama?'

Anna's face drooped with disappointment.

'Hmm, I do not know how we might spend it,' Charles continued, his lip curling with amusement, 'for I've a feeling that Grandpapa has a book to read and Grandmama has so much lace she really doesn't need another piece. I suppose we could buy a ribbon for Aunt Jane, or a paintbrush for Aunt Cassandra. I cannot think who else might like to spend it. Does anyone have a suggestion?'

Anna stood quietly looking up at her uncle. There was hope in her eyes, but she seemed reluctant to speak.

'Oh, Charles, tease her no longer,' Jane cried.

'The pennies are yours to spend, Anna,' said Charles, laughing as he saw the excitement in the young girl's face. 'Where shall we squander them?'

In the pastry cook's please, Uncle Charles!'

I was just joining in the laughter when Emma came to fetch me saying that it was time to go home. There was no more opportunity to talk and all I could hope was that our plans for the next day would not be spoiled before we left Bath forever.

Chapter
22

'My sister and brother have been out on a commission this morning,' Jane said, walking at my side down Great Pulteney Street. 'We are to meet them at the foot of Lyncombe Lane.'

I could hardly believe that I was free at last, it was wonderful to be out of the house and to be able to walk down the road with Jane felt like huge independence. But, I might as well have been in another country as be in Bath; I hardly recognized my surroundings as we followed the river's snaking course. Everywhere looked and felt far more rural, appearing to be a much smaller place than the Bath I knew. As we passed a row of shops at Widcombe, which I didn't know at all, Jane said how much she liked the place saying it reminded her of the small villages in Hampshire where she grew up.

'You must miss your home very much, Miss Austen.'

'I confess I do. At this time of year, it is most delightful in spring and in summer when Bath in the heat becomes unbearable, the old Steventon Rectory comes into its own. It's not the smartest or most modern of houses, Miss Elliot, often flooding in winter, but it's always deliciously cool in summer. And it is when the Syringa is first in bloom heralding the start of summer that the garden is at its best. I can close my eyes now and be sitting in the arbour where I can see the flowerbeds under my father's study and watch his white head bent over his scholars' books. To take a stroll in the garden lost in time itself, watching the shadows on the sun-dial count the hours, or wandering along the terrace walk listening to the scrape of the weathercock, are some of my happiest recollections.'

'It sounds delightful. But, I hope your memories are not too painful to recall, Miss Austen.'

'Oh no, I like to remember them and it is a comfort to talk. I wish you could have visited Cassy and I at Steventon when we had the delight of our own private dressing room. It was a place where we could easily escape and we lived almost entirely amongst the pleasures that awaited us there. I had my beloved pianoforte then, to play at leisure.'

'A room of your own, it sounds delightful!'

'Oh, Miss Elliot, we were most fortunate. There was an oval looking glass set between the windows, striped curtains, a chocolate coloured rug and my precious books arranged on shelves above a painted press. Goodness knows where those old friends are now. So many books we had to sell before we came here.'

'I couldn't imagine being without books that I love.'

'We had little choice. But, in the end, I decided that I knew most of them so well that it did not matter. They will always be there in my head. In any case, above all, there was one comfort they couldn't take from me.'

I had a feeling I could guess what she was talking about.

'Do you ever write, Miss Elliot?' Jane continued. 'Not just letters, I mean, but have you ever tried your hand at writing composition? For myself, there is nothing I'd rather do. It is the greatest passion of my life.'

'Indeed, I have, Miss Austen, and I enjoy writing very much, although my attempts to compose an entire work of any length have come to naught, thus far.'

'Miss Elliot, I knew there was a reason that we are such friends. To think that you are a sister writer and I did not know it before. It is clear we have much in common, as my very own unsuccessful efforts to become published will testify. Tell me, are you writing at present?'

'I am, but my novel is only just started,' I answered truthfully.

'Please, Miss Austen, I would love to hear about your writing. I am certain it cannot be such a struggle for you, as it is for me.'

'On the contrary. I have written several attempts at novels, yet I find I am unsatisfied with any of them. I fetch them out occasionally, but it has been difficult since moving to Bath. I am not so much at leisure to compose here, I snatch whatever time I can.'

'Do you not find Bath an inspiration for composing, Miss Austen?'

'In its way, I suppose it has lent itself to my ideas. I first penned a novel that I set in Bath when I was just a visitor to the city and saw the delights of the winter pleasures through another's eyes.'

'How I should love to read it and discover whose eyes inspired your tale.'

'They were quite my own, Miss Elliot, though I was then a country girl excited with all I saw and quite ready to have my heart broken by the first fellow who danced with me. My heroine declared, "Oh! Who can ever be tired of Bath!" and I felt very much the same. I have never been completely happy with my manuscript and when I look at it now I hardly recognize the delight I found in writing it.'

'I often feel like that when I look back on my work. Perhaps you will return to it one day.'

'I daresay the fashion for gothic novels will be quite over by the time I shall make any attempt on it, and I am not sure if readers are ready to laugh at them with me. No, I think it most likely that this particular manuscript will stay in my writing box for good.'

I noted Jane's disappointed face and it seemed she was

reticent to say any more. I was sure she must be referring to *Northanger Abbey* and wanted to tell her that she would find the opportunity to work on it again, but, of course, I could not.

The subject was changed as we wandered past the shops. Jane pointed out the Mantua maker's where she'd had her cloak made up and Smith's the baker's shop with its slabs of gingerbread laid out on trays in the window.

'I hope Cassandra and Charles remembered to stop here,' she said. 'I am very partial to gingerbread and I did request some for our picnic. It's not far now, we should see them soon hard by the mill.'

I saw Charles before he saw me. Dressed in a dark green coat and buff breeches he towered over Cassandra. I felt so pleased to see him and experienced a sense of excitement that I hardly dared acknowledge. Beechen Cliff above us rose steeply ahead. I was soon out of breath, but Jane and Cassy seemed to find it no effort at all striking out at a march, their parasols shading them from the warm sun. Charles, ever the gentleman, sauntered along beside me.

'Will you take my arm, Miss Elliot? The path is precipitous and if you are not used to it, I fear it will be very hard work.'

A fleeting recollection of Charles's future fate flashed before me. I wanted to protest, to say that I could easily manage but, even as I willed myself to do so, Sophia had other ideas. She, I knew, wanted to take his arm. My body disobeyed my mind, my arm found his and we fell comfortably into step. Jane and Cassandra did not seem to want to wait for us and they soon disappeared from view, screened by trees and hanging coppice.

'It is wonderful to be in England again and to see the beauty of the landscape all around us,' said Lieutenant Austen looking about him. 'You know, Miss Elliot, it is a funny thing but when I am away at sea, all my memories and reminiscences are of home and of being outdoors in scenes like these. I love my life as a sailor and would not wish to be doing anything else. Yet, I often think of those I've left behind. I dream constantly and am often astonished when I wake to find I am in my cabin afloat, so real and vivid are the pictures I see.'

'I do not find that surprising. You are evidently very attached to your family and I'm sure it is only natural to think of them, to miss them so much that they appear in your dreams.'

'Yes, my dreams are always of happy times with family and friends. Never in Bath, I must admit. I am always at home in the rectory at Steventon running through the garden on a summer's day.'

'Jane talked of your old home in just the same way. Tell me, do you also miss it?'

'Very much so and though my brother James lives there with his wife and daughter now, it is not the same. My sister Jane does not like to visit at all. It broke her heart to have to leave Hampshire. Just imagine, Miss Elliot, if you had to leave the home where you had always lived and see someone else take possession of it.'

For a single moment, I could picture our house in Camden, my father standing at the gate waving me off, as I'd set out for Bath. But the image evaporated like the wispy clouds overhead and I couldn't remember any more. A picture of Monkford Hall, like the print we had at home, replaced the vision of the townhouse. Only this time I could imagine it all in colour, see the mellow stone of the Jacobean manor house, smell the lavender bushes lining the paths of soft red brick in the formal gardens and catch the call of a peacock as it displayed its iridescent blue tail. I felt a connection with the place that I'd only ever dreamed of before and experienced a longing to go, to see my ancestral home.

'I should think it the hardest thing in the world to have to leave one's home, the place where you were born and where everyone knows you. And to leave friends behind must have been especially difficult for the Miss Austens.'

'I have not experienced such hardship as my sisters. I went to Naval College when I was a small boy and soon got used to being absent from family life. I've spent more of my time away than at home, but for my sisters who only went away to school for a relatively short time, it has been much more difficult. They have borne it all with such cheerfulness knowing that it was our parents' wish to retire here. Jane, in particular, has not enjoyed the transition from the country to the town. She pretends to be happy, yet she does not know how much I can tell her spirits to be affected.'

'It must be a great comfort for her to have such a thoughtful brother who is so sensitive to her feelings.'

'I hope so, Miss Elliot, I do what I can when I'm here. Jane and Cassy are both such dutiful daughters and carry out their obligations to my parents with true affection, but I do worry about Jane. She has such an independence of spirit, with a lively and intelligent mind. A character like hers is not meant to be so suppressed, or confined to the restrictions of a society where she cannot find time enough to be on her own or follow her pursuits. She may have told you that she loves to write, which is an occupation that many would not consider suitable for a genteel young woman. I know her writing has suffered here in Bath and that she finds it difficult to maintain the daily pursuit she was so used to in Steventon. She is at the beck and call of my mother and her circle of friends. It is no wonder she is subdued in our quiet moments.'

'Perhaps you will be able to take on some of the duties Jane is expected to do whilst you are here. Anyone would appreciate the gift of time that will be hers if you are able to shoulder some of the responsibility. I may speak out of turn, but it seems to me a poor lot for young women to be so completely beholden to their parents. Yes, we must care for them, but surely, your sisters deserve to have some freedoms. It seems to me that men are free to do as they wish. They may go out into the world and make their fortunes without considering anyone else. I am certain your sister has a talent which must be nurtured and it is in your power to help her make the most of her time, at least for a while.'

In a second came the vivid memory that I knew Jane's time was short, that her life was going to end far too soon. It was difficult to equate this thought with the young Jane I knew, the sparkling girl who burned with energy and radiance. I didn't want to believe it. And while I told myself I couldn't really do anything to help, I clung to a new idea. Perhaps I could help to alter this one small part of history. If Jane's years in Bath were productive and happy, could that be enough to change the past. I wanted to urge Charles to do all he could.

'I do understand you. Forgive me, Miss Elliot, for talking so confidentially to you in this manner, but you make me feel that I might open my heart to you. I do not know how to help her or my sister Cassandra, although I will try very much to do all that you suggest. I know they certainly value your friendship. Indeed, having your acquaintance is the very tonic we all require.'

We'd reached the bottom of a flight of stone steps. They seemed to stretch above us heavenwards and it was impossible to see the top.

'Are you ready for Jacob's Ladder, Miss Elliot?' Charles stood with one foot upon the step striking an attitude. His dark green coat was cut away to reveal nankin breeches tucked into gleaming chestnut boots, which delineated every muscle. He held his hand towards me. 'Now, if you please, I will lead you to paradise!'

I took his hand and felt his fingers link mine for a second, before he joined my arm with his. I caught the scent of his skin, a clean fragrance sharp with the aroma of lime and musk and found myself inclining my head towards him to savour it. Not for the first time did I think about how much I liked him, but with those thoughts came the memory that I knew he would one day be married to someone he did not yet know. The details were fuzzy and I began to wonder if I'd dreamt it all. I couldn't imagine any other time but the one in which I stood now and could no more imagine Charles married than I could myself.

The stone staircase laddered above us, turning into steps of banked earth twisted with tree roots. No sooner did I think we must have reached the top than the staircase curved once again climbing higher and ever more steeply. In such restrictive clothing, I found myself having to stop for breath. Charles turned to me with an anxious look. He was so close; I could see the flecks of gold in his eyes like hot embers amongst nuggets of coal and felt his warm breath on my cheek. I was drawn to his eyes, which seemed to swim with mine in that moment, just for a second before we both turned our eyes to the summit almost in view. The surrounding hills spread out like a patchwork quilt of viridian, burnt umber and sienna, hazy under the sun. Wild garlic blooming with white flowers lined the pathway, its sweet perfume rising in the heat against the scent of dark earth and green grass crushed underfoot.

When we got to the top, Jane and Cassy were waiting. They were sitting under a tree in dappled shade chatting to one another and I thought once again how lucky I was to have been invited.

'What do you think of Beechen Cliff, Miss Elliot?' Jane asked.

I was tempted to say that it reminded me of the South of France, as I knew Catherine Morland had suggested as much in *Northanger Abbey*. But, even as I suppressed that thought another came out of my mouth.

'It doesn't feel very English, we could be in an Italian forest or some such exotic place,' I said, wishing that I hadn't voiced anything quite so stupid out loud.

Jane seemed amused. 'Oh yes, I haven't quite thought of it like that before, but it puts me in mind of the countryside one might find in one of Mrs Radcliffe's horrid novels. Is that what you were thinking of, Miss Elliot?'

'Yes, like something from the scenes in *The Mysteries of Udolpho*, perhaps.'

'Beechen Cliff, the perfect scene for a gothic romance,' Jane declared with more than a hint of irony and a chuckle that escaped from her lips to light up her eyes, 'but then, I am not sure if the view of Bath from here lends itself to such horrid inclinations of gloomy grandeur or dreadful sublimity. We may see vast imitations of Italianate villas, crescents and columns enough to satisfy any Roman inhabitant, but we know them to be false, do we not? Bath must be a pale imitation of the real Italy and its inhabitants too tame, too sickly and far too dull to fulfil our romantic notions of a

Valancourt with manly grace and a hunter's costume. We will find no Italian counts within any building, and very sadly, no evil brigands lurking in the solemn duskiness of the forest. I hate to disappoint you, Miss Elliot, but you are far more likely to meet with romance on the open sea with a sailor than you are at Bath.'

I was very conscious that her speech seemed to be directed with her usual precision. Jane's whole expression was one of quiet mockery, her eyes being fixed on Charles and I the whole time. Intent on teasing us, I guessed she was goading him for an answer. A wry smile played around Charles's lips. I sensed that he was biding his time; that he didn't necessarily wish to respond to her teasing. In her usual way, Cassandra immediately stepped in.

'I do think that we should make the most of this fine weather and enjoy our picnic. It is a sad fact that in Bath one never knows how long such sunshine might last. Indeed, there are dark clouds in the distance and it is such a humid day, I fear we may yet be rained upon.'

From her basket, she produced a cloth in which were wrapped chicken pies. 'These are fresh-cooked, and with the gingerbread that Charles and I went shopping for this morning, I hope you will consider joining us in our feast, Miss Elliot.'

It was a relief to hear the conversation changed. Cassy and I exchanged smiles as we set about our meal, uncorking bottles of spruce beer to wash it down.

'I believe this is the finest gingerbread I have ever eaten,' mused Jane, brushing crumbs from her gown. 'There is nothing quite so delicious as a slab of dark, sticky gingerbread. You know if I were ever to be persuaded to seriously contemplate matrimony, it would have to be with Mr Smith whose recipe for this delightful sweetmeat is a celebrated secret. Just imagine being able to indulge your fancy whenever you wished. One might wake to a breakfast of such treats every day.'

'Oh Jane, you do talk such nonsense,' said Cassandra, shaking her head in disbelief, but smiling at the idea of her sister indulging her pleasure for gingerbread whenever she wanted. 'I could no more see you married to a shopkeeper than I could the Prince of Wales!'

'I do not know why the idea should be so offensive to you,' her sister replied. 'If I loved him, I should not care what his occupation.' Jane selected another piece. 'And, believe me, at this very second, I feel myself to be in love most pertinently.'

'But you cannot live on love and gingerbread alone,' commented Charles, 'and unless Mr Smith also has a secret fortune, I do not believe you would truly consider him.'

'You may be right. My love for pewter is undeniably greater than my love for gingerbread, but there's not much in it, I can tell you. Poor Mr Smith, I hope I will not break his heart but, if he should ask me, I should have to refuse him.'

I watched Jane nibble thoughtfully on the rest of the gingerbread relishing every last morsel. 'What do you think, Miss Elliot? If you were to fall in love with a man who had not yet made his fortune, would you consider him as a likely suitor?'

I had a very strong feeling that there was more to this question than there appeared and I couldn't help thinking that she must be referring to her own brother. I chose my words carefully.

'If I truly loved a man, his fortune or lack of one would not make any difference to me. In any case, we cannot always choose with whom we fall in love. When it happens, it is not something we can just dismiss on a whim or tell to go away. There is no rhyme nor reason in matters of the heart.'

Jane smiled rather wistfully. 'I believe what you say is true, yet it is not always in our power to follow our hearts. Obligation and duty are often the arbiters in cases where love has happened by mischance. And yet, still more cruel is the hand of fate, the harshest judge of all.'

Silence followed this little speech. I sensed an atmosphere of discomfort, of unspoken words remaining unsaid. Jane sat quietly for a moment or two, her face averted as if she stared at something in the distance. Jumping up to her feet, she opened her parasol with a snap, holding it over her head and obscuring her face as she walked away. Charles was about to get up to follow her when Cassandra assured him that she would go. It was evident that Jane was upset by something and that it had related to our conversation seemed obvious.

'I hope it wasn't anything I said that upset Miss Austen.' I watched Charles's expression, his eyes following his sisters with concern. We could see them both quite far off now. Cassandra seemed to be making reassuring gestures, taking Jane's arm, stroking her hand as they walked along.

'No, Miss Elliot, do not worry.' Charles looked across at me and smiled, but said no more on the subject, busying himself with the task of collecting the remnants of the picnic together.

Chapter
23

Despite the appearance of grey cloud, briefly overhead, the sun decided to challenge the densest vapour, evaporating all into whipped confections like floating meringues in the cobalt sky. The sisters returned. Jane's mood was bright, but if anything she was overly talkative and I wasn't completely convinced that she was as happy as she appeared. She sat down a little way in front, looking out at the view across Bath. I watched Cassandra reach inside her basket producing a pocket sketchbook, a pencil, a bottle of water and a small box of paints.

'Do not move, Jane,' she called. 'I shall picture you for posterity ... a portrait of unwearied contemplation.'

'Just as long as you do not paint my face!' Jane called, turning her back to us, arranging her dress and striking a pose.

'I would not dare ... I know how much you dislike sitting for me. No, I shall not ask you to turn. I shall capture the folds in the back of your gown instead and paint your elegant bonnet.'

With swift strokes of her pencil, Jane's figure was outlined. Dressed in turquoise blue with her bonnet strings undone, she sat upon the grass, one neat little foot poking out from under her gown, her hand resting upon her knee. Only the most tantalizing curve of her cheek was displayed so it was impossible to guess her expression or sense any emotion. After a few minutes, she protested at sitting still for so long. Ignoring her sister's requests to sit for five minutes longer, she was on her feet in a second and came over to my side. Ever restless, Jane held out her hand to me.

'Shall we walk, Miss Elliot? Sitting about all day is apt to make one sleepy. I am not in the least bit tired but if I know my brother and sister, they shall soon be slumbering.'

Charles and Cassandra laughed as if in agreement. They flopped down together on the grass, lying on their backs, spreading themselves out to watch the skies looking for pictures in any clouds that chanced to float above their heads.

I stood to take Jane's arm and we walked along admiring the view, pointing out the landmarks that we recognized. Bath looked like a toy town far below us in miniature. Up here, amongst the trees studded on the steep slopes, lush and green, it seemed a world very far away.

'I love the scenery up here,' Jane continued. 'If we turn our back on the city, the countryside around is very reminiscent of a favourite spot of mine in Dorsetshire, Miss Elliot. I admit, whenever I come up here, it is to remind myself.'

'I like that part of the world very much,' I answered. 'I wonder; do I know of the place to which you refer?'

'Pinny, near Lyme, Miss Elliot. Do you know it? Of course, the scenery is even more dramatic. It is a place for romance of every kind with its plunging green chasms and romantic rocks amongst scattered forest trees. I confess to having left a large part of my heart behind in Pinny.'

Jane's features seemed to shadow over as if a dark cloud had passed once more overhead. She opened her mouth to speak, but it was a sigh that escaped instead.

'And dare I ask if it was only the place where you left a piece of your heart?' I asked.

Her eyes were bright with tears. I instantly felt embarrassed because I realized if I hadn't been so inquisitive, the moment could have passed before she had had a chance to get upset. She blinked them away, her lips pressed together in determination to fight her emotions.

'I am so sorry, Miss Austen, I did not mean to upset you. I should not have spoken as I did. It is clear that there are some painful memories associated with the place of which you speak so highly.'

'But when pain is over, the remembrance can be a delight. I do not love Lyme any less for having suffered in it because there was so much that I will always look back on with great fondness. I experienced such enjoyment; my good memories far outweigh any other.'

'Do not speak if it upsets you, Miss Austen.'

'When love strikes, Miss Elliot, we must make the most of it and not worry too much about what the future will bring. I learned true romance at a time when I thought I should never know what it was to be in love again. After all, I am an ageing spinster. I shall be twenty-seven this year.'

'Oh, Miss Austen, you cannot believe that age should be such a barrier to love.'

'Perhaps not, but you must also be aware that chances for single women with little fortune and fading charms are few and far between. My sister Cassy gave up all hope of ever marrying and falling in love again long ago. In any case, her heart would only ever be true to her first and only love. She also knows too well the penalties for being unable to take the moment and fly. Be sure that you learn from it. Prudence is one thing, Miss Elliot, but true happiness and love are quite another!'

There was nothing I could say in return and the wind chose to rush through the trees at that moment bringing with it a strong blast of foreknowledge that only served to chill the air around me, and tighten my hold on Miss Austen's arm. I was sure there must be some reason why Jane could not be with the young man I'd seen that day in the Labyrinth and felt certain her heartfelt words had some connection to him.

The descent was in many ways easier than the climb to the top had been, but in long skirts it proved to be more difficult. Jane and Cassandra, used to walking in such clothing, negotiated the steps with ease. Once more, Charles held out his hand to me when he saw that I was struggling. I took it but, even so, there were several deep steps sloping away at a sharp angle that took me by surprise. Walking up them had been one thing, coming down was quite another. Forced to jump down the steep steps, Charles gripped my hand and my confidence soared. However, it was a self-assurance that came too soon. I stepped out too quickly, my boot slipped and I landed awkwardly on a stone ledge. As I turned instinctively towards him, grabbing his arm to steady myself, I felt loose stones shift under my twisted foot and I lost my balance. Charles's free arm caught my waist sharply, pulling me towards him to stop me from falling and dragging us both down the steps together. His fingers gripped the curve of my waist, and a tender pang of desire quickened inside. We were so close I could see the pulse throbbing above the white necklcloth wound round his tanned throat. Pulling away in my confusion, it was impossible not to be drawn by his eyes that crinkled at the corners as he smiled. Now hazel in the sunlight, fringed with dark lashes, they rested on mine.

'Miss Elliot, forgive me, are you quite steady?' he asked, the gentle pressure of his fingers' touch increasing like a caress as he pulled me closer.

I could no longer look at him. 'I am so sorry, Lieutenant Austen. I do not think I am a very accomplished walker.'

'Perhaps not, but you are perfectly proficient in the art of falling down steps which is far more fun,' he said, slowly releasing his arm from my waist, but retaining a firm grip on my hand.

He looked so serious that I didn't know whether to laugh, but then he grinned and I knew he was teasing me again. His dark eyes moved from the top of my bonnet to rest on the curls framing my face, before he glanced momentarily into my eyes. His gaze slowly shifted to stare at my lips, which parted as if at his request.

'There are not too many steps now, Miss Elliot, and they are not so steep. Here, take my arm again and we shall navigate ourselves just a little way further. I am rather mindful of the fact that I've left my sisters to shift for themselves.'

I thought his words rather prophetic as I considered how the men in Jane's life seemed to let her down one way or another, from what I'd read. Perhaps the reason that Jane and Cassandra were so close was because they knew that ultimately no one else had the time or inclination to truly meet their particular wants and needs.

We were soon home, parting at our respective doorways with promises to meet again as soon as we could. Jane and Cassandra said their goodbyes first, leaving Charles who lingered.

'I have enjoyed our picnic together, Miss Elliot, and I know my sisters always relish your company.'

'I am sure that no one could have enjoyed the day quite as much as I did myself. Thank you so much for asking me to come.'

'The pleasure was entirely mine.' He lifted his hat and bowed. 'Until tomorrow, Miss Elliot.'

The door opened to admit me into the cool, dark hallway. I caught sight of myself in the pier glass as I passed, and as the maidservant took my bonnet and pelisse, I examined my reflection turning my face one way and then the other. It certainly looked like my face. The eyes that regarded me were mine and as green as the jade vase on the table below me. It was very strange, but I was not certain if I could see anything left of Sophia at all unless what I observed was really her likeness after all. Was it my own face that I could see or had I simply become used to seeing another in the glass? I tried to remember but I couldn't think about anything very much, except that I thought I might have been someone else a very long time ago. I didn't want to think about that. There were other, much more important subjects occupying my mind. As I mounted the staircase lost in my thoughts about the day and the warmth of my feelings towards Lieutenant Austen, I sensed such a moment of happiness that I couldn't think when I had last felt the same. Jane had talked of fate and in that moment I believed it was destiny that had brought us all together.

Chapter
24

The next day dawned as bright and warm as a midsummer's day. I was looking forward to the gala, but each second and every minute that passed meant we were also getting nearer to the time of our departure from Bath. I didn't want to think about the fact that there was only one more evening left to enjoy the company of friends who'd become so dear to me. That is, if I could manage to spend time with them and I grew anxious that I might not even have a chance to speak to them. Emma was lively and excited, happily chatting about the coming trip to Lyme. I couldn't bear to hear any more about plans and preparations, Emma's instructions on the best ways to pack gowns, or Mrs Randall's enquiries on whether I was looking forward to the trip. The feelings of claustrophobia were overwhelming me again. As the afternoon dragged on, I knew I had to get out into the sunshine or I'd go mad and when I was happy that everyone else was busily occupied, I slipped out before they could stop me.

I escaped to Sydney Gardens. Fine weather had brought out crowds of people who promenaded in their finery. The sun felt very warm on my skin, and I wished I'd brought a parasol to keep me cool. I kept to the shadows and the sun-dappled paths, lingering under tall trees whose leaves rustled in the warm breeze over my head. I'd reached the white gate before I stopped to catch my breath and cool down. All of a sudden, I had the inexplicable feeling that I was being watched. I looked up, and then I saw him. There, not ten feet away was my very own Captain Wentworth, dressed in a blue uniform with a velvet stock about his throat. He carried his hat under his arm so that I saw the dark waves of his cropped hair above his lean and handsome face. It was Charles and I knew, without a shadow of a doubt, that he had come looking for me.

'I thought I might find you here,' he said, a generous smile breaking to light up his face.

'You look lovely,' I said, before I could think of any alternative, and then immediately thought how inappropriate that would sound in this time and place.

Charles blushed but, far from being shocked, he actually seemed pleased by my reaction. 'Thank you for your generous compliment, but it is you who truly does justice to the word. Indeed, if I may be permitted to say it, Miss Elliot, you do look very lovely.'

It was my turn to blush.

Charles continued. 'There's a military parade at four o'clock, to celebrate the Peace.'

'I confess; I did not know. I should love to come and see it, to watch you marching down the road.'

'Well, we are to start at Great Pulteney Street with a march through the town and back again in time for the grand gala opening at six.'

'I will come and wave at you.'

Charles smiled again, but then his expression changed to such a serious one that I wondered what on earth he could be about to say.

'I have enjoyed our discussions, Miss Elliot. It has been an honour to know you and your friendship is one I shall always think on with pleasure.'

I could hardly meet his eyes. 'I wish we were not going away just yet. I should so much like to know you and your sisters better. Thank you for your kindness towards me, Lieutenant Austen.'

'I hope we will meet again.'

'We will meet this evening, I am certain.'

'Yes, I trust we will, but if we are unable to speak to one another, if the opportunity does not arise ... Please write to my sister and tell her of your plans, where you are headed on your journey. Do I ask too much, Miss Elliot?'

'No, it will be my delight to do as you ask. I sincerely hope our paths will cross again one day.'

He paused. 'I must go now,' he said, 'but I wished you to take this in remembrance of a friend who holds you dear.'

From the lining of his hat he produced a small package loosely wrapped in paper. Peeling back the layers, I found a small painted miniature in an oval frame made of gold. A rather serious, but handsome Charles dressed in naval uniform stared back at me from the glass. His skin glowed, his mouth betraying that characteristic humour in the merest hint of a smile and those beautiful eyes, I knew so well, glittered with confidence and hope.

'It was drawn up at Algeciras,' he said softly. 'I hope you will think fondly of me if you ever care to look at it.'

I hardly knew how to reply. Knowing whatever happened, that I would keep it always; there were no words that could convey just how much his gift meant to me.

'I will think of you with pleasure, Lieutenant Austen, and treasure your gift always.'

'I hoped you'd say as much. I, too, will remember the time we spent together. I will never forget it, and I pray that ...'

He hesitated and I waited to hear the words I longed for him to say.

'Forgive me, Miss Elliot, but I must go now.'

I put out my hand to touch his arm, to prevent him from moving just yet.

'Of course, do not be late on my account.'

Taking my hand in his gloved one he pressed it to his lips. I closed my eyes to savour his tender kiss.

'Goodbye, Miss Elliot.'

I wanted the feeling to last. I hardly dared open my eyes because I knew he should have to leave.

Suddenly, I felt the brisk release, he'd let go of my hand and when I looked, to my enormous surprise Charles was gone! Not only had he vanished into thin air, but the whole world as I was coming to know it had disappeared. His world, the time to which I wanted to belong more than ever, had completely evaporated along with the bright sunshine and the portrait I'd been holding. I found myself in the still, quiet gardens, standing alone by the white gate in my own time with spots of rain pattering down on my head, which gathered pace with every second. The mournful cry of a seagull broke the silence as it flew above into the thunderous clouds that were gathering, smothering any patch of blue with a blanket of steel grey. Such a contrast to the happy scene I'd been part of a moment ago made me long for the past. I closed my eyes, hoping against hope that I would feel the sun on my face and feel Charles's hand holding mine. A spot of rain confirmed what I knew before I opened them again to see the gravel paths replaced with concrete, the sinuous walkways amongst towering beeches and chestnut trees and the secret alcoves, all but gone. I couldn't think what had happened, or understand how on earth I could have returned. I could only think that somehow the power of Charles's kiss had been too much, but that didn't seem to make any sense. Not that anything about this whole crazy adventure seemed to work by any logical means. I searched the pockets of my jeans, snatching at the white glove as soon as my fingers found it, pulling it on in an attempt to get back. Nothing happened, and though I closed my eyes and prayed with all my heart to be taken back, it was no use. Willing myself to go back was not going to work; I knew that from experience. I sat down on the path and cried. I knew my tears were completely selfish, but I didn't care. I wept for myself and for the man I was sure I'd never see again.

At least the rain meant I didn't meet anyone on my way home. There was no one in the park to stare at my red eyes or stop me to ask if I was all right. I dodged my way between the cars, not caring if they had to slam on their brakes in an effort to avoid running me over. I let myself into the house. Feeling totally disorientated, I had absolutely no idea how long I'd been away. In the past when I'd travelled back to the present the clocks had stood still, but somehow I couldn't believe that this time had been the same and a pile of post outside my door confirmed my gut feeling. I felt I'd been away so long, but in any case nothing really mattered. All I wanted was to crawl into bed and feel sorry for myself. Fully clothed, I pulled the covers over my head and cried myself to sleep.

When I woke, I really didn't know where I was for a moment or for how long I'd slept, though I recollected that I'd seen daylight come and go more than once as I drifted in and out of sleep. And then when I realized, remembering all that had happened, all my emotions came flooding back to overwhelm me again. I tried to tell myself that I was being ridiculous, that it wasn't possible to have fallen in love with Jane Austen's brother, but I couldn't tell my heart not to be broken at the thought of never seeing Charles again. It simply wouldn't listen. Now I was back once more the feeling that my experience was all part of some weird dream hit me again. What I'd thought had happened was totally impossible I tried to tell myself, but the ache in my heart refused to go away. It was real. Every time I closed my eyes Charles's face was there. I felt my hand in his and saw his lips plant his sweet kiss.

With a lot of effort I managed to haul myself out of bed. I had a bath, put on clean clothes and dabbed on a little concealer to hide the redness round my eyes. Feeling strangely underdressed I decided that the best way to pull myself together would be to go out and get some fresh air though I couldn't bear the thought of going to the gardens. I flicked on the radio. The presenter was announcing the news and when they gave the time and day's date, I knew that this last trip back had been in real time. Days of my life in the present had actually gone missing and I'd been physically occupying space somewhere else. Time travelling was a real puzzle, I decided, resolving not to think too hard on the subject. None of it seemed to make sense. All I knew was that I felt I had been away for an age.

Two weeks passed where I slowly began to accept what I'd learned and even started to convince myself that the feelings I thought I'd had for Charles were not real, not even my own. All attempts to go back failed completely and every time I tried on the glove, it was with renewed hope and excitement. But, the enchantment seemed all but used up. As before, the present swiftly took over my consciousness and the memories, although still present in my mind, were fading like a sepia photograph making me question everything I'd experienced. That's not to say that my feelings did not overwhelm me from time to time, but I did my best to bury them. Feeling so wretched was a pointless exercise. Nothing could change the truth. I was not Sophia, and clearly, Charles had not felt the same. He'd never been in love with her.

I didn't see anything of Josh, and I guessed he was too busy to bother popping up to see me with the last minute preparations for the exhibition and the launch party. The invitation propped against the mantelpiece proclaimed its desire for my company the following evening. Although I couldn't imagine how I was going to cope, I was glad to be seeing Josh again knowing that somehow his company would be good for me.

Chapter
25

As the day of the launch party dawned, I tried not to think about how nervous I was going to feel about seeing Josh again and spent the morning writing. I'd half expected to receive a note saying that he was going to be taking his friend Louisa to the launch instead and wondered if they'd managed to make contact. The day was sunny and it seemed as if the world had dressed itself in finery for the occasion. Over in the gardens flowers bloomed as the lilac trees drooped with heavy, fragrant boughs, their blossoms fading and turning russet in the heat.

When it was time to get ready, I took a deliciously scented bath. I carefully dried my long wavy hair, parting it in the middle and taking the sides back to pin it into place with some pretty slides. Slipping on the dove grey dress which fell in soft folds about my feet, I felt much more confident. A touch of my favourite rosebud lip balm, a flick of mascara and a brush of blusher later, I turned to view my reflection in the long, cheval glass. The whole effect was rather Regency in a way, but far more comfortable. And when I thought about the emotional highs and lows of the last couple of weeks, I was surprised to find that instead of seeing a care-worn harridan looking back at me, the mirror showed someone quite respectable. A spritz of my favourite perfume on my wrists and neck was the final touch, filling the air with the lingering fragrance of Morrocan rose and warm bergamot.

I poured out a glass of wine to help calm my nerves. I didn't know why I was feeling so nervous, but the prospect of being in a room full of people all looking at me and wondering why I was with Josh unnerved me. I really didn't want to let him down; he'd been so kind.

The buzzer went, I opened the door and my mouth followed suit. There aren't many men who have ever made me gasp at their beauty, but Josh Strafford was a vision. I don't know what I'd expected, really, but I suppose I'd only ever seen him in jeans and tees before. He was wearing a black suit, of some fabulous very slightly glazed fabric, that was beautifully cut, fitting him to perfection and making his eyes appear blacker and more glittering than ever. Underneath, a charcoal shirt with a very fine stripe was buttoned to the neck with no tie and had long cuffs that gave a glimpse of silver cufflinks. We looked as if we had planned our outfits together and I suddenly felt rather self-conscious. Josh leaned forward kissing me on the cheek and the smell of his cologne took me back for an instant to the Fashion Museum and that incident I'd almost blocked out of my mind.

'You look divine, Sophie, like a Greek goddess.'

I was so overwhelmed; I didn't know what to say, but he'd already turned and stood at the top of the staircase. 'Shall we go?'

Josh opened the door to the evening air. It was cooler, but it was still warm, which was just as well because I hadn't wanted to wear my old jacket or threadbare cardigan over my gorgeous dress that made me feel wonderful, it was so soft against my skin. I was still reeling from what Josh had said. I did feel good, but I was sure he was just being really nice putting me at my ease like he always did. He was so charming, a perfect date. Not that I meant the use of that word in its proper sense. It was just that he was such a gentleman and I knew I would have a lovely evening.

I needn't have worried about being stared at or worried by the impression I was making on anyone. Nobody looked at me. Several of the men, as well as every single woman in the place positively drooled over him. He was very attentive and saw that I was introduced to his colleagues and he even started to show me round the exhibition. But inevitably, he was the centre of attention. Everyone wanted to be introduced to him, everybody wanted to talk to him. He apologized more than once, but I told him not to worry. I wandered off to look round by myself.

The champagne was flowing and there were plates of hors d'oeuvres being handed round to nibble on but I couldn't eat much. I wandered about trying to look as if I didn't mind being on my own. It felt a bit like intruding in a private club and inevitably after a while people gave up trying to talk to me in favour of catching up on the latest office gossip. I was anxious not to drink too much. It would never do to have copious amounts and fall over, not that I've ever done quite that, but the problem was that my glass kept being filled up when I wasn't looking and it did seem to have gone straight to my head. Feeling a little light-headed and strangely unsettled by the whole event, I took myself round to look at everything. The exhibition was fabulous; Josh had done an amazing job. It was the way he'd pulled all the artefacts together, whether they were prints, paintings, objects or examples of costumes, and it was displayed so imaginatively using pieces of film, or real figures, and tableaux to represent what was being shown. Anyone, whatever their interest, would have gained something from it. I hoped he felt proud of his achievement.

I was halfway round when I couldn't avoid the painting any longer. I didn't want to avoid it exactly, but I knew on seeing it, that it would arouse so many emotions that I wasn't sure I could keep in check. There was Mrs Randall resembling my mother more than ever. Sophie's mother looked vulnerable; so young and beautiful. I wondered what they must have discussed as they sat together having their portrait painted. My eyes wandered to the box on the bookshelf. Even if the white gloves had been draped there for a compositional device, it still gave me the shivers to see them. It confirmed in a way I hadn't wanted to believe before, that there was more to all this than mere fancy. There was also something else. I hadn't noticed it last time because I'd been so pre-occupied by the sight of recognizable objects being there in the painting, but jutting out from the box on one side, ever so slightly open, was what appeared to be a small compartment, or perhaps it was a drawer. It was difficult to see, what with the painting being a very large one and the box on the shelf appearing so much higher than my head, but it was clear that there was also something inside it. I couldn't remember noticing a drawer in the box that Great Aunt Elizabeth had sent. In fact, I was sure I would have noticed it if there had been one.

'What do you think?'

I jumped at the touch of his warm breath in my ear. Josh was behind me.

'Are you having a lovely time? I'm sorry if I startled you and I'm so sorry I've neglected you for so long. Can you forgive me?'

My heart was beating fast. I felt so silly, almost as if I'd been caught out doing something I shouldn't. I tried to answer calmly. 'Of course I can forgive you. People are bound to want to talk to you. It's fabulous ... no, fantastic! It's just brilliant, Josh, you must be so pleased.'

He beamed a wide smile. 'Thanks, Sophie, for coming. I couldn't have done it without you. It's been so good to see a friendly face and one that I knew was not expecting anything from me.'

I smiled back. It felt good that he regarded me as a friend. I could imagine it was difficult for him right now with everyone wanting his attention.

'Oh, and I nearly forgot,' he exclaimed. 'You still have my surprise to see.'

I'd forgotten it also. He grabbed my hand and pulling me through the throng of people took me to the opposite end of the room. Off on one side was a portrait of a young girl dressed in white muslin and velvet slippers with a green parasol in her hand, set in a gilded frame. Seeing her like that in full colour made every hair stand on end. I immediately recognized the portrait of Jane from the monochrome engraving in the book I'd bought.

I stood gaping, unable to say a word.

'Do you know who this is?' Josh asked.

I turned my head to look at him. Something in my expression must have told him that I knew because he looked most disappointed.

'You know, don't you?'

'I think so. It's Jane Austen, isn't it?'

Josh grinned. 'I might have known you'd seen it before.'

'I hadn't seen it until recently, I must admit, and even then it was just a small copy in a book, not even in colour. But, how wonderful to see it like this – it's such a good likeness, so obviously Jane with her teasing expression.'

Josh laughed. 'You'll be telling me next that you know her personally, that she's popped round from next door for a cup of tea.'

I realized how stupid I must have sounded. He'd think I was completely mad. 'It's amazing, Josh, beautiful in fact. Wherever did you find it?'

'I know the family that own it. I have it on special loan for a while. They agreed to let me exhibit it at the last minute. I couldn't wait to show you, I knew you'd love it as I do. Isn't she exactly as you imagined?'

'Yes, it's the Jane I see in my head,' I added truthfully. 'The details are gorgeous and seeing it in colour makes all the difference. She looks so pleased with herself, all dressed up for a party in that divine gown of diaphanous gauze. The sparkle of those tiny spots and the glimpse of pink underskirt just stirring in an autumn breeze, really bring it to life.'

'And the sky is such a dramatic backdrop, almost as if the artist knew he was painting someone very special.'

Standing before the painting got me thinking. I couldn't

remember any specific mentions of portraits or paintings in Jane's books or letters, but one of her novels came leaping into my mind. 'There's a passage in *Mansfield Park* when Fanny Price goes to dinner at the Grants. She wears a new white dress with glossy spots just like that one, a present from her uncle. Perhaps it was a favourite gown of Jane's and why she remembered it when she wrote her novel.'

'I don't think I know *Mansfield Park* that well to comment,' said Josh. 'Isn't that the one where the heroine falls in love with her cousin?'

'Yes, but it doesn't ever look as if it will work out, though Fanny does marry Edmund in the end.'

'Look at the locket, Sophie. It's the painting in it that intrigues me because there's definitely something there. The family says that her Great Uncle Francis had her portrait painted. Perhaps the miniature round her neck is of him.'

I was suddenly reminded of another book of Jane's. 'Oh, that's *Sense and Sensibility*! Now, who is it? I can't remember exactly, I'm going to have to look it up, but it says something like Marianne and Willoughby had not known each other long before she wore his picture round her neck, but then it turned out to be only the miniature of her great uncle.'

As we stood there trying to remember who'd made the comment and whether we'd remembered it properly, Alison the receptionist appeared.

'Excuse me interrupting. You've got a visitor, Josh,' she said, in that triumphant way people do when only they have privileged information.

'Oh? Who is it?'

'I'm not allowed to say.' She winked conspiratorially at me.

'Alison, please. Can't you work your magic and make them go away for half an hour.'

'I can't. She said it's a surprise and she won't take no for an answer.'

'Please tell me you're joking,' Josh said, with a weary sigh.

'No, look, she's over there by the door.'

I saw Josh's eyes follow Alison's pointing finger. His expression changed dramatically from disappointment to one of complete astonishment and joy.

Over by the door was a girl. Tall, dark-haired and dressed in a sheath of peacock blue, which set off her glowing skin and hair, the whole room turned to look at the attractive beauty who presented herself like an extra special birthday package. All she needed was a huge satin bow to undo and the image would be complete. Without another word, Josh was pushing through the crowd, threading his way through the throng of people to reach her side. I watched him greet her with a shout to stun the whole room into a moment's silence, before he picked her up in his arms twirling her round and showering her with kisses.

'Who is she?' I asked Alison.

'I don't know exactly,' said Alison rather coolly, taking it all in with an expression that clearly showed she hadn't taken to the young lady at the door. 'She said her name is Louisa and as far as I know, that's the name of his girlfriend.'

It was a shock to hear that and suddenly, without being able to reason why, I felt completely deflated. Josh had never mentioned a girlfriend, though I remembered hearing about Louisa from Alison before. Why I'd imagined that such a good-looking guy wouldn't have someone is anybody's guess. I'd never heard him talk about anyone, but then we hadn't exactly discussed affairs of the heart.

'I knew she'd be beautiful,' murmured Alison and didn't say anything more, but I could guess what she and every other female in the place were thinking. If they'd only had a slim chance with Josh before, they had absolutely none now. It was impossible not to watch them. They were so animated, it was as if they only had eyes for the other and appeared so clearly in love. Suddenly, I felt completely in the way. I didn't want to hang around any more and I certainly didn't want to play gooseberry. Besides, I was feeling rather woozy from too many glasses of champagne.

'Oh, don't they look lovely together? Josh looks so happy,' I said in my breeziest voice. 'You know, Alison, I'm feeling rather shattered and I'm ashamed to say I think I've probably had a little bit too much champagne. Could you give Josh a message for me when he's not so busy? Just tell him I've gone home and I'll speak to him tomorrow, sometime.'

It may have been my imagination, but Alison's expression looked both haughty and gloating at the same time, as if she had seen through my excuses to some other reason for my early departure. I knew what she was thinking, that I was upset about seeing Josh with his girlfriend, but I really couldn't be bothered to say anything more and knew that whatever I did say would only seem to confirm, rather than deny her reasoning. At the earliest opportunity, I slipped out and made my way home.

Seeing Josh with his girl in his arms left me reeling. I felt an inexplicable stab of jealousy, or did I mean envy? Either way, it made me long to see Charles and I knew that was impossible. I let myself in and managed to get up the dark stairwell before I burst into tears. The living room felt cold, it was too late to light a fire. I turned on the lamp and slid into the winged chair, shivering as I did so, kicking off my sandals to pull my legs up underneath me in an effort to keep warm. I totally misjudged the action, most likely due to my over consumption of champagne and ended up knocking over the occasional table with such a force that I sent a vase of flowers, a photo of my Dad and the rosewood box crashing to the floor.

I saw immediately that the secret drawer in the box had sprung open. I carefully picked up the box to assess the damage and to my amazement found that all was still intact. From within the drawer came a gleam of gold shimmering through the layer of paper that bound it, which made every hair stand on end. I could only just see the curve of the back of a gold, oval frame, but knew before I took it out exactly what I'd found.

Charles's face looked back at me, and the memory of that last afternoon in Sydney Gardens came back with such clarity that it hurt. I held the frame to my face as though doing so would bring him nearer; bring him back to me. I knew it was just my mind playing tricks, but his eyes appeared to look deeper than ever into mine. He seemed to have even more of a smile about to break upon his lips, just like he had on that magical day.

The sound of the front door shutting made me jump. I heard voices, laughter, and then Josh's door shut with a finality that made me feel lonelier than I ever felt in my life before. Rising up through the floor, muffled voices trying not to be too loud were punctuated with giggles and then there was silence. I'm ashamed to say I could only imagine them kissing and that thought brought me back again to Charles. He'd kissed my hand with feeling and tenderness. Such a small gesture, but it was one that had filled me with intense longing.

Another sound from downstairs had me sitting up. Josh's door banged shut once more and then I heard the thump of footsteps on the stairs. I held my breath. There was a knock on my door.

'Sophie, are you in there? Are you still awake?'

I couldn't speak. The truth was I didn't want to answer. Perhaps I shouldn't have rushed off like that, it had been rude of me not to say goodbye, but my feelings were so mixed up. The sight of Josh being so happy had the green-eyed monster inside me whimpering pathetically to myself about my own feelings of insecurity and envy. If I was quiet, he might think I'd gone to bed. I just couldn't face him.

Holding my breath, I twisted into a more comfortable position in the chair and rested my feet on the footstool. I didn't hear footsteps going away immediately, so I guessed he was still outside waiting to hear for a response. It felt like ten minutes passed by but eventually I heard his retreating footfall on the stairs. Heaving a sigh of relief, I felt disinclined to get up now just in case my movements around the flat betrayed the fact that I was still wide-awake. In any case, the effects of the champagne were making me feel drowsy. Still clutching the miniature of Charles, I gave in to sleep which stole over me blotting out the world sending me into velvet darkness. My dreams were so vivid that on waking once more to daylight streaming through unshuttered windows, I couldn't decide which time I occupied at first.

There is nothing like the beginning of a new day for helping you to see things differently from the night before. Once I'd realized I was very firmly in the present, I kept thinking how rude I must have appeared to Josh by just going off like that and resolved on getting up and going to apologize. I'd slept for longer than I'd realized, I had a stiff neck from lying at a strange angle and combined with the inevitable hangover meant not only did I feel rotten, but I looked it too.

Charles's portrait looked even more spectacular in the light. I wondered how long it had been in the box, but guessed it must have been for some considerable time as the painting looked as fresh as if it had been done yesterday. I couldn't think how it came to be in the painting at the museum and then decided that what I'd thought had looked like a similar object might have been something completely different, a piece of jewellery perhaps. Yet, I couldn't get away from the feeling that I had been meant to find it, however it had got there.

By the time I got dressed, attempting to make myself look as if I hadn't got bags under my eyes and a headache that was threatening to turn into a spectacular migraine, it was midday. I was just about to go out and call on Josh when one particular thought held me back. What if his girlfriend was still there? I considered that she might well be and there was also the possibility that they may not want to be disturbed. That thought made me feel uncomfortable without really knowing why. It was silly, but I almost felt that I should have been the person allowed to vet his girlfriend first to see if she was good enough for him. I felt protective towards him, though I knew I had no right to feel like that and rid myself of the thought. I'd just have to wait, perhaps call on him tomorrow.

I was standing in the hallway dithering as I weighed up the pros and cons, when I spotted an envelope wedged under the door. It felt a bit knobbly on closer examination and had "Sophie" written on the front in Josh's handwriting. I snatched it up and took it into the sitting room to open. Inside was a folded letter and a key on a keyring, which incongruously had the words, *"You pierce my soul"*, written in fancy script, not unlike Jane Austen's handwriting engraved on its silver metal tag.

Dear Sophie,

Alison told me you weren't feeling well last night – I'm so sorry, I hope you're feeling better. I didn't have a chance to tell you how grateful I was for your company and it meant so much to me that you came. I must apologize also for not introducing you to Louisa sooner. I really wanted you to meet her, but that can wait for another day.

What I'm writing to say is that we are going away for a few days, heading further west to the Dorset coast, and I wondered if you could do me a huge favour. I'm expecting a package in the post any day now, some books that I ordered last week. I thought they might have come before I left, so I'm sorry to bother you with the inconvenience. If you chance to hear the postman calling, would you mind very much putting them just inside my flat? I've enclosed a spare key, (I hope you like the keyring) and I've left you a very small something to say thank you for your trouble on the kitchen table.

I didn't like to wake you this morning – I hope you had a good night's sleep – take care of yourself!

We're not sure of our plans, but I should be back in a week or so.

Love Josh.

Turning over the keyring in my hands, I wondered if it had been a present. Perhaps Louisa had bought it for him. Somehow, that thought irritated me and I couldn't put my finger on why it should straight away, until I realized that I'd already taken a dislike to her. That didn't seem either very nice or fair, but I decided I wasn't keen on Louisa for three reasons. Firstly, Josh had obviously not been expecting her. Last night, she'd rudely turned up out of the blue, unannounced without letting him know. Secondly, if she really was his current girlfriend, why had he asked me to go with him to the launch? I reckoned she'd turned him down, or worse, she was an ex-girlfriend trying to get him back. After all, he'd talked about broken hearts when we were at the museum. And then there was reason number three. Well, that made me wince with shame, but I just felt that she was one of those people who knew what a devastating effect she had on men and was toying with his affections. Josh, I felt sure, had been completely taken in by her. He was my friend and I didn't want to see him get hurt. Well, there wasn't anything that I could do about it. All I could hope was that Josh would be happy and he had very clearly been deliriously happy to see Louisa.

I am, by nature, a very nosy person and I'm further ashamed to say that I was very curious to see inside Josh's flat. I had a crazy idea that if the glove was going to work anywhere, perhaps it might do there. Without waiting another moment, I let myself out, glove in hand and hurried downstairs. Hesitating at the door, it occurred to me that perhaps I ought to wait for the books to arrive before I went snooping round. And what if Josh and Louisa hadn't really left yet, or if they'd just popped out to get something for their journey? But, the place seemed deadly quiet, so I told myself I was just going to peep in through the door and have a quick look. I was just about to put the key in the lock when I was frightened out of my wits by the sound of the doorknocker and the buzzing of the front door bell going simultaneously. To say that I jumped does not cover it and as I opened the door my heart was racing.

'Package for Mr Strafford. Is he in?' said the postman.

'It's alright, I'll sign for it,' I said, shoving the glove in my pocket and staggering under the weight of the box that he handed into my arms. I put it down, scribbled something hardly legible on his electronic slate and muttered thank you, before closing the door with some relief.

Having now got a legitimate excuse for opening Josh's door, I returned key in hand. I don't know why I felt so nervous as the door opened, but I suppose it was because I knew that I had no intention of just putting the books down and leaving straight away. I tried to justify the fact that I was going to have a look round by pretending that I didn't know where the kitchen might be and so wandered first of all into the living room. I knew Josh would have had nothing to do with any of the decoration as he'd rented on a short term lease, but I was pleased to see that at least he had some updated furnishings and new curtains amongst the inevitable litter of antiques that made up the rest. The mix of ancient and modern seemed to work. A red leather chair by the fireside looked comfy but contemporary and I could just imagine him sitting there listening to music or reading a book. On the table next to his chair were a couple of books. There was a biography about Jane Austen but he hadn't got very far, judging from his bookmark, and the other was about the history of the Royal Navy, which apart from being connected with Charles in the slightest sense did not interest me so much being all about fighting ships and battles. I didn't want to pick anything up, I felt it would be wrong, so I just stood and looked around me noting the jacket left slung across the sofa on the opposite side and a solitary, forgotten wineglass smeared with lipstick on the floor. The box was feeling heavier than ever, so I returned to the hallway passing another room barely furnished with a desk in the middle of book-lined walls and carried on to the kitchen. Painted a fresh white, a range of modern kitchen units and built-in cooker contrasted with the green painted dresser on one side of an old Aga at the other end of the room. The dresser looked a picture filled with pretty floral china, art deco tea sets and the occasional Staffordshire figure, but I couldn't imagine that it would have appealed to Josh. For a kitchen, it seemed a very feminine room with its embroidered samplers on the walls and rose-covered cushions on the rustic chairs. An oak refectory table in the middle of the room gleamed with polish and the markings of many years of use. The delft bowl of planted lilies placed upon the surface perfumed the air with its scent, as the waxy petals warmed in a sliver of sunlight. There was a package next to the bowl which made me feel an almost childish sense of excitement such as I always get when presented with a pile of birthday presents. Wrapped in powder blue paper of Chinese design with twigs and apple blossoms in pale cream, a gauze ribbon bound the whole and was finished in a bow. A tag, cut like a luggage label and tied on with a pink, silk ribbon had my name written on it, and a message.

Thank you for an evening of "exquisite moments", and for everything else.
Yours ever,
J. S.

I relieved myself of the books at last, picking up the package and examining the label carefully. I couldn't work out quite why "exquisite moments" had been written as a quotation, but I was sure Josh had intended it to mean something. I pulled out a chair and sat down to open my gift, which seemed extraordinarily generous for merely opening the door to the postman. Peeling back the thick paper that felt expensive to the touch, I gasped when I saw what was inside. It was an old, yet pristine edition of *Persuasion*. Printed in the nineteen fifties, it had a grey cover with a wonderful illustration by one of the Brock brothers on the front. I'd always wanted a beautiful edition, but my own battered paperback copy showing the old Assembly Rooms in Lyme was a favourite and I couldn't really afford to spend the sort of money on the type of book I now held in my hands. Inside was a bookmark, strategically placed, and then I understood. The "exquisite moments" was a reference to the evening concert that Anne and Captain Wentworth attend after realizing they're still in love with one another. Josh had obviously guessed it was one of my favourite parts of the book and thinking about that made me wish to go home, settle down in a chair and re-live *Persuasion* all over again. I gathered up the paper, pocketed the keys and walked out into the hall. I'd intended to go straight back to my flat but with even more shame than I described before, I decided to take one small peep in the room I really wanted to see.

It was not entirely my fault. At the end of the corridor the smallest glimpse of another room proved too tempting. Josh's bedroom door was ajar. I was going to pop my head round merely to satisfy my shamefully inquisitive nature and then come out straight away again. But I didn't. As soon as my head moved into that space it quickly summoned in the rest of me by what I can only describe as an overwhelming sense of Josh's presence. It was here he'd made the most impact on the flat. I could smell his cologne, as if he had just walked from the room. Everything was neat and ordered from the group of silver framed photos on the tall bow-fronted chest of drawers, to the immaculately made bed dressed in an Indian silk quilt in shades of dark copper and burnt umber. It was impossible not to admire this focal point, which seemed to have Josh's exotic personality stamped all over it. The bed itself was fashioned from rosewood, the headboard and barleytwist posts at each corner, reflecting the skill of the craftsmen who had carved the intricate scrolls, flowers and fretwork at least two hundred years ago and apart from the magnificent quilt that fell in exquisite folds to the floor, a huge pile of cushions in contrasting block patterns were arranged with precision. I sat down for a moment and then thought better of it, but as I stood up, the beautifully positioned cushions toppled over, one or two even falling down on the floor. Looking on aghast at the mess I'd created, I bent down to collect them up only to discover something else. I couldn't believe my eyes. Like a dismembered hand on the wooden boards, the tips of white leather fingers poked out from under the edge of the quilt cover.

I really did feel very strange at that moment. I tried to focus on other objects in the room, a replica of a wooden sailing ship on the window ledge, the ancient-looking telescope in the corner set on a tripod. But, my eyes kept returning to the glow of white leather on the floor. When I picked it up, the smell and texture of the leather instantly brought back such sweet memories that I felt my heart leap and pulling my glove out of my pocket saw instantly that they were a matching pair. If mine had run out of magic, perhaps the other might just work. I knew I shouldn't, but still, I couldn't resist just trying it on.

Chapter
27

'Ooh, Miss Elliot, you have given me a fright! What on earth are you doing in here? I thought you were all settled in the carriage about to go off.' Rebecca, the housemaid was looking at me as if she had just seen a ghost. 'I'm sorry, Miss, but I didn't hear you come in, it's as if you've just appeared in a puff of smoke.' She pointed to the glove I was holding. 'Is Mr Elliot looking for his other glove?'

'Oh no,' I answered quickly, wheezing slightly in an effort to get my breath back, 'it was just here on the chair.' Rebecca looked at me again with a puzzled expression. I felt I'd been winded, the flash through time had been so unexpected and so fast. It took me a moment to realize I was in the same room, though Josh would never have recognized his bedroom except for the long window giving a view out onto the garden.

I could see Rebecca was about to quiz me again, so I quickly said farewell, pocketing the glove before hurrying away through the hallway and out into the brightness of a sunny day, knowing that I'd left behind me one very puzzled and stunned housemaid.

The carriage was waiting outside. Emma's head was poking

through the window and she looked very cross.

'Come along, Sophia!' she cried impatiently. 'I cannot wait a moment longer to be gone from Bath!'

With the best will in the world I couldn't mirror her enthusiasm and even though I'd scarcely begun to take in the fact that I was back in the world I so longed to be, the memory of my last meeting with Charles came back with a freshness that reminded me that in this time it had only been the afternoon before that we'd parted, perhaps for the last time. Knowing there could be no future with him, I was glad to be leaving Bath, but even as I settled into the carriage, all sense of the modern world disappeared. I was here, it was now and I found myself looking toward number four hoping for any glimpse of the occupants within, even though Mrs Randall's figure half obscured the view. When I saw that she was watching me, I promptly turned my head to look out through the opposite side.

I heard the sound of a door opening nearby, accompanied by voices and cries of farewell. It took all my resolve not to turn my head because Emma was scrutinizing me now.

'Oh, look,' she said, 'it's that sailor you're always talking to and he seems to be in something of a hurry.'

All eyes, including Mr Elliot's, swivelled to watch his progress. Charles Austen was walking quickly and without looking either to left or right everyone watched him disappear round the corner into Pulteney Street. I thought my heart would burst. He must have seen the coach, I thought, yet he'd made no attempt to look at us or raise his hat. It should have been obvious to the whole row of houses that the Elliots were leaving Bath with the bustle of servants, grooms and ostlers, and a dray full of baggage and bandboxes. He knew we were leaving but he'd made no attempt to say goodbye. I couldn't help but wonder if something dreadful had happened at the gala evening I'd missed. After all, he'd made no acknowledgement or made any attempt to catch my eye. And yet, I understood that if the situation had been reversed, under the scrutiny of my formidable family, I most likely would have behaved in exactly the same way.

The coachman shouted, the carriage lurched forward and we were off. It was difficult trying to remain calm as we turned the corner and not appear as if I scanned every figure and face in sight, but there were so many people walking and so many carriages, I couldn't see Charles anywhere. We halted at the bridge to wait for a gap in the large volume of carriages crossing and it was then that I heard him. He was hidden from view, but I knew Charles's voice so well. I snatched a word or two, nothing clear, he was talking to the coachman. And then I saw him. Charles drew back into the shadow of a shop doorway, his eyes like a beam of torchlight sought mine. He touched his hat and there was no need for a sign, a sound or a gesture. I could only smile and return his penetrating gaze until he disappeared once more as the carriage moved.

'Pray, Sophia, what has been fixing your eye for so long?' enquired Emma whose expression was so cognizant, that I could only hope she would spare my blushes.

I started with embarrassment because she quite clearly had been watching me. 'I was looking at a hat in the milliner's window,' I replied, knowing this was not so very far from the truth.

'Ah yes, a navy bicorne, no doubt,' she quipped. 'I declare nothing ever caught your attention quite like a sailor's hat.'

So she had seen and even though Charles could not possibly be wearing any part of his uniform being off duty, Emma wanted to make it known that she had observed him. I'd never met another person so cruel. Ignoring her staring eyes and her mouth pursed in amusement, I comforted myself with the image of Charles's face etched in my mind, his warm smile and kind eyes.

It wasn't until we were out of Bath and on the open road that I really thought about my flash through time once more. Clearly the glove had no special significance for Josh or it would never have been forgotten under the bed like that and I couldn't help thinking I'd have to be a bit more careful with this one for fear of being stuck here forever. My thoughts turned to the portrait of Charles and I wondered whether it was still in the rosewood box in my own time. But, recalling that in 1802 it had been left behind, I knew that Sophia would be carrying it with her if she could. Any investigation, however, would have to be postponed until it was safe to do so.

I was feeling drowsy, the combination of the moving coach and the chatter of my companions gradually lulling me into a state where my mind left my body behind. I fell in and out of dreams, so for a while I didn't know quite what was real and what was not. Mr Elliot talked of his pleasure at being in William Glanville's company again as Mrs Randall listened patiently. Emma talked incessantly about how soon she could have new gowns fitted, relating a hundred different compliments made on her appearance by Mr Glanville in quick succession. Soon, even her conversation began to flag as the rhythm of horses' hooves and the sway of the coach lulled all but myself into permanent slumber. When I was satisfied that my fellow travellers had all nodded off, I reached for my reticule, a work-bag large enough to contain all manner of treasures from combs, hairpins and a tiny jewellery box to a small crystal bottle of lavender water and the precious pocketbook that I felt could no longer be completed. Apart from discerning these very necessary items from their shape as I rummaged through the bag, I could hear the crackle of paper and feel the edge of something hard through the fabric. A surreptitious look inside revealed that the miniature was safe inside amongst my possessions. I couldn't wait to see it again, but dared not fetch it out.

The journey that would have taken an hour by car took four in the carriage with stops for the horses and for food at an inn along the way. A meal of roast beef and accompaniments was attacked enthusiastically by everyone and once finished, I couldn't resist the temptation to stretch my legs and look round. The inn was a busy place and more than once, I felt in the way as porters and servants hurried down the passages with trays of food and drink or with vast trunks and boxes on their shoulders. Stepping outside, the landscape rolled in front of me like a vast green carpet, as far as I could see, punctuated with trees and hedgerows, the prettiness of wildflowers and white may. Everywhere we'd passed appeared so much more remote and rural than the England I knew and it seemed as if time had slowed down in more ways than one.

I was standing watching the coaches arriving and departing along with the bustle of travellers in a hurry, as you might see in any age, when the groom approached me, a small package in his hand.

'Begging your pardon, Miss Elliot,' he said, 'the coachman asked me to give you this parcel. It was a gentleman's request at Pulteney Bridge that you should have it.'

I muttered my thanks, but the groom still hovered. 'It was Lieutenant Austen, Miss, from next door at Sydney Place.'

He handed over the small paper package and was about to move off again, but changed his mind. 'I don't mean to talk out of turn, Miss Elliot, but he's what I call a real gentleman with a friendly way and he's always so kind to the horses.'

I was glad to hear someone talking about Charles, to hear him share the same high opinion. 'Lieutenant Austen is an extraordinary gentleman,' I replied. 'He is always kind to everyone.'

'He is indeed, Miss, and ever so entertainin' too! Always full of tales to make you smile, and he never passes by without stopping. He told me about the horse he looked after as a boy, and about his brother's pony that was named 'Squirrel'. That made me laugh, Miss Elliot. You would be diverted to hear him relate the story, I'm sure.'

He grinned, bowed and left me feeling both amused and intrigued. In a very roundabout way, I think the groom was trying to tell me that the coachman had thought it would not be improper for me to receive any item from Charles. And it was typical, I felt, of my friend to be so warm to the men who looked after the horses, the epitome of the perfect gentleman who felt as much at ease with a servant as with the prince I remembered him telling me that he'd accompanied across the ocean.

I tore a small hole in the fine striped paper to reveal a jewel of a summer nosegay. The fragrance of plump, ruby red rosebuds tied into a circle set against dark, green leaves with a flourish of cream lace lifted my spirits and senses as no other gift could ever have done. I buried my nose within the bouquet savouring its perfume and the touch of velvet petals against my skin. That Charles had arranged such a treat touched me to my heart. Even at this distance I felt closer to him than at any time before. But there was precious little time for admiration. The groom appeared to announce that we were leaving, so stowing it away in my workbag that now felt stuffed with forbidden objects of desire, I hurried back to find my fellow travellers.

Once more, I sat next to Mrs Randall who dozed and chatted alternately. 'Marianne should be home from school,' she said, as we passed a signpost for Crewkerne. 'I do hope her sore throat is improved. Well, she's been in good hands with Mrs Dilly to nurse her. We'll hardly know her, I'm sure, she's turning into such a young lady.'

As we passed by the market square I wondered about the sister I'd never met. Surely she couldn't be as spiteful as Emma, I thought.

The town was busy, somewhere not far away the church bells tolled the hour of four. Further out on the western side, the weaving factories followed the course of the river Parrett and here we were slowed down by large wagons bearing enormous bolts of cloth.

'I daresay all this sailcloth is bound for the shipyards, though how many more new sails our ships will require during this time of Peace, I cannot wonder,' observed Mr Elliot, the wagon lumbering slowly before us.

I thought of Charles bound ashore in Bath and selfishly prayed that he would continue to be held captive on land. But knowing his ambition, I knew that his own feelings would not be the same. He was probably already wishing that war would flare again so that he could serve aboard his ship. What was he doing now, I wondered? Perhaps he and Jane were strolling round Sydney Gardens or sampling sweetmeats in Molland's coffee house. I could picture them in my mind's eye and as I stared out of the window not knowing where I was headed, I longed for the familiarity of their friendly faces and their warmth. I hoped Jane was happy. I'd never had a chance to really talk to her, not that she would necessarily have told me about the young man I had seen her with that day. Whatever their problems, even if they were never to be overcome and I had a feeling that might be the case, I could only wish them time spent with the other and of being together.

We left the road after another mile or two to pass through ornate gates and enter a carriageway twisting and turning with no view in sight, but of trees on every side. Broad, leafy oaks and chestnuts, their branches like the arms of graceful dancers made a green tunnel over our heads. At last, the vista opened up to our eyes. Standing serenely in its own remote valley and enclosed by sweeping hills stood Monkford Hall, the gabled manor house of my ancestors, glimmering in golden stone and gilded with afternoon sunshine that winked in the diamond paned windows.

Chapter
28

A young girl about sixteen years old came flying through the door and down the front steps attended by her nurse. Marianne rushed up to the carriage door as we took our turns to step down, her cheeks flushed and eyes shining with rude health.

'Mrs Randall,' she cried, 'I am so glad to see you, for no one here is the least sympathetic about my poor throat. Sophia, it is such an age since I saw you and this last week I had no word from you at school. I could have died of a putrid fever and no one would have cared. You all know my sore throats are worse than anyone else's.'

'I am sorry to find you unwell,' said Mrs Randall. 'You sent me such a good account of yourself on Wednesday!'

'Yes, I did not wish to trouble you; but I have been so very ill, I can assure you. Mrs Dilly has had no time for me either, she's always busy and her sewing is far more important than nursing me!'

'I'm certain that Mrs Dilly has been most attentive,' Mrs Randall replied cheerfully, smiling at the old nurse who looked to be at the end of her tether with Marianne.

'Well, you will soon be better now,' I said, feeling that to jolly her along might be the best course. 'You know I always make you better when you come home from school.'

The words felt so familiar that I guessed I was feeling something of Sophia's emotions on the matter, especially when it soon became clear that Marianne was something of a handful, demanding attention at every turn, and imagining she was hard done by in everything.

Supper was ready; there was no time to familiarize myself with the house or look round. Food was served in the old hall. An Elizabethan space, the vast room was long and tall with windows that were too high to see out of, but which let in the dying light of the sun at twilight turning the walls to chalk pink. Shields and mottoes ran round the top of the room adding to the sense of age and history. Paintings of figures in padded breeches or satin gowns with diaphanous ruffs of starched lawn, followed our actions with their eyes as we moved. A long refectory table placed before the fire at one end groaned with a selection of cold meat, hot pies, and other savouries arranged on pewter plates. Whilst at the other, glasses of lemon syllabub decorated with crystallized fruit, tempted us from a tiered epergne dressed with cut flowers.

Everyone was tired after the journey. Emma and Marianne talked of their excitement at leaving for Lyme the next day, but were anxious to go to bed so that they might be up early. I wanted to explore the house. After all, I didn't know if I'd ever have a chance to see it again. Even though I'd returned in time, I felt cautious about the likelihood of being around in this century for long. It seemed I had little control over my coming and going and so I wanted to make the most of any time I had.

Monkford Hall was a much larger house than the one in Sydney Place. The house in Bath could have been swallowed up several times and although I managed to go all over it to get my bearings, there were many rooms I did not enter. The building as a whole formed a letter H. The earliest and narrowest part was centrally positioned, housing the imposing entrance with its grand oak door and the Great Hall. The two gabled wings comprised of the kitchens, offices and a formal dining room on the east, as well as the drawing room, the oak parlour and the library on the west. It was a lovely country house with rooms furnished in the English style. Stuffed full with ancient furniture, tapestries and tarnished chintz, I fell in love with it all, feeling instantly at home.

'I've missed you, Sophia, why could you not have come sooner?' Marianne said, coming to stand by my side as I gazed through one of the mullioned windows. I felt the weight of her head rest against my shoulder. 'Will you come outside with me before bedtime. We'll sit in the garden as we used to do and I can tell you all my troubles.'

I turned to see a girl who suddenly seemed a lot younger than her sixteen years. With her large, dark eyes, she looked like a bewildered child and if only she could stop scowling, I thought, she'd be a very pretty one. We walked arm-in-arm out into the beautiful garden, damp with dew and fragrant with the perfume of summer blooms. Along the terrace, which ran along the back of the house, our feet crunched along gravel paths until we stepped down a flight of semi-circular steps to pass under an arch in the wide hedge of dark yew that traversed the formal layout.

'Upon my word, I would not be sixteen for all the tea in India,' Marianne cried. 'I was stuck at school whilst you were all being happy in Bath. I do not see why I could not accompany you. I am quite of an age to go dancing.'

'But, Marianne, everyone has to go to school and when you are older, I am sure you will look back on such times with fondness. If you had come to Bath, you would have left all your friends behind.'

'I never want them, I assure you. They talk and laugh a great deal and are so full of their own importance it is too much to bear. Isabella never fails to remind me that she is the daughter of a baronet and therefore requires precedence in all matters, and Penelope is spiteful and unfeeling. Do you know, she said that my sore throats were a figment of my imagination?'

'Oh dear, perhaps she meant that you must try not to think about them too much.'

'She is a heartless girl. I understand her meaning perfectly well, but I do not wish to waste any more of my precious breath talking of her. Ask me instead about my afternoon with Henrietta Coles yesterday. Mrs Dilly and I stayed for tea.'

'Were you well enough to go then? I thought you'd been ill for some days.'

'Of course I went. I could not have stayed at home; Sophia, I should have been missed by all my other friends.'

'Well, I am very glad you were able to go, and have a lovely time.'

'There was nothing extraordinary about it. I knew beforehand exactly who would be there and what refreshment would be on offer. I tell you, if I see another potted shrimp, or wretched seed cake at one of these parties, I shall die.'

I didn't know what to add. Marianne seemed upset with everything and everybody. I decided that what she really missed was the care and attention of her mother and if everything was centred on Emma all the time, being the youngest and left out on the activities of her elder sisters would be bound to have its difficulties.

We entered a small courtyard styled in the old Tudor fashion of parterres with squares of columbines dotted in between low box hedging, their lavender heads nodding in the breeze. I was drawn to the Elizabethan sundial on a plinth in the middle. Carved in a stone spiral with many embellishments around the circular face was the motto: *Time is but a shadow; Too slow, too swift, But for those who love, Time does not exist.*

I shivered. My mother would have said someone had just walked on my grave and the doves up in the church beyond the house flew from the bell tower, their wings flapping against the still air. The words on the sundial resonated with me, but I couldn't think where I had read them before. They seemed so fitting. I couldn't think of a more apt description to the way I was feeling.

Whenever Charles and I were together time did not exist. Time made up its own rules and like shadows we were at its mercy, floating between the layers like sunlight passing through lace to leave its patterns fleetingly marked in shade.

'What are you thinking about, Sophia? You have a most faraway expression. But I think I know and I've guessed why you seem so different since you arrived. You are in love!'

The challenge in her voice brought me up fast. Was that what I was feeling? Was I truly in love with Charles Austen?

'You're blushing, so it's true!' cried Marianne, pulling me down to sit beside her on a stone seat. 'Tell me about him, Sophia. Is he rich like Mr Glanville? What do Papa and Mrs Randall think of him?'

'I am not in love,' I began and hesitated, as I didn't wish to confide in anyone about the complicated feelings I had for Charles. I was doing my best to deny them knowing that his love could never be mine.

'But, I am sure you've met someone,' Marianne insisted. 'I can see that you have and I shall feel most put out if you do not tell me all about him.'

'I did meet a very interesting family when we were in Bath, a set of the most delightful people. I fell in love with them all ... they have such a funny way of saying things that show them to be sincere and openhearted, quite unlike other people who present a smile, but then have no real interest in you at all. The Austens are a creative, artistic family. Cassandra is an accomplished artist and Jane is a talented writer. I also met their parents, a brother James and his family, all literary and interested in books. There is a sailor brother, too.'

'And I believe that this brother is the very one who has stolen your heart.'

'Lieutenant Austen is very gentleman-like, but my heart is intact, I do assure you.'

'But you do like him?'

'Yes, I like him, as a girl might like a brotherly figure. In any case, he has yet to make his way in the world and has no time to fall in love.'

'Oh well, at least there will be one wedding to attend. Emma will be married before September.'

'Marianne, you should not say such things before an engagement is announced.'

'I know, but some sisters keep me informed, whereas others do not. Emma told me that she is certain to get William Glanville now and that he has hinted as much. I've never received so many letters from her on the subject in my life before.'

'However, I think it might be wise not to discuss or use the word, "engagement", especially in light of her previous disappointment. There has been no formal proposal yet.'

Marianne pressed her lips together petulantly. 'I shall be as silent as the grave, but all I know is that she will get him at last, and then introduce me to all his friends!'

It was hard to bite my tongue, and resist the temptation to tell her what I thought, but thinking about the influence her sister Emma must have, I decided it was a pointless exercise. I suddenly felt tired, but knew I had a problem. As in Bath I had no idea which one of the upstairs rooms was mine. When Marianne said she was eager to go inside again, saying she'd like to come to my room to talk, I let her bound up the stairs before me, chattering as she went, to show the way. If she still had a sore throat, she gave no sign of it now.

The door was flung open. White-washed walls and a fire burning in the grate set off a vast four-poster bed, hung with crewel work drapes, along with a huge press and a beautiful cedar chest on a carved stand in the corner. There was also a bookcase, which on closer inspection contained a wonderful selection of "horrid" novels such as Catherine Morland from *Northanger Abbey* might enjoy, and a dressing table set before the window with a toilet mirror, a set of silver brushes and two glass bottles holding scent. It was the personal objects that held the most fascination for me. A doll, dressed in worn Indian muslin with jet-black hair pushed under a satin bonnet, sat on the window ledge next to a wooden cup and ball game, along with another object that I knew so well. I ran to the rosewood box and traced my fingers over the familiar scrolls and inlays, the sight of which filled me with a strong sense of nostalgia.

'What is it, Sophia?' asked Marianne. 'Have you secrets in there?'

'Of course not, I'm just so pleased to see all my things. I really miss my home when we are away and the sight of such a familiar object is a joy to behold!'

'I do understand, whenever I'm feeling upset at school, I wrap myself up in Mama's shawl and imagine she's putting her arms around me like she used to when I was a little girl.'

Her face crumpled as if she might cry and I suddenly felt very sorry for her. 'Do you remember much about Mama?'

'Not as much as I'd like. I remember her voice and I recall the feeling that whenever she occupied a room, it always seemed that the sun was shining and the house was full of laughter.'

I remembered my own mother. It felt as if a light had gone out when she was no longer there and I thought how hard it must have been for the young Marianne to have her mama taken away at a tender age. It was no wonder she was always fancying herself ill. She probably just needed a little more love and attention. I would try to be extra patient and spend some time with her.

'What shall we do in Lyme?' I asked. 'Do you prefer walking, or collecting shells and fossils?'

'I do not like walking, it is so fatiguing and I am not interested in collecting anything.'

'Then, how about some sea-bathing? We will hold hands and go in together!'

'Cold water is perfectly horrid and sea water so salty, that after our visit to Weymouth last year I declared I should never dip my toes in the water again!'

'Well then, we'll just sit on the sands in the sunshine and enjoy doing nothing. I shall read to you if you like.'

'Oh, Sophia, I would like that. Please can you read to me now, just a little of "*The Mysteries of Udolpho*" before I have to go to bed? We'd just got to the black veil before you had to go away! You're the only person after Mama, who can read so well.'

Half an hour later, by which time she seemed in a better humour and tired enough not to protest too loudly about going to bed, I took the candle and escorted Marianne along the dark corridor to her room, tucking her into bed and wishing her goodnight. I made my way back along the creaking floorboards, grateful that I had such a short distance to walk in the dark by the light of one small flame. My chamber felt very homely and quite my own. I can only describe the feeling like a memory, something so deep within my soul that had been awakened by unknown senses. I knew I had been there before, that I had lived and loved in this house. Opening the cedar chest initiated an onslaught of impressions and emotions, most of which were so fleeting that the memories are as hard to write down as a dream on waking. I pulled out the gowns one at a time discovering new muslins, brocade skirts from the past, ribbons and tassels, scented leather gloves, and sheer gauze fichus. Selecting some of the finer muslins for our seaside trip, I threw them over a chair in readiness to take on the journey the next day and turned my attention to the rosewood box.

There were one or two pretty necklaces of cut steel and a tortoiseshell comb inside. When I'd removed these, I set about trying to find the secret drawer. I felt around the interior until I noticed that one corner felt slightly spongy. I prodded and poked; the spring mechanism was set in motion and the drawer popped out. There was only one more job to accomplish and that was to hide Charles's portrait, knowing I could now activate the drawer to look inside whenever it was safe to do so. In the glow of candlelight, Charles looked so handsome my heart turned over. I couldn't resist kissing the glass where his mouth smiled back at me, and it was almost impossible to have to say goodnight to his picture. Climbing up onto the soft feather bed, I slipped between cool sheets at last to admire the beautiful patchwork on the bed.

Trying to ignore the hooting of an owl outside, I was aware of unfamiliar noises and curious shadows moving along the ancient walls.

Chapter
29

Our first views of the sea were captured in sunshine, flashes of blue as bright as a butterfly's wing seen between the rising hills as the carriage climbed ever higher. Turning down a lane from the main road, we were set down at last along the gravel sweep before an imposing house at noon. Nelson House stood about a hundred yards from the brow of a steep cliff-top, which gave glimpses of the little town of Lyme. Its cottages, in narrow winding streets, were huddled together on the steep incline as if to stop themselves from falling into the waves below. In contrast, grandly built with classical proportions, the house before us boasted a wealth of windows on either side of a raised front door. Warm breezes whipped about our faces as we alighted from the carriage, I could taste the brine on my tongue and smell the sea. A line of seagulls called from the top of the parapet in way of a welcome, a sound that stirred feelings of happy recollections and so for the moment, I felt almost pleased at the thought of some time by the seaside.

Mr William Glanville was gracious and welcoming, inviting us all into an elegant room giving magnificent views through a large Venetian window of far distant cliffs and the tops of houses to the sea, dancing and sparkling in the sunshine.

'Not far below us,' he said, 'are local amenities, such as a good milliner's shop and the library, as well as a hotel and billiard room. And from there the principal street begins sending us almost running down the hill to hurry us onto the beach, to the bathing machines and into the water. You'll find everything you desire in Lyme and more besides!'

'This is an outlook, indeed, Mr Glanville,' remarked Mr Elliot, 'a very fine prospect.'

Mr Glanville looked about him with an expression of pride. 'We can boast the finest, purest sea breeze for miles around, with excellent bathing and fine sands. Never was there a happier place designed for a resort of pleasure. What do you think, my dear ladies, will you be happy here?'

'Oh, yes,' exclaimed Emma and Marianne together, eagerly running from one window to another.

Mr Glanville turned to me. 'And you, Miss Sophia, is the prospect to your liking?'

How I wished he hadn't so pointedly asked for my opinion. Still, I had to agree, the view was stunning.

'It's a wonderful prospect,' I admitted, 'you are very fortunate.'

'Do you approve of the seaside and its developments? Is a pleasure resort to your fancy, Miss Sophia?'

I could feel Emma's eyes upon me, glaring in anger at the attention I was getting from him.

'I do approve on the whole; though it is my particular preference that coastal villages remain untouched and unspoiled by tourists. I do not favour such fashionable watering holes as Brighton so much as I do the more natural environs of Lyme.'

'And how on earth would you know, Sophia?' gasped Emma in disbelief. 'You've never ever been to Brighton!'

Life shifted in the folded layers of time with a flash of foreknowledge that was glimpsed for a moment before it disappeared forever. I couldn't think why I'd mentioned Brighton.

Our host glanced at Emma. He'd clearly witnessed her cross remarks and her even angrier expression. My heart sank when he turned to me again.

'I quite agree and I think Brighton is generally known well enough in the scandal sheets without having to witness its entertainments first-hand. Lyme is free from artifice of any kind; the scenery and society suit me very well, indeed.'

Just as I was beginning to think that Mr Glanville and I might have some sentiments in common he spoke again.

'And, of course, here people still understand the meaning of rank and consequence in its truest sense. A man in my position is able to oblige the needs of such simple folk with little expense to myself and yet still enjoy their unwavering deference and devotion. A lady of equal rank might expect so much more in a small society such as this. To be a Lady of the Manor in Lyme is a most fulfilling, rewarding role, one that any parent would be pleased to see accomplished for their daughter, I'm sure.'

He was looking into my eyes with a determination I found not only uncomfortable, but also very intimidating. I looked through the window out to sea, at a sailing ship in the distance, and thought of Charles at once. I wasn't sure that I liked Mr Glanville one little bit. On the one hand he appeared to be the epitome of a gentleman, all charm and good manners, but it was clear he was a snob and I didn't like that at all. He was as self-important as Mr Elliot.

'I do hope you will be able to accompany us into Lyme and show us all the sights,' said Emma, smiling in her prettiest way in an attempt to get his attention.

'It would be my delight,' he readily answered, 'and as soon as we can be ready, I suggest we take a stroll down to The Walk and the Cobb to sample a most refreshing entertainment.'

'Oh, what can it be?' cried Emma, 'please do not tease me, Mr Glanville, I cannot wait to know what you are about!'

Mr Glanville smirked. 'All I will say, ladies, is that you may find it best to hang onto your bonnets. If we're lucky it will be a light zephyr blowing and if not, we'll be able to guess from the whitecaps whether going up on the top will take us off for an early sea bathe.'

The afternoon proved to be a perfect one for walking in the sunshine. The sands were dotted with people staying in Lyme for the season, the bathing machines were all occupied and the sea awash with bodies all shrieking with laughter or terror as the bathers were submerged. Breathing in the tang of the sea took me back to another time I hardly remembered. I saw an image of myself as a small child standing before a seafood stall with my parents. Wrinkling my nose at the pots of cockles and shrimps fragrant with vinegar and the aroma of the sea, I remembered feeling astonished that I actually liked the taste of the pearl-grey creatures and plump, pink prawns. The fleeting vision evaporated as the stronger smells of rotting fish heads replaced it. Slung into barrels, the fishermen's wives were gutting a fresh catch on the shoreline as we walked along to the Cobb, skirting round the little bay. Near the foot of an old pier, a young gentleman emerged from a small house, nodding to Mr Glanville and stopping to exchange a greeting as we passed by.

'That's Doctor Rockingham,' Mr Glanville explained after the brief conversation. 'He looks after our health both here and in Sidmouth where he is much in demand. Not that I've had much cause to consult him myself. Pleasant fellow, a little dour, perhaps, though it's as well not to have a doctor who is too jovial, don't you know?'

I watched the doctor's back disappear. Head bowed and clutching a bag, he looked to be in a hurry. I wondered if he ever had any rest at all. In a place like this, a lot of people would come to recuperate from illness though I suspected many more would be rich hypochondriacs with nothing better to do than spend their money on imaginary ailments.

'Here we are at last!' Mr Glanville shouted, waving his arm in triumph at the harbour wall rising to a great height before us. 'There's not a grander spectacle to be found anywhere else in this part of the country.'

It was a brilliant sight with ships and boats moored alongside and the flurry of people briskly walking along the top. Children running with excitement, and being reined in for fear they might fall, elegant ladies and gentlemen strolling as they admired the scenery, were all full of anticipation as they climbed ever higher. We followed the crowd onto the Cobb where the summer breeze snatched at my bonnet, playing with my ribbons in an attempt to undo them. Mr Glanville walked alongside, halting whenever I paused to take in the view, giving his opinion on its merits. Emma was doing her best to intercept him, but he seemed intent on ignoring her and giving me his fullest attention. I couldn't shake him off so I loudly exclaimed that I had a stone in my shoe before squatting down, taking as long as I could whilst pretending to shake it out and avoiding his eyes that I felt burning into the top of my bonnet. Waiting until I was certain that he'd given up on me and had moved once more to Emma's side, I rose to take Mrs Randall's arm.

'Mr Glanville is a very attentive host and quite everything I expected him to be,' Mrs Randall began.

'Yes, he is pleasant enough, I suppose,' I began, privately considering that I didn't like him.

'I am no matchmaker, as you well know,' continued Mrs Randall, 'being much too aware of the uncertainty of all human events and calculations, but from my observation it seems our host is quite undecided about where his affections lie.'

'Do you not think there will soon be an announcement? Emma will be so happy when they are engaged.'

'My dear, Sophia, only time will tell. Appearances of partiality are sometimes misleading and I have often noticed that a young man disguises the true object of his affections. Whatever Emma's feelings maybe, we cannot be entirely sure of Mr Glanville's at present. Whatever the gossip, he has no more picked her out than you and I own that to see you as a future married lady in her own right would make me very happy.'

I made my way to stand at the end of the Cobb, pretending to look out over the views of the sea all around me and trying to remain calm. I wasn't about to take Emma's place if that was what Mrs Randall was hinting. I felt trapped and knew I must be on my guard more than ever. I was being smothered alive, by the clothes I was wearing, by the stiff behaviour, and by the conventions of a society that thought it was perfectly acceptable to buy and sell women like cattle. I wanted to run away, to tear off my clothes and run along the sands in my petticoat. Of course I couldn't do anything of the sort, but I felt I couldn't bear it for another minute and not for the first time wondered how on earth clever, intelligent women like the Austen sisters managed to cope so well and not go mad. And then I remembered that if not for her writing perhaps Jane might have suffered her own version of madness, brought on by the suffocation of a free and creative spirit. I thought about her escaping to her other worlds and knew that there she had rid herself of real passions where she enjoyed more than a little pleasure in exposing the kind of people that she knew and loved to write about.

'We have hardly been acquainted, Mrs Randall,' I said, as she reached my side. 'I could not be satisfied that I really know his character. Mr Glanville seems agreeable enough, but there is something wanting. I cannot explain. All I know is that he could never be the man for me.'

Mrs Randall said nothing further. Slipping her arm through mine, she patted it reassuringly and for the moment, I breathed again.

Chapter
30

The next week passed in a miserable way to match my mood. The weather turned for the worse. It was impossible to go out and high up on the cliff as we were, any opportunity to venture outside was prevented by the high gales that whipped round the house. The winds shook the glass in the windows and moaned through the cracks in the frames. All day and all night the rain lashed down and I was haunted by the feelings of being trapped with no escape. The mist rolled in off the sea and it seemed as if icy winter had made a return. No one but me seemed in the slightest bit upset by the change in the weather. Everyone else seemed to enjoy the fact that they were all closeted together and were very happy with the same activities, which soon became the routine. Card games were the favourite choice, along with the flirtatious chatter that accompanied the setting up of the card tables, so any chance I had, I disappeared to the library. At least there I could immerse myself in books, escape inside the head of another writer and forget that I might never be able to find my way home. Wherever home might be. When I tried to think about it, I could only see Sydney Place and memories of Charles made me feel sadder than ever.

By Friday, the weather had changed for the better much to my enormous relief. Stuck inside, I hadn't been able to send Jane a letter and if I didn't send one soon, there'd be no chance of her writing to me. The idea that I might not see her and Charles again was one I didn't want to think about.

A request from Mrs Randall to collect a tonic for my father from Doctor Rockingham meant that I had a wonderful excuse to get out of the house. At last the sun was shining, making a perfect day for a walk down into Lyme to call at the doctor's, send a letter, and look at the shops, as well as take a stroll along the sands. Marianne begged to come along so we rushed out of the house before anyone else could join us. I was glad to get away from Mr Glanville's increasing attentions and knew that Emma would be glad that she'd been left on her own with no one to distract the object of her fortunes. Having dispatched my letter, we headed for the circulating library to look at the books and spend Marianne's money that she was desperate to lose on some frivolous item. I bought paper for writing and some for sketching with the idea that I might be able to draw the beautiful scenery and perhaps encourage Marianne to do the same. To my surprise, after she'd looked at all the lace gloves, fans and pretty combs with sighs of adoration, she decided to buy a box of paints.

Clutching our purchases, we set off down Broad Street and turned onto The Walk and along the seashore to find a suitable place to sit and paint. We found the steps leading down to the sands and walked along feeling the warmth of the sun and the soft, sea breeze on our faces. I couldn't help thinking of Charles. I wished he could have been there and thought how much he'd enjoy the wonderful views. The fishing boats were out at sea or tied up along the harbour wall, the fishermen struggling with nets full of gleaming silver fish. They doffed their caps and cried friendly greetings as their wives worked swiftly and expertly at their side. With their skirts hitched and their bare feet planted firmly in the sand, they didn't speak but, I saw their eyes observing us, looking at our clothes with a mixture of envy and curiosity.

'We ought to call at the doctor's house first. It's just a little further along,' I said.

'Oh, Sophia, must I? I'd much rather wait here.' Marianne was not about to be moved. She was already finding the best place to arrange herself and her box of paints, though I did wonder how long it would be before she lost interest in this newfound enthusiasm.

'If you promise you'll stay just there and do not stray, I will not be long,' I said, giving in to her pleas, knowing that any amount of cajoling her simply would not work.

I hurried along to the little house near the Cobb Gate and was invited in by a young woman who introduced herself as the doctor's sister.

'My brother's been called away to a patient,' she said, showing me into a small parlour, 'but Mr Elliot's medicine has already been prepared. I'll fetch it now. Do make yourself at home.'

Packed full of country furniture brightened by embroidered cushions on the oak settles, there were polished pewter plates on a dresser, jugs of wild sea pinks and samphire on every surface and a grandfather clock in the alcove, which whirred into life, striking the hour with eleven bright chimes as I sat down.

At last she returned with a glass bottle twisted into brown paper to make it secure. Miss Rockingham, as pretty as her parlour, chatted away all the time. She knew all about us, she said, and that the Elliots were staying with Mr Glanville.

'For there are no secrets in a place as small as Lyme, you know, Miss Elliot. No one may arrive or depart without the whole place knowing about it.'

'I expect you see a lot of people come and go,' I said.

'Yes, indeed, it's been our pleasure to meet a lot of travellers. Lyme is a splendid place for invalids to recuperate and we try to help those that are sick and in need of good, fresh air. We have a room we let out in the summer months for just such a purpose. But, Miss Elliot, as glad as we are to see them better, we are always sad to say goodbye. People arrive for a month or more at a time and just as you think they are becoming great friends, off they go again.'

'I confess; I've had some experience of that myself in Bath. I made friends with the family next door and now I do not know if I shall ever see them again. I wonder, Miss Rockingham, whether you ever met them. I know they were visiting in the area last year.'

'Well, I don't claim to remember everyone, but perhaps I might know of your friend.'

'The family name is Austen. Miss Jane Austen is the friend to whom I refer. They spent some time in Sidmouth, I believe, and stayed in Broad Street here in Lyme.'

Miss Rockingham's face lit up. 'Oh, my dear, I know Miss Jane very well and her sister, Miss Cassandra. We had the good fortune to become very well acquainted with them during the autumn months. They were happy days! My hope is that we might see them again this year and the young gentleman, who lodged here with us. Forgive me for being so bold, but tell me, Miss Elliot, is it too much to hope that they became engaged?'

I hardly knew what to say. 'I am afraid, Miss Rockingham, that I know of no such engagement, nor of the young man to whom you refer.'

'Oh dear, it was never my intention to talk out of turn, but I never saw two people to suit one another so well. It was a delight to see them together. My brother and I attended poor Mr Austen in Sidmouth many times and during these visits I became acquainted with the young ladies of the house. They duly called here when they came to Lyme and spent a considerable time with us – I feel sure that the young man lodged here on Miss Jane's recommendation. It was a pleasure to see them together. They used to sit just where you are now; a book between them, their heads bowed together, his so fair and hers so dark. He was such a clever fellow and Miss Jane shared all his passion for novels and discussion. I was certain an engagement was about to be announced. Dear me, how I should love to see her again. Tell me, how is she?'

'Miss Austen is well, at least, she was in good health when I saw her last.' I could hardly comment on her low spirits. 'I know they are to travel soon to the West Country but whether they shall come to Lyme, I cannot tell you.'

'Miss Austen and her young man loved one another, that's certain. Well, that is something of a mystery, if nothing came by it. Anyway, it was not my purpose to tittle-tattle. How are you settling in Lyme, Miss Elliot? Mr Glanville is a very agreeable young man, is he not? And I know he loves to entertain when he's here. Nelson House is one of the most beautiful buildings for miles around.'

'It is splendid, I quite agree, and a comfortable home.'

'It is a lovely house, Miss Elliot, but what it really needs is a female hand.'

I couldn't think of anything to say which would stop her thinking that I had any designs on Mr Glanville. Every sentence that jumped into my head seemed to indicate some partiality to him. I saw her smile knowingly and knew it was time to go.

'I hope we shall see you at the Assembly Rooms, Miss Elliot,' she said, as she handed me the bottle. 'I know Mr Glanville loves to dance, so I would reckon it a sure thing. Anyway, you have cheered me up. It's been a treat to talk to you.'

'Thank you, Miss Rockingham, I'm sure we shall meet again soon.'

She waved me off from the door. I could imagine Jane fitting in very well within the homely atmosphere I'd found there and pondered once more on the fickleness of time and place. Miss Rockingham had mentioned a gentleman with fair hair. Could he possibly be the young man I'd seen Jane with in Bath? I didn't really need an answer. I was sure he must be.

When I reached Marianne she was still sitting in the same spot, her painting things had been abandoned and she was looking very cross.

'Where have you been? I've been sitting here for an age and I've quite given up. It's just impossible to paint out of doors. Everything keeps blowing away.'

'Come on, it's time to go somewhere else. Let's walk along

the Cobb,' I said, 'then we will have views on every side to choose from.'

'But, it is so high and very windy up there – I'm sure to get blown off,' Marianne complained. 'And every surface is wet, I am certain I shall slip on the steps.'

'You'll do no such thing. Come along; hold onto me. There's nothing to worry about.'

Complaining all the way, Marianne took every opportunity to grumble. We took the nearest steps to climb onto the Cobb wall. Up on the top, Marianne clung to my arm and her bonnet, screaming partly with exhilaration but mostly with fear, as the fresh breezes propelled us along quite out of our control. But even Marianne laughed like I did, as a gust blew us to the edge. She screamed; the sound carried away on the wind out to the indigo blue sea.

We were coming to the fork of the harbour wall where it split into two. Watching the waves as they crashed and foamed onto the rocks below, I suddenly noticed a gentleman standing at the end near the edge. In complete shock, I stared intently, gasping in disbelief. I couldn't believe what I was seeing, I watched him unable to tear my eyes away. But then, a cloud passed overhead to reveal dazzling sunshine that seemed to get behind everything, winking in my eyes so that I couldn't see. Against the bright light he appeared almost in silhouette, a shade framed against the tumbling water that leapt and broke against the wall. Could it really be him?

Chapter 31

It was Charles, I was sure! He seemed to be enjoying the dangerous game of standing too near the water's edge and retreating just before a wave broke over the surface of the wall, leaping and jumping out of the way of the spray. I started to walk a little quicker, had almost reached him and was about to call his name, when he turned and I immediately realized how much I'd been mistaken. For although there was something familiar about his stance and in the way that he moved with his dark hair curling into his collar, it was not Charles Austen. I felt embarrassed, for he'd turned to see me racing towards him dragging my sister in tow and he now looked at me, as if I were some kind of mad woman. However, he clearly was a gentleman. He quickly recovered himself, bowed, raised his hat and wished us a good day. He was smiling with that expression which still seemed to be extraordinarily like one I knew so well, and his lady who stood a little way off watched us with interest, bobbing a curtsey in our direction as if very slightly amused by our odd behaviour.

All I wanted was to leave quickly so nodded my head and turned; determined to hurry away. In my haste I stumbled. Though

I heard him calling out, to ask if I was quite well, I ignored him, anxious to be gone.

'Who was that gentleman? Do you know him?' Marianne began, as soon as she could speak.

'No, I do not know him. Come, I think perhaps we should go back down to the sands, it is rather blustery up here.'

Marianne persisted. 'But, your face is all red. Are you sure you don't know him? Is he an old lover, Sophia?'

'Don't be so silly,' I snapped, before I had a chance to pull myself together. 'I've never seen him in my life before.'

'You looked as if you did and you almost ran to reach him.'

I couldn't answer without getting cross, so occupied myself with the pretence of looking for something in my reticule and directing Marianne towards the steps down to the sands.

'He reminded you of someone and I think I know who that person might be,' Marianne continued, her face lighting up for the first time that day. 'I think he has a similarity to the gentleman you met in Bath and that is why you could not contain yourself.'

I ignored her, changing the subject to that of picturesque scenes, but her self-satisfied expression told me that she knew she'd guessed right. We sat down on a rock, whilst I fetched out sketchbooks and pencils for the exercise. The tears pricked at the back of my eyelids, but I was determined not to let Marianne see me cry. I drew with passion; scolding myself for being so foolish, yet found I was unable to forget the gentleman and his lady who had since disappeared from view. I had been so sure it was Charles Austen, but however much I'd have loved him to be in the same remote part of the world, I knew he was far away in Bath. In any case, it was useless to think about him and I didn't want to admit that my feelings for him were developing, maturing into something else. Marianne would not sketch again, so I suggested we might walk home. Overhead the sun disappeared and the clouds rolled in changing the colour of the sea from sapphire to a cool, onyx green.

After a weekend of hot sunshine, the following Monday

dawned with more wet weather and the usual games. I couldn't bear the idea of another round of cards with Mr Glanville leering at me when he thought Emma's attention was elsewhere, so I rushed off to the library as soon as I could. It was wonderful to have a chance to be on my own. I selected a couple of volumes from the shelf and curled up on the sofa to read. But, I couldn't settle to any book and the person who'd occupied my thoughts so much lately kept coming into my mind. I wondered what Charles was doing. Would he still be attending the Assembly Balls? I knew how much he loved to dance. I thought there was little chance that he would be sitting out all the dances because he was missing me. Had he found another partner and, worst of all, did he prefer her company to mine? Charles seemed lost to me, even if I could see his face when I closed my eyes and hear his gentle voice in my head.

I heard a noise outside the door and then the creaking sound of the door handle slowly turning had me sitting up promptly, blinking away the tears that threatened to spill over my cheeks. I was too late. My heart sank when I saw who'd come to disturb my peace and I must admit I felt very anxious to see he was alone. Mr Glanville walked in and shut the door firmly. Seeing that I was upset, his face contorted with concern as he rushed over to the sofa and sat far too closely by my side.

'My dear, Miss Sophia, whatever is the matter? Why are you sitting all by yourself? Come now, your pretty face is full of anguish.'

I was trapped. He shifted ever closer; I could feel his breath on my face. As I kept my eyes lowered, I noticed his palms left a damp shadow on his breeches as he rubbed his knees with his hands. I made a move to stand, but he suddenly grabbed my hand, simultaneously falling on his knees in front of me.

'I would do anything to see you smile, Miss Sophia. Just to witness your suffering is to make my very own heart feel the pangs of misery. How you torment me!'

I nearly laughed out loud. It might have been funny if I'd not also realized that he meant every word.

'Do not concern yourself, Mr Glanville,' I cried, pulling my hand out of his grip as my courage rose. 'I promise you I am not suffering and I rather take pleasure in my own company. Indeed, I have sought refuge in the library to enjoy solace and reflection. Besides, I should hate anyone to feel miserable on my behalf, let alone be in any pain.'

'And yet, I remain unconvinced by your rhetoric. Your spirits are subdued; there are tears upon your countenance. But, if I may be allowed to venture upon a course intended from the very first, I think I know how best to make those eyes brighten once more. Please allow me to tell you of my heart's desire.'

The danger of the situation was becoming all too apparent, I knew I must remain calm even as he gripped the edge of my gown and buried his face in the muslin.

'Mr Glanville, please get up, sir. I assure you that I am perfectly well. I simply had the misfortune to have an eyelash lodge in my eye, which produced the tears you saw, but it is quite gone now. Moreover, I do not think Mrs Randall would approve of my being here alone with you. If you will forgive me, I shall leave now.'

He raised his eyes to gaze into mine as if I was truly adored. 'Your perfections are only increased by this little speech and your modesty further enhanced, Miss Sophia, but I promise only to detain you further by a mere five minutes of your time and upon an employment that I feel sure would not be distasteful to our dear Mrs Randall or to any other single female. Besides, I am certain when that lady knows of my purest intentions toward you, she will not only encourage my suit, but be delighted to share in the superior felicity which shall surely result.'

I couldn't listen any longer. 'Forgive me, Mr Glanville, but it would not be seemly for me to remain under such circumstances. I cannot be detained by you for a moment longer!'

Pushing the sofa back with all my force I leapt to my feet running towards the door before he could reach me. Catching a glimpse of his shocked expression, as I closed the door on him, I knew I'd had a lucky escape though I was sure it would only be a matter of time before he declared his "intentions" again. And if he applied to Mr Elliot or Mrs Randall for their assistance, I knew all my efforts would be in vain. What was I to do? I could only hope that I'd put him off and prayed that the weather might improve giving us all an opportunity to get out of the house and be occupied with other things. In the meantime, I should make sure I was never alone again. Knowing that he would not repeat such behaviour if Emma was within earshot, I stuck close by her whenever I could. Occasionally, I found him staring at me in the way he had when we'd first arrived, but by glaring at him I managed to keep control of the situation.

Daily life at Lyme followed a regular pattern of days out if the weather was fine and days of imprisonment in the house when it was wet. Time passed surprisingly quickly and June was heralded in with a blast of heat, fine weather and dips in the sea to cool off. Despite the annoyance of spending almost every moment avoiding Mr Glanville and the illicit pleasure of dreaming of Charles, for the most part I was finding that the days passed pleasantly enough. Excursions, which didn't include the men in our party, were my escape. Miss Rockingham came along on some of these outings and we enjoyed rides in her donkey cart to Colyton and Charmouth, taking long walks to Pinny where I thought of Jane. I couldn't help but wonder if she'd spoken so fondly of the area because she herself had walked amongst its dramatic landscape with someone very dear to her heart. I could see how easily you might fall in love in such a place and I found myself hoping that Jane and her young man had been able to see more of one another in Bath. I pictured them strolling along the Gravel Walk, but decided this was probably a scene that could only exist in one's imagination, as I was sure it had taken root in Jane's. We'd exchanged a few letters, but there was no mention of any gentleman, let alone secret trysts. She hardly even mentioned Charles and I began to worry that he had forgotten all about me. It was hard not to feel quite miserable at times and I realized that the longer time went on; my heart grew fonder of him than I ever thought possible. Telling myself I shouldn't feel that way was utterly hopeless. I'd been in love with him the first time I'd ever set eyes on him and in a way it was a relief to admit it to myself.

I was always the first volunteer to go to the post office to collect the letters and so it was in the third week of June that Marianne and I escaped into town. I had a feeling there might be a letter waiting for me and was excited to see I was right. Waiting until I had an opportunity to read it by myself was going to take all my patience, but the thought of news from Jane and the possibility of even the smallest remark about Charles kept me going.

As we hurried along Coombe Street, the wind picked up to catch at our skirts and snatch at our bonnets. The sky was turning ominously grey.

'Oh, do let us find shelter,' cried Marianne, 'or I shall get wet through and catch another cold.'

We'd just turned onto Broad Street when the first spots of water were felt. The rain was nothing and I wanted to get home as quickly as we could, but Marianne insisted on entering a coffee shop, taking a table by the window and ordering for us both.

I turned to my letter as we waited for our refreshments to arrive. The date on the top had been written a week ago, but I guessed the postal service in this remote part of the country was not as frequent as in the bigger towns. Jane's letter was full of news, describing all she'd seen and heard at the Pump Rooms and the Assembly Rooms in humorous detail, as she always did so well. I couldn't help laughing out loud, until the next paragraph wiped the smile off my face.

Charles is away visiting friends for a few days and in his usual style has sent no word of his return. My mother is anxious that he will change his mind about accompanying us to Dorset, but I know Charles will not let us down. As you know, he's always bubbling with enthusiasm for all he does and I know he will not want to miss his trip to the coast. He's visiting some fellow sailors and I'm sure they're talking over past times like old salts.

Well, dear friend, I hope this letter finds you well.
Yours ever,
Jane.

Although Jane had tried to be reassuring, the thought that Charles might decide to stay with his friends and not come to Dorset after all really bothered me. I wondered where in the country he might be and imagined him being caught up in the entertainments of private parties and balls, most likely at a country house. Perhaps his friends were brothers to a bevy of beautiful sisters and maybe Charles was looking forward to dancing with them. I knew I was getting carried away, but I couldn't help myself.

I was gazing at the bustling scene outside feeling as miserable as the weather looked. The rain was really coming down now bouncing off the cobbles and dripping from the eaves of the shops and houses. Dashing figures hoisting umbrellas tried fruitlessly to dodge the rain and rushed for cover. And then I saw him. As I stared, I was suddenly fixated by one particular figure.

Chapter
32

He was instantly recognizable. Charles Austen was walking down the street! My first instinct was to completely disbelieve what I was seeing; thinking that I'd seen the man from the Cobb again, but there was no doubt. It was Charles; this time I wasn't wrong. My reaction was overwhelming, my heart began to pound and a million butterflies flitted inside. It was such a shock. I felt overpowered with love. For a few moments I saw nothing; I was lost until I scolded myself into being sensible once more, suddenly aware that Marianne was talking to me. But, I couldn't think about anyone else, I really wanted to go to the door. It seemed desperately important to check if the rain was stopping. Why was I to suspect myself of any other motive? Surely Charles must be out of sight by now.

I left my seat and told myself that my reasons for doing so were perfectly innocent and justifiable. After all, we'd soon be making our way home. But, just as I got to the door, Charles was there; he practically walked into me. He was obviously really surprised to see me, more than I expected, for he looked quite conscious and his cheeks were pink. For the first time since I'd met him, I felt that I was showing less emotion. I'd had the advantage of seeing him first; I'd been able to prepare myself. Still, I felt such a desperate mixture of anxiety and pleasure, something between joy and anguish.

'Miss Elliot, it is a pleasure to see you.' Charles didn't seem able to look at me and yet, I sensed that his words were heartfelt.

'It is my delight, Lieutenant Austen, that you are here in Lyme. Are you with your family?'

'No, that is, they are expected in a day or two. I've been visiting friends and as my mother was becoming anxious that I might never rejoin them, I thought I'd restore her faith by riding on ahead to secure accommodation for us all. My mother wishes to be at Dawlish this year for part of her summer tour. I came on to look around the area to find a suitable house and had a fancy to stop in Lyme on the way.'

'Oh, I see. Then you will not be staying long.'

I couldn't stop smiling, nor could I take my eyes from his face. I didn't want to think about the short time we would have together, or the fact that this might be the only chance I would have to speak to him. I just wanted to drink in the image of his handsome face and lose myself in those hazel eyes, which now turned to look into mine. I was suddenly conscious that Marianne was watching us closely.

'Lieutenant Austen, may I present my sister, Miss Marianne Elliot.'

'How do you do, Miss Marianne? How are you enjoying your visit?'

'It is as I expected, Lieutenant Austen. The weather is too dull for words and my sister is only intent on making me sketch or climb steps. Lyme has too many inclinations for my liking and too much wind to make any sitting outdoors pleasurable.'

'Oh dear, I am sorry to hear that,' said Charles, barely able to disguise a smile. 'We shall have to find something to improve on your experiences thus far. I wonder; do you care for violet drops, Miss Marianne? For myself, I always find sweet treats a most agreeable diversion.'

Charles took a small black and white striped box from his pocket and proffered the contents to Marianne. She was unable to resist the sweets and when she'd sampled one and declared it to her liking, Charles made her a present of the rest.

'I think the rain is stopping,' Marianne called, 'we should be going home now, Sophia.'

'There is to be a dance at the Assembly Rooms this evening,' said Charles urgently. 'I will be attending, I do hope you and your party will be there.'

'I do not yet know of our plans, but I hope we will be in attendance.'

'I hope very much to see you there, Miss Elliot.'

'Well, I think we should be leaving now.'

'But, it is raining.'

'Oh, very little, it's just a shower.'

'I have an umbrella, I wish you would make use of it, if you are determined to walk.'

As I hesitated, a carriage drew up outside; the servant came in to announce Mr Glanville before he made an appearance. It was beginning to rain again, though no one inside took any notice of the weather being far too interested in watching what was going on. William Glanville was talking as loudly as he could, making sure that everyone in the shop knew that he was calling to take the Miss Elliots home. He had stopped in every shop along Broad Street, he said, in order to find us. Charles Austen clearly recognized him as the man he'd seen in our party at Bath. Mr Glanville ignored him and made much of me, anxious to get us away. In another moment he had taken my arm. I flashed an embarrassed look at Charles but only managed to whisper goodbye as we passed away through the door and into the carriage.

Going over our meeting in my mind on the way home, I felt myself analyze every gesture, every word that Charles had said. I hardly heard anything that Mr Glanville was saying until he announced that after an early dinner we should be attending the ball at the Assembly Rooms, and it was almost impossible not to give him the impression that my enthusiasm arose from this information alone. I knew my face had lit up at the very mention of going to the ball, but all I could see in my mind's eye was Charles. And, as much as I would have liked to keep my feelings hidden, it was impossible. Mr Glanville's hints about wanting to open the ball with the Elliot sisters at his side gave me several minutes of anxiety. All I could pray was that he would ask Emma to dance first. I knew that he would be asked by local dignitaries to lead the dancers out onto the floor and that if I was chosen to be his first partner, this would signify a certain preference for my company. I didn't want this to happen above everything else.

I dressed with great care, choosing a fine, Indian muslin, embroidered with flowers and French knots along the hem and down the sleeves. A string of coral beads at my throat gleamed in the dying light and two bright spots on my cheeks gave the impression that I was permanently blushing, the work of the sun and sea breezes combined, which had turned my skin to a pale bronze. I felt nervous at the thought of seeing Charles again and for a moment wished I could stay at home and hide away. Seeing him in Lyme had been a shock, I'd felt a certain consciousness between us when we'd met or I'd wanted to believe that I had at the time.

Now, I was not so sure and scolded myself for imagining that Charles had come to Lyme especially to see me. I needed to separate what I wanted to believe from the truth and the facts were that Charles had come to find suitable lodgings for his parents in the surrounding area. That was all, I was determined that I would suppress any other thoughts including those shadowy memories of some other matter that tried to find their way to the surface. He wasn't going to stay in Lyme and even if he did stay for one night, he was soon to leave so that he could organize his family's accommodation. They weren't even going to be in the area, choosing to go to Dawlish instead. His interest in me stemmed from our friendship in Bath and I told myself not to think that there was anything else. If I was not careful, I could so easily betray my feelings, not only to those around me, but to Charles himself. However much I longed to tell Charles about the place he was securing in my heart, I could not reveal my feelings. I knew that now. It wouldn't be fair to him, I decided. He'd made it perfectly clear that he was not about to fall in love with anyone, nor did it fit in with his plans. His career and advancement in his chosen profession were paramount. Besides, a little voice somewhere in my head said it was never meant to be. I could not, and should not attempt to change fate.

The Assembly Rooms set on the edge of the sea gave the impression of being afloat, as if on a great galleon sailing out on the water, for nothing but sea and sky could be seen through the windows. The walls rippled with light and reflections in tones of lapis lazuli, which as the evening progressed bobbed and dipped like the ocean itself, bathing the interior with a rosy glow from the sun setting on the horizon and from the warmth of the candles glimmering in sconces and glass chandeliers alike. What could be more thrilling than dancing with the sea all around us?

The Rooms were very full and even though I searched the place looking for a glimpse of Lieutenant Austen, I knew he was not there yet. I seemed to possess a sixth sense when Charles was around; the air seemed to vibrate differently when he was in the room. I would have to be patient and pull myself together for fear of betraying my emotions to everyone. Conscious that word had got around about our arrival in Lyme, it was evident that our party was the object of much interest as knowing expressions and cognizant looks were exchanged amongst the local gentry and it wasn't long before those acquainted with our host made their presence known. We were introduced to the Barnwells, the Crawfords and the Suttons, all deemed as families of quality by Mr Elliot and Mr Glanville. After their stiff formality, it was lovely to see Miss Rockingham appear with her bright smile and easy chatter. She was with her brother who was immediately introduced and proved to be as welcoming as his sister.

'I believe we have a mutual acquaintance, Miss Elliot,' Doctor Rockingham remarked. 'It is such a pleasure to meet you at last and to know that our friend Miss Austen is well. We were hoping to see her this summer. Have you received any word that she is to come to Lyme again?'

'Her brother is here, Doctor Rockingham, and is hoping to secure accommodation for his family in Dawlish, I understand. I know Jane is keen to come to Lyme once more; her memories of the place are all happy ones.'

'My sister and I will be more than delighted to see her, Miss Elliot, but whether or not we shall have that pleasure, I hope you will honour us with a visit again soon.'

I assured them that I would. It was impossible not to warm to the doctor and his sister who were friendly and kind, quite unlike any of the other people I had met so far in Lyme. When Doctor Rockingham smiled, his eyes lit up his handsome face. If only he had someone to make him happy, I thought, he'd be a changed man.

Before we had been there a quarter of an hour, I had invitations to dance from two or three young men who were introduced. I was relieved that our host would be forced to open the ball with Emma as a consequence, but disappointed that Lieutenant Austen was not there to ask me to dance. Just as I was beginning to give up hope of him ever making an appearance and as the little orchestra were tuning up their violins, the door opened. Charles Austen entered the room, along with two other people who looked very familiar.

Chapter 33

'That's the gentleman and lady we saw that time on the Cobb,' exclaimed Marianne, as everyone stopped to stare at the people who had just walked in. 'I can quite easily see why you were taken aback. There is such a similarity between them, that I confess, Sophia; I am not at all surprised you were in shock. He could be none other than Lieutenant Austen's brother, do you see?'

I could see very easily. Different in looks and manner, yet, there was no doubt that they came from the same family. Both had the same wavy, chestnut hair that framed their handsome faces in dark curls and the same hazel eyes, though perhaps in Mr Austen's brother they reminded me more of Jane in their clarity. There was a look about him that reminded me very much of his sister. He had the same sensitive appearance; the same intelligent look. His lady smiled, as her eyes darted at anyone who glanced her way. She was an elfin beauty. Delicate, yet exotic in style, like a jewelled bird stolen from a foreign land, she was swathed in a silken gown that flattered her tiny figure complimenting her pale complexion. As I stared, quite entranced with the pleasure of looking at her, I knew I was being watched. I only had to move my head very slightly to see

Charles and to be aware of his beautiful, dark eyes. He bowed, his expression giving away little emotion. I felt the intensity of his gaze. So much so, that the spell was broken only by my own reticence to return the expression that I knew I had not misread.

'Who are those people?' I heard Mr Sutton ask Mr Barnwell who were standing a little apart from us.

'Irish, I daresay, by their manners,' answered Mr Barnwell, 'just fit to be quality in Lyme.'

Mr Glanville butted in. 'On the contrary, they're nobody worth knowing. I recognize the taller gentleman from Bath, but I believe he is a sailor, no one of any rank worth our consideration.'

'But the other gentleman,' added Mr Sutton, 'and more particularly his lady have quite an air about them.'

'Now, she is somebody worth our attention,' declared Mr Crawford, turning at their words and joining in, 'for not only is she very easy on the eye, gentlemen, but Mrs Crawford's been telling me she is a French countess! Or, at least she was before her first husband had his head chopped off. Her new husband is a banker, I believe. They are passing through, staying at the Three Cups Inn, I understand, before heading back to their London home.'

I hated the way they talked about Charles, his brother and his wife. I wanted to tell them to stop being so rude. I would have liked to tell them everything about these truly worthy brothers who had not been handed money and riches on a plate, and of how they had more daring, wit, and intelligence than the lot of them put together, but, of course, I couldn't. I wasn't even sure if Charles and I would have a chance to speak on our own. I didn't know anyone that would make it possible for us to meet and talk, let alone dance with one another. We would have to be introduced all over again and I couldn't see any of the gentlemen in my party making that a possibility.

But then, very luckily, Mrs Crawford insisted upon introducing Mr Henry Austen, his wife and Charles to us all. Thankfully, Mrs Randall was her usual gracious self insisting that she was already well acquainted with Lieutenant Austen, his sisters and parents, and maintained it was a pleasure to meet other family members. I'm not sure her words were spoken with true sincerity. I had a feeling that she was aware of my growing affection for Charles Austen and I knew in which direction her hopes for me were going. The fact that we had not acknowledged them in any way was swept aside, brushed away by the polite conventions of conversation. Charles did not speak to me immediately. He hung on the fringes of the circle letting his sister-in-law do the talking. Mrs Eliza Austen knew she had seen me before, she said, though I pretended that I could not remember any occasion of our ever having met.

'I cannot recall,' Mrs Austen said, a frown wrinkling between the dark brows that arched above ebony eyes, 'but I know your face so well. Was it at Tunbridge Wells, or perhaps I knew you in India, Miss Elliot?'

She reached out to touch my arm and her scent, an exquisite pot-pourri of fragrances, sandalwood, jasmine, and attar of roses, perfumed the air in an invisible cloud wafting from her dainty, white kid glove. I shook my head, my cheeks burning with shame. How could I possibly remind her that I'd almost chased her off the end of the harbour wall and that the reason she recognized me was because I'd made such a fool of myself? It was left to Marianne to enlighten her. She spoke out before I could stop her.

'We glimpsed one another on the end of the Cobb, Mrs Austen. My sister thought at first that your husband was the brother she had met in Bath.'

I could have died on the spot.

Mrs Eliza Austen looked at me carefully and then I saw her glance at Charles who seemed to shrink even more readily from our company. A smile passed over her lips and her eyes twinkled as she studied my face. She made no further comment, but merely nodded as if enjoying some private joke.

'Do you enjoy dancing, Miss Elliot?' she asked a moment later.

'Yes, I must admit, it is one of my favourite pastimes,' I

answered truthfully.

'Charles, did you hear? Miss Elliot enjoys dancing as well as you do!'

Charles beamed with a smile that reached his dark eyes. 'Then, I hope, Miss Elliot, that you will save a dance for me. I earnestly trust that I am not too late in my request.'

Before I could answer, Mr Henry Austen spoke to me. 'Miss Elliot, am I to understand that you are the young lady who took pity on my brother in Bath? That you not only danced with him, but that you conversed with him on more than one occasion?'

I could see that he was teasing me, and was struck by the similarity in their sense of humour. I was also secretly pleased that he seemed to know so much because it meant that Charles had spoken about me.

'I have danced with your brother before, it is true,' I answered, hardly able to stop from breaking into a laugh, 'and have conversed with him on more than one occasion.'

Henry Austen nodded sagely. 'I knew it! Then, I beg you do not refuse him. Think of me, and my poor, dear wife who will have to live with the remnants of a broken man if you do.'

I could only smile, turning from one brother to the other. 'No, I shall not refuse and no, Lieutenant Austen, you are not too late. I have three dances marked and then I am free to dance with you if you wish.'

Charles lowered his voice inclining his head towards me. 'I do wish, Miss Elliot, very much.'

The tuning up of instruments started then, the violins and cello filling the room with a sound that brought everyone to their feet if they were sitting or had them marching across the space to find their partners. We were separated as the Crawford's youngest son came to find me, Emma and Mr Glanville stepping out leaving Marianne and Mrs Randall to watch from the side.

Mr Crawford could not dance. He would keep stepping on my toes or leading me the wrong way and it was awful to know that Charles was watching our progress down the room. It didn't seem to matter what I did to help him; it only seemed to make him worse. My next partners were little better and it was proving more and more difficult to show that I didn't mind in the least, nor that I was impatient to dance with someone else.

At last Charles came to claim me and I couldn't have cared if the whole room saw how happy I was to be with him. Everything was as easy as before and happiness was more than just the pleasure of dancing with him again. It flooded every pore of my being, every feeling. Neither of us spoke at first. I couldn't know if Charles felt the same, but for me it was enough to be together. I felt timid in his larger than life presence and so aware that I might say something that would reveal my deepest feelings.

'I have not had a chance to thank you for the beautiful roses you sent me,' I said at last. 'That was so kind, and brought me such happiness at a time when I was feeling particularly sad.'

'I hoped they would cheer you. I wished … ' He paused before speaking again. 'And do you stay in Lyme long?'

'We are here for at least a further week and then I believe we are to travel into Wales, to Tenby, which I must admit feels as far away as the furthest country in the world. I do not wish to think of it, I confess.'

'We will not mention it again, I promise. My plans are slightly changed, I am glad to say. I shall be staying for another two days at least and with all due blessings from my mother who is not so anxious to leave Bath as I first thought. I confess; I did not expect to meet my brother and his wife here. I knew they'd been staying with friends in Dorsetshire, but it was a complete surprise to see them in Lyme, although perhaps understandable in the circumstances. It has been a very distressing year for my sister-in-law, Eliza. Her boy, Hastings, succumbed to a fatal illness after many years of poor health and naturally, Eliza was bereft. Henry does all that he can to cheer her and thought a short spell by the sea would lift her spirits before going home to London.'

'Oh, I'm so very sorry to hear of it. How Mrs Austen must have suffered. What a pity it is that your family cannot also be here to see them. I, myself, am disappointed to hear that Miss Jane will not be coming. I should so much have enjoyed seeing her again and Miss Austen too, of course.'

'Unfortunately, Henry and Eliza will be gone home before the rest of my family make their journey here. I do not know why, but my mother declared a reluctance to return to this part of the coast again. I remember she particularly enjoyed Sidmouth last year, but when I suggested that they hasten down to meet us here, she declared she did not want to come just yet. There were several reasons suggested, but it all seems rather strange. Still, that's the way of my mother. If I don't know her now after all these years, I don't know when I will!'

I had a feeling that I knew why Mrs Austen was reticent to come to Lyme and Sidmouth suspecting she knew something about Jane's gentleman friend or disapproved of him, but I said nothing. 'Well, I am very glad that you are here.'

Charles smiled into my eyes. 'And so am I. To be here dancing with you again is my delight. I hope we shall be able to meet tomorrow.'

I smiled back and declared my wishes to be the same, although in my heart I couldn't see how a meeting would take place. If Charles were to call, I didn't imagine I'd be permitted to see him let alone be allowed to accompany him anywhere even if his brother and sister were chaperoning. It was an impossible situation.

I'd known before the evening started that at some time or other Mr Glanville would be bound to ask me to dance and he stepped in like he'd done once before, as soon as my dance with Charles had finished, even before we had an opportunity to speak further. I hoped Charles would ask me to dance again, but Mr Glanville didn't give him a chance. Hooking his hand beneath my elbow he steered me towards the dance floor, simultaneously cutting Charles as he did so.

'My dear, Miss Sophia, I have not had a chance to speak to you all evening, you have been otherwise engaged. I never saw a young lady so much in demand.' He stepped back to look over me more intently with an expression to make me shiver with revulsion, his eyes devouring me. 'Well, it is no surprise that you are causing such a stir amongst my neighbours, for Lyme rarely witnesses such beauty, such charm!'

'Oh, sir, you flatter me too much.'

'I did not have the pleasure of being in Bath for so long,' he replied, 'without hearing of Miss Sophia Elliot's charms talked of in every drawing room. I am conscious that her modesty denies a true awareness of half her attributes and accomplishments.'

'If I have any attributes or accomplishments, I have to thank my sister Emma who has nurtured any talents I might possess. See, she is over there dancing with Mr Sutton. Her poise and beauty are second to none. Look, watch her dancing. She is so graceful and as fine a dancer as you will see in any ballroom.'

'With respect, it is true that Miss Elliot is an accomplished young woman who has her share of beauty. But, I would not be telling the truth if I did not add that you, my dear, are even more enchanting. I must confess, I find your effortless charm and your unassuming manners quite unsurpassed. You are the more prized, my dear, because you are such an innocent. So unaware of your own attractions, you are the more captivating to me because you are oblivious to your beauty with your flushed cheeks unused to praise and your timid smile.'

I didn't know what to say. Besides not recognizing myself in this description, I couldn't think how on earth I was going to alter his opinion. The more I tried to repel his advances, the keener he appeared to be. I protested again at such flattery, but he would hear no more.

'If I could, I would spend each and every day telling you about the pleasure being in your company brings.'

I couldn't keep silent any longer. 'But, you know nothing about me and I can assure you, that what you think is very far from the truth.'

'I hope to know you better very soon. We have time on our

side, Miss Elliot. Besides, I am not an insensitive man generally unaware of the workings of the heart. I have seen the way Lieutenant Austen regards you. Do not pretend that you know nothing of that gentleman's inclinations.'

I was not expecting that. I felt myself blush as he stared at me.

'He may have a promising career ahead of him, but it will be a long time before he makes enough money to support himself, let alone marry. Do not be taken in by him. He has no intention of offering for you. As far as he is concerned, you are a summer flirtation, a gullible young girl who can be easily manipulated. I say this out of concern for you. Do not be foolish, Miss Elliot, I can offer you so much more.'

My head was pounding. I began to shake my head. Although I wanted to speak, the words wouldn't come out of my mouth. I had no power over my voice, I stood there mute and accepting, which was the most frightening feeling of all.

'I intend to speak to your father very soon, Miss Sophia,' he said. I noticed the distinction he was giving to my name as if we were engaged already. 'I hope that you will come round and understand, that not only will it be in your best interests to accept a proposal of marriage from me, but that you will be doing your duty to your family, as is expected. I know I can make you a very happy woman and that you will come to love me as I do you.'

Again, my lips would not move. I was not feeling at all like myself, and was sure my quiet acceptance would make him think that I was perfectly happy with his proposition.

'Do not worry, my dear, I shall look after you very well and I know, you will make me a very happy man.'

I didn't want to listen to him, but there was no means of escape. I felt like a tiny bird trapped in a gilded cage and imagined that was exactly how I would feel forever if Mr Glanville got his way. I knew that if my father half suspected his intentions there would be no escape, no reprieve. As panic surged inside me, my emotions ebbed and flowed, like the waves I could hear crashing down on the beach below, sucking the life and hope out of my very soul.

I became aware of another figure standing nearby bringing with him an air of calm to pacify the quiet rage growing inside me. Charles, as tall and physically imposing as ever, had a gentleness of spirit. He stood at my side and without saying a word made me feel instantly better. His brother Henry and his wife followed just a little behind him. Mrs Austen immediately commandeered Mr Glanville and I could see how easily her playful manner and quick wit worked on him. I wondered if her husband minded her flirtatious ways with other gentlemen, but he looked as if he were rather used to it. In five minutes, she had praised and teased, flirted and cajoled my cousin into thinking that the invitation he now gave was an idea all of his own.

'A picnic at Nelson House on the morrow, Mrs Austen. Would that satisfy your notion of an entertainment here in Lyme? I am afraid we are not so fashionable as at Tunbridge Wells, but we know how to enjoy ourselves. Please tell me that you are not engaged for other pursuits.'

'We are not engaged, Mr Glanville,' she declared excitedly, turning to her husband in anticipation. 'We shall be delighted to accept your very kind invitation.' And had I just seen her wink at her brother-in-law as her back was turned to the gentleman so keen to make her acquaintance?

'Charles,' she said, breaking into a pretty smile, 'take Miss Elliot for another dance whilst we finalize arrangements. Tell me, Mr Glanville, is Nelson House as handsome as its owner?'

Eliza Austen was outrageous, but I loved her for it. I couldn't help thinking that she had intended the evening to go just this way, that she already knew that Charles wanted to dance with me again and that we could only be together if she engineered it. I worried about what my father would think of it all, but I noticed how quickly Mrs Austen managed to draw him into the conversation. As Charles took me out onto the dance floor, I could see our cousin hanging on her every word. I had no doubt that her rank had won him over, not to mention her dazzling beauty and captivating ways.

Chapter 34

The Austen's carriage rolled along the gravel sweep at noon. I had been watching from the drawing room that gave such a fine view across the town and to the sea that looked like a strip of violet ribbon in the distance. Grey clouds billowed out across the water like a magnificent sail threatening rain and I wondered if the picnic might have to be cancelled. Everyone was gathered to await our guests. Emma had seated herself next to Mr Glanville on a chaise longue, my father and Mrs Randall sat at opposite ends of the room, whilst Marianne could not decide where to be comfortable. One moment she sat beside Mrs Randall, the next minute she came bounding over to the window impatient for any movement below. The second she saw the carriage door open she cried out and there was a general bustle as everyone adjusted their cuffs, their gowns and patted their hair in anticipation of the expected company.

The coachman leapt off his perch to let down the steps. I saw Eliza Austen first, a picture in blue striped silk with a straw bonnet beribboned in the same fabric, followed by her husband, and lastly, the person I most wished to see. Charles glanced up at the window and grinned. I waved and my heart turned a somersault when he waved back.

My father and Mr Glanville jumped to their feet as Eliza Austen made her entrance, pausing a little at the door for most impact. The effect she had on the gentlemen was astonishing and it was all I could do not to laugh as they bowed and preened, fawning over her every word.

A chair nearest to Mr Glanville and Emma was fetched for Mrs Austen who immediately started a conversation with them. Henry Austen came to stand with Charles, Mrs Randall and myself at the other end. I heard our host ask how long the Austens were to be in Lyme.

'Oh, only for another day, Mr Glanville,' Mrs Austen replied. 'Unfortunately, my husband has business in town that must be returned to, and it is impossible to spare any further time. More is the pity, as I am inclined for some travel abroad.'

'But where should you go, Mrs Austen?' Mr Glanville ventured. 'I do not think it safe to be travelling on the continent just yet.'

Eliza Austen patted his arm. 'Please do not concern yourself, sir. I am a long seasoned traveller and I have little fear, especially of those whom I regard quite as my countrymen. I long to return to France where I was first married and, indeed, if ever my property is to be reclaimed, I must go. I do not fear old Boney and neither does Mr Austen. Do you, my dear?'

Personally, I felt Mr Austen did not look quite as convinced as his wife, but he smiled and looked at her with such an expression of adoration, he looked as if he would do anything she asked. They were an unusual couple. He was as handsome as she was beautiful, but I was sure he was much younger than she and I felt most curious about their relationship.

My father spoke up. 'You still have a property in France? Is it not secure?'

Eliza's face saddened and she twisted the mourning ring on her finger. 'Sadly, my first husband, the Comte de Feuillide, was taken from our home never to return. He insisted that I leave France for my sake and that of our poor child, Hastings, who has since been so cruelly taken from us all. I pray that he knows his father once more, now that they are together in heaven. Until the present time, I have not been able to think about the possibility of returning, but with the Peace, I hope very much to claim back our land. The packet boat is sailing once more between Calais and Dover, and I will never be happy until I have seen for myself what has happened.'

'But, is it safe?' asked Mr Glanville. 'Will you not suffer any danger?'

'I believe an amnesty has been declared for all the old families and if we pay our respects to Madame Josephine, we shall escape the effects of Madame Guillotine!' Eliza Austen laughed, a sound that tinkled like a little bell in contrast to the sombre mood of the moment before. 'A little flattery and a lot of bribery will no doubt help my cause. Besides, I long to go to Paris and see all the latest fashions.'

'I would love to go to Paris,' Emma cried. 'I have seen pictures in the monthly magazine. All the women look like Greek goddesses in clinging muslins.'

'Mr Glanville must take you there when you are married,' Mrs Austen continued, without any hint of the embarrassment she might be causing. 'Forgive me, but I could not help noticing how perfectly delicious you appear together sitting side by side on a loveseat. Miss Elliot blushes and you, sir, are looking most bashful. But, everyone loves the thought of a summer wedding and I am certain you will not disappoint us. Besides, the whole town is talking of nothing else!'

Emma beamed and I saw her try to catch Mr Glanville's eye, though I noticed his eyes resting once more upon Eliza Austen. We were all paused to hear his reply, when the room darkened suddenly and the first spots of rain came pattering against the glass of the windows.

Marianne got up to view the scene outside. 'Oh, no, our picnic will be ruined. Whatever shall we do now?'

Our host seemed relieved to have an excuse to consider the situation. He marched over to the window to tell us what we could already plainly see. The rain was coming down steadily. Charles and I were the only people who did not join him. We stood very still, side by side, his arm brushing mine. I felt his eyes on my face, but his nearness was having such an effect on me, I couldn't look up straight away. When I did, his eyes connected with mine striking like the forks of lightning that were crackling in the skies outside. I was only conscious of them and everything and everyone else seemed to fade into insignificance. So much so, that I began to wonder if I was slipping through time once more. I swayed. Charles caught my arm. I felt warm fingers cup my elbow and his looks were so tender, I melted inside.

Thunder rumbled in the distance and the rain came down in torrents. Mr Glanville turned to us all. 'Do not worry, my friends. I have a solution on this wet day. In anticipation, I instructed my staff to serve a cold collation in the Chinese conservatory. Let us not delay a moment longer, we will picnic whatever the weather. Mrs Austen, I hope you will advise me. The conservatory is decorated in the style favoured by the Prince of Wales, you know, and I do not yet think I have quite furnished it with objets d'art enough!'

We followed him downstairs, the conversations of a moment ago replaced by other trivial talk. We passed along a winding corridor toward the back of the house where the walls blossomed with crimson peonies and chrysanthemums and where golden bells and painted fretwork vied with roaring dragon's heads which writhed in the ceiling above, eyes wild and tongues lashing. We soon arrived at a scene from a Chinese fairy tale. The conservatory, a vast glass room was filled with hothouse flora, japanned cabinets, pagodas and bamboo boxes. A series of mirrored panels between the windows added to the sense of theatrical illusion with reflections repeating again and again like the Chinese clock on the table chiming the hour. What seemed to be a flock of faux nightingales in a myriad of gilded cages were strung up in the roof, along with tasselled lanterns of blue, pink and violet glass, painted with mandarins, butterflies and lotus flowers, all hanging on varying lengths of tinted ribbon. The room glowed with colour and soft candlelight in contrast to the misty gloom outside. At one end was a table groaning with cold chicken, pastries, sweetmeats and ices, whilst at the other stood several footmen bearing trays of champagne filled crystal and a band of musicians who started to play as we entered.

I was sure I'd seen Eliza Austen roll her eyes at Charles and smirk at Henry, but she declared that she'd never seen such perfection and immediately asked who had been responsible for the room's decoration. Mr Glanville, unable to stop himself from boasting, declared that he had taken advice from the Prince's own man and though he did not like to appear vain, added that he was very proud of his own additions particularly with reference to the dragon's heads out in the corridor.

There were elements of the room that I liked, but it seemed a little incongruous set against a backdrop of English landscape with views of the sea looking steel grey and unforgiving in the cold wet of the afternoon. We sat down at the table. I had not expected to be seated near enough to Charles to talk to him but contented myself with the occasional glance. I caught Mrs Austen looking at us once and smiling that secret smile of hers before turning again to Mr Glanville as if she were paying him undivided attention. Her efforts seemed to be concentrated between him and my father and, whenever she could, Mrs Randall was drawn into the conversation. Eliza proved she could talk on any subject. I saw Mrs Randall smile with approval as they discussed the work of Samuel Richardson.

Henry Austen was seated next to me. I couldn't help thinking of Jane when he turned with an expression so like hers.

'My sister Jane would be very envious of my visit here today,' he began. 'Though my mother has taken it into her head to go to Dawlish this year, I know Jane is anxious to see both you and Lyme again. She wrote to tell Eliza of your acquaintance in Bath and that is how I first discovered that you danced with my brother at the Assembly Rooms.'

I felt a bit disappointed. I was rather hoping that Charles might have told Henry himself. It must have shown for Mr Austen quickly added, 'Charles has told me since about the time you have spent together, of course.'

I felt myself blushing; the fact that he'd read me so easily was shameful. I asked after Jane.

'Her letters are cheerful and I think she is in reasonable good health, yet, I know my sister's spirits are not as they should be. It will be an excellent thing if my sisters can come and visit you in Lyme. They do not spend enough time in the company of people their own age and if I am honest, Miss Elliot, I do not think I will be talking too much out of turn if I say that Jane, in particular, finds some of the foibles of the society with which they are presently surrounded more than a little challenging. Of course, as two single ladies, there is little chance for my sisters to escape and follow their own pursuits.'

'I understand that Jane is a writer.'

Henry's eyes lit up. 'Do you know, Miss Elliot, I am very proud of my little sister? I think one day she will be a very fine author if she ever gets a chance to pursue her craft. I do not think she is "scribbling" much, as she calls it, at the moment, but one day I am certain that time and talent will collide.'

'I am sure it will and to have such encouragement and kindness from you would mean everything to Miss Austen,' I said and all at once, a memory from the past came to me with such a jolt that my reflection over the way in a slither of mirrored glass between windows displaying a vast landscape open to the sky made me sit up to ask a hundred questions. I didn't recognize myself. The room was full of strangers, and when I looked across the table at Charles I could see someone else. I couldn't think who it could be although seeing him made me feel happy. I felt warmth, a memory that I recognized as a good one. I saw him smile and dark curls tumble over his face as he picked up a knife. I saw the line of his throat as he threw back his head and laughed. The smell of his cologne was sharp and fragrant as if he was in the room. The present flowed around me like the sea swirling up around my toes sucking pebbles and the past away. The clouds through the window passed over to reveal strong patches of blue and the view through windows I no longer recognized looked brighter, the sea changing to a ribbon of sparkling water, the sun flashing on its surface with spots of silver like sequin spangles turning in the light. A seagull called overhead. Life and time stood frozen for a moment. I caught my breath. My body drifted out to sea to dance on the crest of a wave and then the seagull called again.

'Are you quite well, Miss Elliot?' Henry Austen's expression was etched with alarm. The last thing I saw was Charles jumping out of his chair and round to my seat as I slumped forward.

I don't know quite what happened, I suppose it must have been some sort of fainting fit, though as someone who is normally far too robust to do any such thing, I must admit that I denied anything of the sort. I had never fainted in my life before only experiencing giddiness when time travelling, which I supposed would be natural enough. I don't know what caused it or whether I'd started falling backwards through time once more, but the pull was enough to remind me that I really didn't belong there and that these people were relative strangers to me. I knew I was not meant to be in their time and the grip of panic that made my stomach lurch with fear, filled me with dread. I'd slipped away for a moment like a soul freed from its earthly ties, but like one who knows its life is not yet up binds itself to the body once more.

When I came to, Eliza Austen was holding a phial of hartshorn salts under my nose and Mrs Randall was rubbing my hand between both of her own with motherly care. I could no longer recall the details of what had happened. Everything seemed as it had before, with one exception. The rain and the dark clouds were blown right away. There was blue sky as far as the eye could see so that it was impossible to see where the sea ended and the sky began.

'I think what we all need is a walk down to the sea to blow the cobwebs away,' announced Mrs Randall, 'that is, if you feel strong enough, Sophia.'

'Yes, I should enjoy a walk,' I answered, glad that we would be doing something to take the attention away from me, 'and it would be a pity not to enjoy the sunshine now the rain has passed.'

Everyone agreed there could be nothing better than a walk out in sunshine and fresh air. The party that left Nelson House a quarter of an hour later were in high spirits to match the breeze that whipped at our gowns and coats alike hurrying us down the hill past the shops and the library and almost into the water's edge when we got to the bottom of Broad Street. Eliza took Mr Glanville's arm on one side and encouraged Emma to take the other, the former saying that she wished their host to give her a conducted tour of Lyme, as she was sure no one else could be as expert. Mr Elliot took Mrs Randall's arm and so Henry and Marianne, Charles and I, fell into step behind. We turned onto The Walk to join the promenaders who appeared at the first sight of the sun. Marianne, who had insisted on bringing her sketchbook and watercolour box protested at the idea of going any further.

'I do not want to go up on the Cobb again,' she declared. 'I was nearly blown away last time. I want to stay here and paint on the sands.'

'I'll stay with her,' I said immediately, 'we'll be quite safe.'

Before anyone could say another thing, Eliza Austen spoke out. 'Charles, you stay and mind the Miss Elliots. You know, he is quite a talented artist, Miss Marianne, I am sure he will make himself useful to you.' She turned to Mr Glanville. 'I am longing for you to show me the Cobb. I know you will keep us from falling over the edge, and Miss Elliot, we must insist that our companion holds us very tightly. Besides, I simply cannot wait to hear your tales of the sea as you promised. Tell me, are the stories I have heard, about pirates and smugglers in these parts, true?'

I wished to fling my arms about Eliza's neck and hug her. Charles and I would be on our own, or almost by ourselves with a chance to talk much more freely, which seemed heaven-sent. And I knew she had seen the opportunity and forced the situation. I was sure she had been on the Cobb many times before, but she'd made

Mr Glanville play right into her hands. As they all walked away, the only person who seemed to give us a second look was Mrs Randall. I knew she was watching when Charles took my hand to lead me down the steps.

'Mrs Austen said you can paint,' cried Marianne. 'Is it true? Can you really paint with watercolours?'

'I do not claim to be a professional, though it has been said that I have a certain proficiency with a paintbrush,' answered Charles as we made our way across the sands to a part of the beach where rocks and stones made progress slow. 'I like to draw and paint when I'm on board ship. It helps to pass the time away. He bent to pick up a stone and handed it to her. 'Here, Marianne, what do you think of this fossil?'

Marianne examined the ammonite, carved and coiled into a perfect spiral. 'May I keep it?' she asked, looking up at him and brushing a piece of stray hair from her eyes. 'And will I be able to find one myself, do you think?'

'I'm sure you shall. I'll take care of your painting things whilst you look,' Charles persuaded her, 'but don't stray too far.'

It was nothing short of a miracle, the way he dealt with Marianne. With him, she turned into the delightful girl I could see she had the potential to be. He brought out the best in her. Without a single complaint, she roamed around the area collecting any stone or piece of rock she found interesting, putting them into her pockets or running back enthusiastically to show us her spoils.

'Will you paint the landscape?' I asked Charles as we walked companionably along.

'I could if you wished me to, though I have another idea in mind.' He looked rather secretive, but the flicker of a smile played around his mouth.

'Am I allowed to ask what you are going to paint?'

'You may, though I must yet secure your permission before I venture forth.'

'I don't know what you are about, Lieutenant Austen. You are such a tease.'

'I wish to paint you with your permission. May I capture those dancing eyes for posterity, Miss Elliot?'

He was looking at me again with intense, dark looks and I felt another tug on my heart as I nodded, too overcome to speak. More than anything, I longed for him to paint me.

Charles led me swiftly to a suitable rock giving his instructions, directing my every move and wasn't entirely satisfied straight away. He wanted me to sit very slightly to one side, my hands folded and my feet crossed at the ankle in the sand.

'Forgive me, Miss Elliot, but your hands ...'

He took them in his own. His fingers laced with mine for just an exquisite second before he placed them in my lap.

'The composition is extraordinary,' he shouted, taking up his stance several feet away and training his pencil in my direction. 'Miss Elliot, you were meant to sit in a seascape for eternity. Such beauty and sublimity combined.'

I couldn't tell if he was teasing me in his usual way and he was looking at me so intently, I could only look at my surroundings. 'Oh, the view is quite charming, I agree,' I replied. 'Lyme has forever stolen my heart and still more this lovely bay makes it the happiest spot for watching the flow of the tide. I could never tire of this prospect.'

'I am in complete agreement, Miss Elliot,' said Charles, his eyes slowly travelling from the top of my head to my toes. 'This is a view that would never fatigue me. I could gaze at it forever.'

I felt he wasn't talking about the landscape and he said it with such meaning that I could only draw one conclusion, though Mr Glanville's words came back to me just then. I remembered that he'd warned me that Lieutenant Austen only considered me as a summer flirtation. But, I could not and did not want to believe that. Everything Charles said and did was done with sincerity, I would have staked my life on it. Mr Glanville had his own reasons for making such accusations, but I didn't want to think about him now. I was enjoying this sense of freedom and the feeling that I was admired for myself alone. It was impossible not to laugh out loud and Charles saw me return his generous smile with one of my own. When he'd finished, he was as furtive as ever. I wanted to see the painting, but he wouldn't let me. Marianne looked at it with approval before skipping away again with a pocket bulging with fossils, stones and shells. I saw him turn the page. He said he was just signing his name and that he would make a present of the painting when the time was right. We could see the others returning now and as Henry came along in advance to warn us of their coming, I reflected on the fact that there was only one more day for us to be together. Although the sky was still clear, I felt as if the world was grey with cloud again. I climbed the hill with Charles walking at my side. Our sombre mood enveloped us in gloom like the earlier mist that had hung over the cliff tops, unwilling to be banished by the setting sun, which gleamed crimson in the fading light.

Chapter 35

The following morning, I awoke early with thoughts of Charles in my head as soon as my eyes opened. I was so excited at the thought of seeing him and though I realized we didn't have much time left, I knew I should be grateful simply for the chance of spending another day with him. When I heard the carriage downstairs, I leapt to the window without a care for who might see. But I was to be disappointed. It wasn't Charles who stepped out from the carriage, but his brother Henry and the beautiful Eliza. It was so hard to hide my feelings. Why hadn't he come with them, I wondered?

Mr and Mrs Austen were calling to pay their respects, to thank Mr Glanville for the wonderful day they had enjoyed together and to issue an invitation. They wished us all to join them at the Three Cups Inn in the evening as they were leaving the following day.

'Please, gentlemen, I implore you not to break my heart. Parting from dear friends is always so difficult and you will make my happiness complete if you will only spend our last evening in Lyme in the company of my husband and myself. Mrs Randall, I beg you will join us for some supper and cards.'

Eliza Austen looked like a winsome child with her playful

eyes and fine, arched brows raised coquettishly towards the gentlemen, whilst simultaneously managing to bestow her sweetest smile upon the ladies. It was impossible not to love her and I could see how easily she must have captured Henry Austen's heart. She charmed everyone.

'If I cannot convince you by myself alone,' she went on before anyone had a chance to answer, 'I will add that there is a great inducement, a little concert that I am sure you will all enjoy. We have met a very interesting young lady who is staying at the Three Cups. She is a travelling soprano ... a Miss Fanny Howells, though I can vouch for the fact that her voice is most excellent and not as one might think from her unfortunate name.'

Everyone laughed and Eliza smiled with appreciation that we'd all enjoyed her joke. 'By great demand, she is to perform this evening with an accompaniment of pianoforte and harp. Now, tell me, can you think of anything more delightful?'

Mr Glanville readily answered. 'Dear Madam, with such inducements, it is nay impossible to refuse. I am sure we shall all be delighted to accept your most kind invitation.'

With the evening arrangements settled, the Austens rose to leave. Eliza looked at me across the room and smiled. 'Miss Sophia, I simply must beg your company for the rest of the morning. Do you think you could oblige me? I very much need your advice on a small matter that I know will interest you. May she accompany me to our carriage, Mrs Randall? I promise I shall return her later.'

'May I go, please?' I begged.

She couldn't really refuse me.

I followed Mrs Austen out of the room almost skipping with pleasure. Although I wasn't entirely certain, I wondered if she had something to tell me about Charles. When we reached the carriage, to my great surprise, the door opened and there was someone I'd not expected to see.

'Miss Austen!' I cried with delight.

Jane beamed and grasping my arm in her customary way

invited me to take a seat. 'Forgive me for this clandestine behaviour, but I have not been in Lyme for long and I confess I wished to surprise you. We arrived in Dawlish early this morning, and I persuaded Henry to come and fetch me. I could not wait to see how you like Lyme and I have not had a chance to talk to you for so long. I hope you will forgive me for not calling on your family.'

'Well, the delight is all mine, Miss Austen, and there is nothing to forgive. I'm so glad to see you, I did wonder if we might just miss one another altogether.'

Eliza Austen settled herself into the carriage on the other side, all the while chatting about the arrangements she was making for the evening.

'Are you coming back to the inn, Jane?' her brother asked as the carriage bowled away.

'If I know Jane,' Mrs Austen broke in, 'she'll be wanting Miss Elliot to go scrambling over rocks with her, or clambering on the Cobb.'

'You know me too well, dearest Eliza,' said Jane, leaning over to squeeze her scented glove. 'What do you say, Miss Elliot? Shall we walk?'

The carriage set us down outside the inn at the bottom of the hill. Henry and Eliza waved us off and Jane took my arm as we turned towards the steps leading down to the sands. 'I hope you do not mind my very devious methods to get you on your own, Miss Elliot, but I wanted so much to talk to you. I've missed our conversations. You went away when I most needed a friend.'

'Oh, my dear, Miss Austen, how I have needed to talk to you too, I have so much to tell you about Mr Glanville! But, I see from your expression that you look most troubled. Is there anything the matter?'

'My brother has a request that he would never dare to ask you himself. Forgive me, Miss Elliot, but he wishes to know if what he has heard in the town is correct. Does Mr Glanville pay his addresses to you? Are you in love with him?'

I laughed aloud, and saw her smile. 'Miss Austen, I could never love a man like him and with all due thanks to your sister-in-law, I feel I might be spared the fate I was beginning to think I would not escape. With luck, he will marry my sister yet.'

'I am so pleased to hear it and I know that this news can only delight Charles.' I hardly dared think about what she might mean, but my heart responded with a quicker beat. Jane paused, but she still looked very thoughtful.

'What is it, my friend? You look most upset.'

'Miss Elliot, when you went away I realized I might never see you again or have a chance to explain. You must have thought me very remiss. I have never given you a satisfactory account for all that happened in Bath.'

'Believe me, Miss Austen, you do not need to say a word or justify anything to me. I thought that was understood.'

Jane looked out to sea. Dressed in a scarlet cloak over a white linen gown, the bright colour suited her dark chestnut hair. Tendrils of dancing curls were teased from her tam o'shanter by the breeze, quivering like the egret feathers of the military cockade on her hat. I couldn't take my eyes off the locket she wore round her neck on a long gold chain. I didn't mean to stare, but I knew I'd seen it before. I had a memory of seeing it in a painting, one of Jane as a girl. Octagonal in shape, the miniature it had contained in the portrait was now hidden from view, closed over with a circle of gold.

Jane saw me staring, her hand reaching instinctively to cover the locket. 'May I ask, are you in love with my brother Charles?'

I was completely taken aback at such a direct question, and I hesitated. I didn't know if I wanted to admit it to myself, let alone anyone else, but I did want to tell Jane the truth.

'I will speak from my heart. Yes, I believe I am in love with him, Miss Austen.'

'I do not mean to ask out of curiosity, but if you are in love with him, as I think he is with you, I know this will help you to understand my situation.' She paused to look searchingly into my eyes. 'You are so different from people I meet ordinarily. Indeed, I suspect like me, you have something of the wild beast about you, an independent spirit that will not be tamed.'

'I think every woman has that within her which would set her free, if only she could act on her inner feelings and be true to herself.'

We'd reached the Cobb and mounting the steps felt the full force of the wind high up on the topmost level. On either side, the waves crashed relentlessly, white spray misting the air. 'Would not this spot be the very perfect place for a dramatic incident in a novel?' Jane quizzed, her eyes dancing with delight at everything around her. 'Of course, I've often found that the irony of dramatic incidents is that they happen far more quietly in real life. And with such stealth, in fact, that they subside away and disappear as quickly as the spume on the waves.'

I was conscious of a memory, stirring deep inside, which refused to surface. Jane took my arm, pulling me closer. 'I met the man you saw me with when I was just a girl: we were secretly betrothed.'

'Please, Miss Austen, I beg you. Do not make yourself unhappy. You do not have to explain to me.'

'It wasn't until I was nineteen that we really became acquainted and when acquainted we fell rapidly and deeply in love. Oh, the exquisite felicity of youthful devotion! Such a delightful period of happiness we spent together in Kent, that happy county … at least, until his family made sure we could meet no longer.'

'But, why should his family be so opposed to the match?'

'High hopes that I might come into money from my mother's side were not enough where real ambition was concerned and it became increasingly obvious that I was not their preferred choice, particularly after my Great Uncle died. He'd commissioned my portrait when I was a girl thinking that the picture would introduce me to the world as an eligible young lady, and help seal the alliance.'

I knew exactly which painting she was talking about and the

memory of seeing it at the exhibition flashed into my mind.

'So the portrait had quite a significance?'

'At least, it did to those who knew about the painting. I imagine it will never see the light of day now, but will be hidden from the world in some dusty attic.'

'But is there nothing that can be done? Surely, you are both of an age where you may follow your own hearts now.'

'The ending of my great romance is not a happy one, nor can it ever be. My own Robin Adair is a younger son – he has had to make his own way in the world, his profession taking him overseas. Time and duty conspired to keep us apart, Miss Elliot. For almost eight years we were separated, not able to see one another.'

'I cannot think how painful that must have been, to have such a situation forced on you.'

'A young man must seek his fortune and if he is beholden to his parents, he is obliged to carry out their wishes. But, even knowing our case was hopeless and that we could never be together, I could not forget him. My attachment to him was such that no one else could claim.'

'Oh, Miss Austen, women's nature is to truly love with tender feeling. Sincere affection married with steadfast constancy belongs to our disposition.'

'Too true, Miss Elliot – indeed, we cannot help ourselves. It seems a woman's lot is to love longest when existence or when hope is gone. I discovered it was not possible to recover from so strong a devotion of the heart to such a man.'

'No one could who truly loved, I'm sure, Miss Austen.'

'When he arrived back in Bath on leave last year, we found ourselves in the same circles once more.'

'Did no one suspect your partiality?'

'We were careful to hide our feelings and avoided one another in society. Nobody knew, except Cassandra. He sought me out again and again … we snatched precious moments together in the quiet of secret walks in the gardens or along the Gravel Walk whenever we could.'

I felt so sad for her, but so happy that Jane had experienced all that is so magical about being in love.

'And then we met at Lyme.'

'Where you spent a glorious time together.'

Jane nodded. 'Our feelings had not changed and I knew I could never stop loving him, even if all hope of being united was a false one.'

'But you will rally again, Miss Austen. Forgive me for being so bold, but there is time enough to be with the one you love.'

'If it were that simple, Miss Elliot. I am too much of a pragmatist to think I could make either of us truly happy, without the trappings of the life I know he and his family wish him to have. I truly believe sincerely in his regard for me, but his family desires him to make a good marriage, one that will bring in money for them all. Without their approval and help, he would not prosper. And, in any case, I have another person to consider.'

'Do you mean Cassy?'

With a nod, she added, 'I could not leave her to be solely responsible for my parents. Can you imagine a fate more cruel to such a beloved sister?'

'No, I cannot.'

'I shall never marry anyone now. I will stay with Cassandra as long as she needs me, which shall be to the end of my days. Spinsters together, Miss Elliot, and maiden aunts to be useful to our family; I am very much afraid that the Miss Austens have found their roles in life.'

Jane looked as if her heart might break. 'We met for the last time when you saw us that day. He will soon belong to another.'

'But, you cannot believe that he would give you up so easily?'

'It is done. He is engaged to be married to an heiress with a fortune and he will, no doubt, be wed in Bath.'

Lifting the chain from around her neck, Jane grasped the locket in two hands prising apart the cover with her fingers, which acted as a shield against the world. Thrusting the locket towards me, a sombre painting of an old be-wigged gentleman stared back.

'There, how do you like my beau?' she asked, with a teasing smile.

I knew this could not be the man in question. This surely was her great uncle, and the words from *Sense and Sensibility* came to me as clearly as if I'd written them myself: " ... they had not known each other a week, I believe, before you were certain that Marianne wore his picture round her neck; but it turned out to be only the miniature of our great uncle."

Jane said no more, but squeezing the edges of the locket again made the picture swing open to reveal another portrait hidden beneath. She pressed it into my hands.

'I like him very much,' I answered. As if freshly painted, the fair-haired man, captured smiling, was the same I'd seen that day in Sydney Gardens.

Handing it back, Jane's gaze shifted to the locket once more and her eyes flickered over every inch of the painted miniature as if committing the image to memory.

I could hardly bear to speak. 'It's a wonderful keepsake.'

Jane smiled ruefully and with the locket clasped in her fist, she brought her hand to her mouth. With a final kiss, I watched her raise her arm to toss the locket into the sea. The gold chain glinted in the sunlight, as the pendant flew through the air.

I gasped. But, Jane looked back at me with a grin, skillfully hooking the spinning necklace on her finger with a flick of her wrist and deftly catching the pendant. She grasped it in her hand as if she would never let it go again.

'No,' she sighed, clutching the precious jewel to her heart, 'I cannot consign such a prized possession to the waves. Yet, I do not need a picture to remind me of times past. Every single memory is locked like a precious jewel in a treasure box, deep in the recesses of my mind to be brought out and examined, held up in my mind's eye to gleam and sparkle. I cannot change what will be, but I am quite resigned. And one never knows what the future may bring. Perhaps in time I shall receive a proposal I will not be able to refuse!'

Jane laughed and as if the conversation of a moment ago had

not happened she turned to me, a twinkle in her eye.

'I am very fortunate in so many ways and not one to dwell on misery ... or guilt. Besides, I do not know if I was truly cut out for the married state. How could I write if I were a wife and mother burdened with numerous children?'

I couldn't decide if she was being sincere and I suspected that as usual Jane was doing her best to conceal her true feelings.

'It would be very difficult if not impossible, I am certain, but I feel sure, Miss Austen, that you will achieve your dreams of success in writing with or without a husband.'

'You are too kind, Miss Elliot, and you have listened far too long to the rambling discourse of a shrewish spinster. Besides, I have not wished only to tell you of my troubles. I am charged with an assignment. Can you possibly guess what it might be?'

I shook my head.

'My brother wished you to have this mysterious package,' she continued, fetching out a rolled paper tube from her workbag.

I couldn't immediately think what it could be; I was so lost in thought at everything that had just passed and the absolute agony of Jane's situation. However brave she appeared on the surface, her feelings clearly ran as deeply as the currents below us. I took the paper tube realizing with a start, this must be the painting that Charles had made.

'I knew Charles's gift would make you smile,' she said, and gave me one of her most enigmatic looks.

'I am sorry that he could not come himself,' I ventured.

'He promised he would be there this evening at the party Eliza has arranged, if you are well and not suffering a little fever or indisposition, unable to come for any reason.'

I couldn't understand what she meant, though I guessed that perhaps she had learned of my fainting spell of the previous day. 'I would not miss it for the world,' I answered; anxious that she should know how much I wished to spend time with her and Charles.

Jane suddenly reached for my hand squeezing it tightly. 'I do hope that you will be able to come, Miss Elliot. I trust so, most sincerely. And now, I must leave you.'

We descended the steps down onto the lower level together and then I watched Jane hurry away, her quick steps disappearing rapidly into the distance. I felt subdued and wanted to think about everything she'd said. She was so resigned to her fate, which was the saddest knowledge of all.

I wondered what Charles could be doing that was so important. I was pleased that he'd remembered me, but so disappointed that on this last day he hadn't come in person. I didn't want to go home. Someone would be bound to see the parcel and be curious, so I made my way further along to a bench protected by a makeshift shelter and made myself comfortable. The sea was calmer now, lapping against the rocks like whispers spreading round a ballroom of some great-shared secret. The sun poked its head out from behind a cloud, casting indigo shadows on the path at my feet. Carefully unrolling the brown paper neatly wrapped with perfect precision, the parchment inside revealed the painting I'd expected, along with a folded piece of hot pressed paper, which I laid to one side.

Exquisitely painted with deft, fine strokes; delicate hues of turquoise, blue and sand, were the prominent tones, highlighted with a flick of pale coral in the cheeks and lips of the sitter. The portrait of the girl who looked so happy sitting upon her rocky shelf as if she hadn't a care in the world was one I recognized. I looked at her, knowing that I'd experienced every emotion her face and her body betrayed. Every paintbrush stroke revealed every nuance of my own personality. I identified completely with the sitter who was smiling into the eyes of the painter as if she were in love with him. And I knew that to be true.

I set down the painting upon the seat, and turned to the other, smaller piece of paper. It was a letter simply addressed to Miss S. E. My eyes devoured the following words:

I must speak to you by the opportunity that my sister Jane has afforded me. I cannot continue to see you without relating something, which, though I hope will not alter your opinion of me for the worse, is nevertheless a risk I am prepared to chance. I am guilty of giving you false impressions, I believe, not only about the worth of my true character, but of my innermost thoughts. I have misled you at every turn with regard to my true feelings and have decided that even if you should not wish to see me again for divulging the truth to you now, it is impossible for me not to act upon honest emotions, and a desire to declare myself.

You alone have brought me to Lyme. For you alone, I think and plan. I offer myself to you with a heart entirely your own. For it is love that has brought me here and my confession is that I love you, dearest Sophia, and wish, if it is your desire also, never to be parted from you again. These weeks we have spent together have been the happiest I have ever known. Despite every effort on my behalf to remain impartial, and to deny the sincerity of my feelings, the discovery that love will find its way into the hardest heart is mine.

I will cease writing now, uncertain of my fate, but I hope I shall see you at my brother's supper party. A word, or look will be sufficient for me to know whether I shall seek your father's permission for your hand this evening, or never.

Believe me to be your most faithful and loving,
C.A.

I read it again and again committing to memory the words that thrilled every sense and awakened every feeling. How would I ever recover from such a letter? I thought I'd burst with happiness. It was all and more than I could ever have hoped for. Yet, I knew we would face certain obstacles, and I didn't want to think about the reaction of my father to Charles's proposal. My mind was in a complete whirl, but there was only one thing to be done. I knew I must find Charles. Unaware of who passed by or of what was happening around me, I started back towards the shore, hardly able to take in the fact that here was certain proof at last that he loved me, as I did him. I mounted the craggy steps projecting like crooked teeth up to the higher level, gingerly clinging with one hand to the wall as I went. Even on this fine day, the wind was gusting up on the top level. It pulled at my bonnet so I had to clamp my hand firmly to it before it was taken off forever. From this vantage point, I scanned the views all round. I was sure I would see him sooner or later. I revolved slowly, the views of Lyme and the sea like some splendid carousel of pictures, which almost broke my heart by their beauty alone and for the recollections of time spent with Charles.

And then I saw him. As he came along The Walk, I wasn't sure if he'd seen me at first. I stopped to catch my breath; and then found I could hardly look at him. The moment I'd wished for was here and now, and I was as gauche as a schoolgirl. But, I needn't have worried for he looked up at that precise moment and waved. I raised my hand to show him that I had the letter and the painting; and that I'd understood, had revelled in every word he'd written.

He turned onto the Cobb and began to run. I could see someone else just behind him, waving her hand and calling my name. I waved back, shouting their names and was so excited to see them both that I couldn't wait a moment longer to join them. The feeling that there was nothing to fear and that everything was well with the world overwhelmed me.

'Charles! Jane!' I shouted. 'Wait, I'm coming!'

My heart felt so light I thought it might burst and I ran back to the steps skipping down them two at a time. There were several more to go, but with judgement I knew that it would be quicker to leap from the last few. In any case, there was Lieutenant Austen to catch me in his arms.

Don't jump!' called Charles, but I was determined. I knew now that I had to be with him, whatever obstacles might be put in our way. We would not be parted by time or anyone. I saw him, my beloved Charles, his arms outstretched, still running. I closed my eyes and jumped.

Chapter 36

The feeling that my head was splitting open was acutely apparent
before I opened my eyes. The pain was severe, but thankfully
dulled by the softness of cotton pillows under my head, freshly
laundered sheets tucked over me, and the sense that I had been
drugged in some way. I couldn't open my eyes even when I tried,
but I could distinguish voices as if calling me from somewhere very
far away. It must be Charles, I thought and Jane, that I could hear.
Their voices rose and fell sounding both anxious and apprehensive.
I felt someone reach for my hand and it comforted me like no
soothing voice ever could. It was Charles's hand, I was sure, his
warm fingers linked with mine and I allowed myself to fall back
into the tunnel of slumber that I had barely surfaced from. I seemed
to drift in and out of sleep and my dreams were such a strange
mixture of the past and present that I couldn't decide if they were
real or imagined. Time drew me back to a past I had already lived
and beyond to a time I didn't know, only to send me hurtling back
to the future in the next second along dark passageways that
recalled the twisting corridors of Monkford Hall. Generations of
familiar Elliot countenances looked out from varnished portraits,

turning their heads to watch me fly headfirst at speed several feet above the ground over the timbered floor below. Passing through a long gallery and out through open leaded windows, my body floated over the garden at dusk, hovering like a bright Kingfisher above the lake, watching dragonflies dart and shimmer. I saw a figure as I flew overhead, a girl who looked exactly like me sauntered under the yew hedges to pause by the sundial. I watched as she traced a finger along the letters carved into its surface, before I rose again like some great bird into the violet sky swooping with the swallows between clouds flaming with copper light. On I sped flying higher and higher through twilight skies to reach the midnight velvet studded with stars. If I put up a hand I could snatch Arcturus, the dazzling star, to light my way. I was flying or floating so fast I could not bear to look below and only when at last I slowed down did I open my eyes again. It was daylight once more, I smelt the sea, saw the rocks draped with seaweed lurking under Byron's dark blue seas and heard the music in its roar. The sun was high in the sky again with Lyme's sandy shoreline stretched before me, water lapping at its edge. There was the Cobb and a girl who looked quite dead lying on the ground at the foot of Granny's Teeth surrounded by people. Her bonnet had rolled over to one side. The ribbons were soaked through with dark red stains, which left their mark on the cobbles as the wind bowled the hat further away with each gust of wind. Charles cradled the girl in his arms and I could see Jane, too, looking distressed, but as capable as ever as she gave orders for help to the surrounding onlookers.

'Charles, I'm up here,' I called, but he didn't see me. 'Jane,' I shouted again, so that they might hear this time, 'It's me, Sophia! Look, I'm flying! Come and join me. It's easy, I never knew how, until now.'

But they didn't look up and the agitation in their voices was all that I heard.

'She is dead! She is dead!' I heard a woman call. Her dress suggested she was one of the boatmen's wives. I saw Jane turn to her, asking for help.

Charles looked on in silent agony with a face as pale as the girl who lay like a limp doll in his arms. He looked up in despair as if all his strength were gone, 'Can no one help me?'

Jane took over, and then I saw him stand. He started to run and I knew he'd gone to find the doctor. I watched his progress, his long legs sprinting to the house by the Cobb gate. Soon he returned, another gentleman running beside him with his black bag in hand. All I could think about was that seeing Doctor Rockingham again would bring back the most painful memories for Jane. And then I fell. Down, down, I tumbled, hurtling towards the body on the quayside. I tried to shout out to warn them all, but either my voice wasn't heard or it made no sound, I wasn't quite sure. Pain seared through my head and the stench of fresh blood filled my nostrils before I blacked out once more.

When I came to, I couldn't think where on earth I found myself. The voices were there again, but my vision was blurred and though the sounds were familiar, I couldn't recognize their voices. I could just make out the light from a window that was half screened by a sheer blind, and the figures that stood before it, speaking in whispers, were silhouetted like shadow puppets in an Indian theatre.

I struggled to sit up. 'Charles, is that you?'

The figures at the window turned, and I began to see and hear more clearly. I knew I was no longer in the past.

'I think she's delirious. I'm worried. When is the doctor to arrive?'

And then I could make them out. Josh Strafford and his girlfriend Louisa were approaching the bed where I lay.

'Don't try to get up,' said Josh, who came forward to sit on a chair next to the bed.

I managed to speak. 'I don't understand. Where am I?'

'You've been unconscious, had some kind of blackout, we're not really sure. The doctor is on his way to check up on you again. Can you remember what happened?'

'I don't remember anything,' I muttered.

'Sophie, just relax,' Josh reassured. 'Don't worry; you're quite safe, here with us. You're in Lyme Regis. I brought you to my parent's house on the cliff-top. I hope that's okay.'

'But, I cannot stay here and put them to so much trouble.'

'They would insist on you staying if they were here, I know, but they're away on holiday just now. Don't fret, we're here to look after you, and make sure you get some rest.'

The truth was I couldn't remember anything very much. My mind and memories were all so wrapped up in Charles and seeing him in those last moments before I plunged into darkness. I recalled seeing Jane also. In my mind's eye she was calling out trying to tell me something, but either I hadn't heard or the recollection was too difficult being mixed up as it was with so many other feelings and emotions. All I knew was that I had to get back. I had to see Charles again, and let him know that no matter what, I would do anything to be with him, defy my family if needs be, so that we could be together.

The throbbing in my head forced my eyes to close again, as waves of pain seared over me as relentless as the lapping of water on the seashore. I willed myself to return to the past even though I knew that I was giving myself false hope. I felt utterly helpless, and was aware of a single tear smarting in the corner of my eye rising from the very depths of my being to join others that started to flow in an unceasing stream to dampen my cheeks and soak the pillow, Josh's pillow. I must be lying in his bed, I knew that much. How on earth had I got to Lyme? I couldn't remember; the only recollection I had was of holding a letter from Josh saying he was going away, and then it was a total blank until the memories of Charles's beautiful letter asking me to marry him. I felt trapped in the present with only reminiscences of the past and the man I loved. A picture of Charles's handsome face so clear and bright seemed to hover above me and I felt if I wanted I could have reached out and touched him. I opened my eyes to see Josh looking down at me with such an expression of concern that I tried to smile. He looked so worried and I just kept thinking that he must wonder what on earth I'd been doing in Lyme. Josh probably thought I'd been planning all along to spy on him and his girlfriend.

Louisa produced a box of paper tissues. 'Please don't cry. Look, Josh, Sophie's crying.'

I felt a hand. Long fingers entwined with mine, but it didn't help straight away. I could only think of Charles. Josh dabbed softly at my face with a tissue. His voice was very gentle, as he wiped away my tears.

'Please, Sophie, tell me what to do. I hate to see you in tears like this.'

I managed a weak smile for an answer. How could I tell him the reasons for my heartbreak? Instead, I succumbed to his kindness and after a while was surprised that the soothing movement of his fingers stroking my brow and my hair seemed to work their magic. I drifted back into sleep with the same feeling that I was somehow caught between two worlds. I could hear seagulls flying overhead, hear the gentle undulations of rippling surf on the sands, and feel the sun shining down on my face and arms. Charles was stroking my hair and I felt his lips kiss my face. 'Don't cry, Sophia, I'm here with you. I love you, please don't cry.'

When the doctor came, the sound of voices woke me again. Slowly, I became conscious of my surroundings, and the full extent of my pain. I was examined, my head still hurt, but I had a new dressing, and the doctor assured me that apart from a little grazing, a terrific purple bruise and a sprained ankle, the damage was not serious. I began to feel that I was a bit of a fraud, that I should get up and think about getting the first train home, when Louisa came into the room bearing a tray with a bowl of steaming chicken soup with some slices of crusty bread. She looked as beautiful as ever, with her dark hair falling in long curls down her back. There was something quite similar about the way her hair waved into ringlets like Josh's and I could easily see how they'd been attracted to one another. Even her eyes with their thick fringe of black lashes reminded me of him. Though not as dark, more like a clear hazel brown, the way they crinkled up at the corners when she smiled was so reminiscent of Josh's eyes. Twin souls, I didn't doubt. I thought what a beautiful couple they made and couldn't help speculating about the beautiful children they would make together. A perfect couple in every way – surely they would have a perfect wedding, perfect offspring and live perfectly happily in a perfect house for the rest of their lives. Even as she set the tray down and plumped up my pillows, I felt quite ashamed at the uncharitable thoughts that were now surfacing. I recognized them for what they were; I was jealous. I knew there was little chance that I would ever find such happiness without the man I loved. And my heart felt a pang once more with the realization that I was here, so solidly back in the present with no way of going back.

'I hope you can manage a little soup,' she said.

'That's so kind of you, it looks delicious,' I answered, thinking that I would have to at least try a spoonful even if I didn't feel like eating anything.

'I'm Louisa, by the way,' she added. 'It's so lovely to meet you, Josh has told me so much about you.'

I wondered what she meant by that as I managed a smile before I took up my spoon. Had he told her how he'd been practically cornered by a man-crazy lunatic in the upstairs flat? I shuddered at the thought.

The soup was as lovely as its maker and I found I was hungrier than I imagined. As Louisa talked, I ate.

'Josh has been really lonely in Bath and despite having made a few friends, he's never really met anyone that he wanted to spend much time with, so it's been really wonderful that he's had you for company,' she went on. 'My work has kept me away for a while so I haven't been able to spend as much time with him as I'd like.'

'Oh, dear, that must be difficult being separated for long periods of time.'

Louisa smiled. 'Well, to be perfectly honest, as you might expect, it's not that hard and when we do catch up, it's like we've never been apart, so it's fine. It's been good to spend a few days away with him and I needed a break, but I've got deadlines to meet.

Unfortunately, I've just got to get back to work.'

I thought what strange comments she'd made and also about how hard it had been to be separated from Charles even for part of a day and knew that I could never think like Louisa. How could she bear to be away from Josh for any length of time? I remembered the way he'd looked at her that evening and knew he loved her with every breath in his body. I watched her as she straightened out the quilt cover. Efficient, kind and beautiful, I was reminded of someone else. The image of Jane Austen capably dealing with the accident at the Cobb was a clear one. I wished I could remember what she'd been saying to me as I'd rushed along the Cobb. I knew it was something specific, not like Charles's urgent cries not to jump, but for the life of me, I couldn't remember.

'I really must get up,' I said, on finishing the last of the lovely meal. 'I need to think about getting home.'

'Oh, you mustn't say that,' Louisa replied. 'It was the least we could do and I know that Josh isn't about to let you go anywhere.'

'But won't you ... I mean, won't he be needing his bed?'

I wasn't quite sure what sort of sleeping arrangements they had, but in any case, I was starting to feel more like my old self, even if battered and bruised by my experiences and I didn't mean my bandaged head. I really felt I should get out of their way, let them say their goodbyes as lovers like to do and be gone from their hair.

'Josh is going to have my room. I don't think for one minute he'll mind my dirty sheets, and I know he'll enjoy looking after you. It will be a comfort for me to know he has someone to talk to for a few days. This is a big house to be alone in. Please indulge me, Sophie, I'd feel better as I'm just about to go home.'

Well, I knew I wasn't any threat to their relationship, but it seemed, I'd been quite wrong about them sharing a room. Still, it did seem a bit strange that Louisa was encouraging another girl to be staying in her boyfriend's bed, yet she didn't seem in the least bit perturbed by the thought and made her move to go saying she really couldn't delay a minute longer. If she didn't get a move on, she said, her editor would be most displeased and she wanted to avoid that altogether. I couldn't resist asking her what she did. It sounded as if she must be a journalist and I imagined her writing for one of the glamorous, glossy magazines.

'I write novels, women's fiction,' she said. 'I've got to the end of the month to have the last draft finished and I've only just completed the first.'

'Oh, how wonderful,' I cried, 'I'm trying to write a novel. But, you're a proper author. Do you use your real name?'

'My pen name is Cassie Crawford, though I doubt you've heard of me. I'm not at all well known. Goodness knows why my publishers keep taking me on. I'm always thinking that perhaps this will be the last, though I'm ever hopeful that my reputation is growing. My first novel was called *"The Clergyman's Daughter"*, the next was, *"The Sisters"*, and I've another coming out in September, *"A Secret Engagement"*.'

She was right. I didn't know of her or her books and I didn't quite know what to say.

Louisa shrugged her shoulders. 'Don't worry, Sophie, I knew you wouldn't have heard of them. The hope is that one day I will write something that will make the world sit up, but until then, I shall keep trying!'

'I'm sure you've already written it, but perhaps the world doesn't recognize your genius just yet.'

'Sophie, I do so hope you're right. And, I sometimes think I have set myself an impossible task. There are so many novels written these days, it's a wonder any of them get noticed.'

'But, out of all the thousands of books that are sent to editors, yours were chosen and published. That's a huge achievement in itself.'

Louisa smiled. 'Yes, that's true, how kind of you to say so. Sophie, it really has been lovely to meet you. I'd love to stay and chat for longer, but I've got to be going. Just promise me one thing. Please do as Josh asks. He wants to nurse you better ... let him!'

I relented. Louisa was so nice, and I was starting to really warm to her. Josh was a very lucky man, I thought.

When she'd gone, I felt really tired again and those gloomy feelings of despondency swept over me again. I tried to rationalize my thoughts about everything, telling myself that what I thought had happened to me was impossible. But I knew that I had fallen in love for real, that I'd never before experienced anything like it. The fact that I had met Charles two hundred years ago didn't mean anything any more, or that I knew it could never work out. It simply didn't matter.

I did find it difficult at first to let myself be looked after by Josh. But, it became increasingly obvious that I wasn't quite well and although the doctor said there was no permanent damage, he declared he was concerned about me in other ways. He wanted to keep an eye on me and Josh volunteered to be both his eyes and ears. Bit by bit, the story came out though I never quite found out exactly what had happened or how I'd got to Lyme. I learned from Josh that I'd been seen wandering along the Cobb in a kind of trance and that I'd actually taken a tumble almost from the top. He and Louisa had just happened to be in the right place at the right time and had seen it happen. Between Josh and the doctor they convinced me that I needed looking after and that I should be right as rain in a few days if I did as I was told. In a strange way I was happy to let Josh take over. I stopped trying to get up and lay in his bed, which had a wonderful view of the sea in the distance and the town below. It was something of a surprise to find out that Josh's parents owned Nelson House and a couple of days before I got a sense of my bearings. Memories came flooding back of my other existence but, although the house was little altered, I felt I couldn't equate the two. I was looking forward to being able to get up and explore.

Josh was so kind and he kept me from brooding too much by his constant attention and conversation. He sat at my bedside and read to me from *Persuasion*. The scenes at Lyme brought back flashes of images from my memory, but more thought provoking were our discussions of the poetry that Jane Austen had written about in the scenes with Captain Benwick. She'd penned *Persuasion* many years after my flash through time between 1815 and 16, when Scott and Byron were wowing the world with the poems that Jane mentioned like *The Lady of the Lake*, *The Giaour*, and *The Bride of Abydos*.

'I don't really know the poems,' I admitted, 'but I wonder why she remarked on them like that. It seems such a different approach to her usual style.'

'We'll read them together if you like,' said Josh, 'though I'm worried if it's a bit too soon for you to be spending too much time poring over books. The doctor said you should be resting.'

Josh knew the poems well and when I was too tired he read them aloud. His voice was soothing and listening to him was a real pleasure. The themes of love and being faithful to one's heart rang true.

'Although Jane Austen seems to have regarded impassioned descriptions, tremulous feelings and minds destroyed by wretchedness with her tongue firmly in her cheek,' I said, 'I wonder if she is trying to tell us something, though I'm afraid of reading too much into it.'

'I don't know, but there does seem to be a thread which connects them all. Love not easily attained or sustained seems at the root, whether it's between Ellen Douglas and Malcolm Graeme in *The Lady of the Lake*, or the illicit love between the Giaour and Leila. And then there is *The Bride of Abydos*, Byron's love story between Selim and Zuleika, a union denied by their family.'

Like a lightning bolt, I knew why Jane had mentioned these poems; it seemed so obvious. She'd included them as a message to the man she loved, knowing he would read and recognize the clues. *Persuasion* told the truth in so many ways that she would never recover from the love she felt for him. Josh stared, his dark eyes penetrating mine. I came back to earth as he pronounced that if I were to be looking quite so disturbed in future, he would be recommending a larger allowance of prose in my daily study, as Anne Elliot had suggested to Captain Benwick.

Over the next few days we finished *Persuasion* and I couldn't help but be reminded of Charles. When we reached the part where Louisa Musgrove jumps off the Cobb wall Josh looked at me anxiously as if he was worried about reading it, but I assured him it was okay even if every word made me long for Charles. I couldn't see Captain Wentworth any more in my head; the only man I saw was Charles. Thinking about that day brought one particular recollection to haunt me. I remembered a white glove and recalling its special powers I knew I would have to find it if I had any chance of going back. But, apart from some things that Louisa had kindly lent me, I only had the clothes I'd been wearing. I could hardly ask Josh if I'd been clutching a white glove.

Only when Josh went to bed at night and I was left alone did I have time to really think about Charles. The ache left in my heart felt as if I'd been physically wounded and every night my silent tears kept me awake. Part of me wished to take up my old life and make an attempt to start to look after myself again. I wanted to return to my flat or I tried to convince myself that I did and after just over a fortnight of being cosseted, I felt I could make a stand. Also, I longed to see if Charles's portrait was in the rosewood box or lost in time forever. I wanted to read Sophia's diary again, so that I could reassure myself that this whole experience had not been some sort of ghastly dream. I told Josh that I wanted to go home though I didn't want him to think I was ungrateful or that I wasn't enjoying his company. I liked being with him very much, and I recognized that a part of me was so scared to start again on my own especially as my memory had not come back completely. In a strange way, I had started to rely on him and knew that this wasn't going to be good for me. Josh was totally understanding about my bid for freedom although he expressed concern.

'I don't know if you're really ready to go home just yet,' he said. 'I'm sorry, Sophie, I don't mean to sound so bossy, but it was such a shock finding you lying on the ground covered in blood like that. Wait until you've been up for a few days and then I'll let you go.'

'Josh, I can't really explain what happened that day, but it's all to do with me and nothing to do with you. It wouldn't have mattered where I'd been, I'm certain I'd have had some sort of a fainting fit.'

'Do you remember anything about why you came to Lyme yet? You must have been trying to get in touch with me, I think, don't you? Sophie, I'm sorry. I feel it's totally my fault.'

I shook my head and looked beyond him to the distant horizon. 'I honestly don't know exactly what happened, or how I got here.'

He clammed up then, and didn't say any more. He looked as if he had some huge worry on his mind. I felt awful. The last thing I wanted was for him to feel responsible for me.

'Listen, Josh. I'm feeling so much better. I'll get up later, please don't worry about me.'

Josh was silent for a moment. I couldn't make out his expression. He looked so sad. 'The thing is, Sophie, I really need to talk to you.'

I guessed it must have something to do with Louisa. It still didn't seem right that she had just gone off like that. It was all so casual and I was sure he was upset by her behaviour. He hadn't had to say anything these last few days, but it was so obvious that something was upsetting him and weighing on his mind.

'We'll talk later, okay?'

He nodded, but he didn't look happy and the mood in the place seemed charged with something indefinable like electricity crackling in a lightning bolt before a storm. I felt suddenly very aware of his physical presence and his closeness. He put out his hand and touched me briefly on my arm and I jumped in surprise. It was like the feeling I had when Charles came within feet of me and I couldn't account for it except by knowing that every part of me ached for him. I wanted what I couldn't have and as I leaned back against the pillows I thought I'd never felt so miserable in my life before.

Thinking of Charles made me remember Jane and the last conversation I'd had with her came back so clearly. I suddenly realized how completely selfish and stupid I was being. She had loved and lost so much. I wondered if she'd ever managed to see her love again and if that meeting really had been the last they'd enjoyed.

There was a pile of books on the bedside table that Josh had chosen and I reached for a modern biography on Jane, in the hope of finding some clues. I skimmed through the pages, but I soon found there was little written about that particular period of her life when so many letters between Jane and Cassy had been destroyed. There was mention of a romance at the seaside, which had resulted in a tragic ending that didn't quite ring true. Perhaps Cassandra had wanted her nieces to know that Jane had been in love, but hadn't wanted to divulge the whole story. I read that later on that year in 1802, Jane had travelled with her family back to Steventon in October and then the most astonishing discovery leapt out of the page. In November they had been invited to Manydown, home to the sisters' friends, Alethea and Catherine Bigg-Wither. The story was that their brother Harris had proposed to Jane! I'd reached the end of the page and I couldn't have been more surprised.

Just as this information was sinking in there was a knock at the door and Josh appeared with a huge smile on his face. 'I've brought us some lunch. Are you hungry?'

Hours had passed by; I couldn't believe it was lunchtime. I was hungry now I thought about it, but I was also completely intrigued by what I'd just read and longing to find out more. It must have shown.

'Sorry, am I interrupting?'

'Oh no, Josh! I'm the one who should be apologizing; it's just that I've found out the most amazing thing. Did you know that Jane Austen once received a proposal of marriage?'

Josh's black curls shook enthusiastically as he nodded. 'I've been finding out quite a lot recently, I must admit. I think you'll find that she accepted him too, though it didn't quite work out exactly as you might think.' He paused to glance into the bulging bag of shopping. 'I've got smoked salmon. Does that sound okay?'

'Yes, lovely. Thanks Josh, you're so kind, but I insist on giving you a hand. Give me five minutes, and I'll come downstairs.'

I put the book down, got out of bed, showered and dressed. My head felt a little fuzzy, and my ankle ached, but I was feeling much more like my old self. Josh looked up and grinned when I entered the kitchen. He was just setting a vase of plump, scented roses in the middle of the table and I buried my nose in the overblown blooms. The smell of summer made me feel light-headed.

'Sophie, are you sure about this?' said Josh. 'I can always bring your meal up to you on a tray if it's all too much, too soon.'

Ignoring him, I selected two pretty plates from the painted dresser and fetching knives and forks with napkins from the basket on the side, I laid the table and sat down to quarter the lemon that Josh produced from a brown paper bag. I watched him unwrap the salmon carefully arranging the pink pieces on a blue platter, before cutting thin slices of bread liberally buttered from an earthenware dish.

'What did you mean about Jane Austen's proposal?' I asked.

Josh fetched two glasses and a bottle of chilled wine from the fridge. I watched his lips pressed together, a little frown furrowing his brow in concentration as he skewered the cork and pulled it out with the delicious sound that always accompanies a freshly opened bottle of wine.

'She said yes straight away, but changed her mind by the morning. There must have been an awful scene. Apparently, her brother James had to go and fetch them home.'

Poor Jane. She could only have been thinking of her family when she accepted, I decided. Manydown, a rich estate, would have been the answer to a comfortable life, a home for her mother and Cassandra but, unlike the man she'd loved, she herself could not commit to a loveless marriage. In the space of a night, no doubt tossing and turning, she'd known she could never marry without love. And knowing what she'd told me, I recognized that she'd never forgotten her one true love.

'We certainly do not forget you as quickly as you forget us.' The words were spoken before I realized that I'd said them out loud.

'That's from *Persuasion*. Whatever made you think of it?'

'I just wonder if Jane changed her mind because she was still in love with someone else. Perhaps someone who could not be hers.'

'Mmm, intriguing, Miss Elliot. So, do let me hear it, you've obviously been doing a little sleuthing of your own.'

I hesitated. I couldn't very well tell him that Jane had told me herself about the love of her life. I got up and busied myself with slicing some bread to avoid looking at Josh. 'I have been thinking about it. I had a dream, one that was so real. Oh Josh, you'll think me so silly.'

'No, I won't. I dream too. Everyone does and if you feel passionately about something or someone, those things or people have a way of creeping into your dreams too.'

'It was a kind of dream, I think. I met Jane. She told me about the love of her life; a secret tale that's been lost in time. And every single novel she wrote is littered with hints and signs of her own story, from *Sense and Sensibility* to *Persuasion*. Jane and her lover were separated by lack of fortune and family disapproval, a theme that runs through all of her novels.'

'So who was the love of Jane's life? What was his name?'

I suddenly realized that apart from knowing what he looked like, and the clues I'd gleaned about his character, I had no idea.

'I don't know, Josh.' I couldn't recall Jane ever having mentioned a name, only referring to him as Robin Adair, but in a way I was glad. It was nobody's business but her own and I also knew that even if I had known his identity I wouldn't want to share such personal information. 'Captain Frederick Wentworth, I suppose,' I said with a smile. 'I can't tell you his name, but honestly, Josh, it was all so real. You do believe me, don't you? I even met her sister Cassandra, three of Jane's brothers and her parents.'

Josh was silent. How I wished I hadn't spoken. He was looking at me with the strangest expression and probably thinking that the blow to my head had done more damage than he'd realized. His answer surprised me.

'I do believe you. I ...'

He paused. Josh looked into my eyes with such a strange expression. He seemed so upset and so sad; I wished I could do or say something to comfort him. He put the bottle down and came straight over taking my hand in his own.

'Oh, Sophie, what have I done?' he said. 'I have a confession to make, and I'm not sure whether you will like me very much after I've made it. The truth is I've planned something of a surprise for this afternoon; there's a taxi coming to pick us up very soon. I hope that's okay; I know I should have said something before, but I'm really hoping you'll come.'

He wouldn't enlighten me any further no matter how many questions I bombarded him with. The cab duly arrived and although I couldn't wait to find out where we were going, Josh was tight-lipped. We headed out of Lyme and along narrow country lanes, frothing white with cow parsley and dotted with wildflowers. Summer in all her glorious greenery was burgeoning in a riot of nature. We were both quiet and thoughtful for a time and after a while I gave up looking for clues through the window as we passed views of green fields and sheep grazing upon them. After what seemed an interminably long time the road widened slightly again and I was struck by the sense that I knew the territory, that I'd been here before. I lowered the window in expectation and breathed in the sweet air, which only served to heighten the sense of excitement. Further along we encountered a pair of ornate gates and the remembrance of them was like revisiting a dream I'd once had. Before we entered the twisted carriageway with no view in sight, I knew exactly what to expect. I sat on the edge of my seat unable to say a word recalling every moment of my last journey here. Not much had changed, though the driveway appeared slightly more overgrown than when I had visited it in another life. Beyond the green tunnel of thickly wooded trees, the vista opened up to our eyes. There, standing serenely as ever, stood Monkford Hall, the gabled manor house of my ancestors, golden and gilded with afternoon sunshine that winked in the diamond paned windows.

Whilst I sat open-mouthed, Josh leapt out of his side of the taxi and came round to mine to open the door with a flourish and a bow. I couldn't begin to think about why we were there, but when he bent down to take my hand all thoughts of the house disappeared, as his jacket flapped open and I caught the most disconcerting glimpse of white leather fingers just poking out of his inside pocket.

Chapter 38

Josh was gesturing towards the house with one hand and held out his other towards me. I told myself that what I'd just seen couldn't possibly be real and then the memory of being in Josh's bedroom and the glove on the floor came back to me in a flash. Had I really seen what I thought I had? I wanted to demand an explanation about the gloves in his pocket, but at the same time I couldn't believe I was standing before Monkford Hall. Swiftly dismissing the incredulous thoughts that surfaced, I looked towards the house I loved and took his hand.

'Josh, I can't believe it. Whatever are we doing here? Are we expected?'

Josh turned to me with a smile that had his dark eyes sparkling with mischief. 'We are, indeed. I promise I will explain everything now. Welcome home to Monkford Hall, Miss Elliot.'

He was standing so near that I naturally took a step back. I found it almost impossible to look at Josh; he was gazing at me so intently. His dark eyes drew me in and when he bent his head towards me, I felt myself holding my breath. His arms pulled me against him and his lips found mine. I was so shocked, it was a moment before I recognized what was happening, but it felt so exquisitely right that I'm almost ashamed to say I kissed him back immediately without a moment's hesitation. And in that precious moment, time shifted once more. I kissed him with the same passion I'd felt for Charles. Josh's kisses came relentlessly until I no longer knew where I was or where time held me. And when I opened my eyes, I must confess I didn't want Josh to talk. I wanted him to kiss me again.

'Forgive me, but I love you, Sophie,' Josh whispered. 'I have loved you since the very first time we met.'

I was too stunned to say anything at first, but then I felt so shocked, by what had happened between us and at what he was saying. All I kept thinking about was Louisa and Charles. How could I have kissed Josh? What kind of madness had finally taken its toll? I could only think that my desire to see and be with Charles had led me to this dream-like insanity. And worst of all, Josh was looking at me again in exactly the way he had just before he'd taken me in his arms and kissed me.

'I'm totally confused,' I said. 'I don't know quite what is going on or what came over me a minute ago, but I do not think I will ever forgive myself for kissing you just now. I know something's happened between you and Louisa, but she's your girlfriend, Josh. What the hell are you playing at?'

To my utter horror Josh laughed. I couldn't see the joke myself, but he was roaring with laughter.

'Oh, Sophia, my darling, you could not have it more wrong. Tell me, what do you think of my sister? I hope you like her as much as she likes you.'

'Your sister? Louisa is your sister?'

Josh nodded, the curls framing his face taking on a life of their own, as he shook once more with laughter. He drew me towards him again. It was so strange. I knew it must be wrong; but it felt so right. And when his lips kissed mine once more so tenderly that I felt my heart might stop beating at his touch, I just gave in to every delectable sensation. Time paused, the shadows shifted and a seagull called.

'Like you, I've been living a double life,' he began, squeezing my hand as we walked towards the house.

'I don't understand.'

He stopped, and brought my hand to his lips. His eyes seemed to bore their way into the furthest depths of my soul. 'Are you sure you don't understand, Miss Sophia?'

Reaching into his pocket he pulled out the pair of gloves. I started to shake my head, but there was something in his eyes that I recognized beyond anything else.

'No, that cannot be. That's not possible.' I couldn't speak any more.

Josh nodded reassuringly. He pressed the gloves into my hands, and clasped his own over mine. 'You do know me in more ways than one, I am certain.'

'Are you ... can it really be true?' My head swam with visions of everything I'd ever known and seen in the past. So much so, that I pulled away dropping the gloves on the floor, voicing the words I could hardly believe. 'Are you trying to tell me that you are Charles ... my Charles Austen?'

He shook his head. 'No, not really, not any more than you are Sophia Elliot. But, I confess to being the Charles you have known in the past if you can believe that. I have inhabited his body as you did your ancestor. And I know that you will only think the worst of me for not revealing myself sooner, but the truth is I didn't know it was you at first. I only realized when Louisa and I set off for Dorset and having forgotten my glove, I decided to return to the flat. I couldn't understand why it was on the bed or why the copy of *Persuasion* I'd given you was still there, lying next to it. And then when I looked, the glove was not the usual one I'd travelled through time with. It was for the other hand. I had to find out and when I thought about it, I realized it was you who had the other one. Time shifted for us both that day. You were leaving for Lyme with the Elliots and I just got completely carried away again with Charles's life.'

I could hardly speak it was so hard to take it all in. 'I can't believe it.'

'There was a part of me that enjoyed the romance of it all and I thought you'd be disappointed if you discovered that your romantic hero was only yours truly. And then came the horror of your accident. I thought you must have broken your neck at the very least. But, that's when I found your glove and time sorted out the rest. Later, when you came to, I wasn't sure if you'd work it out for yourself or even if you'd remember anything of the past and it's been agony not being able to tell you. I had to wait until I thought you'd be able to take it in. Slipping through time was just a huge adventure for me at first but, when I met you, everything changed even if I didn't know it was you straight away. In any case, I'm sure you felt like me. It was all so weird that I was never really sure whether it was happening for real. I just got sucked into believing the life I was living was true and for most of the time forgot I was anybody but Charles Austen. I admit, I hadn't reckoned on falling in love with Sophia in all of this.'

'Are you sure it's not Sophia you are in love with now?'

'I loved you from the first moment I saw you peeking in through the door at the museum and I couldn't believe my luck when I ran into you at the Pump Room. I didn't know you, of course, but I felt an immediate connection like I'd never felt before. But, how about you? Are you sure you didn't just fall in love with Captain Wentworth? After all, you've admitted you adore him. You certainly gave me the impression that you weren't interested in me. In fact, when I came to supper, you really gave me the brush off.'

I laughed. 'And I thought I'd frightened you off because I looked too eager. No, when I look back now, it was the same for me. I felt an irresistible attraction towards you, breeches or no, but then I thought you were already taken. I can't tell you how I felt when I saw Louisa, though I put it down to missing Charles.'

'I can't tell you how happy that makes me feel, Sophia.'

I was still in shock. 'Can this be real? You mean; you are truly my Charles, the Charles who asked me ...'

Josh pulled me toward him kissing me on the top of my head. "Believe it, Sophie. It's the truth.'

Josh was looking at me with such love in his eyes and with an expression I knew so well, I could not doubt all that had happened between us.

'All I can say is that I have misled you at every turn with regard to my true feelings and now, it is impossible for me not to act upon honest emotions, and a desire to declare myself. Please tell me not that I am too late. Sophie, I love you and can only repeat what I've asked before.'

I saw Josh go down on bended knee. 'Darling, Miss Elliot, will you do me the honour of marrying me?'

'Will I marry you? Josh Strafford, of course I shall!'

As I threw myself into his arms and submitted to his tender kisses, the front door opened, and there stood an older gentleman with distinguished features, dressed in a dark suit, smiling in a most welcoming manner.

'Ah, here you are, Mr Strafford, and it is my pleasure to meet you, Miss Elliot. Mr Strafford's been telling me all about your family history and I must say, I think it's marvellous the way everything has turned out!'

I turned towards Josh but he didn't seem to want to enlighten me as he led me towards the steps. When we entered the Great Hall there was the old table that I remembered gleaming with polish and with chairs I recognized arranged along its sides. The gentleman invited us to take a seat.

'There are a few formalities, Mr Strafford, before you can take possession, but I foresee no problems. I am sure your plans to improve the place will breathe new life into the house again. Now, as I understand it, this property is to be in your joint names, is that correct? Of course, when we have the final papers ready you will both have to sign your lives away.'

He laughed heartily as if he'd made a great joke before picking up his briefcase. 'Well, I'll be going now, but I expect you'll want to explore the house. The keys are at your disposal for as long as you wish.'

I couldn't believe what he was saying. I looked at Josh, my eyes filled with tears.

Josh spoke at last. 'My fiancée is very keen to take a look. She's not been here for some time.'

I couldn't help but laugh as the old gentleman left. 'No, only for about two hundred years! But, can it really be true? Josh, is this to be our home?'

Josh beamed and nodded his head. 'If you think you'd be happy to live here. There's even a little church at the back of the house where we can be married if you wish.'

'I don't know what to say,' I muttered incomprehensibly. 'I'm thrilled and yes, of course I should love to be your wife, but I confess, Josh, to being a little troubled. How can we possibly afford a house like this?'

And besides the problem of buying it, I couldn't imagine how we would pay for all the improvements and renovations that would have to be done.

'I'm afraid I have a few more confessions to make,' admitted Josh. 'But before I go into all of that, I have another surprise waiting for you upstairs.

Chapter
39

I duly followed. I had an idea where we were headed when I saw in which direction we turned at the top of the stairs, but my surprise couldn't have been greater. The bedroom looked as if I'd just left it a moment ago with the same huge bed, but now adorned with the prettiest linen and with primrose curtains flapping in the breeze at the open window with a wonderful view over the garden to the sundial.

'Have you seen what I found on the shelf?' he said. Sitting exactly where I'd left it in that other time was the rosewood box.

'Josh, I don't know how you've managed that, but it's wonderful. How can I ever thank you?'

'Oh, I'm sure I'll think of something,' Josh said, drawing me into his arms again with the look I was becoming accustomed to.

'You haven't finished telling me everything,' I half protested, as he kissed his way down my neck.

'Ah, yes,' he murmured, pulling me ever closer. 'You remember when I said my family came from Lyme? That was partly true, my parents have lived in Lyme for the last five years. They moved when the upkeep of this place became too much for them.'

I stared in disbelief, but somehow it didn't seem such a surprise. 'Do you mean to tell me that your parents owned Monkford Hall?'

'They did and do, and I grew up here. It was a wonderful family home for us, but my parents are quite elderly now and eventually they were anxious to move to a place where they felt they could still be independent with views of the sea that they love so much. Of course they know nothing about your connections, although they soon will. I hope you understand why I kept all of this quiet. I didn't want to tell you at first because I suppose in a way I felt you'd been cheated out of growing up in your proper home. I thought you might dislike me on the spot, as it was one of my ancestors who wrested it away from yours.'

'Oh, Josh, I could never have disliked you. I love the house more than I can say, but you must know I have no money.'

'Besides inheriting the house, I've managed to make quite a bit of money of my own and will also come into some money on my birthday, some that's been held in trust for me until I reached a responsible age. Don't worry about money, Sophie. In any case, I just know that one day, you'll make all the money you wish from your writing.'

I couldn't take it all in and trying to imagine not worrying about money was impossible. But, I trusted Josh implicitly and knew that every word he'd spoken was true. That he believed in me was the most wonderful tribute. I now knew how Jane must have felt to be supported by a family who believed in her work too.

'I still don't understand the Jane Austen connection,' I said, as a sharp image of her came into my mind. 'There must be one. I've never felt so strongly that we were meant to find one another and that somehow she had a hand in it. Does that make any kind of sense?'

'Yes, without a doubt there is a link. I found a box of Charles Austen's possessions in the museum containing amongst other treasures, his white gloves, a key to the Austen's house and a letter saying that the gloves were donated by a far-flung family connection of mine, which made me instantly curious. I'm afraid I can't possibly explain how, why, or even if the gloves work as we think they do. Who knows what really happened to us? But, you might also be very distantly connected to the same family, I think. From the day I found out about the Elliots I think I've known that our lives would be linked as our families were in the past.'

'What do you mean?'

'Well, you said yourself that you saw some of the parallels between your family history and the Elliots in *Persuasion*. I think Jane was writing about events she witnessed or at least in part. Charles, we know, was in the Navy. He was certainly in Bath in the summer of 1802 when he visited his family. Perhaps he did fall in love with the girl next door. Don't you think that Charles could have inspired the character of Frederick Wentworth? People always assume that Jane was writing about herself in *Persuasion* and that's obviously partly true, but she was also writing about her brother's love story that didn't work out. Mr Elliot must have refused Charles permission to marry his daughter because he had no money, just as Wentworth was refused permission in *Persuasion*. Jane wanted a happy ending; she hoped some day that the love story would be a real event between the families. She was looking forward to a time when a woman could live her life, as she wished and be free to marry whomever she wanted. Her own happiness had been denied and so too had her brother's. And besides all that, I'm now certain Jane knew that the families would be united someday.'

'But, that doesn't make sense, unless Jane Austen was a fortune teller or a time traveller too.'

'Oh Sophie, I was going to wait until I knew for sure that you were strong enough and ready to take in everything I have to tell you. I've had enough difficulty trying to believe it all myself.'

'What is it, Josh? What are you trying to tell me?'

'The thing that you ought to know, Sophie, is that I've only just realized that Jane has been as much a sister to me as Louisa.' He paused and looked deeply into my eyes with an expression I could hardly fathom. I wondered what on earth he was going to say. 'You've met my sister, haven't you?'

But, even as he said the words I read the truth in his eyes and besides, I knew I'd seen her hazel eyes before.

On the day that I married Josh Strafford, the day was heavenly. A bright, autumnal sun shone out of a larkspur sky over the Somersetshire countryside as I entered the cool, dark church on my father's arm. Reunited with him once more, he'd taken the news extraordinarily well considering that it had come out of the blue as it did, but he and Josh hit it off straight away. The interior gloom of the ancient building was bathed in candlelight, scented by the profusion of white roses, stephanotis, and greenery, garlanded in swags or arranged on the altar in tall silver vases. Ahead, at the altar I could see Josh waiting for me, a smile on his lips and his beautiful eyes on mine.

I'd chosen a simple silk dress reminiscent of the muslin gowns I'd worn in the past. It felt beautiful on my skin, the cream silk rippling behind me in a train that slipped over the ancient steps leading to Josh's side. A lace veil found in one of the attic trunks at Monkford was pinned in place on the top of my head with a tiara of diamonds and moonstones, given to me by Josh's mother, who was as sweet as I'd imagined she'd be. The sense of the occasion was so unreal that for a moment I wondered if I'd slipped into some other dimension, until Josh took my hand, and we voiced our vows together. Louisa got up to speak during the service; saying how thrilled she was for our happiness. As I listened, I remembered Jane's words on that fateful day when I had fallen from the Cobb. 'But, for those who love, Time does not exist.' I now knew the truth of that motto and recognized the twinkle in her eyes as she read from *Persuasion*. I felt she was looking particularly at me when she said, '*Anne was tenderness itself, and she had the full worth of it in Captain Wentworth's affection.*' Taking her place in the congregation once more, it was with enormous pleasure that I watched the young, fair-haired man, at her side, take her hand in his own, squeezing it with undisguised affection.

Great Aunt Elizabeth was there to share our happiness. Dressed in blue to match her forget-me-knot eyes, she told me how she'd known that I would find the answer to my dreams in Bath. I took her into the house as we left our guests drinking champagne in the marquee on the lawn. I wanted to show her the sitting room that we'd made as cosy as we could with furniture that my aunt said we might borrow from Sydney Place for the time being until we could furnish it ourselves. The old, silvered looking glass looked very much at home above the mantelpiece as did the Sèvres clock whose pretty chimes struck the hours. My favourite winged chair sat on one side of the fireplace and, in the alcove, the painting of Sophia sitting on the sands looking as radiant as I felt today was hanging on the wall, luminous with sunbeams which danced over the surface of the glass, making the memory so sharp that I could smell the sea. The wonderful watercolour had given up one more secret when I'd gone to collect it from the picture framers in Walcot Street. The shopkeeper had found a letter tucked behind the painting, a letter I realized now that was written in Josh's handwriting expressing his heartfelt love for me. A love letter to cherish forever, I'd asked for it to be replaced and sealed within the frame. Whatever the real truth was about Sophia and Charles, the only relationship that mattered was the one I shared with Josh. I would never forget the time spent in the past and knowing that Sophia would always be a part of me, all I wanted now was to look ahead to a bright future with the man I loved.

My aunt looked up at the painting as I did. There was one question I needed to ask more than any other. 'Great Aunt Elizabeth, do you know what happened to our ancestor, Sophia Elliot?' I asked. 'I've been wondering about her. She must have married, but who was he?'

'She did, indeed,' answered my aunt with a reassuring smile. 'Sophia married the local doctor in Lyme. Not the match her family wished for I don't think, but she went on to have a fine family of seven children, I believe.'

Suddenly, I had that feeling again, as if someone was whispering in my ear telling me it was so. It seemed too much to hope that Sophia might have found love with a gentleman I'd known, if all too briefly. 'Was his name Rockingham, by any chance?'

'Why, yes, I believe that's right. Apparently, they met when she was travelling with her family. I remember my granny telling me a tale that she and the doctor were thrown together after an incident where Sophia had some sort of accident. She was ill for some time and they fell in love when he nursed her back to health. There was a story that she had fallen for him on the rebound, that the young gentleman she had first been in love with had been rejected when her father disapproved of the match, but I know little about the details. All I know is that she would not be persuaded against refusing her second chance at happiness, and her resolution carried the day!'

That seemed to make complete sense to me, and I had an idea exactly what had happened. I couldn't imagine how heartbroken she must have felt when it all ended with Charles, but I was absolutely thrilled to realize that Sophia had escaped marriage to Mr Glanville and found happiness in the end. Their story could not have been more fitting or more romantic. I couldn't imagine that her father had consented to the match easily, if he had at all, but it was wonderful to know that their love had won the day. My eyes met Sophia's, and as she smiled back at me, I knew she had known true happiness.

I had something I wanted to give back to my aunt. When I handed her the rosewood box she seemed to understand. 'You know, your mother had possession of the box for a while,' she said. 'And when she met your father, she gave it back to me.'

I remembered the diary entry that my mother had written all those years ago. I still didn't quite understand what had happened to her, but perhaps she had experienced something similar to me. It didn't matter; none of it mattered. I didn't need the box any more or its contents. I could let Charles and the past go now that I knew

I hadn't really been in love with him, even if he would always have a part of my heart. I hoped he'd been happy and from what I'd discovered in these last few days about him, it seemed very likely, even if he had never quite had the luck of a certain hero in *Persuasion*.

'And I think you are probably ready to write that book at last, Sophie,' said my aunt.

I smiled, and looked to the French windows where Josh was walking over the smooth green lawn towards us. He waved and blew a kiss.

'I shall write it very soon, I promise, but just for now, Great Aunt Elizabeth, I am simply going to enjoy my happiness with the man I love most in the world, my very own Captain Wentworth!'

The End

ABOUT JANE ODIWE

Jane Odiwe is a lifelong Jane Austen enthusiast. She is the author of
Effusions of Fancy, Lydia Bennet's Story, Willoughby's Return and Mr
Darcy's Secret. Born in Sutton Coldfield, England, she holds an arts
degree and spent many years teaching History and Art in Birmingham and
London.

Jane is lucky enough to live with her very own Captain Wentworth,
their children and two cats, dividing her time between North London and
Fairyland, Bath.

www.austeneffusions.com

www.janeaustensequels.blogspot.com

www.twitter.com/janeodiwe

ALSO BY JANE ODIWE

Lydia Bennet's Story

"Odiwe pays nice homage to Austen's stylings and endears the reader to the formerly secondary character, spoiled and impulsive Lydia Bennet... devotees will enjoy."

- Publisher's Weekly

Willoughby's Return

"Odiwe's elegantly stylish writing is seasoned with just the right dash of tart humor, and her latest literary endeavor is certain to delight both Austen devotees and Regency romance readers."

- Booklist

Mr Darcy's Secret

"Jane Odiwe writes with skill and charm, and her latest novel will delight the thousands of readers for whom just one book about the Bennet sisters is not enough."

- Jane Austen's Regency World Magazine